She cou 5 JUL 2

"Sophia?" He reached ~~~~~~~ ~~~~~~~~ d falling over her tightly laced ones. "It's okay. It will be okay."

The warmth and the way he leaned in as he dropped his voice was her undoing. The stuttering sob issued from her and she pulled her hands from beneath his in order to cover her face. Tears spilled and the sobs got worse. Right here on the squad floor, she realized, she was going to have the cry she had kept inside since that night.

Jack rolled his chair to her so his legs straddled hers, and he drew her forward. She nestled against his chest, clutching the soft fabric of his button-up shirt. His hands rubbed up and down her back. The man was really good at this. Was that why she'd finally let go—because she knew he'd be there to catch her?

THE WARRIOR'S WAY

BY
JENNA KERNAN

MILLS & BOON

First Published in Great Britain 2017
By Mills & Boon, an imprint of HarperCollins*Publishers*
1 London Bridge Street, London, SE1 9GF

© 2017 Jeannette H. Monaco

ISBN: 978-0-263-92892-1

46-0617

... yclable
... he logging and
... regulations of

Jenna Kernan has penned over two dozen novels and has received two RITA® Award nominations. Jenna is every bit as adventurous as her heroines. Her hobbies include recreational gold prospecting, scuba diving and gem hunting. Jenna grew up in the Catskills and currently lives in the Hudson Valley of New York State with her husband. Follow Jenna on Twitter, @jennakernan, on Facebook or at www.jennakernan.com.

For Jim, always

Acknowledgments

Many thanks to Lt. Christopher Knurr of the Brown County Sheriff's Office for his expertise and advice.

Any mistakes regarding the use of explosives are the author's.

Chapter One

Amazing how much a simple favor could cost you. FBI explosives expert Sophia Rivas waited for her escort to finish introductions. She held her tight smile firmly in place as she shook hands with the chief of tribal police, Wallace Tinnin. The man looked well past the age of retirement, judging from his deeply lined face. He ushered them from the station floor, such as it was, into his small, stuffy office, where everything seemed as old and worn-out as their chief.

Her gaze flashed to the CRT monitor on his desk that looked straight out of the 1990s. Those things still had cathodes and vacuum tubes inside.

Her escort, FBI agent Luke Forrest, had moved into the office and now gave her a look of warning.

Sophia met Luke's gaze. He was her cousin and the reason she had been recruited into the Bureau. She owed him a lot, but that didn't mean she agreed with him. This entire thing continued to feel like a bad idea.

She opted to remain standing in the chief's office rather than sit in either of the stained chairs facing his overcrowded desk. Chief Tinnin headed the Turquoise Canyon Tribal Police Department, which consisted of nine officers, all male, and one dispatcher, female.

"He should be here soon," the chief assured them.

Who were they waiting for again? Luke told her she'd be working with their best man. Best of nine, she realized. What was his name? Bear Trap. Bearton. Something like that.

With luck he could take her to the reservoir and she could give her opinion and be heading back to Flagstaff by dark. It was midafternoon on Friday and the days were still long. She'd be leaving well after the rush-hour traffic, but would still be heading back to the refuge of her little apartment after the longest week of her life. She usually loved the sanctuary of her place, but this week, on leave, it had become a kind of holding cell, where she paced and obsessed over the review team's findings on her use of deadly force.

Forrest was more than a decade her senior and his short black hair and pressed suit did not hide the fact that, like her, he was Apache. But not of the Turquoise Canyon tribe. They were both Black Mountain, both spider clan, making them kin. They also shared a grandmother, so the connection was especially close. And even though Luke worked in the Phoenix field office, he had heard she was on leave during the investigation.

Had she made a mistake that night, one that could cost her the thing she valued most in this world—her job? No. They would clear her.

She glanced from her cousin to Wallace Tinnin, who moved behind his desk. She wondered why he used an old rusty spur as a paperweight. Had he once ridden in the rodeo? That would account for the limp.

What was happening back in Flagstaff? She knew the protocol because they'd explained it all to her. But she didn't know how long the investigation process would take. "As long as it takes" was not very helpful, but was the only answer her supervisor provided before placing her on mandatory leave.

This was the process. She had to trust it. But she didn't. She didn't trust anything that threatened her job.

Tinnin set down a cup of water before her and asked her to take a seat. She politely declined both.

"Coffee?" asked Tinnin.

She glanced at the well-used drip coffeemaker on his sideboard.

"Maybe just water."

It was delivered in a Dixie cup instead of an unopened bottle. Her smile remained but she cast her cousin a certain look. He seemed to be enjoying himself, judging from the smirk.

The chief opened the top drawer of his desk, drew out a silver foil packet that she recognized was for nicotine gum, popped a white cube into his mouth and chewed. The pouches beneath his eyes spoke of a man running a department that she knew must be understaffed and underfunded.

There was a polite knock and her cousin opened the door. In walked a mountainous man who surveyed the room with a quick sweep before he fixed his stare on her.

"Sophia?" said Forrest, motioning toward the new arrival. "This is Detective Jack Bear Den."

The first thing she noticed—that anyone would notice—was how damn big he was. Big, tall and broad-shouldered, with a body type very unlike the men she knew from her reservation on Black Mountain. The second thing that she saw was the cut across his lifted eyebrow—not a cut really, but more like a blank spot where a tiny white scar bisected the brow and made him look roguish, like a pirate.

What he did not look like was Apache.

Was their best detective really from off the rez?

"A pleasure to meet you, Ms. Rivas. I'm roadrunner, born of snake."

She answered automatically, giving her clan affiliation. "I'm butterfly, born of spider."

Since the Turquoise Canyon people were Tonto Apache and she was Western Apache, they did not share linguistic roots, so she spoke in English, her second language.

Her brain was still sending her signals that he was not roadrunner or snake or Apache. He did not fit. Did not look like any other Apache man she had ever met. Still, she extended her hand.

He stepped forward, meeting her gaze. She saw his eyes were hazel with a shift of color toward brown near his pupil, which blasted outward to give way to a true green at the outer rim of his iris. Most Apache men did not have green eyes.

The rest of him was equally appealing, particularly his strong square jaw and welcoming smile, which disappeared as their hands brushed. Tingling awareness zinged from their melded palms all the way up her arm. His eyes glittered and his brows descended. Then he broke the contact as if reconsidering the wisdom of a custom of the white world and not of theirs. He drew back, wiping his palm across his middle as if the touch was somehow dangerous. He left his hand stretched across his flat stomach for a moment, his long fingers splayed on the blue cotton fabric of his button-up shirt. Her stomach did a nervous little flutter as her senses came alive. His fingers were thick with a dusting of hair near each knuckle. His fifth finger brushed the top edge of the silver belt buckle bearing a medicine wheel inlaid in black, red, yellow and white. The four directions, the circle of life, the seasons and a compass to guide a man as he walked through life. Why did he wear that symbol?

Her attention dipped below the buckle and stayed fixed long enough for the room to fall silent. The detective's hand shifted toward his personal weapon. Holstered at his hip was a .45 caliber. Then his hand dropped to his side, at the ready.

They'd taken her Glock for the investigation and offered a replacement weapon—a .45 caliber, just like his. She didn't like the stronger recoil. It affected her aim on multiple discharges.

Tinnin cleared his throat and motioned Jack forward. He took a position near her, in front of the desk between Tinnin and Forrest, in only three strides.

Her hand continued to tingle as if she had touched the hot wire of a horse pasture.

She wasn't attracted to Jack Bear Den. She couldn't be. She didn't mix business with pleasure and she wasn't planning to stay one minute more than it took to deliver the bad news.

All three of them were now staring at her. Had they asked her a question?

"What's that now?" she said, her voice sounding odd above the constant buzzing in her ears.

Tinnin fielded that one. "I said, we would like you to advise us on where we might be vulnerable. Specifically, how to protect the reservoirs above us."

"You're on low ground. No protecting you if any of the dams blow." She gritted her teeth as both Tinnin and Bear Den exchanged glances. She should have thought before she spoke.

The councilors told her that she was bound to feel

some anxiety after the shooting and that she would question her own judgment. They hadn't even a clue at how this investigation was messing with her. She was usually way more thoughtful.

"I'm sorry. I spoke out of turn," she said.

She met Bear Den's steady gaze. Her skin felt clammy as the stirring sexual desire crashed against her determination to avoid entanglements. If she'd met him in a different place and time, maybe. But he still looked dangerous. Some part of her liked that, but not the part that liked to eat. Protecting her job meant keeping things professional. What would they say at headquarters if they heard she'd used her leave to bed this guy? Her stomach tightened in dread.

Sophia glanced away from temptation, past the window and the dusty venetian blinds. It was a fine bright September day. The air was cooler at this elevation and it made her homesick for Black Mountain. Everything was green now after the annual monsoonal rains and those, too, reminded her of home.

"I'm sure I can make some useful suggestions," she said. Suggestions like recommending they all move to higher ground if they believed the threat was viable.

She looked to the yellow-and-white rock face that rose on the far plain beyond the flowing water. The Hakathi River threaded through the wide plain. This land, even this office, had once been river bottom. But that was before the dam had captured the water—before the government stole this land and then gave it back to the Turquoise Canyon people.

Bright September sunlight glinted on the glassy surface. The placid winding river didn't fool her. It was dangerous, the vanguard of what lay above their settlements.

"Will that be all right, Sophia?" A man's voice snapped her back to attention. It was Luke who had posed the question.

She lifted her brow at Luke in a gesture that she hoped would alert him that she had not heard a word.

Luke steepled his hands together as if preparing for prayer. "Sophia has been in all the recent briefings, but the Bureau did not put forth your theory. I think it would be of benefit to share it now."

She agreed with that. And listening to their problems sure beat worrying about hers. The minimum administrative leave was five days. But she was already past that. Was that bad? And when exactly would they give her the "pertinent information" they promised her? Last she'd heard the autopsy was complete. When would they release her weapon?

"Yes, I'd appreciate that," she said as she turned to the chief, but she could not resist another look at the detective.

His hair was short, dark and thick with a definite wave. She'd like to rake her hands through that hair.

Chief Tinnin pushed the gum to his cheek, placing it there like chewing tobacco.

"Ms. Rivas, our tribe isn't convinced that the threat of the eco-extremist group BEAR has been neutralized by the death of their leader, Theron Wrangler."

Her office had gone over this in a briefing before the shooting. During the devastating wildfires in July, a prominent citizen and eco-advocate had been murdered. Suspicion had been cast on his wife, Lupe Wrangler, but no evidence was found and she was cleared.

"We feel BEAR is alive and well and that our reservoir system is a likely target for attack."

BEAR was the acronym for Bringing Earth Apocalyptic Restoration. In layman's terms, they wanted to blow man back to the Stone Age, where he couldn't destroy the planet. Some part of her believed man was the earth's biggest threat. But she was no eco-warrior.

Luke surprised her by revealing information she felt proprietary.

"The FBI believes that the death of Theron Wrangler has crippled their organization," said Luke.

Bear Den took it from there. "A member of our society witnessed Lupe Wrangler shoot her husband."

Luke rubbed his forehead and then picked up where Bear Den had left off. "We could find no proof, no evidence to support this man's claim that Lupe Wrangler killed her husband."

Bear Den broke in, his voice now containing a dangerous edge. "Her daughter also witnessed the shooting. You have two witnesses."

"Nonetheless, the Bureau could not break Lupe Wrangler's alibi."

"She should be in custody," said Tinnin.

"I agree and I'm here doing what I can." He had his hand on his neck again, massaging away the tension that now crackled in the room.

"We believe the witnesses. It's not over."

She now recalled the theory that Wrangler's death might trigger sleeper cells to action. Could these men be right? She decided to proceed as if the threat was viable, as she had been trained to do, until she knew otherwise.

"Tribal Thunder contends that this is not over," said Jack Bear Den.

"Tribal Thunder?" she asked.

"These men are Tribal Thunder." Luke motioned to Tinnin and Bear Den. "It's the warrior sect of their medicine society."

She knew about medicine societies—mostly that they were misogynistic groups, all male and secret as heck. Sophia looked from one to the other and speculated on their activities. Certainly protecting their people would be their prime objective.

"Just a few ground rules before you two visit the dam." Tinnin pinned her with his eyes—he no longer looked tired, but was rather deadly serious. "You will be with one of my men at all times."

Her gaze went to Bear Den. It was him, of course. She knew it and the prospect excited and terrified her.

"Detective Bear Den will escort you."

"That's not necessary."

Tinnin glanced to Luke and then back to her. "Your cousin wants assurances you are protected because of the recent incident. He and your supervisors feel there may be an ongoing threat."

She doubted that. Sophia glanced at Bear Den. He looked capable, but an FBI agent did not need the protection of a small-town cop.

"Detective Bear Den is very good and knows the territory," said her cousin. "He's an ex-marine. Weapons specialist. He's been a tribal detective for seven years here and knows the terrain. He is an honored member of his medicine society, the Turquoise Guardians, and of the elite warrior society, Tribal Thunder. He's their best."

Best of nine, she thought.

"You can trust him to keep you safe."

Bear Den spoke to her and his voice was deep and rich as dark coffee. She loved the sound.

"My honor," he said.

She cast him a dubious look and he inclined his chin, as if readying for a fight.

"Detective Bear Den will make sure you are safe," said Luke. "It's a condition of your consultation."

"My supervisor onboard with this?"

"He had no objections."

She blew out her frustration. "Fine."

"So you will have protection 24/7," said Tinnin.

"Maybe twenty-four. Certainly not seven. This won't take as long as you think," Sophia assured him. Her confident smile was met with silence. "I'd like to get started."

Because the sooner they started, the sooner she could get out of here.

"Detective Bear Den will bring you up to the closest reservoir now," said Luke. Bear Den cast her a wicked smile.

And that was when it happened. Her body, always reliable, and her mind, always predictable, both short-circuited at once. Her stomach flipped as she squinted at him trying to figure how the upturning of his lips could make her go all jittery inside. She met the steady stare and the challenge with a smile of her own. The connection grew. He had an air of confidence and a physicality that inspired her to all kinds of bad ideas.

"Check in with me tonight, okay?" said her cousin. "Let me know when you expect to be finished your consultation and I'll come get you."

She tore her gaze from the detective.

"Sure thing," she promised.

"We'll make sure she stays in touch," said Tinnin.

He handed her a large boxy black Motorola radio that looked a decade old. She clipped it to the waistband of her slacks.

"You ready for a tour?" asked the detective.

"Absolutely. I look forward to it." She didn't, because the idea of being trapped in a vehicle with him made her skin itch.

Chapter Two

"Agent Forrest said you were on leave. But he was unclear why you were on leave."

She glanced at him cautiously, perhaps recognizing a fishing expedition when she heard one.

"Was he?" She made no excuses and offered no answers.

He snorted at her posture. Jack Bear Den slowed his stride to match that of his charge. Sophia Rivas was a beauty, but she wasn't very big, reaching only to his shoulder.

She looked straight ahead with her chin up, as if nothing bothered her. Well, *she* bothered *him*. Had certainly gotten under his skin in record time.

Jack accelerated to reach the passenger side door of his SUV before she did. She increased her speed and then let him go. He had the vehicle door open when she reached him.

She looked younger than thirty-three, with wide dark eyes that shifted to scan the vehicle's interior before she cast him a dubious gaze.

"Is that your mobile data terminal?"

The laptop was old and looked like it had been kicked down a flight of stairs, but it worked. Mostly.

"What about it?" He knew he sounded defensive. The

FBI had all the toys and nearly unlimited resources, and he'd had to fix his side mirror with duct tape.

"Nothing," she said, wisely closing her mouth.

Her gaze met his and locked in like a sniper zeroing in on her target.

For a moment he saw the trained FBI agent instead of the most appealing woman he'd seen in…forever. He was just dying to know why she was on administrative leave. He was also dying to know what she looked like naked, but that was an incredibly bad idea. He'd been assigned as her protector. It was a sacred duty and nothing came before his duty.

She carried no weapon at her hip. So she preferred a shoulder holster beneath her blazer. He couldn't see it, but could see just a little honey-brown skin at the modest scoop of her collar. His higher vantage allowed him to also see the slope of her breasts. He glanced away, placing a hand over his own service weapon, which was clipped in a leather holster to his belt. You had to rock it backward to get it clear. Most folks wouldn't know that. But Sophia Rivas sure would.

She glanced at his hand, his thumb locked under the belt just before his weapon. Then her gaze swept up over him in a way that made his entire body flash between alertness and sexual arousal. Finally her gaze held his. She had big amber eyes framed with dark spiked lashes and the kind of mouth that made a man do stupid stuff.

Oh, no. This was not happening. He was not having sexual fantasies about a woman who looked at his headquarters, vehicle and person with a cool disdain.

How had she ended up in explosives? Forensic explosives expert. Odd choice, that.

He reached for her elbow to assist her and she gave him a certain look that made him hesitate.

"I can make it," she said and climbed into his vehicle. He moved to close the door, resisting the pull to step nearer to her. Then he rounded his SUV and slid into the driver's seat.

He wiped his damp palm on his trousers before turning the key. He gave a cough meant to clear his dry throat.

"Thank you for agreeing to help us."

"I'm not sure how much help I can be. The canyon walls are steep on both sides and we are clearly in a gap in what used to be riverbed."

"You wouldn't want to be here if any of the three reservoirs go."

"Can we tour the interior workings of the dam system?"

"Yes. I've arranged a tour for tomorrow."

She gave a little laugh and shook her head.

"What?"

"My cousin knows that we aren't seeing the interior until tomorrow?"

"Yes, I mentioned it to him."

"And yet he sent me up here today. Where is it I will be staying? I didn't see a hotel or casino."

"Yeah, we don't have a hotel, or rather we do and it is connected to the casino, but it's being renovated. Grand opening is this November. Maybe you can come back."

"I highly doubt that."

"Don't worry, I have a bed for you."

Agent Rivas was out of the car and marching toward the station before he could turn off the ignition. He didn't see her again until he reached the squad room and that was only her back as she entered his chief's office without knocking.

He slowed as Olivia, their dispatcher, gave him a look.

"I wouldn't," she advised.

He took her advice and waited. It didn't take long. Rivas emerged red-faced and panting, her fists clenched. She cast him a murderous look and continued past him. He let her stride away, following until he returned to his seat beside her in his SUV.

"Ready?" he asked.

"Not even close," she said. "Why didn't you tell me that we would not be alone?"

"You didn't really give me a chance. It's on our tribal gathering grounds. There are several cabins. I'll be there along with some of the members of Tribal Thunder. But you'll have a private cabin. It's a beautiful place beside the river and we have a lodge with a generator for gathering at nights."

"Nights? I only packed an overnight bag. You think there will be more than one?"

"Tinnin said we'd have you until Tuesday. Time enough to see all four dams, inside and out."

She rubbed her slender neck and looked straight ahead. "Four days. After that I'm going home, even if I have to walk."

They sat in silence, the A/C blowing in their heated faces. The air between them seemed to move with currents all their own. He hadn't felt this kind of attraction, ever.

"Can I call you Jack?" she asked.

"Sounds fine. Shall I call you Sophia?"

"Fine."

"You want to know why I'm stuck up here in the hinterland instead of working on a case?" she asked.

Jack shifted in his seat. "Sure."

"I was involved in an incident of fatal force."

That was a euphemism that told him she'd killed someone. Likely shot them.

"I'm sorry to hear that."

"So I'm on administrative leave until they finish the investigation and clear me."

"FBI conducts their own investigations, right?"

"Yes."

"So you should be fine."

"What's that supposed to mean? You think they'll sweep any mistake I made under some rug bearing the FBI seal?"

He shrugged and set his vehicle in motion.

"Well, they won't. I could be relieved of duty, permanently. And that can't happen."

"If you say so."

"And they wanted me to see a shrink. When I said no, they extended my leave.

"It wasn't even the assignment I'm working, which is going to hell, I'm sure. Luke thought I might like to go home to our rez." She shook her head. "Can't do that so he came up with this to distract me. A welcome diversion. Ha. Oh, anyway, it doesn't matter. I'm stuck here until they take me back."

"You can't go home?" he asked.

She cast him a look and then turned to stare out the window. Only then did he realize he had asked Luke nothing about her upbringing. All he knew was that she was of the Black Mountain people, butterfly born of spider.

But who was she deep down, where it mattered? Jack wanted answers.

"You want to talk about it—the investigation?"

She shook her head.

"Okay. I'm a good listener. Just saying. So, do you have brothers and sisters?"

She didn't look at him. "Yeah. And tons of cousins. My mom came from a big family. Where are we going?"

"Top of the canyon. I thought I'd give you an overview. Okay?"

She nodded.

"I've got three brothers," said Jack. "Carter is the oldest. He's my twin and he's coming home soon. He's under protection by the Department of Justice."

That sure got her attention. Her posture changed and she half turned to stare at him.

"Why?"

"Witness. He went with his wife, Amber, who survived the mass shooting at Lilac copper mine. She was going to testify in a federal case against Theron Wrangler."

"But Wrangler is dead and so they don't need witnesses."

"That's right." She was quick and pretty.

"Then there are Tommy and Kurt. They are younger. Kurt flies in the air ambulance out of Darabee. Next town over. And Tommy is a Shadow Wolf on the border."

"Border patrol?"

"They work under Immigration and Customs Enforcement—ICE. But he works with border patrol, too."

"Shadow Wolves. That's the all–Native American outfit, right?"

"Exactly. They're on the Tohono Oodham lands."

"I've been down there. It's hot."

"Most of Arizona is."

"But not here and not Black Mountain." She seemed

to have lost some of her bristle. "Listen, I'm sorry your people feel threatened by BEAR."

"What's your take on it?"

"I'm not briefed. Really, I only know that group has been connected with the Lilac shooting and might be involved with the Pine View wildfire in July."

On the drive he told her what he could. Carter had rescued Amber Kitcheyan from the Lilac copper mine and placed himself between her and BEAR's assassins, and the Lilac shooter had been caught. She knew that the mass murderer had been subsequently executed and that the assassin was a member of the Turquoise Canyon Apache tribe, Detective Bear Den's tribe. She did not know that the shooter had been terminally ill, or that his death had brought suspicion on his daughter, Morgan Hooke.

"Our men set up protection for Morgan Hooke as a precaution."

"What happened?"

"She helped us recover the blood money paid to her dad. And she and her daughter are safe. You'll meet Ray Strong soon. He's one of our men and her assigned bodyguard. Soon he'll be her husband."

She made a face that showed her disapproval of that turn of events.

"You know about Meadow Wrangler?" he asked.

"More than you do, I'd suspect."

"She witnessed her father's death."

"I know that. I also know she has a history of substance abuse resulting in rehab."

"She got drunk at eighteen and swam in a country club's fountain."

"She's an unreliable witness."

"We believe her."

Sophia shrugged. "Your prerogative."

They crested the top of the canyon rim and Jack brought them to a halt.

"This is it. From here you can see Skeleton Cliff Dam above our land and also Piñon Forks and Koun'nde, our two main settlements. Turquoise Ridge is out of sight and also above flood level."

"Let's have a look." She exited the vehicle and their doors closed simultaneously.

Jack walked easily to the edge of the rim, where the rock bluff ended, leaving the dizzying drop to the valley below. The river had once cut this canyon from solid stone and spanned the gap where the town of Piñon Forks now stood. He had never seen the river roar with the yearly monsoonal rains because the dam and reservoir system had been installed in the 1920s, long before the stretch of his memory. But the old ones remembered. Few had seen it tumble and rage and then shrink like the belly of a woman after giving birth. The floods left rich fertile soil deposited yearly. They also left wetlands that burst with mosquitoes and that brought yellow fever. Crops were raised in the rich earth, but now the land was fit only for grazing livestock and none died from yellow fever. Was it better now than before the river was tamed?

He didn't know. He only knew it was different. They had electricity, mobile phones and no crops.

"That's quite a drop," she said.

"Nine hundred meters from that point above us. Over a half-mile deep." Jack smiled. "See that spot over there?" He pointed to the arched cut in the yellow sandstone. From here it looked close to the water. "That's just short of eleven meters—higher than an Olympic diving platform. We used to jump off it into the deep water."

"That's foolish."

"Fun. It was fun."

"You and your friends sound reckless. I don't take such chances."

"Too bad. It was a thrill. What did you do up on Black Mountain for fun?"

Her eyes went sad and then she looked away, leaving Jack to wonder what kind of a childhood she'd had on her rez.

"So what do you want to show me?"

Back to business then. He pointed out the landmarks, towns and road system along the river and bridge east of the reservation. Beyond sat the great gray wall of Skeleton Cliff Dam that allowed just enough water to keep their livestock alive and their towns above the waterline.

"That looks like a very healthy vein of turquoise," she said, motioning to the line of blue threading through the canyon wall beyond the river.

"Yes. It is good quality, too. We don't mine by the river anymore. Too much overburden," he said, pointing to the dangerous overhang of rock created by undercutting the hill to retrieve the turquoise below. "But we have some nice veins farther north at Turquoise Ridge. Very hard and nice nodules. Turquoise varies by looks and quality. That over there is brilliant blue with a webbing pattern called 'bird's eye.'"

"I know it."

"We also have bright blue with flecks of iron pyrite up on Turquoise Ridge. That's our main mining sight now. It's pale blue to dark blue. We get a little green sometimes. But that's rare."

"You wear it on your belt," she said.

He tilted the buckle. "Yeah. This is from that ridge," he said, grazing a thumb over the brilliant blue outer inlay that surrounded the medicine wheel. Then he lifted his hand to brush the grey Stetson on his head. "My hatband, this paler blue with the fleck of black chert matrix, this is from Turquoise Ridge."

"Chert?"

"Those are the blackish inclusion of the host rock that makes the cut stones more valuable, similar to spider web veining. Some collectors prefer the veining and inclusions to the solid blue stone."

"You know your turquoise," she said.

"Major biz here. Digging it, selling it at the rock-and-mineral shows. We go as far as Australia for shows. And we make jewelry." He looked back over the rim to the blue river of turquoise that threaded through the dark stone. He pointed. "We derived our name from that vein of turquoise. It would be a shame to cut it all away. We do collect what erodes and you'd be surprised."

He followed the direction of her gaze as she glanced from the mineral vein down to Piñon Forks and then returned her attention to the opposite rim a mile up from where they stood, pausing on the yellow rim of rock. This was the narrowest section of the canyon. Here the walls became pinched so the canyon was wide enough only for the river that touched the cliffs on both sides. He always thought that this spot must have been a heck of a rapid before the dam.

He tried to picture the surging torrent that once climbed far of the smooth walls and hoped he'd never see the water forced through that narrow gap.

Now her attention flicked to the wide flood plain, where his rez had placed their major settlement, Piñon Forks, then lifted to fix on the Skeleton Cliff Dam.

"That is really close," she said, folding her arms before her. The gesture lifted the tops of her breasts so that he saw the mounds of firm tempting flesh over the scoop of her maroon blouse. His mouth went as dry as the cliff stone.

She turned to him and opened her mouth to speak, then caught the direction of his stare. Her hands dropped to her sides. Her amber eyes and sinking brows sent a clear message of displeasure.

"Sorry," he said.

"I was about to say that the reservoir system in total is at a high-water point for the year. August rainfall set a new record and so a break in any of the dams would theoretically compromise the one below. If I was trying to destroy the system I would focus on Alchesay Canyon Dam because it's the largest and holds back Goodwin Lake."

"Your cousin told us that the FBI presence is focused on that dam as well. But what if they hit this one? Skeleton Cliff Dam is very close to our land. It wasn't even land before they dammed this river."

"Listen, with the force of that water and the speed, I have to be honest. If the dam goes, there would not be time to evacuate. And that break would carry enough water and debris to at least overflow Red Rock Dam below your lands. Likely Mesa Salado Dam, too."

"That one is above the Yavapi Indian Reservation."

"It would shut down the power grid for Phoenix." Her hushed voice relayed the gravity of her thoughts.

"Your cousin told us he can't discuss the surveillance methods on the dam system, just that they do have eyes on all the dams, have taken preventative action and established rapid response for various scenarios."

"We do our job, Jack."

"So what steps do we take?"

"Other than evacuate all low-land areas indefinitely, I can't really offer suggestions." She waved her hand toward the opposite rim. "Your best hope is to protect the dams."

"They aren't our dams. We can't protect them."

"We're protecting them."

Jack sent a look her way that he hoped relayed his lack of faith in the government protecting his people—history was on his side on that one. She rolled her eyes, returning her attention to the flood plan.

"Evacuate now," she said.

"We have nowhere to go." She made a face. Then she shook her head and her voice took on a sarcastic edge. "Well, you could blow up that entire ridge up there. That would stop anything. Theoretically."

He'd never considered fighting an explosion with another one. But it could work.

Her eyes rounded. "Jack, it was a joke. Just a stupid offhanded remark. You can't blow up that canyon wall."

"I can't. But you could."

Chapter Three

"That's crazy. I'm not blowing up anything. I'm here to advise you," said Sophia. She was sweating now, but it was a cold sweat and her skin had gone to gooseflesh.

One thing she knew with certainty—there was no way in hell she was ever, under any circumstances, doing anything that could affect the outcome of her fatal force investigation. Destroying federal land in a massive unauthorized explosion qualified.

"No," she said. "No way and hell no."

Jack's smile told her that this wasn't over and she felt like kicking herself for opening her big mouth. What if they did something incredibly stupid, like tried to blow that opposite wall and then they told her supervisors that it was her suggestion?

"You can't be seriously considering this." She tried to make her voice reflect her incredulity, but instead there was a definite tremor.

"I'll consider anything that keeps my people from drowning."

"We're protecting the dam system, Jack. You and your warrior society don't have to do anything. This is federal land. All of it. It falls under federal jurisdiction."

He pointed toward Piñon Forks. "That's Apache land and we will protect it as we see fit."

31

"I hope you like federal prisons, because that's where you're heading if you blow one single rock of this canyon. This is a wetland system. It's crucial to the power grid and it's beautiful."

"You have a better idea?"

"That wasn't an idea! It was a joke."

"How would you set the blasts, in your joke?" he asked.

"You must think I'm crazy to answer a question like that. Besides you don't have access to the kind of explosives you'd need."

"We have mining explosives, det cord, blasting caps and rolls of shock tubing."

He used the abbreviation for detonation cord, used to trigger explosions of the main charge and his knowledge caused her to lift her brows in surprise. "Turquoise mining," he said, answering her unspoken question. "The community operation is mostly underground now, following the veins as they run deeper. Plus we have lots of smaller claims. My friend Dylan Tehauno has a really good one up there on Turquoise Ridge. Lots of blasting material here."

"If you are considering this, I have to report you."

He smiled as his eyes challenged her. "Just a joke. Like yours." He glanced toward the west. The town below was already cast in shadows, but up here it blazed orange as the sun made its final descent.

He sat on the canyon rim and glanced up at her. "Want to watch the sunset?"

She sat beside him, close enough to feel the heat of his body but not quite touching him.

"Turns the river into a ribbon of gold." He pointed to where the river flowed a deep orange color that changed by the minute.

"Jack, I'm in the middle of a fatal-force investigation. I cannot be involved in blowing anything up. This is a consult. Remember?"

"Back to the investigation again. Why are you so worried? Did you screw up?"

"No. I—well, I don't think so. Maybe."

"You can tell me, Sophia."

She lowered her head, staring at nothing that he could see.

"I'm a former US Marine. I've shot people before."

"That's different." She waved a dismissive hand. Then squared her shoulders and drew a breath. She was going to tell him and the realization filled her with both hope and terror.

"Do you know that there is not one person in my office that has even discharged their weapon, let alone been engaged in a significant-use-of-force incident? Well, Mel drew on a pit bull but he didn't shoot because he got over a fence in time."

"It happens to a lot of us," he said again. "And if you can't sleep or think or eat, that's all just part of it. The crappy part, but it's necessary. Eventually, you live with it. Mostly the memories stay down."

He sat beside her overlooking the river as the clouds changed colors before her eyes. *Clouds*, she thought. That meant more rains would be coming.

"I shot a young Hispanic male," she said.

He nodded. Saying nothing but somehow his silence encouraged her to continue.

"Here's what happened. I'm going to say it fast so I don't have to think about it all night." She drew a breath as if preparing to submerge in deep water, then let it out. "Okay, I was off-duty and in my new car. I had just leased a BMW, black, Two Series. I mean I just left the dealership and I got bumped. I considered that it was a scam and so I had my weapon out when I left the vehicle. The male driver told me to step away from my BMW. Actually he said, 'Give me the keys.' And then he called me a…well, it doesn't matter. He demanded the keys and reached for something in his coat. I saw the handgun before I fired. He died at the scene."

Jack scratched his chin, feeling the stubble growing there. Seemed like a home run to him. She'd defended herself and from her version he saw no reason for her to worry.

"Seems justified."

"But it wasn't a handgun. It was a phone. He did have an unregistered handgun on his person. But that was not what he pointed at me. And he kept the phone pointed at me, even when he went to his knees."

"You think he meant to photograph the damage?"

"I'll never know."

"Sophia, he told you to give him your keys. There is only one reason to hit a new Beamer and then demand the keys. He was boosting your car."

"Probably."

Jack's anger took him totally by surprise. He tried to understand why he was so furious at this unknown perp. And then it struck him. He'd be murderous with anyone who threatened her. How had she gotten under his skin so fast?

She could have died and he would never have had a chance to know her. He wanted that chance. Trouble was, she didn't. She had made it very clear that she could not wait to be out of here and back on the job.

"Does he have a criminal record or history of stealing cars?"

"I don't know. They won't tell me anything, and I

don't have access to the system. I do know his name.
Nothing else yet. I've made my formal statement. I met
with the union rep and our attorney. They gave me the
protocol."

"Referral to mental-health professional?"

"Sure. And contact with an agent who also had a
deadly force encounter in Phoenix. But he was on a
raid of a grow house and everyone inside was dirty and
heavily armed. Not the same."

A grow house was a home, usually abandoned, taken
over and converted to an indoor greenhouse to grow
marijuana. The drug producers were often well armed
and prepared to defend their crop.

He said nothing. No one's life experiences were the
same, but all could be used to help every person find
their path.

The silence stretched as the first star, Venus, appeared in the western sky.

"They've been investigating since Sunday. SAC said
he'd keep me updated. He really hasn't."

"SAC?"

"Special agent in charge. He's my liaison to the thir-
teen-member SIRG. That's 'shooting incident review
group.'"

"Really?" Thirteen seemed like overkill. But this
was the FBI. He knew that their investigation would
be exhaustive and in-house.

"I haven't heard anything since Thursday, when
he told me the autopsy had been completed and that I
should get my personal weapon back next week."

"Any results from the autopsy?"

"He's still dead."

Jack almost laughed, but reined it in. She looked
so grim.

"So what's next?"

"Interviews with the two witnesses. Photographs. Diagrams and the report by the administrative director of the office of inspections."

"That's a real thing?"

She cast him a scowl. "Of course. He's chairman of SIRG."

"Supervising the cast of thirteen."

"Twelve, minus himself."

"I can see why you're nervous."

"No. You can't. Your shooter had fired at you. My shooter was pointing a camera. One of the witnesses also had a phone and may have taken a photograph or video."

"More evidence."

"Yes."

"You feel you made a mistake?"

"No. But what matters is what SIRG thinks. If they rule my actions unjustified, I could lose my job. Everything."

There was a definite note of panic in her voice.

"All the schooling, training, work…gone." She snapped her fingers. "Like that. And I'm not going back…" Her words trailed off.

Back where? To her reservation? He cast her a questioning look, but Sophia had clamped her mouth shut and laced her fingers so tightly in her lap her fingernails were going blue.

Jack offered her the only thing he could think of. "You have his name. I can run him through our system."

Her eyes shifted to him.

"You'd do that?"

Jack didn't say so aloud, but he'd do a lot more than that for her because despite knowing that she could not wait to put him and his tribe in her rearview mirror, he was desperately attracted to her.

"I would."

She wrapped her arms around her knees and rocked back and forth. He lay a hand on her shoulder and she stilled and glanced up at him.

"Thank you." She placed a hand over his. It wasn't until her hand slid away that he could breathe again.

"Yeah. Don't mention it. Name?"

"Martin Nequam."

Jack asked for the spelling and she provided it.

The light had changed again, casting the sky in bright fuchsia and red. He glanced away from her, taking in their surroundings.

"It gets pretty dark up here at night," he said. "And the road can be tricky. We'd best head down. Get you settled. And I want to introduce you to the others."

She followed him back to the SUV. "What others?"

"The men of Tribal Thunder, Dylan, Ray and my brother Kurt. Carter, when he gets home. And Ray's wife, Morgan."

"You're not talking about the daughter of the man who murdered the Lilac gunman?"

"The very same. Also Dylan's fiancé, Meadow Wrangler."

"*The* Meadow Wrangler? As in, daughter of the murdered prime suspect and leader of BEAR."

"It's her mom. Even Meadow says so."

"Interesting attack team. You have at least two members who might be working for BEAR."

"They're not."

Sophia got back into his vehicle and clipped her seat belt, saying nothing to that. She would not be offering any more advice and she would sure as heck not be making any more jokes.

"You wanted to be sure we weren't alone."

"So instead we have a party."

"Planning committee."

"If you really feel threatened, then they should be planning an evacuation."

They drove along the road that was more switchback than straightway. The angle of descent was jarring and Sophia had to hold on to the handgrip above her passenger window to keep from jostling into Jack Bear Den, whose wide body spilled across the center console and into her personal space.

She was not sure what to make of him. He was a detective, sworn to protect and serve. Did blowing the opposite ridge qualify? Only if he was right and the dam failed. But then there would be no time to set the charges. They would have to be placed early.

Why was he so darn big? She was attracted to big, muscular men. Jack unfortunately ticked all the right boxes except for one—he was trying to get her mixed up in a career-ender. She'd worked too long and hard to get off the Black Mountain rez to jeopardize that. Having a career gave her money, respect and purpose, and it kept her from having to ever rely on the system to protect her.

He held the wheel as he flexed his arm muscles and stretched, showing thick fingers nicked with white scars on the knuckles in the golden light of sundown. He had strong hands to match the rest of him.

Sophia liked men, but she didn't depend on them. She glanced at Jack, his face now cast in shadows as they crossed below the line of sunlight. Sleeping with him would be dangerous, but perhaps the thrill would be worth the risk. As long as she remembered that after she toured the dam system, she was out of here and he was not coming along for the ride.

Jack angled his head and shoulders, making his joints give a popping sound, without ever releasing the steering wheel.

"We'll be down soon."

The road did finally level out to a rolling pasture. He flipped on his headlights. They continued through the town. She glanced at the tribal headquarters, which had lights illuminating the great seal of his people. It featured the river, of course, the cliffs and a single sacred eagle above them both.

They continued downriver as the sun set, and drove past the neat houses and fences that held the cattle. Cattle, ranching and rodeo were all a way of life for her people as well. Signs warned to watch for horses.

"You don't pen the horses, either?" she asked.

"No. The river and canyon does that," said Jack. "We're just up here." He slowed and turned onto a dirt road, lined with barbed wire on each side. She could see the cattle, dark shapes in the fields. The headlights made their eyes glow green as they passed.

She lifted her phone and called her cousin, checking in as he requested. But she didn't tell him about the misunderstanding about her flippant suggestion which the detective seemed to be seriously considering.

Jack pulled off the main road and drove toward the river again.

"This is the place where our medicine society gathers. It has a large outdoor meeting space, sweat lodge and fire pit. But most importantly for you, the tribe uses it for ceremonies, so we have several cabins on site. You'll have a one-bedroom with working bathroom.

Hot and cold water, too. I'll take the one beside yours. Ray Strong has the one on your opposite side and Dylan Tehauno the one after that. Ray's wife, Morgan, and her girl will be here for dinner, then she's got to get their daughter back home. Lisa is Ray's stepdaughter, actually. But Meadow Wrangler will be spending the night. Couldn't keep her away."

"I see."

She was about to say that it wasn't necessary for the others to chaperone. But the way he looked at her gave her pause. He seemed hungry and that simple glance was all it took for her heart to pound and her stomach to twist. Oh, she wanted Jack Bear Den in all the ways a woman wanted a man. And since she could not leave, having chaperones might be a really wise idea. She needed to either stay away from Jack or get it over with. After all, he was just a man. Getting him out of her system might be the wisest course. There was no regulation against sleeping with him. He was not a colleague or a suspect. He was the friend of her cousin.

Fair game.

Sophia ignored the internal warning alarm sounding in her mind. She'd had short affairs before. They were the best kind, allowing her the excitement and physical contact of a man's company without the entanglements. Leaving before they did was just self-preservation, because, sooner or later, they all left. But she'd never been this interested before. In fact, she had intentionally picked men she had minimal interest in. Made leaving easier.

"Sophia? Will that arrangement work for you?"

"Seems fine, but not Wrangler. She's connected to an ongoing investigation. It would be best if I had no contact with her."

"See, I'd think you'd want contact. Especially if you think she's involved."

"Not my investigation," she said.

"We don't think she's involved."

"Why is she still up here? I'd think a woman like her would be bored to death."

"Well, if she leaves, the highway patrol or Flagstaff PD will arrest her as a person of interest in the Pine View fire."

"Ah," said Sophia.

"She didn't do it. But you make up your own mind. If you don't want her to stay, I can speak to Dylan. But it's an insult and he's my friend."

"They're a couple?"

"Yes, but they don't live together."

That surprised Sophia. From all accounts Meadow was a wild woman with numerous short, public affairs.

Sophia took the irresistible bait to meet the infamous heiress, Meadow Wrangler.

"She's your guest," said Sophia.

He gave a toot on his horn and hit the lights of the SUV. A moment later the headlights illuminated a large square structure, the lodge she supposed. Onto the porch spilled five men, two women and a child. She recognized only one—Wallace Tinnin.

"That's our tribal director in red. The rest are all members of Tribal Thunder."

"The men, you mean."

"No, all. Our warrior sect includes women. But not children. Lisa, the girl, is not yet a member. But if we are successful, she will live to join someday."

The gravity of his words struck her. What for Sophia was a hypothetical problem to be considered and quickly set aside was for the Turquoise Canyon Tribe a matter of life and death.

Jack made introductions on the porch. Sophia shook every hand as if she was running for public office. She recognized Meadow Wrangler from her photo, but the blue hair was new. Sophia tried not to stare. When she met the executive council president, she both shook his hand and bowed her head in respect. She did the same when she met Kenshaw Little Falcon, their shaman and leader of their medicine society.

The formalities complete, Morgan Hooke offered to take Sophia to her cabin to freshen up.

"Where's Agent Forrest?" asked Sophia.

Kenshaw Little Falcon took the question.

"He had to return to Phoenix. I drove him to the airport in Darabee. But he left the car for you." He motioned toward the dark portion of the field, where she had seen the vehicles parked when they'd arrived.

Luke had abandoned her. Nasty trick, she thought. Sophia tugged at the hem of her blazer and forced a smile. She was now alone among strangers.

"I see."

Morgan lifted a lantern from a nail and motioned Sophia down the steps.

Sophia knew of Morgan since her cousin had been lead on the FBI investigation into the shooting of the Lilac gunman. Morgan's father had killed the shooter, a paid assassin, according to Luke. How had that affected this woman and her child?

"Let me show you to your cabin so you can freshen up before supper," Morgan said again.

Under the bright starlight, they picked their way to the cabin. Morgan preceded her through the door and set her lantern on a small wooden table. Then she fished in her pocket for a book of matches, lifted a second lantern from a nail beside the cabin door and lighted the wick. The smell sent Sophia right back to the home of her childhood, making her stomach roil.

"Everything all right?" asked Morgan. "It's not much, but Dylan cleaned it up and Meadow changed the bedding. It's all new."

Meadow changed the bedding? The woman she believed to be a spoiled little rich girl had made a bed? Sophia couldn't believe it.

"Meadow?"

"Yeah. She's not so bad."

Oh, Sophia had to disagree. If she wasn't bad, she lived in the same house with bad for most of her life.

"It's lovely," said Sophia.

And it was so much nicer than her childhood home on the Black Mountain rez had been.

"Well, you can't beat the view of the river and the canyons across the way. You can't see it now, but tomorrow, from the porch, it's beautiful."

The river again. It seemed to be taunting her now.

"Plumbing works. Hot water, too. Just no electric. You know how to light a kerosene lamp?"

Sophia was all too familiar with how to do so, but had hoped she would never have to use a lantern again.

She forced a smile. "Absolutely."

"They brought your bag in. It's by the bed."

Sophia followed the direction Morgan indicated and found both her briefcase and the bag Luke suggested she pack "in case things run long."

"Do you want me to wait for you and bring you back to the lodge?" asked Morgan.

"I can find my way."

"Well, I'll leave you to get settled."

Sophia just wanted to slip into her yoga pants and a loose T-shirt and climb into bed. It had already been a long day.

"I'll be over in a few minutes."

"Bring a lamp," said Morgan as she hesitated at the door. "We are so grateful to you for coming to help us. Luke told us all about you, and we are hopeful you can give us advice so we can protect ourselves. I don't know if Jack told you but I lost my father to cancer. But before that I lost him to BEAR. It's a dangerous group and none of us believe they are done. They still have the Lilac explosives. If this is their target, we are in terrible danger."

Sophia did not have the first idea how to reply. Mostly she felt guilty for wanting nothing more than to get out of here. Being so close to the river now gave her the creeps. And she realized why. Because she believed her cousin and Morgan. BEAR was still out there. How would she feel if she could not pack up and leave in four days?

Had they planned all this, Luke and their shaman, Little Falcon? To show her the pastures that lined the river and the town and this gathering place, the very heart of the reservation, so she could see what would be lost? The problem that had been theoretical was now all too tangible.

Morgan hesitated, lingering. "I have a little girl. We live right in Piñon Forks. Her school is there, too." Morgan's hand went to her stomach and Sophia saw the definite bump she had not seen before. Morgan was expecting a child.

The two women stared across the silent cabin.

"I'll do what I can," said Sophia.

Morgan cast her a sad smile and left her with her

troubled thoughts. For the first time in five days, the investigation was not the most important thing on Sophia's mind.

Chapter Four

Sophia unpacked, then used the bathroom, checked her hair and reworked her ponytail before heading back across the open ground with the darn kerosene lamp held high to light her way.

She knocked and entered. The smell of fry bread made her mouth water and brought her back to some of her earliest memories. Meadow motioned her to a chair and the group sat to eat baked chicken with a tangy sauce, mashed potatoes, corn, three different types of casseroles, including one of a noodle pudding that was especially good, and the fry bread, golden brown and piping hot. Sophia knew how much trouble it was to turn the simple ingredients for fry bread into dough and appreciated the effort as much as the flavor.

After the meal, several newcomers arrived and both Morgan and Meadow were absent. Their shaman greeted her formally, as if they had not just shared a meal, his smile flanked with vertical lines. Then he motioned her forward to meet an older man, who wore his hair cut blunt at the shoulder. About his neck was a bolo of the tribe's great shield inlayed with stone. The river, she noted, was a fine blue spiderweb turquoise.

"Sophia, this is our executive director, Zachery Gill." The older man extended his hand as Kenshaw continued speaking. "Gill is the new leader of our tribal council. Zach, this is field agent and explosives expert Sophia Rivas."

Gill had a fleshy tanned face and was dressed simply in a cotton shirt and jeans with no indication of his rank outside the ornate bolo.

"Welcome to Turquoise Canyon, Agent Rivas. Thank you for answering our call for help," said Gill. He motioned a broad hand to the empty chair and she took a seat. Gill sat to her left as everyone took their seats. The circular dining table had transformed into a war room.

Each attendee introduced themselves by clan, family name and first name, and ended with their position. They were tribal law enforcement, tribal council and warriors of Tribal Thunder.

When Jack spoke her stomach fluttered and she mentally scolded herself for her very physical reaction to the man that was seated on the far side of the table, which she now realized resembled a medicine wheel with each section made from a different color of wood. Jack sat at one point and she at another of the four directions. Did he notice that the line bisecting the table seemed to connect them?

Finally the circle came back to their shaman. Kenshaw rose as he addressed the gathering. "Some of our tribe have been elected to protect the language, some care for and teach our young people, and still others guard our heritage. These men and women have one mission, the survival of our people, and each and every one is prepared to defend our tribe with their lives. They are at your service, Agent Rivas."

"While I appreciate the offer, no one is going to die as a result of my visit. I'm just here to have a look at the reservoir system. I'll report back to my field office if I see any gaps in their existing protective plan. I can assure you that no one is going to compromise the power grid."

There was a general shifting of chairs and postures. You didn't have to be a master at reading a room to know that the tribe members here disagreed.

Director Gill spoke to Sophia. "Jack was just telling us about your plan to create a makeshift dam with a series of controlled blasts at the narrow point of our canyon."

Her eyes flashed to Jack's and held. "That was not at all what I advised."

Gill continued as if she had not made an objection.

"We feel, that should the Skeleton Cliff Dam fail, we would not have time to evacuate our people."

"I can assure you, it is very safe, protected by our Bureau and the state highway patrol."

"Yes, we know. We have seen them and our warriors have gotten past them. Back to my point—if the dam was to fail, how long would we have to evacuate?"

Gotten past them? That wasn't good at all.

"That would depend on the scale of the breach."

Gill lifted his thin brow at her. "Total breach."

She drew a breath and released it. There was no way to deliver hard news but directly.

"Minutes," she said.

JACK WATCHED SOPHIA'S face as she delivered the news that the two settlements along the river, Piñon Forks and Koun'nde, would not have enough warning to evacuate.

"But they could be moved to higher ground now. You have three towns. Those in the lower two could move to…" She lifted her gaze to the ceiling as she tried to retrieve the name of their third and smallest town.

"Turquoise Ridge," Jack said.

She smiled at him and his stomach trembled in a way that he hadn't experienced since middle school, when all his hormones had been popping in different directions. He grimaced. The woman was near desperate to be clear of them all. He knew that, but still he could not deny that, even knowing she couldn't wait to be rid of him, he was still imagining what she'd look like out of that suit.

"They could relocate there," said Sophia.

Zachery Gill took that one. "We have only sixteen hundred members. Over nine hundred live on the rez, nearly all of whom live along the river. Turquoise Ridge is for our miners and loggers. There's nothing up there but rock and ponderosa pine."

"But it's high ground," she said.

"It's impossible. We even asked FEMA for temporary housing. I'll bet you can guess the answer."

Judging from the pressing of her full lips, Jack felt that she did. FEMA would not provide emergency housing before an emergency and the federal and state officials had indicated that all was safe regarding the reservoir system.

"Did you say you got men past the security?" she asked.

"Men and women. The road across the top of the dam is blocked with one concrete barrier on each side and a state police vehicle on the east side. We were allowed on tours with only our tribal identification cards and saw the inner workings of each dam during public tours. We were allowed to walk up to the top of the dam."

"Single individuals could not carry enough explosives to destroy a dam. At worst they'd damage the power station."

"We have a twenty-four-foot police boat, which had been seized from the property of a drug dealer convicted on their rez. We use it for water rescues and search-and-rescue."

He had her attention.

"We were able to bring it and a flat fifteen-foot Zodiac with a load capacity of 250 pounds simultaneously within ten feet of the base of the dam. We were there nearly forty-five minutes before there was a response."

Sophia was no longer meeting the director's gaze. Instead she was staring into space. A moment later she reached for her phone.

"I need to check in."

"You're on leave," reminded the shaman.

"But if what you say is true then I need to report this."

Zach smiled. "We tell you this for two reasons. One, because we wish you to see that we are vulnerable."

They waited but Zach said no more. Sophia glanced at Jack, the look of confusion evident. He did nothing but glance back to the executive director. But now there seemed to be a steel band around his ribs squeezing away the air from his lungs and making it hard to draw a full breath. If just looking at her did this to him, he really, really needed to avoid touching her. Yet he could think of nothing else.

Sophia inadvertently rescued him by directing her expressive dark eyes at Gill.

"What is the other reason?"

"You are here and you are listening."

"Yes, but I can't help you blow up the canyon. It would be an ecological disaster for the river, not to mention destroying the water supply to both Red Rock and Mesa Salado Dams below this position."

"We disagree," said Kenshaw. "Creating a temporary dam of rock and debris would actually save both dams from the flood and debris that would at best test the limits of their infrastructure. All reservoirs are at their limits now after a record rain. We believe this is what BEAR has been waiting for. The rains have come and gone and the water is high."

"I can't help you do this." She folded her arms. The action lifted her breasts.

Jack stared and when he finally tore his gaze away, it was to meet Ray's knowing glance. Jack wanted to knock the smirk off his face. Ray had settled down since marrying Morgan and taking on the role as father to Lisa. They were now expecting their first child, but there was still devilment in him. Ray leaned toward Dylan Tehauno and whispered something. Dylan's gaze snapped to Jack, and he stared with wide eyes full of surprise. Jack had a reputation for being very selective when it came to women. Jack shook the thoughts from his head and realized Kenshaw was speaking, his voice as hypnotic as the wavering notes of a flute.

"No need to decide and no action to take. Tonight we will pray and dance and perhaps then know better what direction to go."

"Folks will be arriving soon," said Gill to Sophia. "You are welcome to join us. Tomorrow Jack will take you to the reservoir system. You can see if you think the protection is adequate. After that we will talk again."

Sophia stood. "Then if you'll excuse me, I think I will turn in. Early start tomorrow."

Actually they would start late. Jack wanted her to see the day tours, but also night surveillance because

Kenshaw was right. It was not that hard to get past one state police car parked at one end of each dam. Closing the bridge spanning the dam was a predictable security measure. But one Humvee followed by a tractor trailer could knock the concrete barrier aside without even slowing down.

There were many things Jack wanted to show Sophia Rivas. But he would stick to the ones relating to the reservoir system. For now.

Jack followed Sophia out of the council lodge. He paused to grab her kerosene lantern. The lantern was unnecessary really, because of the waning moon, now in its quarter. The silvery light reflected back on the placid surface of the Hakathi River.

"You forgot your lantern," he said and offered her the handle.

She made a sniffing sound. "I don't like them."

"Lanterns?"

"Yes, lanterns—they smell," she said.

"I like it—it smells like—"

"Poverty," she said, finishing his sentence.

He cocked his head at the odd association. Did she mean that people used kerosene when they had no electricity? For him the association of the lantern brought back memories of camping along the river as a boy, but perhaps she did not have electricity in her home on Black Mountain. His tribe had some homes on propane up in Turquoise Ridge, but most everyone had electricity and septic tanks. Hadn't she?

"Well, we don't need it. It's bright enough."

She just kept walking until she reached the front porch facing the river. All the cabins faced the river so he understood why she had picked the wrong one.

Close, just one off, but this was his cabin for as long as she stayed with them.

"Um," he said. Should he tell her or let her figure it out on her own?

She rounded on him. "You had no right to take an offhanded comment and present it to everyone as if I had suggested blowing up your reservation as a viable option."

"Seemed like a plan."

"It's a disaster. It will ruin the canyon and it will boomerang back to me. Your little stunt in there could cost me my job."

She worried about protecting her career while he worried about safeguarding the lives of everyone here.

"It wasn't a stunt, Sophia. I'm trying to save my people."

"That's *our* job—the FBI's. And we can do our work more efficiently without a bunch of lunatics performing a ghost dance and then blowing themselves to smithereens."

The ghost dances had been used in a vain attempt to remove the scourge of white men from the west by the Sioux people, who followed the great spiritual leader the Anglos called Crazy Horse. His real name was *Th´ašúŋke Witkó*, which literally meant "His Horse is Crazy." But Jack understood the reference. Their shaman called for all the people to come and pray and dance tonight. Like Crazy Horse, Kenshaw Little Falcon believed in the old ways. But he also honored the new. In other words, pray but also act. Her comparing his tribe's gathering to the ghost dance was both insult and honor.

"How about you wait until tomorrow to see what you think of the job the authorities are doing?"

She stiffened and placed a hand on the latch.

Behind them the string of headlights marked the arrival of the tribe, as they wound along the river road like a great, brilliant snake.

On the great open area between the main lodge and the cabins, the central fire was being lit.

"Are you sure you won't come?" Jack motioned to the gathering place. "I'd love to watch you dance."

"I haven't danced for a long time." She sounded wistful.

Dancing was a form of prayer for their people, a way to communicate to the great divine while still connecting to the earth.

"You could just sit on your porch and watch. Then come join us if you like," he said.

"Maybe." She pulled the latch and the door cracked open. She regarded him now, really looking up at him.

He went still under her inspection, hoping that she liked what she saw. His nostrils flared as he tried to bring enough air to sustain him, but each breath brought her delicate floral scent to him. He breathed it in, making it a part of him. He swallowed but his throat was still dry. He was looking at her mouth now, thinking what it might be like to kiss her slowly at first and then...

"I'd better go," she said.

"Sophia?"

She stepped closer. Oh, boy. He was about to tell her that she was at the wrong door, but maybe it was no mistake. Maybe she knew exactly which cabin this was. That thought made his wiring short-circuit. His blood rushed and his breathing quickened as the desire drowned the rational part of his mind.

"Yes?" She brushed the tips of her fingers down the center of his chest.

"This isn't your cabin."

She stepped back. Damn, he should have kissed her first and then told her. But then he might not have wanted to tell her. Not when his bed was only a few short steps away.

He wanted her in that bed more than he had wanted anything in a long time.

Car doors slammed and headlights swung into the field they used for parking. Voices reached them as the people began to gather.

Sophia looked around her. "Which one is mine?"

Jack pointed and watched her go. He didn't follow. Not just because he was needed in the drum circle, but because they needed Sophia's help. Kissing her, sleeping with her, might make it easier to convince her. But it also would lead to the bloody same questions women always asked.

Why don't you look like your brothers? Why are you so big? Have you ever thought about speaking to your parents?

Jack let his hand trail over his wallet. Inside were the answers. But he just couldn't bear confirmation that his mother had deceived his father and he was the visible sign of that infidelity. Everyone suspected. No one spoke about it. Except the women he dated. That seemed to make them feel they had some right to turn him inside out. It didn't. Never had. Never would.

Chapter Five

Sophia stood on the porch of the little cabin and listened. The men sat in a circle around a huge drum, each with a leather-tipped drumstick, collectively beating the rhythm for the dance. She could see them all by firelight and recognized many; Ray sat next to Dylan, who was beside Kurt Bear Den. Then came three men she could not see because their backs were toward her. Adjacent to them, Jack Bear Den sat in profile. He was a full head taller than any of the others and that was while he was sitting down. His appearance raised all sorts of obvious questions. The investigator in her wanted answers. But the part of her that kept her own secrets did not.

Much of her childhood had been horrific and blocking it out just made sense. No different than blocking someone on social media. Except those drums. They brought back something she hadn't remembered, the good part. Belonging to something bigger than herself. Walling herself off, avoiding going home, it was logical but now she felt a longing that made her weep.

So here she stood, leaning against the porch rail and watching the Turquoise Canyon tribe dance in unison around the central fire. Her head bobbed in time and her feet shuffled from side to side. She knew this dance, knew the meaning and the purpose.

There in the light of the fire went Morgan Hooke and beside her was the Anglo Meadow Wrangler. She did not seem to care that she was an outsider, as she matched her steps perfectly to the others. Sophia studied Meadow and how the other women reacted to her. From Sophia's perspective, it seemed that this tribe accepted the heiress despite her outlandish ocean-blue hair and relations with the known head of BEAR. Sophia longed to join them but something kept her rooted to the porch. If she were similarly welcomed, it would be harder to leave.

She wiped away the dampness on her cheeks and straightened. It didn't matter. She didn't need to move in slow harmony around the fire or sing the songs to earth and sky. But a prayer might help the outcome of the internal investigation. A song sung with so many voices was a powerful thing. Was it strong enough to give her back what was taken…her badge, her gun, her position?

She needed them. Needed to be away from here and back where she belonged. On the job.

Sophia sang softly to herself. The song was a prayer, her tiny voice mingling with the people. Their languages were different. She hoped it wouldn't matter as she returned to the language of her youth, her terrible wonderful youth beside the high black-capped mountain. She sang the next song as well and was still there when the logs fell inward and the drums went silent. Still there clinging to the porch rail when the gathering broke and the engines of the cars and trucks started. She watched the vehicles cruise away. Saw Jack Bear Den lift the drum as big as a truck tire and carry it single-handed into the lodge.

She retreated to the shadows as his friends made

their way to their cabins. Ray chased his new wife past her door as Morgan giggled like a girl.

Next came Dylan and Meadow, strolling arm in arm, their heads inclined so they touched. They paused at the river and shared a long kiss that was so full of love and desire that Sophia had to look away. She turned toward the lodge and saw Jack Bear Den standing before the steps leading to the cabin beside hers. His eyes were pinned on her. The shroud of darkness wasn't cover enough to keep him from locating her.

"You didn't come," Jack said. His voice was low and only for her. Had he been watching for her? That thought made her tingle all over.

She glanced over at Dylan and Meadow and was surprised when Meadow kissed Dylan good-night and then retreated alone through the doorway. Sophia blinked in confusion as what she knew of Meadow's wild reputation for men and parties clashed with the chaste kiss. Dylan walked alone to the next lodge and vanished inside.

"They don't?" Sophia asked.

Jack shook his head. "Nope."

"But why? They are clearly in love."

"Because to marry her is to give Meadow federal protection from the local wants and warrants regarding the wildfire. Meadow won't have the people thinking she married Dylan for that reason. Someday, she will marry him. When the matter is settled."

"That could be years." Sophia looked at the dark lodge. Beyond the window Sophia thought that Meadow must be preparing to sleep in her empty bed. "It could be never."

"Her choice," said Jack. "And a difficult one. But one that has earned her much respect here."

Sophia returned her gaze to Jack, taking in the readiness of his stance and the way he was now angled away from his cabin and toward hers.

"I was hoping you would join us," he said.

"I did not want to intrude."

"We want you here, Sophia. Everyone. And they want to meet you."

"I won't be here that long."

He nodded. "More reason."

"You want to sit awhile?" He motioned to the bench beneath the single window on his porch.

Sophia knew with certainty what would happen if she crossed the distance between them. It wouldn't be sitting.

"Detective Bear Den, I want you to know that I'm not in a relationship at present."

His brows lifted at this change of direction.

"By choice. I like men, I just don't like them encroaching, you know, on my space. I need privacy."

"I wouldn't think I'd be encroaching for long. Like you said, you're leaving."

"Yes."

"Just as well. I need my space, too."

She was so tempted to walk right over to him and lace her hands behind his neck and kiss him with everything she had. That's what she wanted. But it wasn't wise.

"I'm not getting mixed up with you," she said, narrowing her eyes at him.

He walked to her porch, placing one large foot on the bottom step as he gripped the rail and broke into her personal space.

"If you say so."

She backed toward her door.

"If you change your mind on the encroachment thing, you know where to find me."

Men were like that, just like stray cats. But they didn't stay. Not for long, and a woman who was wise knew to take care of herself. Relying on a man was a lot like working with explosives. You kept clear if you could and if you couldn't you wore protective gear.

"Good night, Detective."

"Good night, Agent Rivas." He followed her with his eyes. "Did you hear me singing to you?"

She had—his voice was low and deep and distinctive. He'd sung one full song alone. It had made her insides ache.

"Was that for me?"

"Couldn't you tell?"

Sophia stopped backing away and took one step toward him. He was up the steps in an instant.

"I just want to kiss you good night," he said.

"One kiss."

His arms went around her and she felt the restrained strength as he leaned her back. She angled her head so their mouths met. The touch of his mouth was firm and enticing, the contact quaking through her like a shock wave. That had never happened before. If she was smart she'd pull back. Instead she wrapped her arms around his neck and pulled him closer.

Jack moved toward the door, opening it with one hand as he swept them in a slow circle until they stood inside. The kiss that he'd planned had gone quickly off the rails. Sophia's response had left no doubt that she felt the burning want with the same fierce intensity as he did. But as soon as they were inside, she pushed back. He resisted the silent request for release for just a moment and then let her go.

He held back the curse and only just kept from reaching out to reel her back in. It couldn't end like that, half-finished with both of them panting and unfulfilled.

"Sophia, there's no reason not to. You and I aren't colleagues. You're here as a favor to a friend."

"I'm still a federal agent on leave awaiting an investigation."

"This, what is between us, has nothing to do with that. It won't impact the investigation in any way. You're hurting and worried. Let me comfort you, help you forget all that."

"I don't sleep with men I've only just met."

He nodded. "You just kiss them silly."

"You kissed me. I did say one."

That was a qualified no. Perhaps she needed to know more about him before trusting him. He could do that. She wasn't staying and he was trustworthy, as long as she didn't start up with the same hard questions they all asked.

She had not yet asked. Surprising for an investigator.

"So what is it you want, Sophia?"

"I want to see the reservoirs and get back to Flagstaff, back to my job and my home and my life."

"But you felt it, too, Sophia. I know that was no ordinary kiss."

"We'll talk about it in the morning," she said.

"Talk. Sure. We can talk." Not happening, he thought. "Breakfast in the lodge in the morning. Coffeepot in there if you are up before seven. Good night, Sophia." He didn't turn until he reached the porch. If she was still in there or if she closed the door then he'd know she wanted no more from him. But if she followed him...

He turned at the edge of the porch. She was in the

doorway, one hand on the latch and one on the frame. Sophia wanted him. She just didn't want to make a mistake. Jack smiled. She wouldn't be here long, but time was still with him.

"See you in the morning."

He could feel her watching him. He paused before his door, facing her across the distance that separated them.

"You know where to find me." Jack stepped inside and closed the door, leaving the bolt open. She wasn't going to follow him. But she was going to think long and hard about what would have happened if she had.

Chapter Six

Of course, Sophia couldn't sleep. The minute she set her head on the unfamiliar pillow, the worrying started. She went over her initial interview in her head and then her formal statement. The special agent in charge had looked at her so strangely when she had declined to call a family member the day of the incident. What was so odd about that? Lots of people had no family. Only she did have some. Her mother and sisters and brothers, some of whom she did not remember or had never met. Five days mandatory leave. Two weeks until the investigation had to be completed. Eight days before a ruling. Everyone said she shouldn't worry. They'd rule she'd been justified. But if they didn't she'd be referred for a disciplinary review.

She could smell the wood smoke though the open window. She glanced out at the side of the adjoining cabin and the open window. Jack's window.

Now she couldn't sleep because she was thinking about that kiss and his big warm body just next door.

Sophia rolled to her side, giving the window her back. If only she could just lie next to him and tell him everything. That would make her feel better, wouldn't it?

Thinking about it sure didn't help. She sat up. If she walked over and then just asked to talk…

Sophia thumped back on the mattress. If she crossed his threshold, it wouldn't be for pillow talk. It would be for the kind of comfort a man gave a woman. Her body hummed, preparing for him even as she kicked at the covers and pounded the pillow.

Tomorrow they would see the reservoirs.

The flute music intruded into her thoughts. It was so low that at first she thought it was in her mind. But then she knew that it came from the cabin beside hers. Jack Bear Den—that giant of a man—was playing his flute for her. And just as in the old legends the music made her heart beat faster and her eyes grow misty. Was he wooing her or was this what he did before sleeping?

He was awake. She rolled to her side and propped her head on her hand to listen. She didn't mean to fall asleep, but the music was so sweet, each note a reflection of his breath. She breathed with him and soon slipped into slumber.

She woke to a birdsong and blinked her eyes open, disbelieving that she had slept the entire night. She hadn't woken once. That had not happened since the incident.

Sophia sat up and glanced toward the open window, smiling. He'd given her comfort without touching her or intruding or asking for a thing.

It did not take long to wash up since there was no shower, just a sink. She dressed in a different blouse, but the same trousers, donning her shoulder holster and then her blazer. Outside the sun blazed, streaking across the floor of the single room and heating the cabin.

A new fragrance wafted through the open window—coffee and bacon. She took a moment to fix her long hair in a knot at her nape. She had packed limited cosmetics, but did apply a tinted gloss to her lips and used the liner and mascara before slipping into her shoes and heading out.

Kenshaw Little Falcon sat on the porch and was the first to greet her, first in Tonto Apache and then in English, inquiring as to how she slept.

She was cautious of him because Luke had told her of the shaman's involvement in BEAR. He was a federal informant, but also possibly an eco-extremist with a long history of activism.

"I slept well, thank you," she replied.

"It's the river. The sound of the water is very soothing."

The river. Sophia pressed her smile into a tight line as she continued into the lodge to find three men crowded in the kitchen. There was Ray, Dylan and Jack.

Morgan was nowhere to be seen, but Meadow sat alone at the table with her coffee. She offered a bright smile.

"There she is," she said.

This brought all three men around. Jack cast her a dazzling smile that made her stomach tighten.

"Coffee?" asked Ray.

She nodded. "Black."

He grinned. "Do all law personnel take their coffee black?"

"I believe it's regulation," she said.

That made Jack laugh. The sound vibrated through her insides and made her skin go to gooseflesh. Their eyes met and held. His mouth quirked and his eyes sparkled. Was he thinking about the kiss?

As if in answer, his gaze dipped to her mouth.

"Help yourself," said Dylan, motioning to the counter that separated the circular gathering table from the kitchen. "We have eggs, bacon, fry bread and grits."

Her gaze turned to the fry bread. Her mother didn't often make the Apache staple, but when she did, it was fine. Her mouth began to water and she took the plate Dylan offered. She joined Meadow and wondered if she should keep the conversation light or try to find something useful about the eco-extremist group her parents ran.

Jack joined them first, leaving Ray and Dylan to manage the kitchen.

"How did you sleep?" he asked. His warm smile shone on her like sunshine. She wanted to scooch her chair closer just to be nearer to him. Instead she lifted her coffee mug in salute.

"Well, thank you. When will we be leaving?"

"Soon as you're ready."

She focused on her breakfast, pausing only for a second cup of coffee. Meadow finished first and left them alone at the table. Dylan and Ray had begun to argue about the importance of using butter versus oil in cooking. The discussion quickly changed to light-hearted insults.

Jack motioned his head toward the two men. "They always do that."

"Most men do."

He sipped his coffee and the act of pursing his lips made her go all jittery inside. He lowered the mug.

"Something wrong?"

Really, really wrong. Wrong time. Wrong place. And wrong man.

"Nothing at all. I enjoyed your flute playing. Do you always practice at night?"

"Naw. That was for you. I've been in a deadly force encounter, Sophia. I remember the investigation and I remember not sleeping much. I'm sure it's more formal at the Bureau. But they still put me on leave. I hated every minute."

She was staring now. He'd been where she was.

"Will you tell me about it?" she asked.

"Sure. On the way to Skeleton Cliff. Okay?"

"That'd be great."

"Anything more?" he asked, motioning to her empty plate.

Had she eaten all that fry bread? Generally her morning repast was coffee and yogurt mixed with flaxseed. This was better.

"Yes." She stood and took her plate to the kitchen, where Dylan relieved her of it. "Great fry bread."

He looked pleased. "My mother's recipe. Few ingredients, but lots of work."

Pulling and stretching the dough. She remembered because she'd learned how to make the staple with her mom. Seemed they always had flour, salt, milk and shortening, even when they had nothing else.

"Delicious," she said.

"You shouldn't eat fry bread," said Dylan. "Too much fat and carbs."

"Listen, there is nothing better than carbs for energy. It's what we run on."

"It gives you diabetes," said Dylan.

Jack touched her elbow and motioned with his head toward the door.

She let him drive. He flexed his fingers and then gripped the wheel, waving at Kenshaw as they left the compound.

"You have enough air?" He fiddled with the direction of the vent. "Usually ride alone."

"I'm fine. So..." she began, trying to sound casual,

and watched him brace himself. "You were in an offi-cer-involved shooting?"

His shoulders relaxed. What had he thought she was about to ask?

He chuckled. "I thought you might ask about that, but I was hoping…"

"What?"

"You'd ask me if I was seeing anyone. I thought after last night you might want to know that."

"It was just a kiss."

"Was it? To me it was more."

"So. Do you have a girl?"

"Currently unattached."

"The same. Most men aren't very understanding of the hours I keep."

"I hear that."

His smile lit up the compartment and made her in-sides squeeze. Her cheeks went hot and she had to look out the window at the river to catch her breath.

"So…" she said, bringing the conversation back to safer ground. "About the officer-involved shooting."

Chapter Seven

Jack didn't like to talk about it. Every law enforcement
officer knew the risks. Knew they might die on the job.
But most didn't really consider the impact a deadly force
encounter would have on the rest of their lives.

"First off, I was a US Marine. I saw action in Iraq
and lost a good friend there. Dylan, Ray, me, my brother
Carter and Yeager Hatch all joined up together. I almost
lost my brother and Ray. Hatch didn't come back. We
miss him all the time."

"I'm sorry. I've never lost a colleague."

"He wasn't a colleague. He was Ray's best friend
and the five of us were inseparable."

"Yes. I see."

"We were attacked by insurgents. I wish I could say
that I felt something for the men I killed over there.
Mostly I still just feel anger. But the deadly force incident was different. I knew them."

She sat in quiet attention as he continued driving
along the river and into Piñon Forks.

"There was a warrant out for the driver. I pulled him
over and found he had a passenger. His kid brother,
Donny, was eighteen. They were both dressed all in
yellow and black."

"Yes?" As if she wasn't sure what that signified.

"You don't work gangs then?" he asked.

She shook her head. "They don't use explosives, generally."

"Yellow and black are the gang colors favored by the Latin Kings."

She nodded her understanding. "What was the warrant?"

"Skipped on his hearing. Used Donny's 18 Money to make bail and then pulled a no-show."

The accumulated per-capita dividends from the tribe's revenue sources, including their casino, was called 18 Money. She'd used her own 18 Money to get out. The funds were enough to pay for her education, her first apartment and a very old Toyota. Her mother expected her to turn the money over to her for her use. When she didn't, her mother threw her out.

"I had both of them out and had the driver cuffed when Donny pulled a gun on me. I wish I could say I saw it coming, but I didn't, and he got a shot off before I drew my weapon. They never found that bullet, but his gun had been fired so all clear on that. I hit him three times in center mass. He was wearing leather and that loose clothing the gang members wear so he didn't die right away. I had to watch it happen with his older brother cursing and crying and swearing he'd kill me."

"That's awful."

"His brother's in jail. Donny's in his grave and I was cleared. Justified use of force. I was on leave for ten days and rode a desk another two. We use outside agencies to investigate and they took their sweet time. Just about drove me crazy."

"Were you hit?" She pointed at the scar through his eyebrow.

"This? Naw. I cracked this on a rock jumping off the

canyon wall into the river when I was sixteen. We all jumped from that ledge as kids. As young men we all had to scale the canyon wall. I was the first one in my group to reach the top. Carter was second."

She drew a deep breath and said nothing, but her jaw was clamped tight.

"Thank you for telling me that."

He nodded and tried to focus on the road, which was a challenge with Sophia sitting beside him.

They left Piñon Forks and drove along the river. Just past the casino he saw a familiar bright yellow pickup with black pin striping. He knew the truck and the driver, and knew he had warrants for skipping a tribal court appearance on a drugs and weapons charge.

He hit the lights. "Hold on."

"Wait a second. I can't pull someone over."

"Just stay in the SUV."

She didn't, of course. Just as soon as he had the vehicle pulled to the shoulder and was out of the SUV, she was out as well and she had her hand on her replacement weapon as he made his approach.

SOPHIA FOLLOWED JACK, noting that he had his hand on his weapon as he reached the driver side and ordered the driver to put both his hands out his window. He had the driver out of the vehicle in short order as she covered him and kept an eye on the passenger side door. There was no telling who was inside because of the tinted windows, which she hated. But when Jack made the collar, the passenger side door opened and a woman poked her head out.

"Back in the vehicle. Now!" Sophia ordered.

She couldn't see the woman's hands. Sophia kept her hand on her replacement weapon and felt the unfamiliar grip. The loaner pistol made her even more uncomfortable with the situation. This wasn't her personal weapon and she was not accustomed to using a .45 caliber.

Was he crazy, putting her in this position? The passenger stared at her from the open door.

Sophia repeated her order and the woman retreated but called to her associate.

"Trey, we got any female cops on the rez?"

Trey was pressed against the bed of his truck, feet spread wide and hands cuffed behind his back. Jack was efficient at least. Trey lifted his head to stare at her. Sophia watched the emotions play across his broad face. The look of disgust changed to one of interest. Finally a smile curled his lips as he looked at her as if she was the bounty.

"Well, well. What we got here?" he said.

Jack ignored him, keeping one hand on Trey's neck as he asked if his suspect had anything sharp on his person.

"No, man. No weapons, drugs. I'm clean. Why don't you introduce me to your bitch?"

"That her?" asked the woman from inside the truck.

Is that who? Sophia wondered.

"How 'bout you come over here so I can get a look at your fine ass," said Trey.

"Shut your mouth," said Sophia, releasing the grip on her weapon as Jack called for backup.

"Uppity little thing, too. Sassing me." Trey turned his head to speak to Jack. "She my woman, I'd crack her across the mouth. She never talk back again. I guarantee you that."

Jack escorted him by the collar to his SUV. "Yeah, well, good thing she's not yours."

She could already hear the siren of the second unit.

With Trey in the back of Jack's SUV, Sophia kept her eye on the passenger in the vehicle as Jack went to speak with the young woman.

"You own this truck, Minnie?" he asked. He knew her, of course.

"Naw. I gave it to Trey. Early birthday present."

She gave it to that jerk? Sophia found her jaw clamped. She knew what this was because she'd seen it before. There had been older men suddenly interested in her during her seventeenth year. At first Sophia had been flattered. Her mother had been on to them, ready for them actually, and had chased them all off, even the gangbangers. Though Sophia later realized it was for her mother's own selfish reasons and not to protect her daughter's best interests. It was a minor miracle she had gotten out.

"You use up all your Big Money?" asked Jack.

Minnie raised her chin. "I got some left."

Sophia stared through the open window at the girl and realized with little imagination that this could have been her future, she could have squandered her one chance on someone like Trey.

This woman was actually little more than a girl, Sophia realized, and Minnie had used up her accumulated portion of the annual tribal revenue on this jerk.

"You should keep it. Don't spend it on some guy."

"He ain't some guy. He's my fiancé."

"Yeah, well, your intended is going to jail."

"He didn't do nothing," said Minnie without hesitation.

"And then they impound his property and sell it at police auction. In other words, you lose this truck."

That got her attention. She stepped out of the vehicle and Sophia plainly saw the gun in the woman's hand. Sophia had hers out and aimed. Minnie kept her weapon at her side.

"Put down the gun, now," barked Sophia. She was already in a cold sweat just thinking about shooting someone else.

The siren grew so loud that Sophia couldn't hear what Minnie replied. But she did see her drop the pistol into the sand that lined the shoulder of the road.

Tires crunched behind her and car doors slammed. Jack shouted something and Sophia kept her attention and her aim on Minnie. A uniformed tribal police officer rushed past her and ordered Minnie to place her hands on the roof of the truck. Sophia waited until the woman was in cuffs before holstering her weapon.

At Jack's direction, the officer came back with an evidence bag and gathered Minnie's gun. Then both Trey and Minnie were transferred to the marked unit and read their rights. Sophia was trembling when they pulled away.

Jack came over to where she stood by his SUV and gathered her up in his arms. She let him hold her for a moment, felt the comfort of his embrace and the callused hand that stroked her neck, lifting the tiny hairs there. Then she pushed off of him.

"Are you out of your ever-loving mind?"

Chapter Eight

"He has outstanding warrants," said Jack, as if this was reason enough.

"I'm on administrative leave. You're my escort. I'm not here to help you make a collar."

"It was a good one."

"I had to draw my weapon!"

"You sure did."

She pressed her hand to her forehead and then growled at the sky. Finally she focused back on the detective, who smiled at her with a new appreciation. She ignored the tingle that smile caused and stuck with her fury.

"Now I have to report that I drew my weapon."

He seemed puzzled now. "You *have* to do that?"

"Of course I do! While they are reviewing my fatal force encounter I have to explain why I was making arrests up here on the mountain."

"It's federal land. Your jurisdiction."

"I am on administrative leave!"

"Got it. No more collars."

"Oh, for the love of…" She got back in his SUV and slammed the door. She still had her hand pressed to her forehead when he climbed in and set them in motion. Eventually she could not stand the silence.

"My cousin told me you are the only detective up here. Is that true?"

"Yeah, but not for long. One of our guys is getting his gold shield soon."

"Not the guy that took over our collar." She hadn't really gotten a look at him except to see he was Native and young.

"No. That's Jake Redhorse. He's so green he still has that new car smell. Good kid." Jack sighed.

"Yeah?"

He stared at the road, thinking of the Redhorse boys, Ty, Kee, Jake and Colt. He feared he'd have to arrest Ty if he didn't straighten up, and Colt...

"He's got three brothers like me. Two were in the service, like me and Carter, and they both..." Jack's words trailed off.

"They both, what?" she prompted.

"Changed. Ty is raising hell and it seems self-destructive to me. Like he's punishing himself. He won't talk about the war. At least not to me."

"Keep trying," she said.

"Colt, well, that boy is just gone."

"Mentally?"

"No, he left. Ty said he's living like some Apache survivalist in a cabin up past Turquoise Ridge. Still on our rez, I'm told, but no one but Ty ever sees him."

"What did Chekov write...? Happy families are all alike, but unhappy families are unhappy in their own way." Hers certainly had been.

"Tolstoy," said Jack.

"What?"

"Tolstoy wrote something like that."

She lifted her brows at that but said nothing. Did she think he could not or did not read?

"And he was right, I think."

Approaching from below the man-made structure, they made it to the Skeleton Cliff Dam. The dam itself spanned the river from canyon wall to canyon wall in a great gray concave ellipse that vomited water back into the river through a controlled spillway gate. A narrow road ran along the top of the dam far above them.

"According to your shaman, there is a highway patrol vehicle up there, angled to block the east entrance with the help of a movable barrier."

He cast her a look of skepticism. "I could knock him clear with this vehicle, not to mention a dump truck or tractor trailer loaded with explosives."

She turned her attention back to the gray wall looming above them.

"Placement of explosives at the top would cause minimal damage. For real compromise you would need to be inside the working of the powerhouse or at the base of the dam."

"I've been up here in our police boat."

"Is that the little fishing boat tied up near the station?"

"Yeah. I took it up here more than once on search-and-rescue, right to the foot of the dam."

"Well, do you think the words *Tribal Police* on the side improved your access?"

"Heck, anyone who can untie a knot could take that boat. Keys are in the ignition."

"Maybe you should reconsider that policy. And that little boat couldn't carry enough to do any real damage. A bigger boat would bottom out."

"That twenty-four-footer has a gross-load capacity of over fifteen hundred pounds. That's a lot of RDX," he said, mentioning the explosive he'd used in Iraq.

"They'd see it. The explosives."

"Who? There's no one up here but the guys working the dam. I could fill the livewell with explosives and they'd never see them," he said.

"The what?"

"The livewell. On our police boat. It's an insulated fiberglass container built into the hull. A livewell is used to keep fish alive after hooking them. It's water-tight and locks, so we store our rifles in there."

She shook her head, dismissing this option.

"You haven't seen the size of that livewell. I can get four twenty-pound bags of ice in there and have room to spare."

"Something the size of a car trunk might do super-ficial damage to the base. I doubt it would crack the structure. Plus, foam is a bad choice to hold the load because it's a shock absorber. No projectiles."

He continued to the smaller utility road leading to the powerhouse. "Good to know."

There was no more than a metal gate across the road with a simple keypad for admission. He did not press the call button, but used the key code. The gate rolled back.

"They haven't changed it in a while," he said in reply to her silent question. "Carter's wife has two sisters. One of her kids went on a field trip. The gate was open in preparation for the bus."

Sophia shifted in her seat. "I see your reason for concern."

"This is only the second dam. We know it is smaller and less vital than the one at Goodwin Lake."

"Alchesay," she offered.

"Yes, but Two Mountains Lake above this dam is still more than big enough to decimate our reservation."

"It would look like the Johnstown Flood," she said. "Let me have a look inside."

Jack drove through the gate. They did encounter a locked door at the powerhouse and a keypad. Jack tried the same code as the gate and came up empty so he used the call box.

They were buzzed in.

She pointed at the camera over the door. "They can see your uniform and you are expected."

He hoped his expression showed how not reassured he was by her observation. Inside the powerhouse they were toured around. Sophia asked questions about the capacity of the various pressurized gases that he didn't really understand. He did understand that the giant white cylinder held something explosive from the amount of time she spent on it. Their guide was very free with information and offered to have them rappel down from the top to the bottom of the dam.

"Is that access road the only way to reach the bottom?" asked Sophia.

"Unless you can swim, but I wouldn't recommend that," joked their guide.

"Boat?" said Jack.

"Not permitted past the signage, ropes and floats."

Jack looked at Sophia. "Ropes and floats. Can't think how a person could circumvent protection like that."

Sophia held her tight smile but she also seemed less than reassured. The slam dunk she had hoped for had trickled away. He thought she saw the reason for their continued worry. Whether she would admit it was something else.

She waited until they were outside to address his concerns.

"Yes, I see some issues that need addressing and we

will deal with them. But BEAR has been disbanded. They are a nonentity."

"Not according to our shaman."

"Who is a member of BEAR."

"He was."

"And also an FBI informant."

"He believes in protecting the environment."

"Through terrorism."

"Without him you'd never have discovered Lupe Wrangler headed the organization."

"That's not been proved."

Sophia knew from briefings that the Pine View Wildfire had been caused by an explosion that took down the iconic private residence that broke the ridgeline. The eco-extremist group BEAR claimed credit for the disaster sending a message to others not to build in the pristine area. Whether BEAR intended the resulting devastating wildfire touched off by the blast was unclear. The FBI had determined via exhaustive investigation that Meadow Wrangler's father, Theron, headed BEAR. But she knew that Jack and his warrior society believed that Theron Wrangler was merely a figurehead and that it was her mother, Lupe, who ran the organization. Meadow's statement regarding her father's death had been considered and dismissed. There was no evidence her father had been murdered by her mother. And Meadow's statement was self-serving as she was implicated in helping her father set the fire.

"Kenshaw says that the death of Theron and the exit of his wife serve as a signal for sleeper cells to activate," said Jack.

"I've heard that." She didn't sound as if she believed it.

"We told the FBI this."

"You very well may have. But I'm an explosives expert here to consult on your concerns. I don't work on domestic terrorism except in how it relates to explosions."

"They stole a heck of a lot of explosives."

"Yes, we are aware."

"Still missing."

"Also aware. Generally, I come in after the boom."

"Well, we are trying to avoid that."

"Understood. But let me remind you, this is an unofficial visit. I do not represent the Bureau. I'm doing my cousin a favor. Now you have pointed out some weaknesses, and I can have our people contact highway patrol to shore up these holes in security. But that's all I can do."

"What about BEAR and the sleeper cells?"

"I'll share your concerns, but I am not abreast of the BEAR investigation except to say there has been progress and arrests have been made."

Jack's phone vibrated in his pocket, making him jump. He drew it out and glanced at the screen. It was Chief Tinnin.

"Hi, Chief."

"We've finished processing Trey Fields," said Wallace.

"Okay," said Jack as he waited for the other shoe to drop. His chief would not call about such a routine matter.

"He made his phone call to an unlisted number," said Wallace. "We think he mentioned Sophia."

Jack plugged his opposite ear with his finger and leaned forward to listen as his stomach roiled. "What did he say?"

"'We saw her. She's here with Detective Jack Bear Den. Right here on our rez.'"

Jack scowled as he tried to think of someone else that Trey might have been referencing and came up empty. Not good. Having a gang member use his one call to report the position of an FBI field agent was bad. Really bad.

And it was his fault. He'd forgotten his duty to protect Sophia the moment he spotted that truck like a poorly trained hound scenting a rabbit.

"We need to find out who he called."

"Working on it now."

He turned to Sophia, raising the phone so he was not speaking into the receiver. "That fatal force encounter with Nequam, did the suspected carjacker have gang ties?"

Her lovely brown eyes widened. "I don't know that."

"How was he dressed?"

"Loose clothing. Flat-brimmed ball cap."

"Yellow?"

She closed her eyes and blew out a breath, as if thinking back to the incident. Her eyes opened wide, meeting his, and she nodded.

"Yes."

"Latin Kings," said Jack.

"Yellow and black," she said, repeating what he had told her earlier in the day.

"You know how they get in, right?" he asked.

She nodded. "Women by sex. Men by crimes."

"They have to kill someone."

She nodded.

"I think you were targeted. That's why there happened to be someone right there filming."

"Because I'm FBI?"

"I doubt they knew that. Maybe just because of your black Beamer. Flash car like that makes a great target."

"I told the SAC that the witness may have been there to film the heist as evidence of the crime," she said.

"Returning with the car would do that. What they were filming was evidence of murder."

She gave an almost imperceptible shiver and folded her arms around her middle.

"We have a problem."

Jack gave her the details.

"I have to call in and report this," she said.

"They're going to pull you out of here."

"I sure hope so."

THEY CANCELED THE second visit to the second power station and headed back toward the compound. Jack called for an escort but they were still alone as they crossed into and out of the adjoining town of Darabee.

They'd had some trouble with crooked cops here so he had not called to them for assistance. It was the Darabee PD that set up the opportunity for the hit on the Lilac shooter and the nest of corruption was still being sorted out.

Sophia had been in contact with her office supervisor. As she expected, the shooting had set off alarm bells and they wanted her home. Her people were making arrangements.

She had other information. Her field office was on high alert after some intel on a possible terrorist threat to the federal offices in Phoenix. Something was happening, but they didn't have the important information, like where or when. They did know who. BEAR had sent a message by US mail warning of an impending attack.

"They've got their hands full," said Sophia. "I may need to sit tight until they can get to me."

"We'll take you to the compound. There is one road in and we can protect that."

"There is the river," she reminded him.

He nodded. "Tribal headquarters, then. The station is a defensible position. Plus, I can get us information on Martin Nequam. Seems like this all points back to him."

"Sounds good."

Somewhere between the phone call and this moment, he and Sophia had ceased pulling in opposite directions and become a team. His police force was small, and he'd never had a partner. But having Sophia beside him felt like a partnership and he liked it.

Jack never saw it coming. One moment he was discussing strategy and the next he was showered with cubes of glass as the front windshield exploded.

Chapter Nine

Sophia spit out a piece of glass and ducked. She had her pistol drawn and her seat belt released just before Jack reached across the seat and shoved her to the floor of the SUV.

"Stay down," Jack ordered.

That was no rock hitting the windshield. It was a bullet, and he was darn sure they weren't shooting at him. But taking him out would make it easier to get to Sophia. And they were not getting to Sophia.

Not today. Not ever.

"What's happening?" she yelled as dust billowed in through the empty space before him.

"Someone's shooting at us."

"Location?" she asked, spinning so she could crouch down with both elbows on the seat and her pistol pointed at the ceiling.

He marveled at her dexterity. He could not even fit in that tight space, let alone maneuver in it.

"Unknown. Forward, possibly in the rocks to my left."

Another bullet struck behind him on the passenger side. He glanced back and saw daylight through the hole. Large caliber, he thought.

"Rear position," he said and accelerated. They had

to be on the ridge, across the river. Using a scope. He lifted the radio and called it in.

He left the road, choosing the cover of the pines. Within a few moments he reached the narrow gap cut through the rock for the road. This position gave no shot from across the river, but if there were someone on the rock above them he had drawn them into a shooting gallery.

He braced for more gunfire.

Sophia glanced from one side of the shorn rock to the other.

"Bad spot," she said.

"But out of range."

"They could be up top." Her words mirrored his thoughts.

"If I leave this gap they have another shot at us from across the river."

"Hold then," she said, pistol raised and ready.

The radio barked as Wallace Tinnin called for a status update. Jack lifted the radio and responded. Tinnin was sending his only available men, three units, to them. Jack lifted his cell phone and called Ray Strong, told him the situation. He sent Ray and Dylan to check the opposite ridge.

"We're en route," said Ray. "You sit tight."

"Will do."

"Oh, and your mom called," said Ray.

"What's wrong?" asked Jack.

"Don't know. Call her when you can. Gotta go. We're rolling."

"Let me know what's happening when…" He glanced at the phone and saw that Ray had disconnected.

"Now what?" asked Sophia.

"We wait." Jack wondered if there were more of

them. If they had forced him onto this road cut and were now approaching their position.

Sophia rose, sending the cubes of broken glass showering to the floor mats. She ran a finger into her mouth and along her cheek and dropped a bloody cube of glass to the floor with the rest.

"You all right?" Jack asked.

She didn't look at him when she nodded. All business, as she scanned for any approaching threat. From far off came the welcome sound of sirens. His department was on the way.

"That's a good sign," said Sophia.

A few minutes later Jack and Sophia continued to the station under police escort.

They reached tribal headquarters, where Chief Tinnin waited, greeting them with a Kevlar vest in hand. Jack exited the SUV and took the vest, then gave it to Sophia. She needed no instructions but slipped into the oversized gear with fluid grace. The second the last strap was secure, he had her out and running for the doors, his arm around her waist and her body tucked close to him. They ran with matched strides, like a thoroughbred teamed with a draft horse.

Jack wouldn't feel safe until he had Sophia through the station doors.

Sophia panted, with hands on knees, the dizziness a result of the aftermath of her fright. Studying the effects of adrenal reaction in the academy was far different than experiencing it, and she did not object when Jack sat her in a chair and offered her a bottle of water.

She'd been prepared when she needed to be. It was all right to let her body recover now. Still it bothered her that Jack's hand was steady as he handed her the cool plastic bottle.

"This is my fault," he said.

His supervisor nodded. "It is. She's a guest. You're her escort. You don't pull over a suspect when you have a passenger."

"They might have been shooting at Detective Bear Den," said Sophia.

"Maybe," said Tinnin to Sophia, hands on his hips as he regarded them. "But it's your side of the window that's missing."

Sophia's ears buzzed and her dry throat made her cough. She sipped the water and said nothing further. Jack did not leave her side. He stayed squatting on his heels, his head nearly eye-level with hers until she finished shaking. He also held her hand. Was this just an act of comfort or did he also feel the connection between them strengthening?

"I'm all right, Jack," she said and gave him a smile.

"Still pale," he observed.

She pulled her hand back. He wasn't her sweetheart or her mother. She could deal with this like she did everything else—on her own.

"Can I get you anything? You hungry?"

She shook her head. The idea of food made her stomach clench. A glance at the station's ancient analog wall clock told her it was nearly two in the afternoon. A man Jack's size must be starving by now. She took pity on him.

"Could you order something in?"

His smile made her heart flutter. Based on the heat flooding over her skin, she'd guess the color was also returning to her cheeks.

"Fine. Turkey, ham or roast beef?" he asked.

"Roast beef with lettuce, mayo and tomato, if they have it. No onions."

He moved to the phone and placed an order with someone named Willy, adding drinks, chips and brownies.

"Want to look up Martin Nequam while we wait?" she asked.

"You recover fast," said Jack. But he sat at his desk and tapped at a keyboard so old the space bar had a shiny spot exactly where his thumb touched.

She cast a dubious glance at the cathode monitor. But soon after he'd logged in and up popped the image of a young woman.

"Who's that?" she asked.

"Missing person," said Jack. "Her name is Kacy Doka. She disappeared in February. Teens run away but she's the third since November."

"That's a lot on such a small reservation."

"I agree."

"Home troubles?"

"Don't know. Wallace just pulled me in. I've only started investigations on them collectively. Up until now they've been treated as separate cases. We want to be sure their disappearances are unrelated."

He closed the window and the bright smiling face of Kacy Doka disappeared.

Jack was searching on the Crime Information Center database. It wasn't as sophisticated as the tools available to the FBI, but would do in a pinch.

It did not take long for him to get hits on Martin Nequam.

"All right," said Jack, leaning forward.

The criminal history page popped up and displayed Nequam's date of birth. The age of the youth hit her hard, and she was glad she was still seated beside Jack's desk. A lump rose in her throat and she swallowed several times to choke it back down.

Nequam had three entries under names used. Below that came known associates, his arrest record, including the agency making the arrest, and the charge.

"Juaquin Nequam, twenty-three. Martin have an older brother?"

She shook her head. "I don't know."

Jack used the computer to look up Juaquin's information. Then he lifted the phone and called the state highway patrol, relaying the information on the shooting and the make, model and plate of his suspect. Then he repeated the call to the Flagstaff PD, asking them to check the location for Juaquin Nequam.

Jack flicked his attention back to the screen and read aloud from Martin Nequam's criminal history. "'Fleeing, convicted,'" said Jack, reading the list. "'Robbery, convicted.' Another robbery and conviction, battery and substance-abuse charge. Looks like he had some charges pending." He turned to her. "Your boy was bad news."

She couldn't meet his gaze.

"Sophia?" He reached out to her, his big hand falling over her tightly laced ones. "It's okay. It will be okay."

The warmth and the way he leaned in as he dropped his voice was her undoing. She let out a stuttering sob and pulled her hands from beneath his in order to cover her face. Tears spilled and the sobs got worse. Right here on the squad floor, she realized, she was going to release those tears she had kept inside since that night.

Jack rolled his chair to her so his legs straddled hers and he drew her forward. She nestled against his chest, clutching the soft fabric of his button-up shirt and holding it before her. His hands rubbed up and down her back. The man was really good at this. Was that why she'd finally let go—because she knew he'd be there to catch her?

"I'm s-sorry," she stammered. Her fingers were wet and his shirt damp.

"Don't be. You're under a lot of pressure. Best to let it out."

She released him to wipe her eyes and his hands continued to rub in long strokes down her back. She turned her head so that her cheek pressed to his chest. He lowered his chin, cradling her.

"I got you, Sophia. You're not alone."

She managed a nod and another sniff escaped her, but the sobs had ceased, rubbed away by his strong, gentle hands.

Sophia straightened and he rolled back in his chair, reestablishing their personal space and leaving her with a disturbing desire not to let him go. Silly. He was comforting her. Anyone would do the same. But anyone would not have left her feeling breathless and dizzy with an entirely new kind of unwelcome emotion. She wasn't sorry she kissed him last night except that now that she had done so, she wanted to kiss him again.

"You all right?" he asked, his gaze now cautious.

Oh, yeah, he could read her. She met his inquiring gaze and his brows lifted as he sat back.

"Well, here we are again," he said. "Just like last night."

"Except we are in your squad room."

"True."

"And my office is sending transport. I'm leaving tomorrow at oh-eight-hundred."

"That just adds a time clock."

"No, it makes it impossible. I don't play where I work."

"A consult. You don't work here," he reminded her. "We aren't colleagues."

"What are we then?"

"Real question is what could we be. I'd like to find out."

She glanced around and found the small room blissfully empty and the chief's office door closed. One of the advantages of a small squad room.

"I forgot to tell them I drew my weapon." She pressed a hand to her forehead.

"You okay?" asked Jack. "You're going pale again."

"I forgot to tell my supervisor I assisted in making an arrest and that I drew my weapon."

He sat back, testing the mechanics of the chair, which creaked in protest.

"Really? That's your big worry?"

"I'm on…"

"Administrative leave," he said, finishing her sentence "Yeah. Got it. But someone tried to kill you. That's not your top priority?"

That *was* messed up, she realized.

"Yeah. I know." But they could have been shooting at Jack and either way, they had missed and that was not going to go on the report that would be considered in the ongoing investigation.

"Excuse me." She lifted her phone and found the battery in the red because she hadn't charged it.

"You can use mine. I have to talk to Tinnin."

He left her and she made the call to Captain Larry Burton.

"Are you in a secure location?" asked her captain.

"Yes."

"Okay. Great."

The conversation did not go well from there, but the gist of it was that she was not to be consulting while on leave. Favor to a friend or not, her opinion as a federal officer entangled the Bureau.

When she told him about the gaps in the security at the power station, he told her he'd handle it, have the state highway patrol increase their presence.

Burton tried to get her off the phone before she managed to tell him about the shooting, but she got it in. She had his full attention, judging from the silence on the other end of the call.

She told him about the collar and her role in covering the passenger and that the suspect seemed to have mentioned her to someone during his one phone call.

Then she made a mistake, telling her captain that Martin Nequam had gang ties.

"And how do you know that?" asked her captain.

Sophia stopped talking.

"You were warned not to do any background on the deceased."

"Technically, I didn't do it."

"You're blowing it, Rivas. You know that your fishing trip could influence the outcome of your investigation. I thought getting away for a few days would be good for you."

"Captain—"

"Stop. Just stop. Your little side gig or whatever this was, it's over. I'm pulling the plug. You stay put and out of trouble until we get you home in the morning."

"Yes, sir."

"I'll be in touch." He hung up before she could give him the number at the station.

Jack emerged from the chief's office, rubbing his neck and looking equally glum.

"We're taking you to the compound."

"There's no phone service out there."

"I have a radio."

"I need to charge my phone."

"You have a charger?" he asked.

"In my car." Which was back at the compound. "Fine. Let's go."

They reached the parking lot when the food delivery arrived. Jack would not let her pay for her lunch. They took the food along in his unmarked, white F-150 pickup and were followed by Chief Tinnin. They had no further trouble en route.

Kenshaw Little Falcon greeted them at the compound, walking out to stand beside the truck and speaking to Jack the instant he opened the door.

"First I must deliver a message from your mother," said Kenshaw.

"What's wrong?"

This was the second message from his mother, and she believed that he had not returned her call.

"She said that she is coming here to see you. She can tell you why when she arrives, but you should stay until she speaks to you."

"I have to help with the investigation. The shooting. And she shouldn't come here. It could be dangerous."

"Too late. She's coming and she doesn't carry a phone. So just stay awhile. Ray and Dylan called me. They found the shooter's position and shell casings. He was driving a pickup, which tells us very little."

Sophia slid down from the high bucket seat to the grass.

Jack grabbed their lunch from behind his seat and

then walked with Little Falcon toward the lodge. She followed, glancing toward her car and wishing she could get her phone charged, but not wanting to miss what else Kenshaw might say.

Jack passed Sophia her lunch and then filled in his shaman on their two encounters and turned it over to her for a recap of the visit to the dam and power station. She shared her observations and did not hold back any of her concerns as Jack munched his sandwich. She'd be gone tomorrow morning and this tribe needed all the information they could get. Some small part of her wished she could stay, not just because Jack Bear Den made her entire body flash on and off like a Christmas light, but because she was coming to agree that they had reason for concern.

She took the seat on the porch beside Kenshaw, who faced the river. Jack preferred to lean against the porch rail in front of her, causing a visceral distraction that interfered with her ability to think and speak. The man was one giant temptation.

Perhaps her imminent departure was a blessing. One more night with him in the adjoining cabin was going to be tough. Well, it was out of her hands. Her field office was yanking her out of here and she'd be lucky not to receive a reprimand.

No good deed goes unpunished, she thought, and snorted at the truth of that.

Kenshaw listened as she finished up her description of the security concerns and fell silent.

"I do not know what you have been told about me," said the shaman. "But I would tell you some things that I do not think are in my files."

She'd read those files, of course, at least all that she'd had access to.

"I worked with a man named Cheney for a long time, since we were young men."

Her mind provided intel on Cheney. Cheney Williams, deceased. Killed in the explosion that triggered the ridge fire. Known member of BEAR and Theron Wrangler's second in command. Death ruled accidental.

"He was my friend and my contact in BEAR, but not my only one. That is why I am so concerned. My cell has been activated with the others, but I only know the target of my cell. Still, I was aware of various potential targets."

"Did you share this with my department?"

"The one in Phoenix. I worked as an informant with that field office. And I will tell you what I told them. Each cell will attack their target as soon as feasible after the death or departure of Lupe Wrangler. She has left the country. That is the signal."

"And you believe the reservoirs are a potential target."

"I know it. But since it is not the target of my cell, I do not know how or when."

"Isn't the purpose of a cell to keep their mission secret from the others?"

"It is to insulate itself and work independently. But Cheney Williams knew each cell's mission. He was to pass that information to Dylan, but Cheney was killed on the ridge in an explosion. You know where those explosives came from?"

She did. The theft at the Lilac copper mine.

"What is the target of your cell?" she asked, not really expecting an answer.

"Pipelines in Phoenix."

She sat up straight. "Does my office know that?"

"Of course. But not where and when. I have not been activated and so I have no more information."

He turned to her and held her gaze with eyes that reflected great sadness. "We were trying to save the earth. When the organization became radicalized, I had my doubts and reached out to the FBI. I hoped they could stop BEAR."

"I'm sure they will." She needed to get to a phone.

"I do not share your confidence. A small dedicated group prepared to die can accomplish great and terrible things."

That, she knew, was true.

"Which is why we need you to protect us and help us set those charges on our canyon as a fail-safe in the event BEAR succeeds in destroying that dam."

"I can't do that."

"You are our last hope."

Chapter Ten

"I can't blow up a public waterway, no matter what the reason." Sophia gripped the arms of the pine rocker angled beside a similar one holding the tribe's shaman. "You asked me here to give an opinion. Your best course is to have your leadership voice their concerns to state and federal authorities."

Jack chuckled and she glanced at him. He stood casually, leaning against the porch rail with his thumbs hitched on either side of his belt buckle.

"That hasn't gone so well in the past, historically, I mean."

The number of egregious breaks in federal contracts to Native people was a debate for another time. She wasn't here to defend the US government. But she was trying to be part of the change she wanted in the world.

"I can't do it," she said.

"We understand. And we are sorry for the trouble you have had here," said Kenshaw. "I am embarrassed and concerned that a guest would be attacked on our land."

"Thank you."

Kenshaw gazed toward the gently flowing river, which was carefully controlled by the outlet of the powerhouse and dam just northeast of their land. She watched the water, trying not to think of the millions of gallons contained by concrete and steel. What would happen to his people if the dam was destroyed.

"Perhaps moving your population would not be a bad idea," she said. "Just temporarily."

Jack's radio crackled and the police officer stationed at the top of the road reported the arrival of Jack's family.

"Family?" he asked, straightening.

Kenshaw turned to Sophia. "Jack has his parents and three brothers. Kurt works in Darabee. Thomas is with ICE on the border, a Shadow Wolf hunting drug traffickers. And Jack's twin, the oldest, Carter, is with his wife."

"With the Department of Justice." She knew that, of course, and knew that the trial for the men who had tried to kill his wife was now underway.

Jack was already off the porch and standing by the twin ruts that served as a road.

"We believed Carter and his wife, Amber, would need relocation. But the man she was testifying against is dead."

"I understood the trial was moving forward."

"Not those men. I mean Theron Wrangler."

Now *that* she did not know and she was instantly curious as to what information these witnesses might have.

Kenshaw watched her with intent eyes and a knowing smile.

"Amber Bear Den, Carter's wife, is the only link between the Lilac mine massacre and Theron Wrangler. It was why BEAR tried so hard to kill her."

"And she's no longer in danger?"

"The information is useless now. She has nothing on Lupe, Theron's wife."

She'd heard the theories that Lupe ran BEAR. It was her department's belief that Theron was the leader and not a front. But now she began to wonder.

"She was careful," said Kenshaw. "I will give Lupe that."

Sophia could hear the roar of a truck engine now and the creaking of old struts. Jack lifted his gaze toward the vehicle she could not see.

"Carter has a wife and Jack has been missing his brother. Jack has friends and Kurt, but he has still seemed to be very lonely, to me."

"Jack, he's not…attached?"

Kenshaw smiled as he continued to watch the river and she continued to wish she could go back in time and not ask her last question.

"Jack feels unattached. His appearance has been a great burden to him."

"Because he's so big?" She liked that.

"Because he is so different. Anyone with eyes can see, but it is always his women who ask. They make him face what he would ignore. He cannot stand that and so he is alone."

Note to self, she thought—*don't ask him why he looks different than his brothers.*

"Well, that's too bad," she said.

"Yes. But he needs to face his differences to accept himself as we have all accepted him."

Get him to accept himself but don't mention the differences. Check. How did she do that?

"Could I borrow your phone?" she asked.

Kenshaw passed her a small black older-model phone. She called her department in Flagstaff and relayed what Kenshaw had told her about the pipeline.

They took down the information. Then she called Luke to be sure his field office was aware. They were.

"And I don't appreciate that you ditched me up here," she said.

"Mountain air will help you sleep and having problems bigger than your own is good for you," said her cousin.

"They sure are bigger."

"Call if you need me," said Luke and the line went dead.

A problem bigger than herself. Sophia's gaze lifted to the road and landed on Jack Bear Den.

JACK STOOD IN the road, facing the approaching vehicle. He couldn't see it yet. But he could hear it, caught the sound of an engine and a radio playing classic rock.

A familiar truck rolled into view. He knew his father's vehicle on sight. The older model Ram had four doors and both front and rear seats. Judging from the sag in the suspension, that rear seat was full. Jack recognized his father, Delane, driving and his mother, Annetta, in the passenger seat. Between them he could see Kurt. But as they drew closer he realized that he was not looking at the face of his youngest sibling, but the thin face of Carter.

Jack broke into a run, charging the truck like a bull. His father hit the brakes and his mother managed to slide out of the seat before Jack reached into the truck and hauled Carter Bear Den to him and squeezed.

"They didn't tell me!" he said, hugging his twin and feeling the changes. Carter had lost weight.

"Easy, bro. You're crushing me."

Jack eased his grip and drew back to stare at the familiar face he had so missed.

"You back?" he asked.

Carter nodded and wiped the tears from his cheeks. Jack swallowed at the lump in his throat.

"I missed you, brother," said Carter.

Jack glanced away to keep from blubbering and met his mother's tear-streaked face. It was his undoing. He couldn't seem to get enough air.

"We wanted to surprise you," she said, her voice quavering like a bird's. "They just got back."

From the smaller rear door emerged Amber and Kurt. Amber stepped forward and he gave her a kiss, careful not to crush her as he had his brother. She also looked drawn, with circles under her eyes. The ordeal of witness protection and the trial had taken an obvious toll.

Kurt slapped Jack on the shoulder. "Surprised?"

Jack grinned and glanced back at the porch, where both Kenshaw and Sophia watched the reunion. Kenshaw knew, of course. But Sophia did not. She beamed at him, clearly pleased at his joy and his heart squeezed a little tighter.

He motioned her to join them. Her smile vanished and she shook her head. He motioned again. She set her jaw, but descended from the porch.

Jack made introductions and Carter and Amber politely shook her hand, but it was clear they had both had enough of FBI and DOJ officers. Kenshaw called them all into the lodge.

"Casseroles," he said. "I sent out a call and have them in the oven."

They all gathered in the lodge at the circular table and Jack was astonished at how much Carter and Amber ate.

"Didn't they feed you out there?" asked his mother.

Out there. It was how the people referred to anywhere that was not right here, on their land.

Sophia sat between his father and Kenshaw and
seemed to Jack to be trying to disappear. He did not
have to be the most perceptive of men to realize she
was genuinely uncomfortable surrounded by his family.

Tommy arrived in time for dessert, adding to the gai-
ety and the volume of conversation as they each talked
over each other in a rush to catch up on the missing
months.

In the evening they lit a fire outside and brought out
the large drum. Kenshaw and his father set the rhythm,
with all three of this brothers and him keeping pace.
Jack thought they'd never sounded so good as they sang.
Sparks from the fire rose into the clear dry air and lifted
skyward to the glittering stars.

Amber and his mother and Sophia clapped to the
rhythm. They broke their song only to greet Ray,
Morgan and Lisa, who'd arrived. Amber noticed immediately that Morgan was expecting and offered con-
gratulations. The two old friends linked arms and were
just heading toward the drum circle when Dylan and
Meadow arrived.

Then the circle formed again and Jack thought of his
medicine wheel talisman and the circle of friends and
family that formed this living sacred hoop.

The men drummed and the women sang, Meadow
keeping the general melody, though not knowing the
language, her attempts to sing made everyone laugh.
The party broke up very late. Carter and Jack walked
toward the river. Jack knew in his head he would see
Carter in the morning, but it was hard to let go after
missing him for so long and so very much.

"It's been tough without you here, brother."

"I missed the ridge fire," said Carter. "Heard Ray stepped in. Always figured it would be Dylan as captain."

He was talking about the historic Pine View wildfire. Of course, as a Hotshot, it would have killed Carter not to be able to deploy with his crew. The Turquoise Canyon Hotshots were among the most elite crews in the country.

"He couldn't. Dylan was caught in it with Meadow. Had to deploy his fire shelter over both of them."

Carter's eyes widened. "No."

"He can tell you all about it. Love to, I'm sure."

"I've got a lot of catching up to do," said his brother.

Jack tried to imagine missing all that had happened since his brother had followed his wife into witness protection in February. Eight months.

"How did things go with the test results? Did you get your answers?"

Jack looked away.

"Jack?"

"Never opened them," he admitted. Though he'd carried them in his wallet every day since they'd arrived in March.

Carter placed a hand on his shoulder. "Want me to do it?"

"No." He faced his twin. "I'll do it. Now that you're home. I will."

Headlights rolled across them as his father pulled the truck around.

Carter stared back across the darkness, hearing Ray and Dylan bid each other good-night as they made for their cabins with Amber and Meadow.

"You want me to stay? Help keep an eye on Sophia?"

Jack took one look at his brother and made the call. "We got it. You go home with your wife."

"She's pretty," said Carter.

"Who?"

"Don't give me that. You couldn't take your eyes off her when she was singing."

"That's because she doesn't speak our language."

"Western Apache. Yeah. They're different. Not as different as Dylan and Meadow. Boy is that a mismatch. Can't even believe Dylan is going to marry her. He's always been so traditional."

"The heart leads where it leads," said Jack, quoting their mother.

"Right. Well, good night."

"'Night. Glad to have you back, brother."

"Likewise."

Jack watched him walk away, knowing his mother would be making fry bread in the morning and Carter would begin gaining back the weight he had lost. Still smiling, he wandered back to the porch to wave his family off.

Kenshaw turned in, leaving Sophia and Jack standing alone by the road.

"You have a lovely family," said Sophia. Her voice held an undertone of something, a kind of stiffness that resonated inside him. What was wrong?

"Yeah. You know, my mom looks so happy. She'll probably put this in the classifieds, too."

"The classifieds?"

"Yeah. It's silly, but she makes announcements there. Stuff like 'Carter and Jack are back from overseas. Welcome home, boys!' She always posts one for birthdays and when something big happens."

"Might not be a great idea to say her eldest son is back from witness protection," said Sophia.

"You got that right.

"Do you have siblings?" asked Jack.

"Yes, lots. But we weren't raised together."

His brows lifted, and he wished that just once he had not been right.

"No?" he said, half hoping she'd keep her problems to herself, the other half recognizing that she was about to share something personal.

"Fostered. All of us. I was number eight. They broke us up when my father went to prison. It's a common story."

All too common.

"Mom?"

"She's around. Can't really take care of herself, let alone her kids. Doesn't stop her from having them, though. I stayed with my granny until she passed. She raised me."

"That's tough, Sophia." And made her current position with the FBI even more impressive. The odds had definitely been stacked against her.

"All I ever wanted was to get off the rez. When I was a kid I wanted clean clothes. Once I got to foster care, I wanted a room that was mine."

"And you have that now."

She nodded, meeting his gaze with sad eyes. Was she thinking of losing all she had gained? She would if she did as his tribe wished. How could he ask her to risk losing everything she had achieved? Jack glanced over his shoulder to the river and knew the answer. If they didn't do something, all he knew would be washed away.

"Let me walk you back to your cabin."

They strolled across the grass, neither in any hurry to arrive.

"I'm sorry to put you in this position, Sophia."

She shook her head. "Don't be. I've given you my suggestions. Tomorrow my escort will be here and I'll be back home. But, Jack, you should move your people. Send them up to my reservation. They'd take them in."

"My tribe fought long and hard to establish a reservation of our own. We are not leaving it."

They passed the fire pit as the drenched embers smoldered and smoking logs shifted. The members of the Turquoise Canyon Hotshots knew better than to leave a fire unattended and had carefully doused the flames and scattered the fuel inside the stone fire pit.

Sophia and Jack continued on, pausing on the porch of her cabin.

It was their last night together. Jack gazed down at Sophia.

"They're coming for you in a few hours," he said, the clock ticking louder now.

"Oh-eight-hundred hours, yes. I won't have time to check the uppermost dam."

"Sophia, I'd like to kiss you again." He'd like to do more than kiss her if she'd let him. He wanted to know her as a man knows a woman and keep some part of her here in his heart.

"Will you come in?" she asked, opening the door.

Chapter Eleven

"I'd like that very much," said Jack in answer to Sophia's invitation.

She moved aside and Jack stepped past her into the darkness. His eyes adjusted slowly, the light from the windows casting blue starlight across the floor. Each cabin was identical within, with a table and chairs, sitting chair and a full-size bed centered on the back wall next to a bedside table. He waited for her to close the door and throw the latch, then gathered her in his arms.

He leaned in to inhale the sweetness of her neck, but she drew back, making him pause.

"You understand that I'm leaving tomorrow?" she asked.

"Yes."

"This won't change anything."

It would change everything, he knew. But he murmured, "Yes," as his lips brushed her neck.

She trembled as he trailed kisses down the column of her throat and into the vee left by her prim, professional blouse. She worked the buttons, releasing them until the garment flapped open. He breathed in her sweet scent.

"Lavender," he whispered against the swell of her breasts.

She backed away, gripping his shirt in both fists as

she led him across the room to the bed. Halfway there she released him to slip out of her shoes and drop her blazer, then unfastened the clip that held her shoulder holster. She lay the weapon on the bedside table. He placed his beside it with his wallet and radio. His fingers trembled as he groped for the square packet in his wallet, causing the letter to fall to the floor. She stooped and retrieved it as he found the condom. She set the folded envelope on the table beside the weapons and shucked out of her slacks. He watched her shrug out of the blouse, which fluttered to the floor, leaving her in only her white lace bra and matching panties. Her skin glowed blue in the starlight. She was all soft curves and smooth skin. He was all coarse hair and muscle, by comparison.

He unbuttoned his shirt slowly, hoping she would not have second thoughts when she saw him shirtless. He didn't often remove his shirt because it emphasized the dissimilarity between him and other men here. His body type was so different and his chest was covered with thick curling hair. He dropped his shirt and waited.

Sophia's gaze raked over him. Finally she lifted her eyes to meet his. He did not see revulsion or fear, but hunger. He released a breath. She reached for his jeans and let her unzip them before he sat to tug off his boots and then his jeans.

She moved to stand between his legs, her thighs brushing his. Jack lifted his hands and rested them lightly at her waist.

"I'm not too big?" he asked, voicing aloud the fear he carried with him like his skin.

"Not for me." Her fingers raked down his chest, scraping through the chest hair and over his muscles.

"You look more like a lumberjack than a guy riding in a police unit all day."

"Sometimes I ride a horse," he said. "A lot of our rez is easier to get to that way."

She moved closer, allowing him to brush his hands up the long muscles of her back. He lifted her and spun her to the bed, easing her down beside him. He pushed the bra up and away. She lifted to let him drag it off. She shrugged out of her panties.

Jack remained on his side, giving himself the gift of seeing her completely naked and stretched out before him wearing nothing but a seductive smile. There was something dark on her breast—a tattoo? He thought it unlikely, but the possibility made him grow even harder. Sophia was full of surprises, including giving in to the heat and hunger roaring between them, if only for one night.

God, he hadn't even had her and he wanted her again. But he waited for her to make the approach.

He looped a thumb under the tie holding her thick hair and dragged it free. Her hair fanned the pillow.

"You're beautiful," he said, his fingers trailing over her shoulder and back up to her hair.

"So are you."

She rolled to her side, facing him now, and inclined her head so that her cheek brushed the back of his hand.

"Not too big?" he asked again.

She chuckled. "I like big."

The tension crackled between them as he waited and prayed she would reach out to him, his hand trailing down her arm and back to the blanket.

Sophia moved closer, dragged a hand down his naked chest, her fingernails making his nerves blast awake.

He growled in pleasure, the sound vibrating through his chest.

"I have protection." He reached back for the condom, already wishing he carried more than two.

"Me, too."

She was cautious. That was smart. Her caution was probably why she'd made it out of foster care and avoided getting pregnant as a teen. He admired her for so many reasons. But right now the aching want was descending over his brain. He needed his skin pressed to hers, to feel her breath on his neck and her nails rake over his back.

He loomed over her and she looped her arms around his neck and pulled, sending a barrage of hot kisses down his neck and chest, trailing lower until she reached his waistband. His arms, usually so strong, began to tremble as her fingers slipped beneath his underwear. She released him, peeling back the fabric that separated them.

She tore open the condom package with her teeth, pushing him to his back. He complied, falling to the mattress and letting her slip the protective sheath over the length of him.

His stomach twitched and tightened as she kissed her way back up his body, finally finding his mouth. He cradled her head as he kissed her long and deep.

When she slipped a leg across him and straddled his hips, he watched them come together. She lowered herself and Jack closed his eyes to savor the bliss that carried them both late into the night.

They slept tangled in sheets and blankets. He felt her shivering in the heart of the night and dragged the blanket over her, tucking it up around her shoulders and then pulling her close to his chest, sharing his heat. She snuggled against him and he breathed a sigh at the perfect moment. The sense of calm and the ache of want mingled to form an unnameable desire that beat with each stroke of his heart. He closed his eyes to better sense each warm breath that flowed from her and across his chest. Jack cradled her head and kissed her forehead. Deep in sleep, Sophia muttered something that was an attempt as speech. He stroked her head, his fingers tangling in the satin of her hair, loose at last.

"Shhh," he whispered.

She relaxed back to slumber. Jack tried to stay awake a few minutes more. But the satisfaction of their joining and the lethargy that followed was too much and he tumbled to sleep, still cradling her close.

This was special, his heart murmured. She was special.

He woke when she slipped from his arms before dawn. He grasped her hand to stay her.

"Be right back," she promised and he let her go.

She would be. But Jack did not fool himself. Sophia would not stay with him for long. He'd been okay with that when she arrived. But things were changing and he wasn't sure just what to do about that.

The bathroom door opened and closed, water ran and she was there beside him again. She slipped over him, one thigh gliding across his stomach until she lay on top of him like a second skin. Her body was warm and her muscles slack. He stroked her back, gently but with purpose, to rouse her from her sleepiness. Her breathing changed first, then she started to move, climbing up until her mouth met his. Her kiss and the rocking of her hips left no doubt that she wanted him again.

This time was slow and sweet. Their pleasure vibrated like a taut cord until they broke together in a hot rush of sensation.

Would he ever get enough of his spider woman? Not if he had a thousand years, he decided. He'd had women, but none was Sophia's equal. She was poised and strong and experienced in the ways of the world, with enough sexual confidence to keep him guessing.

She was a survivor who had beaten the odds and made something of herself with very little help. His admiration only strengthened his desire.

They dozed and when he next woke the light was pink, giving everything a rosy glow. He scowled at the window and the light that peeked through, knowing they were coming for her today and that they would take her from him.

He wondered if she would agree to see him again, or if this was, to her, just a one-time affair.

She slipped from the bed and back across the room. He could see her scoop the white bra from the ground and slip it around her torso, fasten the clasps and spin the undergarment back into place. He understood the meaning. She was back to business and preparing for the day.

Her cousin, Luke Forrest, was coming to take her back to Flagstaff under escort. It might be safer for her there, but he didn't like the idea of relinquishing custody. He knew their force was small and resources were limited. His mind knew it, but his heart wanted to be the one protecting her.

Sophia slipped into her panties.

She stood beside the bed. Jack sat up, the sheet and blankets covering him from midthigh to his waist. If she wanted modesty, he would go along. But after what they had just shared, it seemed sad.

Things were always different in daylight. He knew that.

"Good morning," he said.

She cast him a bright smile. "Yes. It is."

He did not know if she referred to the lingering satisfaction from their night together, or her anticipation at leaving. Jack did not like the uncertainty that settled in the pit of his stomach.

"I wanted to be ready when they come for me," she said.

"I understand." *Say something,* he thought. *Ask her to stay.*

Sophia leaned forward, her fingers brushed along his neck and then she lifted the cord to his medicine bundle. The small leather pouch had been beaded with a medicine wheel in white, black, red and yellow, the wheel segmented into four sections, the symbol as sacred as the cross to many in his tribe. His father said that all things of importance moved in a circle. Inside the pouch were a few blessed objects he used in ceremony and to help ground, protect and inspire him.

"Very traditional for a guy who wears his hair cut so short." She ran her hands through his hair in emphasis.

He didn't address the comment about his short hair. If she saw his natural curls, she might understand why he preferred to keep it short, eliminating the sight of one more difference between himself and his people. He looked away and glanced at the folded envelope from Relative Finder Lab in California.

He forced his attention back to the medicine wheel, the symbol that had been chosen for him by his shaman. The hoop had special powers for healing and protection. He supposed a lawman could use all the protection he could get. But his shaman had not picked this emblem to protect, or to mark the seasons or the stages of a man's life. He had chosen it because it marked the four directions. And Kenshaw had told him the medicine wheel would help guide him.

"I have one here, too." He placed his fingers on the back of his neck. He could not see the tattoo except in his mind. "My shaman said it would help me know which way to go."

She leaned forward, her stomach pressing momentarily to his chest. It was hard not to capture her there, her skin felt so amazing against his.

"Hmm," she said. "Did he pick the symbols for your friends, too?"

"Yes," said Jack.

"It's different than the others. Isn't it? I mean they are all medicine shields and all have five feathers. But I saw Carter's. It's a bear track on a shield. And your friend Dylan also had a track. Seemed like a puma."

"Bobcat," he said, correcting her.

"And Ray's is the head of a bald eagle, also on a shield."

Sophia drew one finger down his back, counting to five. "You each have five feathers but there are only four of you."

He wished for a moment that she was not an investigator.

"We got them after leaving the service. Kenshaw helped us pick the symbols and placement. We picked the feathers. One for each of us and the fifth feather is for Yeager Hatch. He was the friend who didn't come back."

"Bear is your family's symbol. Shouldn't you have a bear paw like your brother?"

Jack nodded. He had always thought so.

She laced her fingers behind his neck and leaned back to look at him.

"Why didn't you put it on your right arm, like the others?"

He lowered his head. He had done as his shaman had suggested, but he had wanted the tattoo on his arm.

One more way he was different. He didn't know the reason his shaman had chosen to place the medicine wheel on his back and had never found the courage to ask him.

"It doesn't show under my uniform or a short-sleeved shirt," said Jack. It wasn't the reason. He was sure there was more.

"I suppose." Sophia seemed to be humoring him. "Carter has scars all over that arm and one right through that tattoo."

"Bullet wound. He got it saving Amber," said Jack. "The other scars are older. Burns from the war."

She nodded, absorbing that admission. "Why is Dylan a bobcat?"

"Bobcats have stealth. Dylan needs that quality, needs to see what is hidden."

"Then the eagle is to give Ray perspective?" she asked.

"Yes, and to remind him that he is holy, like all things. Ray was very hard on himself about Hatch. He's better since Meadow joined him."

"What did Kenshaw say about this?" she asked, her finger circling his tattoo.

He didn't want to tell her.

"I'll show you mine," she offered as compensation.

He let his gaze rake down her perfect skin. Sophia stood before him. She reached across her body with one hand and lowered the strap of her bra, revealing her right breast beneath the white lace cup. There was a dream catcher the size of a silver dollar. Inside the web was a tiny black spider.

Jack moved to sit at the edge of the bed, so he could get a closer look.

"Spider born of butterfly," he said. He touched the mark on her perfect skin. Her nipple hardened instantly, though he had not touched it.

His body went hot and pulsed to readiness.

"Exactly. She's a hunter, like me—catching bad guys is what I do. Seemed appropriate."

"In our legends, the four spiders wove the cords that hold up the world," he said.

She turned to him. "Same with us."

They were both Apache. But the differences extended beyond their languages.

"I also have a butterfly. Want to see?" Her thumb hooked the waistband of her panties.

He did, but if it was where he thought it might be, showing him would drive him into the most obvious of actions. He wanted his brain working for a few more minutes, but not as much as he wanted to be inside her again.

He met her gaze. Her lips curled in a smile of anticipation and her attention dropped to the sheets and blankets now doing little to conceal that he was beyond ready for her.

"Well?" she asked as their gazes locked.

He nodded, hungry for her now.

She presented her back, peering over her shoulder at him. Then she lowered the lace panties to reveal a perfect monarch butterfly on the curve of her buttock.

"Butterfly born of spider," he whispered.

He reached for her and she stepped away, waving a finger at him.

"I'd love to, Jack. I mean it. But they're likely on their way. I don't want them to find me like this." She waved at her matching bra and panties.

He thought she never looked more appealing. Then his mind flashed images of their night together. He'd seen her look more appealing because last night her eyes had flared with desire for him.

"No, I understand. But maybe you'd be safer here."

"This is where they shot at me, Jack."

"I meant here at the compound." He meant here in his arms, he realized.

She made a face. Was it too much like her childhood, the rugged little cabin with no air conditioning or electricity? He liked hearing the birds and the wind, but she was a city girl now.

"You don't have enough men to guard me 24/7. The Bureau has resources."

"I'd guard you 24/7," he said.

She cast him an indulgent smile, perhaps assuming a double entendre that he had not intended.

"Would you like coffee? I'm heading to the lodge to make some."

"Yeah. Sounds good. Wait for me."

"I think I can make it." She slipped into her blouse and then shrugged into her shoulder holster, and picked up her pistol.

Jack got up and into his jeans. He'd use the lodge bathroom, he decided, because she was not walking around unescorted. He trusted Jake Redhorse, the tribal officer who covered the road overnight, but the river was still a highway and anyone with a small craft could reach them via the Hakathi River. Which reminded him, he needed to be sure they relieved Jake, who had volunteered to cover the road. The young officer was rapidly becoming Jack's go-to man for important assignments.

Jack ducked into his shirt and clipped his holster and his radio to his belt. Then he tucked the envelope back in his wallet and put them in his front pocket.

"You want to talk about that?" she asked, glancing in the direction of his wallet.

"Over coffee maybe."

She followed him out and across the wide open stretch between the row of cabins and the lodge. The scent of ash from last night's fire reached him and made him smile.

"You have a wonderful voice," she said.

"You could hear me over the others?" he asked.

"Of course. You don't sound anything like them. Your voice is much deeper."

His proud smile vanished as she pointed out just one more way he was different.

He let the conversation die as he held open the door for her. What was the use? He needed her to help the tribe. That was why she was here and that was what he should be focused on.

Chapter Twelve

Sophia headed straight for the large drip coffeemaker, filling the reserve with water and then measuring out the coffee into the filter. Then she flicked the switch and stood back to watch.

"Can't seem to get moving without a cup," she said.

Jack excused himself to wash up. When he returned, she was sitting at the counter sipping her coffee. Beside her was an empty stool and a full steaming mug.

He sat and they drank coffee side by side as they watched the river roll beyond the picture window. The familiarity struck him, and the longing. He swallowed it back with the next gulp.

"You got me dead curious about that letter. Looks like lab results. You okay, Jack?" Her dark eyes regarded him and he saw the investigator again.

"Not sick, if that's what you mean. But you are right. It's a DNA test. Carter and I sent in a swab from each of our cheeks."

She didn't ask why but cut straight to the point. "You want to know if you've got different parents."

"Parent. My mom. I think, suspect…"

"I see. Easier to sneak around behind her back than come out and ask her?"

He cradled his mug, rolling the base in a circle.

"I asked. She said she's never been with anyone but my dad."

Sophia's look told him that she didn't believe this, either.

Jack muttered a curse.

"Why haven't you opened it?"

He couldn't explain it. He just hadn't yet.

"Maybe I'm drumming up the courage."

She snorted at this. "You don't lack courage, Jack."

He didn't argue.

Sophia released her mug and spun the stool that turned in complete circles.

"But if you don't open it, you don't have to face what's inside. Me? I'd need to know."

He reached for the envelope and extracted it from his wallet. He held it between a thumb and index finger for a moment. Then he placed it on the counter and pushed it toward her.

She looked from the folded offering and then back to him, brows lifted in a silent question. He nodded.

"Okay." She straightened the envelope and ironed it once with the side of her hand. Then she unceremoniously tore open the side. Sophia upended the contents and the pages dropped out into her open hand. She spread out the pages and studied them for just a moment. Then she glanced at him, a frown on her face. It was all he could do not to snatch the letter and shove it back in the envelope. But like Pandora's box, the damage was done and at least one person knew his secret.

"What does it say?" he asked, displeased at the squeak in his voice.

"Your mother told a half truth."

"A lie."

"Misrepresentation," she amended.

Jack pressed his hands on the counter. "Sophia. You're killing me."

"Well, it says that siblings with common parents share all the same DNA, basically scrambled."

"Are you going to tell me what the results say, or not?"

"Yes, that's what I'm doing. If you have a different parent, say your father, then you'd share half the DNA as your brothers."

"Sophia, just give me the results." He extended his hand.

She drew the pages away, holding them to her chest and meeting his impatient stare with one of worry.

"Okay, fine. See?" She pointed to a table and read the first column. "Parent-child, full siblings have fifty percent shared DNA. Half siblings, your suspicion, share twenty-five. That's the same with aunts, uncles and the grandparent-grandchild relationship. First cousins share only twelve-point-five percent. Half cousins even less."

He stared at the ceiling. Then he let his head drop. Finally he met her gaze.

"What does all that mean?"

"Carter is not your brother."

Jack felt a pain in his heart as the information sliced into him like a jagged shard of glass.

SOPHIA KNEW THAT LOOK. It was the look of a man whose world was coming apart. The fabric that glued him to this place and to his family had been shredded by this information.

"Give it to me. I'll put it back." He groped for the pages, his hands trembling now. Sweat beaded on his brow.

She pressed a hand over his. "No, Jack. Just listen."

"I can't. I don't want…" He was tugging at the pages now. She lifted her hand and he made a terrible job of folding the sheets. Then he tore the envelope trying to cram the pages back inside it.

Finally he sat still, gripping the tattered envelope in two hands as if the information inside could be crushed by the pressing of his thumb and fingers.

"I knew it," he whispered. "Always."

You only had to have eyes to see he wasn't a Bear Den, she thought.

"Jack, your mother isn't your biological mother."

He looked at her, his eyes red-rimmed. His shoulders rounded. He looked completely defeated. She felt a righteous indignation on his behalf.

"What?" His head was cocked to the side like a dog trying to understand speech and failing badly.

"They should have told you, Jack."

"So what does that mean? I'm adopted?"

"I'm not sure. But your test says that you and Carter are first cousins, so you share two common grandparents."

"Two?" He shook his head, still lost. His broad hand now rhythmically rubbed his forehead.

"If I had to guess, I'd say Annetta's parents are your grandparents. It could be your father, Delane, of course. But I don't think so. You both resemble Annetta more strongly around the eyes."

"What are you talking about?"

He'd been vested in the secret that his mother had cheated on his dad for so long. But now she was switching his secret and his mind just couldn't grasp it.

"In other words, you are the child of Annetta's brother or sister."

"She doesn't have any brothers or sisters."

Now Sophia angled her head, lifting her brows at the same time to give him a look that said *I don't think so.*

He shook his head in denial.

"I wouldn't be too sure about that."

"What are you saying, that my mother left me with my aunt and disappeared? And not one member of my tribe happened to mention it to me? That's not possible."

"When you have eliminated the impossible, whatever remains, however improbable, must be the truth."

He blasted out a breath from his nose. "You're quoting the writing of Arthur Conan Doyle now?"

"It's what happened. I don't know why she kept it from you, why everyone here kept it from you. But in a way you are lucky."

He wouldn't look at her now. "How do you figure?"

"You have a family that loves you and something else. You have possibilities. Who and why? I'd give anything not to know who my parents are and where I come from."

She slipped from the stool and took the envelope from him, folded it and attempted to return it to his front pocket. He turned to face her, extending his leg so she could push the report away. Then he captured her around the waist and pulled her into the vee of his legs. She rested her hands on his chest and smiled at him.

"You are who you make yourself, not who you were born. Don't spend too much time back there in the past, Jack. It's not healthy."

"It doesn't matter to you?"

"Your roots? Nope. Not at all. Who I am is not where I come from or how I look. To know me you have to look much deeper than all that."

He kissed her then, his mouth hungry as his tongue

slid into hers. He tasted of coffee mingled with desire. Sophia laced her fingers around his neck and leaned in.

"You two still at it?" said a male voice from the doorway.

Sophia stiffened and drew back. Jack kept the pressure on her lower back, allowing her to retreat only so far.

She turned to see Ray Strong stride into the room. His face seemed freshly scrubbed and his short hair was wet. He wore jeans, moccasins and a tight T-shirt…and a cocky smile.

"I thought you'd be worn out by now," said Ray.

Jack winced at the comment. Clearly they'd been overheard last night.

Sophia's eyes widened and she broke away from him like a bucking bronc out of the shoot. Her face went pink and her mouth dropped open.

Jack cast Ray a glare that should have dropped him in his tracks. Instead Ray held that stupid grin that had gotten him into more jams than Jack could count. Well, this time his antics had dragged in both Jack and Sophia.

"Shut up, Ray," Jack said.

Ray scratched his chest and yawned. "When you said you'd convince her to help us, well…I misunderstood. Good for you two. Morgan says you're perfect for each other."

Sophia hurried past Ray to the door.

"Sophia, wait," said Jack.

She didn't, of course.

Jack glanced back to Ray. "What is wrong with you?"

"I was congratulating you." Ray seemed oblivious to the damage he had caused.

Jack grabbed him by the T-shirt and yanked him forward. Ray lifted both hands in instant surrender.

"You made it seem that I used sex to make her help us."

"Didn't you?" asked Ray.

Now he really was going to hit him. What did Ray think Jack was, Mata Hari?

He drew back his fist.

The door crashed open. "Hey!"

Jack looked up toward the female voice. Morgan stood in the doorway and her glare was aimed at him. Jack pushed Ray away, sending Ray staggering back several steps.

"What did you do?" asked his new wife.

"Nothing. I was congratulating them."

Morgan made a sound of frustration in her throat and stared at the ceiling. Then she met Jack's gaze.

"I'm sorry, Jack."

Not as sorry as he was. He had to make Sophia understand that last night was not about getting her onboard. He cleared the door and scanned the yard. She hadn't gone far, just to the end of the porch. She stood facing the river, arms clamped across her chest.

He had covered half the distance when his radio sounded.

It was Cecil Goseyum, one of their tribal council members. Not only did Cecil do some of the best leatherwork in the tribe, but he also volunteered with the fire department. On the weekends and evenings, when Olivia was off, they covered the incoming calls to the station.

"Jack, you there?"

He lifted the radio. "Yes, Cecil. What's up?"

"I just called Wallace. He said to call you, too. I got

the Phoenix news on here. There's been an explosion in the city."

Jack stopped walking.

"What kind of explosion?"

Sophia turned, her arms dropping to her sides.

"High-pressure pipelines. It's bad, Jack."

Sophia's steps were brisk. "I have to go."

He clasped her arm as she walked by him, halting her so they stood facing in opposite directions, staring at each other.

"You're on leave."

"They'll want me back for this. I've got to go. Now."

JACK GOT HER to the police station in Piñon Forks. There Jack saw the news on the television as she tried unsuccessfully to reach her supervisor.

Someone had hit three locations in Phoenix at once. Apparently dressed as employees of the natural gas company down there, they had blocked and dug up the streets right over the major pipelines. They used backhoes and took out the major excess flow valves first, then waited for the gas to accumulate before igniting the free-flowing stream.

You didn't need to be an explosives expert to know what happened next. They had it on every downtown security camera. The workers, the breaks and the resulting fireball. Three sites. Two downtown, both banks, both among the largest buildings in the city. The third site was south, on the edge of town, an industrial complex used by a mining company as a distribution center. It was unique, Jack thought, because of its size, 250,000 square feet, and because it was owned by a company that violated the earth. Mining again. Just like the Lilac copper mine.

It was BEAR. He was sure of it.

That meant Kenshaw was right. The eco-extremist group wasn't broken. The cells were all working independently now and each had their own target. He couldn't keep himself from glancing out the window at the gently flowing river. The river where he learned to swim, canoe and fish had become an enemy.

Chapter Thirteen

This could not be happening. Sophia hunched over the phone and spoke to her captain, Larry Burton.

"But I should be there," she said, working hard to keep her voice level.

Burton's tone was rushed, as if he was on the move as he spoke. The man did not have time to chat.

"You're still on administrative leave."

"But—"

He cut her off. "I asked. It's a no. You are *not* to report."

"That can't be right."

"You need to be requested back." He spoke slowly now, as if to be certain she heard and complied. "That's an order. Now I have to go."

She gave up on the voice-modulation thing. "I'm an explosives expert!"

"And you are not the only one in the Bureau, Rivas. We can manage without you. Okay?"

"What am I supposed to do? Sit up here twiddling my thumbs?"

"I'm sorry, Soph. Gotta go. I'll call when I can."

"Wait. Is it BEAR?"

There was silence. "I can't talk about an active investigation."

"There's a shaman here. He told me yesterday that the pipeline was a target."

"And why didn't you call that in?"

She wanted to say because she was on administrative leave.

"I did call it in. I left a message with your administrative assistant and I phoned Luke Forrest and told him. He said the Phoenix field office was aware that the pipeline system was a potential target."

"Next time speak to me directly."

"Yes, sir."

She thought she'd gotten through to the right people. Had she made another mistake?

She saw her position eroding like a tree undercut by floodwaters.

"Maybe I should just drive down there."

"No. I gave you an order. And, Rivas? Keep your head down and your mouth shut. Okay?"

She closed her mouth but then opened it again. Sophia regretted her words even as she spoke but she could not remain mute.

"The tribal council up here on Turquoise Canyon believes that BEAR will strike the reservoir system. Anytime now, since the first cell has hit their target."

"We don't know it's BEAR."

She did. She felt certain and until she had credible evidence to the contrary, she was sticking with that theory.

"Can you at least send up the National Guard?"

"Sophia, they're deploying the National Guard and every available law enforcement agency to Phoenix."

"Highway patrol?" she asked, her voice a croak.

She was met with silence.

"Larry?"

"Yes. Highway patrol, too. Listen. I got to go. Stay out of trouble up there." The line went dead.

Sophia stood there with the phone pressed to her ear, the line buzzing with her mind. They blew up the pipeline, just as Kenshaw Little Falcon had told her they would. And they would hit the reservoir, too. And if the larger Alchesay Dam was as poorly secured as Skeleton Cliff, it would make an easy target. Easier now if they also pulled the highway patrol.

She lowered the phone to its cradle and met Jack's gaze. He was waiting for her. Waiting for the awesome weight of responsibility to settle over her. She could choose to do nothing, wait and see. If she did that, she might still be reinstated, but this place and his people might be washed away. Or she could act and lose everything.

"They pulled the highway patrol," she said.

Jack's forehead furrowed as his brows dipped low over troubled eyes.

"We should leave," she said.

"There are too many of us. Our senior center is in Piñon Forks. Our day care. Our schools. Our medical clinic. Our new woman's health center. Even if we got every single person clear, for how long? Days? Weeks? It's not possible."

She wanted to get him to leave with her but could not find the nerve to ask him.

"We can't leave," said Jack. "You can. You should."

He was trying to save her. Well, she was not leaving Jack Bear Den here to die. Even if he had tried to seduce her into staying. And it had worked, darn it.

"Take me to see Alchesay Dam."

The frown vanished. On the way she mentioned her reservations. Not the obvious ones, like losing her job, being arrested and prosecuted, and likely spending a very, very long time in a federal prison. No, she stuck to the practical.

THEY REACHED THE larger dam and power station by mid-morning. She was relieved to see that Alchesay Dam was better guarded than Skeleton Cliff. They had the National Guard on site in plain view with the highway patrol. The barricades were larger than at Skeleton Cliff Dam and there was more than one. A truck or car could not gain access via the road that crossed the dam from either side.

The National Guard sat in a Humvee at the barricade before the power-station gate. In addition, there was a floating barricade on Goodwin Lake supported by a patrol boat ready to intercept any leisure boater who ventured too near.

Clearly they believed this was BEAR's target. What if the beefed-up security here actually served to make Jack's reservation more vulnerable?

If she was in charge of an attack, she would certainly move her aim to Skeleton Cliff and possibly Red Rock Dam below his reservation. Breaching them both might create enough hydraulic force from the released water in Canyon Lake and Two Mountain Lake to destroy the smaller Mesa Salado Dam. No question that the water would overflow. And with three power stations knocked out, the city would go dark. All those humming air conditioners, which made life in the desert possible, would go silent.

"We're on our own, you know," she said after scouting Red Rock Dam and finding it vulnerable. "No one is coming."

Sophia glanced at Jack. Last night she had thought

that she had found a man who was different. He was strong and self-contained. He had purpose and vision. And it had all been an illusion. Had he used her to get this help, or had he been as moved as she was?

They needed to talk. Her about last night. Him about the personal bomb that just went off when she opened those test results. But that wouldn't happen because she needed to circle the wagons.

Regret scalded her. She wished, hoped… It didn't matter.

She'd come and consulted. Now it was time to go.

Nothing was going to stop her from getting through this inquiry and getting reinstated. Nothing. Not him. Not his tribe. Not the senior center that sat beside the river.

"How do I get the explosives to set up the blast?"

JACK HAD THE miners of Turquoise Canyon on the ridge site within the hour. They knew how to blast away a boulder and how to drill a hole for a charge. They did not know how to take down the tonnage needed to completely block the river and be strong enough to hold when the flood waters crashed against it. If the explosion went wrong, all they would do was add rolling jagged torpedoes of rock to the destructive force of the water.

Did Sophia have the expertise they needed?

Wallace Tinnin arrived as the men were drilling the holes in the rock.

He regarded the operation with hands on hips and the kind of grim acceptance he often used when facing an unpleasant task.

"Sorry I'm late. We have another report of a runaway."

Jack swiveled his head toward his chief. "Another since Kacy Doka?"

"Yeah. That's four."

"Another girl?" asked Jack.

Wallace nodded. "I've got a bad feeling. These girls aren't tied up with gangs. All I can find, they're sweet and never been in trouble."

"Their families?"

He looked toward the sky. "Awful. Single parent. Drug users. Drug suppliers. Multiple run-ins with us and outside law enforcement. I swear, some of them hardly noticed their kid was missing."

That made Jack's heart ache.

"I want you on this."

Jack rested his hands on his hips, considering his argument. He was not going to leave his escort duty, especially after the attack.

"But I'll send Redhorse out to do preliminaries for now. We need you here."

Jack nodded, his hands sliding to his sides.

"I spoke to Kenshaw," said Wallace. "Asked him if he knew his cell had been activated."

Jack lifted his brow. Kenshaw had told them that his cell of BEAR had been assigned to the pipelines.

"He said he wasn't contacted," said Wallace.

Jack scowled. "You believe him?"

Wallace inclined his head.

"If what he said is true, then they know he's working with the Feds," said Jack.

"Looks that way."

"You think they'll try to get to him?"

"Maybe."

Jack added Kenshaw to the list of people needing protection.

Tinnin looked out at the men crawling over the rock.

"We got enough material?"

"We have the blasting caps, batteries and DET cord. She needed two burner phones. Those just arrived."

"She's not using shock tubing?" asked Wallace.

His chief's family had a claim, and his chief knew how to handle explosives.

"She said anyone could set that off. She wants full control. So she's using an electric initiator. I'm not sure about the main charge. She seems worried," said Jack. "She also wants everything we have left moved here to the station."

"Why?"

"To secure it, but also to have it close at hand, near the river."

The station was in tribal headquarters and sat across the street from the river. If they got much closer, they'd need the tribes' twenty-four-foot police boat.

"She's about to destroy her career. You know that, right? That hill goes boom and she's just another unemployed Indian, maybe one going to prison."

"We can protect her."

Tinnin didn't look convinced. "Maybe. She's on our land. Unfortunately the FBI thinks it's federal land."

He knew that. Knew the risk she was taking and it made him sick. In spite of whatever he did, there were some things he couldn't keep from happening. His mind flashed back to Yeager Hatch, the comrade that none of them could reach in time.

Jack watched Sophia moving along the ridge. She progressed with an intensity of focus and alertness that he had not seen before. But he had not seen Sophia on the job until today.

The sun was descending toward the canyon ridge

when she finally climbed up the rock to speak to them. The woman was as agile as a monkey.

"Almost done," she said. Her breathing was still heavy from her exertions. Sweat beaded on her brow and she worked to fill her lungs with air.

"The explosives are set in two separate sequences. The first will take down that lower section and the second will remove this ridge. They're going to feel it down in Piñon Forks. The debris will go a quarter mile, but shock waves will easily travel a mile. Might take out some windows."

"You think it's coming, don't you?" asked Jack.

"I wouldn't be up here if I didn't. I'd like to ask that your department help guard Skeleton Cliff Dam. Maybe we can stop them."

"Better to be proactive," said Wallace. "We've got Tribal Thunder watching the dam and we have snipers and drone surveillance. But we don't know when or how."

"Drones?" she asked.

"My son owns one," he said. "Short range. Good images, though, in real time."

She nodded.

"Any chance this will go off accidentally?" asked Jack.

"None. I trigger the blasts with this." She lifted her phone.

Jack was about to remind her that any of the miners would know how to bypass any initiator she devised when Tinnin interrupted.

"Couldn't anyone do it from over there?" Tinnin pointed toward the ridge.

"Anyone that wants to die. The shock wave from the blasts will kill anyone up here." She pointed over the cliff. "Or down there. You'd have to be that close to manually fire the blasting caps."

"That's your security system?" asked Jack. "You have to die to set them off?"

"No. If there was time, you could run additional nonel tubing. Get far enough away or behind adequate cover."

"I think we should run that cording now," said Jack.

"There is no adequate cover," she said.

"We have nonel tubing in thousand-yard rolls."

"Which we are securing at the station. Right?" she asked.

Tinnin nodded. "Yes, ma'am.

"You plan to set it off remotely, then?" Wallace asked Sophia.

"Yup. I'm using two burner phones and nine-volt batteries to boost the charge. Only I know the numbers for each phone and my phone is password protected."

Jack and Tinnin exchanged a look and Jack knew his chief was not happy that they could not initiate the blast without Sophia.

"If the dam goes, will we have time to trigger both blasts?" she asked.

"We've got eyes on the dam 24/7 and the power company has a siren they sound at noon and for emergencies."

Sophia surveyed her work and nodded. "I'm done here."

"All that's left is to pray we never have to place those two phone calls," said Tinnin.

Waiting, Jack realized, was going to be hell.

Chapter Fourteen

Sophia and Jack reached Piñon Forks after dark, hot, dusty and thirsty. The cool interior of the tribe's casino bar welcomed as they arrived with ten minutes to spare before the happy hour food specials ended. He picked a booth and asked for menus. She studied hers and he lowered his to the table. He had to be starving, she thought, because they had missed lunch.

"You already know what you want?" she asked.

"Got it memorized."

When the waitress returned, he asked for water and then ordered chicken wings, southwest egg rolls and cheesy spinach dip. He asked Sophia to choose a drink and she picked soda, thinking she could use the sugar rush after the exertions of the day.

The waitress made an efficient turn and retreated toward the bar to get her soda.

"You don't drink?" he asked.

"Mom has a problem with alcohol." Among other things. "I figure I won't risk it."

Jack nodded. Alcoholism ran in families and she'd wager he'd seen his share of drunken brawls, domestic violence and the removal of a child or two from reckless endangerment or neglect. She rubbed her forehead, trying not to go back there in her mind. Still, she thought she heard her mother screaming at the cops and her husband and her kids.

Sophia thought she was doing so well. She didn't often think of the home she'd left. Home. She snorted. If you could call it that.

Her siblings had been scattered by the foster care system or their own sadness. She didn't know her older siblings, Brenda or Amanda. They were taken before she had memory of them. She recalled Marvin and Velma and when Wilbur was born, though she'd not yet been two. How many did her mother have now? She doubted Vera even knew. None of her siblings had tried to find her and she had not tried to find them.

The drinks arrived. She finished hers before Jack had even taken a sip.

"You okay?"

"Yeah." She said it automatically, as people do when someone asks how they're doing. *Fine. And you?*

Not fine. Not okay.

She scoured the menu, already knowing what she was having but needing the privacy the shiny laminated booklet allowed.

Oh, no, her eyes were not tearing up. She refused to allow it. Sophia dragged in a breath and blew it away.

Jack placed one finger on the menu and pushed it to the table, pinning it beneath his index finger. She glanced up to find concern in his eyes.

"Sophia?"

"Was Ray right, Jack?" she asked. "Did you sleep with me to get my help?"

The waitress returned with the appetizers and asked if they'd made up their minds. She ordered a burger and sweet potato fries. Jack told her he'd have the same, mostly, Sophia believed, to be rid of her.

Jack pushed the egg rolls in her direction.

She glanced from the peace offering back to him, waiting.

"No. He wasn't right. Sophia, you don't know me that well, but I'm not like that. I don't use women."

"I think you just did."

"You said you'd help us."

He was right. Much as she'd love to put this on him, she'd set the charges and laid the fuse.

"So I did. Amazing what bad choices I've made since coming here."

He looked away. Seemed he didn't like being labeled a bad choice. He faced her again just a moment later. The man was either a sucker for punishment or as strong as he looked.

"Sophia, I know you came up here to give an opinion. I know that getting involved with me and that ridge line were not in your plans. But what you did for us today—I hope we never need it, but if we do, it might save us all."

"*If* it works. There's no guarantee it will. I've never set an explosion even a third that big." Was she actually excited at the prospect of seeing if those charges would block the river?

"I'm only staying until the pipeline is secured and they can increase security up here."

"I understand."

She reached for a neatly sliced half of the egg roll that oozed cheese and hot chili.

"I have a life down there in the valley. I've made a life and I am not coming back to the rez to live on my portion of the per capita payments from the tribal trust. I don't need it."

"That's your prerogative," he said.

She felt a bubble of pain in her throat. She couldn't swallow. Sophia dropped the untouched appetizer back to the plate.

Jack reached across the table and took both her hands.

"Sophia, you're saving us."

"Maybe so. But when they find out, they'll terminate me. Ask for my shield. How would that make you feel, Jack?"

He drew back. "It was a lot to ask. Too much, maybe. But I'd ask again. I'd have to. We have no choice. If we believe Kenshaw, we have to act."

The burgers arrived. Sophia choked down what she could. Jack finished his burger first, of course, and offered her the wings. When she declined, he polished them off, too, along with the remains of the egg rolls. The man could eat, but judging from his size, he needed to.

The waitress checked in and finally cleared away the plates.

"Y'all save room for dessert?"

She shook her head and Jack looked disappointed when he asked for the check.

They settled up and headed out. Jack waved to the patrol car waiting in the lot.

"You have them following us?" she asked.

"Seems prudent after yesterday."

Was that only yesterday that someone had taken a shot at her? It seemed days ago.

He held open the door to his white truck and she slipped into the passenger seat.

"My grandfather says 'don't borrow trouble,'" said Jack. "But my dad says 'when you have trouble, go help someone with theirs.'"

"I think that is why my cousin, Luke, sent me up here."

"I was talking about my troubles, Sophia."

He stood beside her seat in the space beside the open passenger door to his truck, shifting as if trying to get comfortable in his own skin.

"I want you to come with me to see my folks. I need some answers."

He had dear friends in Dylan and Ray. He had a twin brother just returned from witness protection. Yet he did not ask them to come with him. He asked her.

"Why me?"

"Sophia, I've been an outsider here all my life. Seems like you know something about how that feels."

"But they love you. Have accepted you."

"And, if those results are correct, they have lied to me since I was born. I want to know why."

JACK TRIED TO stand still as he waited for Sophia to respond to his request, but he couldn't help but weave like a snake to the sound of the flute. It wasn't the sort of thing you asked a woman whom you had known only a few days. But it seemed so much longer and his knowledge of her so much deeper. Perhaps it was the crucible of danger, but she had risen in his estimation each hour of each day.

At last she nodded, accepting his request to come with him. It was Sunday night. They'd be home, all of them except Thomas, who had returned to the border south of Lilac with the Shadow Wolves.

It wasn't far from the casino to Piñon Forks, where his parents lived. Just a short drive along the river that had changed from friend to enemy in the last few months. They were at the modest home of his birth far too soon. He pulled up on the flat pad, extended by his father because his boys all drove trucks and mostly came home for supper on Sundays.

Jack pulled past Kurt's blue Ram pickup, parking beside Carter's red F-150. Carter liked red because he was a Hotshot, fighting wildfires all over the west. In fact, he had been captain of the tribe's team, the Turquoise Canyon Hotshots. But Ray had taken his place during his absence and done a great job, by all accounts. Jack wondered who would lead now.

Jack turned off the engine and the truck fell silent.

Sophia sat quietly beside him in the dark.

"Changing your mind or just gathering your nerve?" she asked.

"Neither. I'm reconsidering you witnessing this."

She had just met his family and he did not want his second visit to be unpleasant. He didn't know why it was important for them to like her and for her to like them, but it was.

He pressed his hand to his forehead as understanding dawned. He'd brought Sophia to meet his parents at their home. The first girl and the first time. Only he'd disguised the visit even from himself because he knew she wasn't staying, despite their obvious compatibility in the sack.

"You worried I will think badly of them because they kept this secret from you?"

He lowered his head, not knowing what he thought or what he wanted. Answers, he supposed. Something to fill up this empty hole in his chest he carried day in and day out.

"It might be rough," he said and lowered his hands to grip the wheel of his vehicle, as if already planning his getaway.

She made a sound that might have been a laugh. Jack

turned in the seat to look at her. The light from the living room filtered out through closed curtains and illuminated the yard in yellow light. He could see Sophia's face in shadows and she was smiling.

"Jack, I'm going to say this quick, because when you uncover a wound, it's best to get that Band-Aid off as fast as possible."

He tensed, bracing for whatever she would say.

"You are supposed to honor your parents. I mostly avoid mine. I don't visit my father." She laughed. "Though I might see him real soon if I have to trigger that blast."

Did she mean her father was still in prison and that she would be joining him? He wanted to ask but did not want to interrupt.

"My mom still lives up there on Black Mountain rez. But she isn't well. Too many years of hard drinking. But I'm still lucky. You want to know why?"

He nodded.

"Because she had me early and I'm not like my younger brothers—Ned and Talbert both have fetal alcohol syndrome. And they didn't have my grandmother, not for long. I had one good loving parent in my grandma, and I had an excellent example of why I needed to get my degree, keep my 18 Money and get off the rez. I can't thank my mother enough for that. Now, I only just met your folks. But I know they love you. They'll have a good reason, Jack. Let's go find out what it is."

She didn't wait, just threw open the passenger door and slipped out. A moment later she was holding open his door and motioning to the yard.

"I won't be embarrassed, Jack. But I'll be there for you. You give me the sign and I'll take you out of there."

Funny, to look at them, you'd assume he was the strong one. But it was Sophia who had the backbone needed to get answers, because she'd faced far worse. He knew too many girls who had similar upbringings that had not done so well. Five of them were missing right now. Tinnin had told him he'd assigned their new man, Jake Redhorse, to look into the disappearances. Jack felt he should be investigating, but both he and his chief believed that the threat from BEAR and protecting Sophia from possible gang attacks took precedence.

Sophia held out her hand. He took it. They walked hand-in-hand up to the front door. He reached for the knob and she grabbed his wrist.

"Wait!" There was a note of panic in her voice.

"What?" he asked.

"I forgot your mother's first name."

She looked so worried it struck him as comical. His entire life had been a lie and here she was worried about this?

"Annetta. And he's Delane. Brothers are Carter, Kurt and Thomas. Thomas won't be here."

"Back on the border. Got it." Her hand dropped to her side.

He was still smiling when he opened the door. If she didn't care about him, it wouldn't be important to know those names. She said she was leaving and didn't want any attachments. But she acted as if she did.

His mother spotted him first. "Well, Jack! This is a surprise. Look at you two, all dusty." She swept forward and kissed him, and then kissed Sophia. "We just finished dinner but I can heat up the casserole. Are you hungry?"

"We just ate, Mom."

"Oh, that's a shame. Just some dessert then? I have

pumpkin pie, lemon cake or chocolate ice cream." She waited for them to choose, ready to dart into the kitchen and fix them something.

They left the entrance, his mother leading the way, and paused in the small living room. Carter waved from the sagging sofa where he sat beside Amber.

In the living room the ballgame blared as the Diamondbacks took on the Padres. His father lowered the sound and stood to greet them. Kurt sat on the couch, closest to the set, with Carter's wife in the middle between her brother-in-law and her new husband. Amber placed a bookmark in the novel she read, waiting for Kurt to rise so she could clear the coffee table to greet them.

"We just…" Jack's words failed him.

His father looked from him to Sophia.

"They're not here for dessert," said his dad.

"What happened?" asked his mother, dessert forgotten for the moment. Her hands laced before her, gripping tight as if preparing to pray on a moment's notice.

Carter rose to his feet. He was a big man and he wore his hair in the fashion Jack admired—long, loose and, of course, straight. He stepped clear of the coffee table. Amber trailed behind him, blending seamlessly into his family as if she had always been here.

"You opened it," said Carter.

Jack nodded.

"Opened what?" asked their mother.

Carter stared at him as if trying to learn what he had discovered with a look. Jack reached in his wallet and passed him the wrinkled, torn envelope. Carter held it as if Jack had just served him a subpoena.

"What's going on?" His mother's clasped hands had

now reached her throat. "What is that? Is it from the marines?"

His mother's biggest fear was that her boys would be called back overseas by the marines.

Carter was now scanning the page.

Jack couldn't find his voice to ask the questions. His throat was burning and tight. He looked to Sophia.

"Me?" she asked.

He nodded and she gave his hand a quick squeeze.

"They're test results, Mrs. Bear Den."

His mother's hands pressed flat over her chest. "Jack, are you ill? You're so pale."

His father stepped up to support his mother, holding on to her elbow and draping one arm around her lower back.

"He's not ill. No one is," Sophia assured them.

"What is all this?" asked his father.

"It's a sibling DNA test," said Sophia. "Jack and Carter sent a sample to see if they shared the same genetic markers."

Now his mother had gone pale.

"Why would you do that?" asked his father.

"I knew it," whispered his mother. "I knew."

Knew what, he wanted to ask, but here, now all he could do was stand mutely by and wait for Sophia to ask the next question.

"Let's go sit down," said his dad, escorting his wife to the dining room and a seat. He did not take his place at the head of the long rectangular table, but slid into the adjoining bench beside Annetta.

The family all took their places, with Jack sitting in the chair belonging to his father. Sophia sat to his right. Carter dropped the damning evidence on the table and took his seat, and Amber and Kurt joined them a moment later.

Sophia looked to his parents as she spoke. "Jack is interested to know why he was not told that he is not your child, but rather a nephew to one of you. Could you explain that, please?"

Chapter Fifteen

Sophia felt like the rain cloud pouring down on this wonderful family. Carter, Jack and Kurt all stared at their parents with looks of utter astonishment.

Annetta sat ramrod-straight with her husband's hand still pressed to her lower back. Tears coursed down her cheeks, but her chin had taken on a defiant tilt.

"You are my son."

Jack and Carter shared a look that seemed to involve some silent communication all their own. Sophia returned her focus to Annetta, waiting. She'd interviewed enough suspects to know when one had not finished speaking.

"But…" Annetta said.

Here it comes, thought Sophia. Jack reached under the table and squeezed her knee so tightly she flinched. She slipped her hand into his, mainly as self-defense to keep him from crushing her kneecap.

"But you were born to my older sister, Ava."

Kurt said, "I didn't know you had a sister."

"She had to leave," said Annetta. "She saw something terrible, a murder." She looked at Jack now with such sorrow that Sophia found herself squeezing Jack's hand. "Your father's murder. He died before you were even born."

Jack's jaw went to granite.

Annetta's shoulders slumped and Delane took over like a relay runner relieving a teammate.

"Your father's name was Robert Taaga. Your mother called him Robbie. He was Hawaiian. A really big guy."

"They met in Phoenix," said Annetta. "He was going to the university, too. Classmates. He was helping her get through physics. So smart. She said he was so smart."

So Jack had gotten his size and features from a man of South Pacific descent. Sophia had seen some pro athletes and actors who were Samoans, and they had been epic in size, like Jack. And his father had been murdered.

Annetta was shaking her head and staring vacantly at a spot before her on the table.

"What happened?" asked Carter.

Their father answered. "There was a robbery attempt. Robbie stepped in. Ava said they shot him the minute that he took a step in their direction. Even with two bullets in his heart, he still got the killer's gun."

Sophia imagined Jack's strong heart trying to beat against the blood loss and the picture in her mind washed her cold.

"Ava saw both attackers. She made a positive ID, she testified and sent them both to prison, but they were in a gang and the Justice Department said they wouldn't stop. That the gang would send a message by killing Ava if they could," said Delane. He blew out a breath. "Your mom did not want you raised out there. She wanted you to know your people and your tribe. So she made a hard choice. She asked Annetta to raise you as her boy."

But how had they managed to keep this secret? The tribe must have known or at least suspected.

"She made it a condition of her cooperation. They were both pregnant at the same time. Annetta with Carter and Ava with Jack. So when Ava delivered, they brought us to her. We said we were visiting my brother in Fort Collins, Colorado. He was on a survey crew up there for an oil and gas company. We left and we didn't come back until you were born, Carter." Delane looked to his oldest son.

And then they brought home the twins that were not twins. Three sons, Sophia realized. Not four.

"You were so tiny," Delane said to Carter, measuring the distance with his hands.

"He was not," said Annetta. "He weighed six pounds, six ounces."

"But Jack was two months old by then, and he was over nine pounds when he was born. Our twins came home and Annetta kept you both close."

"People must have known," said Sophia.

"They did, some anyway."

But this was a tribe, Sophia thought, and not like Black Mountain, with several towns and so many members spread out over so much land that it would be impossible to know everyone. But here they did know everyone and everyone knew how to keep a secret, especially an important one. And they kept it even from Carter and Jack.

Jack looked at his twin.

"We're not brothers," said Jack, the pain raw in his voice.

Carter reached across the corner of the table that separated them and pulled Jack close. The hug was fierce and possessive.

"We are. We are."

Kurt stood and joined the two. The rest of them all seemed to hold collective breath. Finally Jack pulled away.

"You guys are wrinkling my shirt." His shirt was filthy with dirt and dust, so his comment broke the tension and made everyone laugh.

"Let me up," said Annetta to Delane. She stood. "I have to get some things for Jack."

They sat waiting for her return, hearing her thumping around the bedroom down the hall.

"I can't see her?" said Jack to his father, meaning Ava, Sophia was sure.

He shook his head.

"Call or write?" he asked.

"Talk to your friend Agent Forrest. Maybe he can arrange something. They haven't let us see her. We don't know a thing except that she's alive. Nothing, for all these years. But she knows about you, Jack."

Sophia's brow wrinkled. That wasn't possible.

"The classifieds," said Jack.

Delane smiled. "That's why you're the detective. Yes. She and her sister worked it out. Ava can go online and read the news. Classifieds are always in there. She's let her know you played baseball and when you graduated from school. That you were safe after your tours of duty. Something on your birthday—the one we picked for you both. Right between February 2nd and April 2nd."

Carter and Jack stared, realizing they had been celebrating the wrong birthday their entire lives.

"I'm keeping it," said Carter.

"Me, too," said Jack.

Annetta returned with a shoe box.

"This was my sister's. I kept them for you even though they told me not to. That I should destroy anything that would reveal who you were. She made me promise never to tell you, Jack. I promised her the day you were born. I didn't lie about you being my son. You are mine as much as you are hers. And I told the truth when I said I'd never been with a man other than my husband. But I didn't tell you that you were Ava's child before you were mine. I promised her, Jack. I'm sorry."

Because she was protecting him, and Sophia saw exactly why keeping that secret was so important. Suddenly Jack rose to his feet.

"What was the name of the man who shot my father?"

"He's in federal prison. Life sentence."

"The name?"

Delane shook his head. Sophia knew that Jack could find the information easily. Everyone did, but still the name was not coming from his parents.

"Before you run off after him," said Kurt, "maybe you should remember your promise to Kenshaw, and that BEAR just blew up a pipeline in Phoenix and that we are probably next."

Jack sat back down in front of the box Annetta had left him. Carter pressed a hand to his back, high up, directly over the medicine wheel. Was Carter reminding Jack to use the wheel to help find his direction?

Jack blew out a breath and then lifted the old box from the table, as if it was fragile, like an eggshell. He tucked it under his arm and looked to Sophia.

"We need to go."

"Jack, don't run off," said Annetta.

"I'm not going after him, Mom. I just need some time to..." He looked at Sophia. "You ready?"

She followed him out of his parents' house with his family trailing as far as the front steps. Sophia held out her hand.

"Keys," she said.

He turned them over without a word of objection. She had the seat adjusted by the time he was belted into his.

"Where to?" she asked, backing them out.

"I'd prefer to be in Piñon Forks in case something happens."

She headed toward the town.

"You said the casino hotel is closed for reno."

"We're going to my place."

She saw the squad car on the shoulder. It pulled out as they passed.

"One of your men?" she asked.

"Hmm?" He turned to glance out the side mirror. "Yeah. That's Wetselline. He's our shadow tonight."

She had not seen him on their way from the canyon and that bothered her. Jack was a distraction and she was getting all tied up in his problems. It had made her forget her own, just as Luke had promised. She had never been so completely overtaken by anything other than her job in years. She didn't like it. Didn't like that being with Jack was more appealing than returning to her position and that the problems on Turquoise Canyon were becoming her problems. Somewhere along the way in the consultation, she had taken a wrong turn. She needed to get back home to her job and her life.

Jack thanked her for coming with him.

She made the obligatory reply and flicked on the radio to static.

"Local station goes off at seven."

"I have to get out of here," she said. But instead she drove to Jack's place. Not because it was closer to the dam and got better mobile phone service, but because whether she would admit it aloud or not, she wanted to be here with Jack.

Chapter Sixteen

Sophia sat beside Jack on the couch of his comfortable ranch-style house. He had too much black leather furniture and not enough food in the refrigerator, but the space was clean. She especially liked the wall decorations. Instead of paintings, he had hung various drums. Some were elaborately adorned art pieces and others looked ancient, with rawhide heads so thin the center of the leather was transparent.

Jack had been exceedingly quiet on the ride to his place. "Your things are in the spare room. I had Ray bring them over."

She slipped a hand onto his knee. It was obvious he was feeling lost and the confusion was etched in lines across his forehead.

"It's not what you expected. Is it?" she asked.

He shook his head. "I…I'm just… Am I supposed to get a surfboard now? I've never even seen the Pacific Ocean."

"You don't need to do anything except keep the secret that your family has kept for you. They were protecting you."

"But all this time. They wouldn't still be after her."

"Gang hits have no expiry date. Once you are targeted that target stays on your back unless they withdraw it."

And now Sophia had the same target on her back, as his mother had once had. Would they take her into protective custody, too?

"She should have taken me with her."

"Is that what you would have done, in her place?"

He sighed.

"She might be living in Detroit or Dallas. She's cut off from her family and friends. And she did nothing wrong. It was just really horrible luck," she said.

"I knew I was different, that we had different fathers."

"And mothers. That's the surprise. But you still have Annetta. She's more mother than many."

"I feel sick," he said.

"Take some time. Time helps." She knew something else that would help ease his mind, soothe his body. Sophia admitted the truth, she was not some angel of mercy. She wanted Jack again. It was possible that the investigation on her use of force might take longer than usual because of the pipeline explosion. Or it might be expedited for the same reason. And if they ruled in her favor, she'd be back on the job. She looped her arm around Jack's stronger one and lay her head on his shoulder.

"You can't change it."

"Change what?"

"The past. I've been trying to bury mine. You've been trying to uncover yours. Uncovered or ignored, it's still there like an infection in your jaw. Eventually you have to deal with it."

He turned to her. "But not tonight."

Her body tingled with anticipation as he leaned in

and kissed her, slow and deep. She laced her fingers around his neck and he eased her down to the thick leather cushions of his couch.

"I need you, Sophia," he whispered, hot breath fanning the hair at her neck.

"Me, too." How had this happened? She should be keeping her distance. Reminding him that she was here only to give her opinion and to distract herself from the investigation.

Well, Jack was the best darn distraction she'd ever had. And when his hands covered her breasts, she ached to have those big hands pressed to her bare skin.

She unclipped her holster and slipped out of it and her blazer. Then she unbuttoned her blouse. His mouth found the bare skin at her stomach, traveling up as she released each button. Then he pushed the fabric off her shoulders. She sat up and he let her go. Sophia did not know where she got the nerve, but Jack's hungry eyes made her bold. So she dropped her blouse and released her bra, letting them fall to the floor. Then she slipped out of her shoes and slacks. She stood in only her panties. Jack sat on the edge of the couch, both hands on the couch cushions as his gaze devoured her.

"So beautiful," he whispered.

She hooked a thumb in the elastic of her panties and lowered them over her hips, then kicked them away.

Sophia stood wearing only a smile. Their eyes met.

"Your turn, Jack."

He rose from the couch like a charging bull, but instead of disrobing he lifted her up into his arms and ran her toward the back of the house.

She squealed as he tossed her onto his bed and then flicked on the light on the side table.

"I never do this," he said.

"I think you did this last night."

"I mean here. I don't bring women here. I don't bring them to meet my parents, either."

"Why not?"

"Never found one I liked that much. Didn't want to give them the wrong idea."

"But I'm safe. Right? Because I'm leaving."

"No, Sophia. You're dangerous because I don't want you to leave."

The smile left her.

"Jack, I have to go. You know that."

"I do. It makes this sweeter and sadder."

This was a bad idea. The man had been left behind by his mother and now she was preparing to do exactly the same thing. Sleeping with Jack wouldn't make him feel better. Not in the long run, because whatever was happening between them, it was growing stronger. Just the thought of leaving him made her chest ache. But she could no more leave his bed right now than she could stop breathing.

Sophia extended her hand. "Come to bed, Jack."

SOPHIA WAS STILL ASLEEP. They had spent much of the night tangled in each other's arms, sharing the passion that seemed to burn between them like wildfire. But well before the dawn, he woke, his mind racing with his heart. He needed to see what his mother had left him. So he rose and headed for the kitchen and then out to the concrete drive and his truck. He returned to the dark kitchen with the shoe box and flicked on the light. Then he sat alone at the kitchen table.

Inside were photos he had never seen. Photos of two sisters. The photos of the sisters as young women showed the differences. His mother, Ava, the oldest, was smaller than Annetta. Ironic, he thought, as he studied each image of his mother. Maybe he'd see her sometime, someplace. Unexpectedly. But she was now twenty-eight years older. What did she look like now?

There was a diary, written by his mother. He did the math and realized she began the entries at fifteen and continued on and off into her first year of college. He flipped to the end and saw his father's name written out in bold letters:

> Robbie Taaga and I went to the movies. I really like him. When I'm with him I'm so happy and when we are apart I hurt inside.

Jack lowered the book. He had not been away from Sophia. But just the prospect of her departure filled him with gloom. Was it because of all this? Maybe this was about his mother leaving and not Sophia at all.

He closed the diary and placed it carefully back in the box. It wasn't about the past. He was now haunted by the future. What would happen if that dam broke? What would happen if she left them before the strike? He knew the attack was coming. He believed Kenshaw Little Falcon's prediction that the dam, their dam, was the new prime target of one of the cells.

So why did he want to follow Sophia back to Flagstaff when she left them? His life, his duty and the legacy his mother had given him were all here. But soon Sophia would not be.

"Hey, there," she said.

Her voice had been just a whisper but he still startled.

"Sorry," she said.

"Didn't hear you."

"I was standing here awhile. You seemed lost in thought."

She stood in bare feet in a familiar flannel robe. It belonged to him and reached nearly to her toes. It also gaped at the chest, revealing a wide swath of smooth skin and the curves of her breasts.

"Borrowed this." She tugged at the worn collar.

"It never looked so good."

She came forward, stood just behind him with a hand on his shoulder. "Interesting?"

He handed her an envelope he had not yet opened marked *Jack*.

She slipped into the seat next to him and opened the flap.

"Photos," she said, flipping rapidly through the stack, her smile growing wider until she grinned. "These are precious."

She moved to sit on his lap and she went through the pictures again for him. It was his mother, pregnant. Then in a hospital bed, with circles under Ava's eyes, smiling joyfully as she held a dark-headed baby. Beside her bed was Annetta, obviously pregnant as well. What she saw as happy, he saw as sad. One of the photos showed a guard at the door. It was the last time he would ever see his mother, and he could not remember her face.

"Can you find her?" he asked.

She stilled and then lowered the photos to the table surface.

"Perhaps. But it would put her in danger."

"Why? Anyone who is still looking for her would not know she has a son."

"That's true. I'll see what I can arrange." She glanced

toward the stove and the digital clock there. "Too early to call. Coffee?" she asked.

"All ready. Just hit the switch."

Sophia flipped on the drip coffeemaker and left him, heading for the bathroom and a shower. Jack put away the box. Sophia might be able to arrange a meeting. He felt butterflies in his belly at the thought. He wanted to meet her, but what if she was disappointed in him?

Sophia called to him. When he reached the bathroom, he opened the door enough to peek inside. She asked him to come in and he did. The view of Sophia's naked, soapy body through the textured glass was something he would never forget.

"Come in before the water gets cold."

As it turned out, the water did get cold before they left the shower's stream. His legs were trembling and her smile curled his toes. Sophia was generous and inventive and full of surprises. He toweled her dry, which started them off again, and they ended tangled up in damp towels and sheets in his bed. They dozed with Sophia's warm clean body draped across him until his phone woke them.

He lifted the mobile and saw it was Wallace Tinnin and that it was after nine on a Monday morning.

"Yeah, Chief," he said.

"You coming in?"

He was generally there by eight.

"On my way."

"Listen, we got something on Trey."

Tinnin was speaking about the gangbanger Jack had picked up. The one who had used his one phone call to reveal Sophia's location.

"Minnie said that Trey got a video on his phone. He showed it to her. I've got his phone and I watched it. It's a carjacking and Sophia is the driver of the car. She's clearly visible and they recorded the shooting."

It was on the phone of Trey Fields. Why?

"Minnie said there was a still photo, too. Can't find that. Might have been deleted. But Minnie says it was an Instagram shot made up to look like a wanted poster with Sophia's image. Minnie said they don't know her name. Just that she killed one of their guys."

"He recognized her when I arrested him," said Jack.

"Seems so."

Jack had put Sophia in danger by making that collar. He'd seen Fields and just reacted. But he was supposed to be escorting Sophia. She was law enforcement so he had not considered any consequences of involving her.

"Who did he call?" asked Jack.

"A friend here on Turquoise Canyon. Real question is, who did the friend call?"

"I'm bringing her into the station now," said Jack.

"Seems prudent," said Wallace. "I've alerted our guys to keep an eye out for suspicious persons."

"Wearing yellow and black," said Jack.

"Yeah. They know."

Jack disconnected and set the phone aside.

"So they know where I am," she said.

"It's not safe for you here anymore." So soon. His mind was screaming for him to stop her, keep her. Too soon, she would be leaving him, too soon.

They were up and dressed in record time, all business now as if the night and morning had happened in some different place to two different people.

"I wish I could stay awhile," she said in the truck.

Like forever, he thought.

"Yeah."

Her phone chimed. She slipped the mobile from her pocket and glanced at the screen.

"My captain," she said and took the call.

Jack could hear her captain through the speaker because his voice boomed. So he heard the conversation.

Her captain had good news. They had expedited the investigation and ruled the shooting justified. He was ordering her to report to Phoenix and the pipeline explosion ASAP.

She glanced at Jack. They both knew that she had set the explosives so that only she could trigger the blasts. Of course, his miners could bypass the system she set with time. If they had time.

Sophia told her boss the new developments.

Her captain swore. "Sit tight. You'll need an escort."

"Will do."

She disconnected and glanced to him. Had she intentionally bought them time?

"Justified," she said, then closed her eyes and sank into the passenger seat. "They ruled justified," she whispered.

The relief she expected never came. Instead she felt a kind of tearing inside her chest. It came with the words whispered in her soul...*now you must leave him.*

No. Not until she was sure he'd be safe.

"They'll still be looking for you," Jack said.

"Up here. Not in Phoenix. You said yourself, they don't know my name."

"That information could be wrong. I'm not betting your life on it."

"We better go," she said. Her throat squeezed so she said no more.

As they reached the station, Sophia received another call from her captain, Larry Burton.

"Highway patrol found the older brother of Martin Nequam. Juaquin is being detained on a gun charge."

"Rifle?" asked Sophia.

"Yup. And a handgun. They found a rifle with scope in his trunk."

Sophia blew out a breath.

Burton continued. "We're sending an escort to retrieve you."

Sophia's heart sped. She couldn't leave Turquoise Canyon now. The pipeline was a forensic investigation. But the threat here could still be prevented.

"I can't come back right now," she said and then held her breath at the audacity of her words. She had never refused an order before.

"What did you say?"

"I can't. There is a credible threat up here. We need more agents on Turquoise Canyon. Not less."

"Sophia, we have multiple explosions down here. You're an expert. I'm ordering you to report."

"Requesting personal leave, sir."

"Denied."

She closed her eyes and pictured everything she fought so hard to win destroyed by her own undermining. Then she looked at Jack's strong, solemn face.

"You'll have my resignation today, sir."

"What?" he howled.

Sophia disconnected and met Jack's gaze.

"That was the bravest thing I've ever seen."

"I'm a fool," she said.

"No. You're a warrior. And you just might have saved us all."

"What if your shaman is wrong? What if the dams are well protected or not even a target?"

"You saw the protection. And we are a target."

She nodded. "I know it."

Chapter Seventeen

Sophia had been singled out for a hit by the Latin Kings thanks to the work of Martin's brother, Juaquin. They had not figured out that she was FBI, but they knew she was on Turquoise Canyon. Just outside Tinnin's office, Jack called Luke Forrest and told him what was happening—the attempted hit, the death order, Sophia's resignation and the threat they still faced from BEAR.

The agent didn't take it well. But he could not come riding up the mountain to the rescue. There was too much chaos down in Phoenix. It was all over the news. Scenes of gas explosions and fireballs. Neighborhoods destroyed. Industrial parks in flames.

"You going to be able to keep her safe?" asked Luke.

"I'll protect her with my life," Jack said.

"Not what I asked," said Luke.

"Yes, I'll keep her safe. I swear."

On the other end of the phone there was a deep sigh. "Let me speak to her."

Jack passed off the phone and Sophia pressed the phone to her ear.

"Hi, Luke," she said.

Jack felt sick and proud all at once. She was staying. Was it because of him or them? Or did she just see the need of protecting his tribe? Some deep animal part of him wanted it to be because of him.

Sophia was Western Apache and exactly the sort of woman he always wanted and never felt he deserved, because he was different. Now he knew why and he wasn't certain that knowledge changed anything.

"I understand," she said. "Yes, I'm sure. I know what I'm doing."

Most Apache women he knew stayed on the reservation, close to their families, their language and their culture. Sophia had broken free, left her tribe and made a life for herself down in the desert. And she had thrown it all away for this.

He'd never be able to repay her, but he hoped she'd let him try.

Tinnin met Jack's gaze. His worried face told Jack that his chief wasn't sure they could handle what was coming. He motioned toward his office and Jack followed, leaving Sophia in the outer office on the phone.

"Will it work?" he asked Jack, motioning his head toward the river.

"I hope we never find out."

"She can't stay forever," he said. "Eventually she will have to show one of us how to trigger the blasts."

"That was a condition of her supervision."

"But our guys can bypass the ignition system she set up."

"I'm not sure they can. I wouldn't want to mess with the ignition system. It might blow up before the dam is damaged."

"I don't like it. What if one of those gang members gets by us and kills her?"

Jack's body surged to life at the hypothetical, preparing to fight. "We have to keep her safe."

"For how long, Jack? Protection detail is straining our resources. I need you on the runaways."

Jack's curiosity was piqued. "Did someone else go missing?"

"Yes, Lawrence Kesselman's kid."

"Which one? He has—what? Thirteen?"

"It's Maggie. She disappeared yesterday."

"How old?"

"Fourteen. She's the youngest to go missing. The others were between sixteen and eighteen."

Jack glanced to Sophia, who was still on the phone, and then to his boss. "How's Jake Redhorse doing with the investigation?"

"He's fine, but he's not you," said the chief.

Tinnin was putting him between a rock and a hard place. The crimes on Turquoise Canyon did not stop because of the outside threat. If anything, Jack's inattention to his normal rounds had allowed crime to increase. The stack of paperwork on his desk was rising. He needed to get back to work and he needed to protect Sophia.

"I'll check in with Redhorse. See what he's got so far."

"Do that," said Tinnin.

Jack turned his back on his chief and walked away making a mental note to speak to Redhorse as he worried about the missing teens. Right now he needed to focus on BEAR. If Sophia was willing to risk everything to protect them from the river, he would do the same.

Jack returned to the squad room and his desk, taking a seat before the stack of unreturned messages. Sophia was off the phone and he was on his computer answering his email. She took a seat beside his desk.

"Funny," she said. "You have too much to do and I have not enough."

"That's a good thing," he said and smiled. But it wasn't. They decided it was best for her to stay here, close to the river and the protection of the squad room.

He took her with him in the afternoon to speak to two witnesses in one of his open cases, but he could not go on calls where she might be exposed or in danger. That evening, they ate together at his home in a kind of pall.

"This is bad," she said. "I don't want the dams to go. But I can't stay up here indefinitely."

But she now had nowhere else to go. He knew she would not return to her tribe. He wanted her to stay here with him, but how did he ask her that? She was an FBI agent, or she had been.

"How did you leave it with your captain?" Jack asked. He wanted her to choose him out of love, not need.

"He gave me one day to report. After that I'm insubordinate."

"I'm so sorry, Sophia, for dragging you into this and so grateful you are here to help us."

"I keep thinking of those explosives on that beautiful ridge. You understand that some of the rocks will fly over a mile and rain down over Piñon Forks. It will damage cars, buildings and people who don't take cover."

"The tribal council has the word out. The warning sirens mean take cover. Not evacuate."

"But what if I figured wrong? What if the blast is too small or too big or it doesn't completely stop the flood?"

"You set the charges, Sophia. What do you think will happen?"

"I've never set one that big."

"The miners were there. They tell me you got it right, exploited every fault and fissure. It will work, Sophia."

Sophia's mobile phone rang and she glanced at the screen. "It's Luke." She stood as she took the call, as if coming to attention in front of a superior officer as she spoke her greeting.

Sophia listened for a few moments then glanced at Jack and excused herself, stepping away from the table and disappearing down the hallway to take her call. She returned a few minutes later and stood beside him at his dining room table.

"What's up?" asked Jack.

"He's worried about me."

"Understandable," he said.

"Let's go sit in the living room," Sophia said. She offered her hand and he grasped it, allowing her to lead him along to the leather sofa. He sat closest to the arm and she in the center, half turned to face him. He found his fingers gripping into the soft padding as he braced for whatever was troubling her.

"I asked him about your mom earlier today. He was getting back to me with some information."

Jack stiffened as hope mingled with dread. Was his mother alive? Was she safe?

"He couldn't get much out of his guy at the Justice Department. But he did find out that your mother is alive and living somewhere in the Midwest. Your mother is employed and she has remarried."

Jack pressed a hand flat on the armrest as his other hand squeezed the cushion edge flat. His mother had started again. Started a new family.

"She has children, Jack. You have sisters. He couldn't find out how many or their ages."

Sophia slipped from the sofa and kneeled before him,

taking his hands in hers. "You have sisters, Jack! More than one."

He couldn't take it all in. He was confused and unreasonably happy. Should he feel joy or sorrow at knowing that he had siblings that he would never meet? His mother had given him a great and selfless gift, leaving him here to grow up an Apache man of the Tonto people. He wished he could thank her for that. He had his roots and his legacy, but he did not know his father's people or his mother and now he added three more relations to that list.

"I wish I could see them."

"Luke told me that you would ask that and told me to tell you that that is not possible."

"After all this time she still in danger?"

"Relocation is a permanent step, Jack. Once you go in, you don't come back. The Justice Department has never lost a single person who was relocated unless they broke cover. It's the single most dangerous thing your mother could do."

"A photo then," he said, knowing that a photo could be used to identify his family and therefore put them at risk. Even the simplest landmarks in a photo could reveal the part of the country and perhaps even the neighborhood where they lived.

Sophia did not directly deny his suggestion, but simply glanced away and then slipped back to her seat beside him.

Jack thought back to last February and remembered something. "When Carter had to leave us, my mother said something. It makes sense now."

"What did she say?"

Chapter Eighteen

Jack recalled exactly what his mother had said upon learning that Carter and Amber were being taken into witness protection. He repeated Annetta's words for Sophia now.

"She said, 'Not again.'"

Sophia cast him a puzzled look.

Jack explained. "She had already lost her sister to the Justice Department and she was about to lose her oldest son. Ironic. For a time she lost Carter and kept the son that was not hers."

"Jack, I've seen your mother with you. You *are* her son."

Jack bowed his head. He knew that was true. His mother, Annetta, had never treated him any differently than the children she had had with Delane, except, perhaps, to minimize his concerns about how differently he looked than his brothers.

"You're right. Annetta has been a wonderful mother and Delane has been a doting father. I'm lucky. So why do I hurt inside?"

"I don't think you have to know your mother to miss her." Sophia cuddled up close to him on the sofa. She collected the hand he used to deform the sofa cushion beneath him and lifted it to give him a kiss on his knuckles. "Funny, you have two good women in your life. I'd be happy to just have one."

Jack had been so tied up with his own erratic feelings that he had forgotten Sophia's troubled childhood. He did not think to speak platitudes or trivialize her pain. But what could he say to comfort the woman who now comforted him?

"I'm sorry."

"Don't be. I'm lucky. I survived that and I'll survive leaving the Bureau."

"You have a home here for as long as you like."

She gazed up at him with a look of curiosity. Did she understand his invitation was personal and not a general announcement of the tribes' gratitude? He should make it clear that he wanted her to stay. But somehow the words failed him.

"Jack, there is one more thing that I learned from my cousin. It's also about your mother."

Oh, no, he thought, *she's ill.*

"Is she sick?"

"No," said Sophia, squeezing his arm and resting her chin on the top of his shoulder. "It's nothing like that. I'm just not sure how to, that is, I don't know how you'll take this."

He meant to tell her that whatever it was he could take it. But instead his mouth hung open and he waited as if he was a punch-drunk boxer unable to lift his arms to defend against the knockout blow. But he did see it coming. She had held it back perhaps deciding whether or not she should tell him.

"The Justice Department said she broke cover to come to Phoenix. As far as they could tell she never had contact with anyone from her tribe. They even checked the surveillance tapes to confirm she made no contact. In other words, she did not break the terms of her agreement. If she had, she would lose her status as a relocated witness. Just coming to Phoenix didn't do it. But it was close.

"She flew in and out on the same day. She was in the Phoenix airport for less than two hours. Surveillance tapes showed she did not speak to anyone other than the waitress who took her order. They checked on the waitress. She was not a relative."

"What was she doing here?"

"I think she was here to see you."

Sophia gave him the date of her breach of agreement. He recognized the month and date immediately and that he had been in Phoenix, in the airport at the same day and time.

"She came to see me."

"Yes. The Justice Department says your family was all there. Was that the day you came home from overseas?"

The closing of his throat hit him so hard and so fast that all he could do to answer her question was nod. He squeezed his eyes shut and felt the hot sting of tears roll down his cheeks. His mother had been there. Ava had seen him come off the plane. Drop his bag and hug his mother, father and two younger brothers. Carter had still been overseas, beginning his third tour. Jack had been certain after only one that the marines was not in his future. He had wanted only to come home to the place of his birth and return to the life he had left.

Sophia's arms went around him. She pressed her head to his chest as she continued to speak.

"She was at the gate directly behind the one from which you disembarked and met your family."

Jack thought back to that day. Pictured her there

across the wide polished floor, watching him greet the family she had given him. But unable to cross the few short steps to welcome him. Jack pressed a hand to his face as the sobs broke from his throat.

Sophia held on tight and cried with him. Her words were strangled but he still managed to understand past the sound of his own cries.

"It must've been the newspaper classifieds. Your mother, Annetta, must have posted the time and date of your homecoming."

Jack could only nod and sob.

Sophia stroked his arm and pressed a hand over his chest. She made soothing sounds in her throat and ran her fingers through his hair. Gradually the tension and pain drained away leaving him spent. He wiped the moisture from his face and blew out a breath.

"I haven't cried since Carter came home from overseas."

"It's cleansing, I think. Nature's way of helping us grieve."

Is that what he had been doing? Of course, she was right. He was grieving for his mother, Ava.

"I wish I could do the same and see them just once."

"I think if the Justice Department figures out what your aunt and mother are doing they might revoke her protected status. You would need to think long and hard about using the classifieds to arrange a meeting. It would be dangerous for her."

Jack let that wish die.

Sophia sidled forward until she sat on Jack's lap. She held his face between her two small hands and looked at him with a sweet expression of empathy.

Jack's heart still ached. But the pain was deeper now and mingled with joy. The dark feelings that he had harbored about not belonging were gone. He did belong here on Turquoise Canyon. These were the people who loved him and protected him and raised him.

"I'm a lucky man," he said.

"Yes. That's true."

They smiled at each other. Jack felt a rising awareness of Sophia as she draped her arms around his neck and her mouth turned upward in an inviting smile.

"You hungry?" he asked.

Sophia shook her head, and her brows lifted as she gave him an enigmatic smile.

"Thirsty?"

Another slow shake of the head.

"Sleepy?"

Sophia giggled. Jack stood, carrying Sophia up with him. It was a short walk to the bedroom and the large welcoming bed. Jack did not know if Sophia meant only to comfort him, but he did know that for him this was so much more. He had found another person that he did not want to lose. Somehow, someway, Jack needed to keep Sophia with him. He began with soft, hot kisses to her neck and worked downward from there, each kiss a tribute.

Sometime in the night she roused him from his sleep stroking her leg along his as her fingers danced circles over his chest. He pulled her up so she straddled his hips, giving her leave to claim what she had summoned. This time was slow and quiet and joyful as Jack tried to show her what he could not yet say…*I love you.*

Afterward he held her as he slept, his slack fingers still tangled in her hair. It was there, naked and sated, that they still were when the siren sounded just after dawn.

Chapter Nineteen

Sophia scrambled out of bed first, pressing her hands to her ears as she tried to understand what was happening. The siren, it meant something. Jack sat up in bed, his eyes wide.

"The dam. Skeleton Cliff. That's the warning."

She knew it, of course, because she had heard it sound every day she was in range at noon. But that had been a short friendly toot. This was a shrill shrieking blast that went on and on.

"Dam breach," he shouted, leaping from bed and dragging on his clothing.

She glanced at the bedside clock. The time read 5:51 a.m. Nearly everyone in Piñon Forks would be asleep.

Sophia scrambled to do the same, but he was already dressed and clipping his holster as she hopped on one foot in an attempt to tug on her second shoe.

Jack grabbed his phone and punched in a number, then frowned. He tried again.

Sophia had her holster on now and was dragging her hands through the tangle of her hair. She found the clip on the floor beside the bed and used it to hold back her long hair.

"What's wrong?" she asked.

Jack continued to jab at his phone. "No service."

An icy cold washed down her spine. She needed cell service to detonate the explosions. A terrible thought rose in her mind.

"Where is the cell-phone tower?" she asked.

Jack's eyes widened and she had her answer. She knew before he spoke, the flaw in their plan becoming obvious too late.

"It's right beside the power station at Skeleton Cliff Dam."

She made the obvious conclusion from the siren and the absent service. The dam was gone. Between the dam and Piñon Forks lay twenty-two miles and one bridge. How long until millions of gallons of water spilling from Twin Mountain Lake filled the canyon? How long until the hydraulic head, the wave of water, reached them?

"Jack. I need mobile service to trigger the fuses."

He stared at her and she could see the gasp, if not hear it. Then his jaw clamped shut and he pointed toward the door.

They ran to his SUV. Inside the compartment, the siren's wail was muted enough to be able to speak.

Jack lifted his radio and called in to the station. Somehow Chief Tinnin was already there.

"I radioed the highway patrol boys. The dam's gone. Used a school bus full of something, they said."

"Kids?" she cried.

Jack relayed the question.

"They don't think so. Empty bus. They were expecting a field trip. Let it right by. And the two highway boys both got off the bridge before it collapsed."

Jack explained about the fuses.

"What do we do?" asked Tinnin.

"We need to get across the river," she said.

"A boat," said Jack. "Our patrol boat."

They reached the police station. Already the town of Piñon Forks was responding to the siren and everyone was attempting to reach higher ground, choking the narrow, poorly maintained road that was the single evacuation route from town. One of the tribal officers was directing traffic, but Sophia knew it would be too little, too late. The flood would find them here in their vehicles and everyone would become just part of the rolling, tumbling debris sweeping down the canyon. Unless she could stop it.

Sophia knew the main charges were all in place. But without the initiator, the cell-phone call, the detonator would not fire and the main charge would not explode. She needed another way to start the explosive chain reaction.

At the station, she collected the two rolls of a thousand feet of nonel shock tubing. This was her nonelectric initiator, a modern-day version of a burning fuse, replacing the iconic wires and TNT blast box. Only this was faster because the hollow tubing was coated with HMX, military-grade explosives that relayed the charge from the blasting cap to the det cord, which fired the main charge. With luck, this length of cord would give the distance they needed to protect them from the flying debris and blast wave. Her training had taught her that it was the blast wave that killed most people. She also gathered additional fifty-grain det cord just in case. Det cord, short for detonation cord, looked like shock-tubing cord. But it had a key difference. It did not transmit the blasting caps signal to the booster and explosives. It *was* the explosive. Wrap it around a tree trunk and bye-bye, tree.

Jack helped her carry the supplies to his SUV. They

found that Wallace Tinnin was already at the river in the police boat that they used to patrol the portion of the river that adjoined their tribe's rez. The three of them loaded the blasting materials aboard.

Sophia climbed into the bow of the boat and sat facing Tinnin. He had a hold of the controls for the outboard motor and set them off the instant Jack had centered his body weight in the middle of the small craft, sitting on the white fiberglass livewell.

The chief ferried them straight across the river, but halfway to their destination the sirens went silent. The sound of the outboard motor filled the space as Jack and Sophia stared at one another.

"What happened to the siren?" asked Sophia.

"Not sure," said Jack.

"They could have taken that out, too," said the chief.

She had not thought of that.

"How long until it reaches us?" asked Tinnin.

"Depends on the size of the breach," said Sophia. If it was only a minor hole, the flooding would be minimal and the water would rise slowly. If the entire hydroelectric dam was gone...she couldn't imagine it. That huge grey structure, destroyed. But it could happen. Had happened to larger targets in military operations.

"I've had spotters from Tribal Thunder upriver since we identified the possible target," said Tinnin. "Today, it's Ray Strong. He radioed in. It's gone. Dam, power station—all of it."

And Ray's pregnant wife and Lisa were likely in the snarl of traffic in Piñon Forks. Sophia felt the weight of their lives pressing down on her. They had to get to those detonators.

Jack and Tinnin stared at her as they jolted across

the water—both seemed to be wondering if she could pull this off. She wondered with them.

"Okay." She turned her mind to the math problem. Water, volume and force. "The water from the lake will be forced through the gap in the dam. The flood will move outward as well as downriver. It has to fill up the canyon," she said. "There's a bridge between us and the dam site. That will slow the water and block the debris for a while. When it fails, the debris will be rolling toward us with the water in a wave."

"How long?" asked the chief again.

"Twenty minutes would be generous."

She needed to bypass to ignition sequences set with cell phones. That meant getting up close and personal. Way too close and much too personal with the amount of explosives lining that cliff wall. It also meant that both she and Jack would need to be in different locations to detonate the two respective sequences of charges she had laid.

She looked to Jack and his troubled eyes told her that he had already come to the same conclusion.

"How are we going to do it?" asked Jack.

Sophia wondered the same thing.

"We will each need to trigger one of the sequences. I'll take the first. You handle the second."

Jack's brow lifted as he seemed to realize that she had taken a more dangerous sequence.

"How about we reverse that. I'll take the first. You take the second."

"You can't." She was so glad to have a reason he would accept because she knew saying she needed to protect him would not fly. "I'll never scale that cliff face in time. And you've done it before." She pointed at the wall in question. The one he'd climbed as a young man. The first in his group to reach the top, he had said.

He could have driven upriver and over the bridge to reach the canyon ridge, if they had time. They didn't.

"We should stay together," he said, but he was accepting the truth. He needed to leave her to save his people. He didn't like it but could find no alternative. They would separate to initiate sequences or they would let the river take it all.

"How long will it take you to get up there?" she asked.

Jack considered the problem. Studying the route once taken by the ancient ones to the cliff dwellings in the caves she was about to destroy. These were left by the indigenous people who lived in this place far before the Apache moved over the land bridge with the Athabaskan peoples to this place. There were steps cut into the inclines to ease the way for the women who carried water vessels on their backs. On the steepest sections, the steps had been worn smooth by the rubbing of countless hands and feet of those who walked here before.

"How much will I be carrying?" asked Jack.

She organized what he would need as Wallace Tinnin opened the livewell, rummaging past their gear for the nylon bag that held survival equipment. He dumped the contents of the red nylon bag onto the deck and began loading up the blasting supplies she selected.

Sophia spoke quickly, feeling the pressure of time pushed by the oncoming water. Jack knew how to set the charges. He had been with her but still she reviewed how to use the detonator after the shock tubing.

"Get behind whatever you can. Something solid and as far back as possible. You need something to break the blast wave. Something solid and far back from the ridge."

He turned to go and then did an about-face. Jack grabbed her wrist and tugged. Then he gave her a quick kiss and whispered, "Come back to me."

She nodded. Her throat was too full of pain and grief to answer.

The chief pressed a radio into her hand.

"Tell us when you are clear."

Jack was already scaling the steps. She watched him a moment more and then turned to Tinnin.

"I might not have time to get clear."

He held her gaze. "Then radio us that you're clear anyway. He won't hit the initiator otherwise."

She understood. Telling Jack she was safe would ensure that he initiated his sequence.

Sophia clipped the radio to her waistband, scooped up the roll of shock tubing and took the seat vacated by Tinnin. Then she pointed the flat skiff upriver, toward her position.

In her plan, they would be across the river in cover when she made the two phone calls to the burner phones to trigger the blasts. Then she would blow the sequence upriver first, blocking the flow of the river. The second sequence would bring down more of the cliff above and reinforce the existing temporary dam. Without the second blast, she was certain the force of water would at least break over the smaller debris pile. At worst, it would take the pile of rubble and use it like a scouring pad to wipe away every structure and living thing along the river.

Unfortunately, after setting her sequence, she would have to travel above the range of the first blast site. She'd have to face the ensuing floods from the riverbank or she would have to race under the cliff face that was destined to fall in the second blast.

How much time had passed? Ten minutes? Fifteen? It would be a miracle to just get to the cell-phone initiator before the waters reached her. She glanced back, seeing Jack scaling the steepest section of rock with Tinnin still far behind him. They'd make it to their position and then it would be a race to lay out the tubing and take cover. They had a chance.

Sophia continued running along the flat riverbank, her gaze searching for the flood.

"Not yet. Please, not yet."

And then she saw it—the brown wave swept toward her from canyon wall to canyon wall.

Sophia reached the initiation site for the first blast and tied the tubing into the line she had set. Then she ran back toward the boat, unrolling the yellow tubing as she went. She threw the roll into the skiff and unrolled it into the river. Then she set the boat to drift. All the explosives were inside the tubing. It was waterproof, so no need to keep it dry.

Sophia glanced at the motor. If she engaged the motor, she could make a faster escape, outrun the cresting wave and possibly the debris from the second blast. But then the tubing might pull away from the initiator and there would be no first blast, no foundation for the second. Neither her sequence nor Jack's would provide enough of a debris field to hold back what was coming. They needed both. So she drifted along in the current, faster than normal in the swell of water already lifting the river's depth. As she went, she spooled out the tubing until she was directly beneath the site of Jack's sequence. Sophia glanced at the approaching hydraulic head, judging the speed and distance it covered. She wouldn't make it.

Then she lifted the radio. "Jack, over."

He answered immediately, out of breath. "Here. We're in place. Your position? Over."

"I'm initiating first sequence now. You're next. Over."

"Are you clear? Over."

"Clear. Jack, I see the flood. Initiate immediately after my blast. Over."

"Roger that."

Sophia couldn't save herself. But she could save Jack and all he loved.

She hit the trigger. The tubing flashed a brilliant white as it carried the signal back upriver. A moment later rocks and debris shot into the air as the canyon wall collapsed into the river.

Sophia hit the throttle and flew downriver, knowing she'd never make it to the still water she could see beyond the rock wall engineered to collapse.

Chapter Twenty

"She's done it."

Jack and Tinnin took cover behind the wall of rock at the top of the canyon rim. From this position he could not see the river directly below him. More importantly, he could not see Sophia. But he could see far upriver to the narrow gap between the walls of rock, and he could hear the echoes of the first blast rumbling through the stone beneath his feet as the dust billowed up into the blue sky.

If she'd calculated correctly, rock from the lower bluff should have collapsed into the river, blocking its normal flow. His sequence of blasts would bring down the overburden and cliff rim to fall on top of the first mound of rubble adding weight, depth and height to the new temporary debris dam.

"Hit the charge," said Tinnin.

Jack lifted the button. He needed only to press his thumb to send the canyon rim down into the river. But instead he held the control aloft and still, as if he, too, had turned to stone.

"Hit it!" yelled his chief.

"Hear that?" said Jack.

"What?"

"The motor. It's the skiff."

Jack dropped the control and stood. "She's not clear. She's still in that skiff."

"Maybe." Tinnin reached for the control and Jack snatched it back.

"She's under us! We have to give her time." If Tinnin thought to wrestle the control from Jack, he'd never make it. Jack faced his chief ready to fight to give Sophia the seconds she needed to escape.

But Wallace Tinnin did not lunge for the control, or take a swing at Jack. Instead he pointed upriver. Jack stepped back, suspecting a trick, a diversion to distract his attention for the moment his chief needed to make a play. Then he glanced toward the gap in the canyon. What he saw frosted his heart.

Brown water roared through the opening, blasting forty feet to the top of the canyon walls. The hydraulic head—millions of gallons with only one way to go, straight at his reservation.

The anguish surged with the flood waters as he realized he faced a devil's choice. She could die in the blast or in the flood. He held the trigger in his hand and turned his gaze to his chief.

Tinnin lifted his chin, indicating the trigger. "That's quicker."

Jack turned back to watch the water. He could see pieces of metal in the debris field that Sophia had forewarned. Soon it would pummel everything below. Unless he stopped it.

He waited as long as he could, until the sound of the crashing wave drowned out the sound of her motor. Until the flood had reached the point where he could no longer see it run.

Jack pushed the trigger.

Tinnin jumped on top of him, upsetting his balance

and forcing him back to cover. The earth beneath them heaved and groaned as the blast wave passed over them. Then the rock that had been there all Jack's life, and the lifetime of every person who'd ever walked the earth, dropped away. Where it had been was only dust and gravel and chunks of stone flying high, up and up.

"Get down," yelled Tinnin, pushing Jack's head to the warm sandstone.

All about them the rocks fell, raining down like a meteor shower. Mercifully, the debris missed their heads, which were pressed close to the outcropping they had chosen for cover. But one hit Tinnin's leg. He yelped and rolled from side to side as he clutched his thigh.

Jack checked his chief's leg. The deformity of the tibia and immediate swelling made it clear that both bones of his lower leg were fractured, and he could not walk down the way they had come.

"Call for help," said Tinnin. "Tell them I need transport."

Jack crouched beside his superior.

"I can't come with you, Jack. Go see if anyone is left down there."

Jack lifted the radio, issuing a prayer under his breath before pressing the button necessary to transmit. Please let his dispatcher be there. Please let everyone be there. Please let Sophia's death not have been in vain.

"Jack Bear Den, here. Are you there, Olivia?" Jack released the button and held his breath, waiting for their dispatcher to answer. As the seconds crawled by with the settling dust, Jack's heart beat so hard he could not swallow.

"They're not there," he said to Tinnin.

"Try again. She leaves that radio on her desk all the time."

"Olivia! Pick up! Are you there? Over."

The radio squealed and then Jack heard Olivia, out of breath.

"Yes. We're here. We're all here! I was at the window. I can't believe it. The rocks flew everywhere. It broke windows. But it worked. It stopped the water! Over!"

"Thank God," said another voice. Ray Strong, Jack recognized, who had spotted the flood from far upriver and whose new wife was there in Piñon Forks.

Jack pressed the radio to his chest and bowed his head to also give thanks. But the tear in his heart grew wider and he pressed his hand to his eyes. He wanted her back. He wanted to tell her that he loved her and that he was so sorry for what he had done to her. If not for him, she'd be back on the job she loved, alive.

Tinnin put a hand on Jack's shoulder.

"She's a hero, son."

He nodded and looked at the sky, still so filled with dust, it seemed like a cloudy day. He lifted the radio again and asked Olivia if she saw a boat on the river.

"A boat?"

"Our boat."

"Not from here. No, Jack."

"I see it." Another voice broke in. "It's Jake."

That was Jake Redhorse—one of their newest and most promising hires.

"I'm at the river. I see the boat. It's downstream on this side. Over."

"Where's Sophia? Over."

"Checking. Over."

Jack spoke to Olivia. He told her to call Kurt in Darabee and get the air ambulance ready.

"I'm not that hurt. It's just a busted leg," said Tinnin.

Jack glanced at his chief. "It's not for you."

Jack half expected him to tell him to give up. That all they'd find was Sophia's body, if that. But he couldn't give up.

"I'm going to the cliff edge. I'll be right back."

"Be careful," said Tinnin.

Jack crept forward. He crawled the last few feet on all fours until he got his head over the edge.

Below, a lake was forming behind the dam of canyon rock that Sophia had devised, the water threading up the box canyons and flowing out into the pastureland above the tribe's casino.

The river flowed in a fury, but it did not overflow the banks. He swept his eyes across the scene and found the fiberglass craft they had taken across the river together.

Why didn't you tell her you loved her?

He watched the patrol unit pull to the shoulder and saw Jake Redhorse jog down the bank. Jack looked downriver for her body, fearing he would see it floating in the current or worse, snagged on a log.

He saw nothing but the unusual brown muddy water. He returned his gaze to Redhorse, who searched the boat. From Jack's position, he could see the boat rested on its side against a large boulder. The contents of the craft were strewn along the bank. He looked again.

But the contents were all upstream from the boat. Wouldn't they be below the craft or in the river?

Instead he saw the life preservers, medical pack, flares and small shovel all thrown in a pile on the bank. It looked as if someone had dumped everything they routinely stored inside the fiberglass livewell onto the bank.

He looked at the boat's position again. It lay above the high-water mark. That meant it had been thrown up there or...

Could she have grounded the vessel? Sophia would know, or at least be able to guess, how far the rock would fly and how high the river would rise before they blocked the flow.

Jack lifted the radio. "Redhorse. Check the livewell!"

"The what?" Redhorse looked across the river and waved his arm above his head to show that he had spotted Jack.

"The bin where we stow that gear. Check it."

The livewell, designed to store large-mouthed bass on fishing trips, was also fiberglass, but Jack knew it had good insulation.

Redhorse affixed his radio to the front shirt pocket of his uniform and walked to the boat. The cooler was on its side. Redhorse lifted the two latches that locked when the lid dropped to the base.

Sophia spilled out onto the ground like a mermaid. She lay on the riverbank, motionless and pale.

Jack lifted the radio. "Is she breathing?"

Redhorse dropped to one knee and rolled Sophia to her back. Her arm flopped lifelessly above her head. The young officer lowered his ear to Sophia's lips and listened.

Jack spoke into the radio again. "Olivia. Call Kurt. Send the air ambulance to your position now!"

Redhorse sealed his mouth around Sophia's and blew. Jack knew what it signified. Sophia was not breathing.

Chapter Twenty-One

Jack lay on his belly on the canyon rim staring back down to the river. The route down had vanished in the blast. The bridge above them was gone and he was stranded on the wrong side. He glanced across the water to see several people now gathering around Sophia, so many that he could not see her.

He prayed as he watched. His shaman had chosen the medicine wheel as Jack's guide. The circle of life and symbol of all things that were important. You knew they were important because they moved in a circle, like the sun and the seasons and the years in a man's life. Kenshaw Little Falcon said Jack would need to know the direction to go and the wheel would guide him. Four quarters, four directions and the fifth direction that was the place in the center.

He'd found his center. It was Sophia.

He'd found the direction he needed to go. Toward her and with her. If he had the chance, he would not let her go. He had done his duty to his people, the tribe of his mother. Now he would follow the hoop and the woman and ask her to pass through the circle of their lives together.

But first she had to live. She had to.

Jack studied the makeshift dam she had made. The

temporary structure allowed natural spillways between the huge boulders and rubble that blocked its course.

Jack lifted the radio and hailed Jake Redhorse.

"Is she alive?"

Across the river, Redhorse stood holding the radio to his mouth. Jack could read nothing from his expression as he squeezed the radio so hard he feared it might crack.

"Affirmative. She's breathing. Over."

Jack closed his eyes and glanced up at the sky.

Thank you for this day and all that are in it. Thank you for her life.

Jack lifted the radio. "Get me down there, Jake. Get me to her. Over."

Olivia's voice broke in. "How's the chief?"

"He needs transport. His leg is busted."

The thumping of the helicopter blades flashed Jack back to Iraq, but he kept his attention on the group across the river. He knew it was the air ambulance.

"Jack, your brother is hailing me. Over. He wants to know where you want him."

"Set it down over there."

It seemed an eternity as he waited for Kurt to leap from the open door of the chopper and dart between the parting crowd to Sophia. He left her to fetch the stretcher. Jack knew that was good because his brother must have decided she needed nothing from him at the scene before transport.

"Is she critical? Over," he said.

"Negative. Coming around. Breathing. Good pulse, he says." Redhorse waved at Jack from across the way. "Kurt says they have time to land up there for the chief."

"Yes. Tell him yes." Sophia was loaded, Kurt disappeared aboard and the engine revved as the bird ascended. A moment later, Jack was shielding his eyes as dust and sand swirled beneath the landing chopper. The pilot set the runners on the plateau, where Chief Tinnin waited with Jack.

Jack ran to the open door as one of the crew emerged and ran past him with his bag. Jack wedged his shoulders past Kurt to get a look at Sophia. She was strapped onto one of two stretchers beneath a white sheet and her color was gray.

"How is she?"

Kurt rested a hand on Jack's shoulder. "You did it."

"Yeah." His attention remained on Sophia. "Is she all right?"

"I think that cooler protected her. But it locked on her. She ran out of air."

That was bad. Brain damage. Jack pressed his hand to his forehead.

"She's got good vitals, but she may have ruptured her spleen. Possible other damage—"

Jack cut him off. "Okay. Let's go."

Kurt slipped past him with the spine board and he and the other paramedic carried Tinnin to the chopper. Jack was already aboard.

"Aren't you in charge now?" asked Kurt, motioning his head to the tribe's side of the river.

"They'll have to wait."

Kurt's brows lifted in surprise. Then he took his seat and replaced the headset.

"Good to go," he said into the microphone.

The pilot gave a thumbs-up. The motor shrieked and then lifted into the air.

The canyon, the rubble dam and the river grew smaller and smaller and then fell away behind them. They landed in the parking lot beside the hospital in

Darabee. Two teams awaited and buzzed forward, taking charge of the patients and leaving Jack with Kurt standing on hot pavement.

"Can you get me into the OR?" he asked.

"Not in a million years. Waiting room. Now I have to go back to work."

"Piñon Forks?"

"Minor injuries. We're taking the ambulances."

His brother left him and Jack headed inside. Over the next three hours, Carter called to update him on the tribe's status. Officer Redhorse called on the direction of the chief, who was already back in Piñon Forks. They were moving everyone to Turquoise Ridge temporarily, or out to Darabee. The FBI was on site and FEMA was coming in with temporary housing and still he heard nothing on Sophia's condition.

It was well into the evening before he received any news. The doctor met him in the waiting room, where Jack had about worn out the carpet pacing.

"How's she doing?"

SOPHIA FORCED HER eyes open and glanced about, struggling to figure out where she was. It didn't take a forensic explosives investigator to recognize she was in a hospital bed hooked to an IV, a finger monitor for her pulse and... She shifted, stifling a groan at the sharp abdominal pain and the tug that told her she was hooked to a catheter. She hated hospitals and instead of being glad to have somehow survived, she began immediately plotting her escape.

The room was dimly lit by the headboard light. The white curtain that circled her bed prevented her from seeing the window or, presumably, the second bed.

Night time, she thought, and relaxed her head back onto the thin foam pillow.

She closed her eyes against the pain. Something was definitely wrong down there in her midsection. She moved her feet, grateful they were both there and still worked. Her hands balled into fists, minus the one encumbered by the dreaded finger clip. She turned her head, continuing her inventory, and spotted the call button looped around the raised side rail.

The sharp pain in her middle had morphed into a constant escalating throb that forced her to grit her teeth. The act of reaching for the button made her break out in a cold sweat.

What had happened to her?

Sophia pressed the button, which made a dinging sound. Something on the opposite side of her bed moved. She turned and saw Jack Bear Den lift his tousled head from the mattress beside her hip. His gaze was groggy from sleep.

"Sophia," he whispered, his tone echoing the relief that lifted his features. He straightened and she saw that he sat in an orange vinyl chair pulled close to her bedside in the dusty clothing he'd been wearing when she last saw him ascending that cliff.

"What time is it?" Her voice was a rustling thing, like dead leaves rattling in the wind. She pressed her dry lips together, realizing how much her throat hurt. That was very bad because it likely meant she'd needed a breathing tube and that meant either her heart had stopped or she'd had surgery.

Jack glanced at his phone. "Three in the morning."

"Which morning?"

"Wednesday."

"Lost the day," she said and gritted her teeth against the pain. Tears leaked from her eyes.

Jack stroked her forehead.

"You in pain?"

She nodded, eyes now squeezed shut. She had no energy left for words.

"I'll get someone." He rose and left her. She heard him meet the nurse outside the door and caught some of their conversation.

Then the nurse was standing on her opposite side offering soothing words and an injection in the backside. The relief was almost instant. But she also felt the world receding again and she did not know what happened. Had they done it? Had they saved his reservation and ended her career in two spectacular explosions?

JACK MET WITH Carter and Dylan and Ray in Sophia's hospital room that same Wednesday afternoon. They crept in trying not to wake Sophia.

"Sleeping?" whispered Carter.

"They gave her something for pain," said Jack. "She's out."

Ray, ever blunt, told him that he looked like he'd been blown off the mountain.

Dylan, ever the diplomat, asked how Sophia was doing.

"They took out her spleen. She lost a lot of blood from the rupture and they said she had at least one bruised kidney."

"In other words," said Carter, "she's lucky."

"And smart," said Dylan. "Using the livewell for cover. Brilliant."

"Nearly killed her," said Jack. "She ran out of air."

Ray was now peering at Sophia, as if judging her condition, and Jack had to resist the urge to shove him back.

"How's her…?" Ray pointed at his skull. "You know."

"No brain damage. Redhorse got to her fast enough." And for that he would be forever grateful. "She'll be fine in time."

"You hear back from her supervisor?" asked Carter.

"He'll be here soon. We need a plan. She saved us all and we need to be sure it doesn't cost her the job she loves."

"You said they ruled in her favor," said Ray.

Dylan turned to Ray. "He's not talking about the investigation. She just blew up the whole ridge. That's not what FBI agents do."

Jack could not have said it better. He knew what was most important to Sophia. It wasn't his tribe or the land. It was her career. She'd fought great odds to get clear of Black Mountain and make a fresh start. She was doing good work and if that was what made her happy, he was going to do everything he could to protect her from the fallout from their transgression.

"You have any ideas?" asked Carter.

Jack told him what he'd come up with. They added their opinions and suggestions on how to make the story believable. He hoped that they'd be ready when Burton and Forrest arrived with their posse of federal investigators. They came to an agreement and stood ready to protect her from the FBI. Jack wished they were on their land as they would have a better chance of guarding her. But the FBI would not take a woman recovering from surgery from her hospital bed.

Would they?

Chapter Twenty-Two

Carter cleared his throat in that way he did to indicate serious matters. Jack glanced up from Sophia's pale face and gave his brother his attention.

"Mom asked me to give you this." Carter extended an envelope.

"You know what's inside."

Carter nodded once.

"What?"

"It's information on your grandparents. Your father's people."

Jack tore off the end of the envelope, drew out the page and flipped it open. Ray crowded in to read over his shoulder as Dylan and Carter waited for whatever Jack decided to share.

Ray pointed at the page. "How do you even pronounce that?"

"I don't know," said Jack, staring at the name of his father as he realized he was no longer roadrunner born of snake. He looked at the page. What clan was this? He read the names of his father written in Annetta's hand.

Hawaii
Keanae, Maui
Maua Kahauola (grandmother)

Clifford Taaga (grandfather)

Robert Taaga (father)

Jack glanced at Carter. "Mom said this is all her sister told her."

It was enough—the proper way to introduce a man beginning with the place of his birth, the names of his parents and finally the name of the man.

He tucked the page into his wallet, in the place where he had carried the results of the DNA test for eight months.

"Thank her for me."

Carter nodded.

"Why don't we wait out in the lounge for the agents?" asked Dylan.

Ray filed out of the room after Dylan, leaving Jack behind. The nurse bustled in and woke Sophia, then chased Jack from the room.

When he returned it was to find Sophia sitting up in the bed and looking more pale than before. The grayness of her complexion made the circles especially dark.

"You all right?" he asked.

BY ALL REPORTS, Sophia was healing, but she still felt mostly on the wrong side of terrible. Her nurse let her use the bathroom while Jack spoke to his medicine society in the hospital lounge. He stepped back into her room just after the lunch tray was delivered. The pain made her jaw lock and the welcoming smile felt forced.

His gaze swept over her. "You hurting?"

"They just gave me something," she said. "I will be dopey again soon."

But before they gave her the shot, they had tugged

out her catheter and changed the dressings. Everything from her chest down was aching.

He kissed her forehead and she closed her eyes at the touch that was light and comforting. She was done here. The tribe was safe and her purpose complete. He didn't need her and she was free to go. But go to what? They'd ruled on her use of deadly force. Now she faced a new investigation over her actions. She had no defense. She would lose her job and her career. It mattered, but not as it had before. Was that because she knew she had done the right thing?

Jack pulled back.

"Burton is en route," he said.

She snorted. "Just when I thought I couldn't feel any worse."

"I'm going to tell them that you only advised the tribal council on how to remove dangerous overburden from the canyon rim."

"I blew up the whole canyon," she said. "Pressed the trigger."

"No. We blew it up. The tribe. All the miners of Turquoise Canyon will swear they set the charges."

"Under my supervision." She arched a brow, catching on to what he was attempting to do.

"Not according to them. They were removing overburden from the turquoise vein and added too much to the main charge."

"They are not going to believe that you set those charges off immediately after the dam failed."

"It didn't fail, Sophia. They blew it up."

"Who?"

"No one taking responsibility. Just like the pipelines in Phoenix. The FBI will question the timing. But our guys laid the explosives. They caused a landslide." He shrugged. "It happens."

He was offering her a way out. A way back to her position and her life. All she had to do was to go along with the cover-up.

"I can't, Jack."

"Well, I'm not letting you get arrested. You saved us, Sophia. Everything we have, we owe to you."

"No one held a gun to my head. I made the choice and I'll take the consequences."

"No. You won't."

"It was illegal."

"Kenshaw often says what is legal is not always right and what is right is not always legal."

She thought about that then said, "Convenient. Your shaman is a known member of the eco-extremists group."

"He also works with your agency."

"Jack. I blew up federal land. They're not going to ignore it."

"That's true," said a familiar voice from the doorway. "Might give you a medal for it, though."

Luke Forrest stepped into the room.

His confident smile waned when he took a good look at her. She had seen herself in the bathroom mirror when the nurse had forced her up. She thought that she would frighten small children in her current state. Grown men, too, it seemed.

"Oh, Sophia," he said and moved to the opposite side of the bed. "I'm so sorry."

"I'm alive. I'll be back on my feet soon."

"That's great news. Burton should be here soon. I wanted a chance to thank you and to apologize for putting you in this position."

She let him off the hook without regret. "I made my own decisions, Luke."

"But if not for me, you would never have been here."

"And everyone in Piñon Forks would be dead," said Jack.

She never would have met Jack. Her gaze flashed to him. He scooped up her hand. When she glanced back to her cousin, it was to see him looking at the place where their palms met and then back to her. His brow quirked as he likely connected the dots.

"Well, then. You'll be on disability for a while. After that, you planning on coming back to the Bureau?"

She looked from one man to the other, resisting the pull to stay here with Jack. What would that be like? Then she remembered, though he had extended the hospitality of his tribe, he had not asked her to stay with him. Had not asked for anything more permanent than sharing the time she had here. They'd gone in knowing she would leave.

But he was here with her in the hospital. Never left her side, judging from the dark stubble now growing on his face and the dusty clothing he still wore.

Did he want her to stay?

"You think they'll take me back?" she asked Luke.

"I think so. You not only saved this reservation, you kept that flood from taking out Red Rock Dam below the rez and possibly Mesa Salado Dam as well. If that had happened, we could have lost three of our four hydroelectric dams. The results would have crippled the electric grid. You did that, Sophia."

"She had help. If they're going to pin a criminal charge on her, then I have forty miners who will swear she advised against it."

"I think that won't be necessary," said Luke.

"They won't prosecute?" asked Jack.

"Can't guarantee. But I highly doubt it. You were on your land. Federal land, true. I think they'd be foolish to pursue a case. It would be nothing but bad press. But if they do, you'll need more than forty miners. The Bureau will know Sophia was there. She's left physical evidence. They'll find it."

Jack's grip on her hand tightened.

"You have a suggestion?"

"For starters, I'd move her out of Darabee and back to Turquoise Canyon. That would delay them. If she can travel, then consider taking her to her own reservation on Black Mountain. There are other ways to protect her."

Now he met Jack's gaze and Jack nodded.

"I understand."

She didn't. "What are you two talking about?"

Luke leaned down to kiss Sophia's cheek and whispered words of encouragement. Then he straightened and looked to Jack.

"You know what to do."

Chapter Twenty-Three

It was not how Sophia pictured being proposed to. She lay in a hospital bed hurting all over, a pulse monitor and IV connecting her to equipment beside her. In her mind's eye, her would-be groom would not have been rumpled and tired and covered with fallout from a recent explosion. And he would not have proposed to her out of duty and an obligation to protect.

Her mother's choices had taught Sophia many things. One was never to trust a man to take care of you. It was why Sophia needed her job. And no matter how much Jack tempted her, she was not putting her foot in that trap today or any day. One made decisions from a position of power, not from one of weakness, and she had never been so weak.

"No," she said and stopped talking.

Jack's brow furrowed. "But it would make you a member of the Turquoise Canyon tribe."

"I just blew up your canyon. You might need a new name. Turquoise Valley?"

"Sophia, this is serious. If you marry me, we can claim you have federal protection on our reservation."

"Jack, I'm Black Mountain Apache and I've spent my adult life trying to leave that legacy behind. But if I needed it, I have the protection of my tribe."

"You want me to bring you there?"

"No!" Oh, it hurt to raise her voice.

"Your captain will be here soon. I can have you out of here before he arrives."

"I don't need a husband, Jack. What I need is my old job back."

"Forrest thinks that might not work out."

"Well, I'm going to try. I'm sure not going to quit because they might fire me."

He blew out a breath. "Is that your decision?"

"Yes."

"You could come to work for us. We need more women on our force."

"You don't have any."

"Our dispatcher, Olivia. She's ten percent of our force," he said, rubbing his neck. "And she does a great job."

"I appreciate the offer. But I don't think you need a forensic explosives expert just yet. Maybe think about a second detective first."

"I don't want you hurt over this."

Did he mean more than a ruptured spleen and a bruised kidney? She was really tempted to just accept his offer. But she wouldn't. She wasn't going to be his act of selfless duty. No matter how good they were together, her ego could not tolerate that.

When her captain arrived with three investigators, they asked Jack to leave the room. The last thing she said to him was to tell them the truth.

He was a lawman. But she feared that his need to protect her might make him forget that. It wasn't something you could do halfway. Either you followed the law or you didn't.

They asked her a series of questions, the interview stretching so long she feared she'd have to call for her

pain medication. When they left, she felt totally drained.
The medication helped her sleep. When she woke, Jack
was back beside her bed.

"You don't have to stay. I'm doing well."

"I want to stay."

"Jack, go home. Take a shower. Sleep in your own
bed and come back tomorrow."

"You ordering me out?"

"I need to rest."

He kissed her forehead and something unexpected
happened. Despite the pain and fatigue, that familiar
tingle of awareness was back. This man, only this man,
could rouse her to want something her body was in no
way ready for.

"I'll see you in the morning," he promised and disappeared.

She ate and slept and watched television with the
sound off, dozing and waking to find the windows dark.

In the morning, her breakfast came, but Jack did not.
She tried to hide her disappointment and worry.

That afternoon, Executive Director Gill of the Turquoise Canyon tribe came to her room dressed in full
regalia to formally thank her for her efforts to save
their tribe. Chief Wallace Tinnin accompanied him, on
crutches, his leg in a cast from hip to toe. Also there
were the members of Tribal Thunder—Ray Strong,
Dylan Tehauno, and Carter and Jack Bear Den.

Jack looked especially appealing in his high beaded
moccasins, bright camp shirt festooned with blue rib-
bons sewn horizontally across the yoke. Across his forehead he wore a red band of folded cloth ornamented
with a string of silver and turquoise medallions on a
leather cord. Two eagle feathers hung by his temple.
His appearance was so distracting that she had to con-

centrate not to keep staring at him. Each time she cast him a quick look, her stomach gave a familiar quiver. Perhaps she was healing faster than she thought.

The tribe presented her with a sacred eagle feather adorned with red cloth and elaborate bead work and a simple leather cord to allow the feather to be tied on whatever she chose. The eagle flew closer to the heavens than any other creature and was therefore the most sacred. She had earned one such feather before from a bald eagle presented by her tribal leaders to mark the milestone of graduating from high school. The entire brief ceremony at her bedside made her proud and she accepted the golden eagle feather with two open hands from Executive Director Gill. The feather, a symbol of strength and power, was holy to her people. There was no higher honor and she felt humble indeed.

"You are one of us now," said Gill. "And welcome on our land and in our homes. Know that we are forever grateful."

"I'm honored."

The room seemed very empty after they left. She had come to know them. What would it be like to stay here with them?

The longing welled up inside her. She sat with the feather before her on her lap, bright against the white blankets. Then she lowered her head and wept. She didn't want to leave them. She didn't want to leave Jack. But how could she stay?

He had so much work to do with his tribe and with the FBI, who were now investigating the dam explosion and the secondary blast that saved his reservation. She had no right to detain him when she was healing well. They needed him, she didn't. Only she did and that was the most concerning thing of all.

The nurse surprised her a few minutes later. Sophia swiped away the tears.

"Well, they're finally gone," said her nurse, clipboard firmly gripped in her hand. She spotted the feather. "Isn't that pretty."

"Sacred," she said, correcting the woman.

The nurse shrugged. "I have your discharge papers."

Sophia blinked. She had been told she would be released tomorrow and the switch caught her by surprise.

"Oh, well, that's good."

"Someone has to pick you up. Do you have someone to call?"

Jack, she thought.

"Um, yes. Of course." It was in that moment that Sophia realized that she had the FBI, an office, a job and coworkers. But she did not have a friend to call to come get her or a family member ready to drop everything to drive her from Darabee to Flagstaff. Suddenly her career seemed cold company by comparison to the warmth of Jack Bear Den's arms.

She lifted her mobile, called her office and asked for her captain.

"I was just going to call you. How you feeling?"

"They're releasing me. I need a ride."

"I'll send someone. Listen. We have good news."

She could use some. "What's that?"

"The ballistics came back on Jauquin Nequam's rifle. It's a match for the bullet fished out of Bear Den's vehicle."

"Great."

"We have him in custody. I've met with Mr. Nequam. He's removed the hit order as part of a plea."

Sophia bristled. She didn't want him getting off after taking a shot at her.

"Really?"

Burton might have heard the aggravation in her voice.

"Sophia, he fired at the highway patrol and fled the scene before arrest. We got enough on him. He's not getting out."

"That's good. How's the highway patrol guy?"

"He didn't hit him," said Burton. "I understand the shooter put a hole in his hat. But he's fine and his hat is in an evidence locker."

"Any progress on the dam explosion?" she asked.

"Lots. Listen, I've got to go. We have a driver on route. Should be there soon."

She thanked him but he'd already ended the call.

Sophia dressed in the clothing Jack had brought her from his apartment. Then she added the eagle feather in its presentation box to the top of her overnight bag. But she paused before closing the bag, retrieving the feather and tying it in her hair.

Sophia was done pretending she was other than what she was. She was Apache, Black Mountain tribe, and she would not let her mother's bad choices keep her from claiming her heritage.

She tried not to be disappointed that Jack did not appear to say farewell and resisted the urge to call him to tell him of her early discharge. Instead, she waited on her bed until a stranger from the Bureau appeared at her door, presented his ID and walked beside the wheelchair she was required to use. On the ground floor, she could not keep herself from searching the lobby for Jack, as if wishing would conjure him. If she wanted to say goodbye, she should have called him.

But she didn't want to say goodbye and that was exactly the problem.

JACK HEADED FOR the station after another sixteen-hour day. He had never been so busy or so distracted. He knew from Forrest that Sophia had been discharged and had been back on the job for eleven days. Everything was as it had been. He had his work. She had hers. That was what she wanted, wasn't it?

He knew she didn't want him. He'd not said a formal goodbye to her. But he had asked her to marry him and she'd turned him down. He'd seen her at the feather ceremony. It had been very hard not to linger after the tribal representative had left. Not to grovel and beg her to come back.

He placed a hand over the medicine wheel he wore around his neck and felt the presence of the one upon his back as he wondered what direction to go.

His shaman said he needed the hoop to help him find his path. When the temporary dam was shorn up and the FBI finished with their investigation, perhaps he would take a trip to Hawaii to find his father's people, see the land where Robert Taaga had come from and learn exactly how to pronounce his grandmother's name. He imagined flying to Maui with Sophia and frowned.

Jack pulled into the lot at tribal headquarters and stared across the river at the dam Sophia had built them in two separate blasts. The woman knew her business. He was on dry ground now only because of her.

Repairs were underway for the damage resulting from the blast. There had been few injuries, which was miracle enough.

Jack headed in and checked his messages. There was nothing from Sophia and the rest could wait. He was expected at his parents for supper. Sunday again.

He was the last to arrive as it was after eight. But they had waited. Tommy was back home because of Jack's urgent call for help after the dam's destruction, but his brother would be returning to the border tomorrow. So this was a final chance for the Bear Den boys to share a meal until they gathered again for Christmas. Carter and Amber greeted him at the door. He kissed his mother in the kitchen and they all came together at the round, scarred wooden table that showed the marks of having survived the raising of four boys.

Jack enjoyed the company as much as the food. He was starving, having missed lunch again. His mother commented that he was losing weight. He usually just wasn't hungry anymore.

"Any word from Sophia?" asked Carter.

The table went silent as all eyes turned to him.

He shook his head and pushed the remains of the noodle casserole around his plate.

"That's odd," said his mother, her brow furrowing.

"Anything from Forrest on those responsible?" asked his father.

His mother made a sound of frustration and stood to clear the table. Amber and Carter helped her carry out the dishes.

"They're collecting evidence. I understand they have the school bus, or what's left of it."

"What about Lupe Wrangler?" asked Carter. "They going to extradite her?"

"According to Forrest, she has family in Mexico and they still have not broken her alibi for her husband's murder."

"So she gets away with it?"

"They are making progress and they've locked up her money. That's all I know."

His mother called from the kitchen. "Jack, come help me with this."

All eyes flicked to him. Tommy gave him that you're-in-trouble look and lifted an index finger. Carter grimaced and Kurt rubbed his face. Every last one of them knew he was being summoned, and not to help in the kitchen.

His father rose. "Boys, it's a lovely night. Let's get a fire started out back."

Jack's father was abandoning him and taking all Jack's backup along. He pressed his hands on the table and rose to face the music.

Chapter Twenty-Four

"You going to read me my rights first?" he asked, folding his arms across his chest and staring at his mother.

"What?" she asked. Her mask of innocence did not
fool him for one second.

"You know, my right to remain silent?"

"Don't be silly. I want to hear about Sophia. Why
haven't you called her or gone to check on her? Isn't
she still under a hit or something?"

"Removed. She's safe."

"So you think she doesn't need you. Is that it?"

"No. Yes." Jack flapped his arms. He was used to
being the one doing the interrogation.

"Jack Bear Den, I saw the way you looked at that
girl. And I saw the way she looked at you. She's beautiful, smart, serious, works in law enforcement, so she'll
understand the ridiculous hours you keep. Is it because
she's Mountain Apache?"

"Is what because she's Mountain Apache?"

"That you're letting her go. Because, if you want my
opinion, she's in love with you."

"You're wrong there," he said, unable to keep the
edge from his voice.

His mother thrust a fist to her fleshy hip and lowered her chin. Jack's ears went back as he recognized

the signs indicating he should take cover. Instead he dug his hole even deeper.

"Mom, Sophia doesn't want to stay up here in the pines with us Tonto Apache." There had been long-standing animosity between the Western Apache and his people and it was easier to blame that than voice his confusion.

Her mouth dropped open but she rallied. "It's because you're Tonto? I don't believe it."

"I don't know." He rubbed his neck. "I was just supposed to escort her and protect her while she was here. She's gone now." He flapped his arms.

"I see that. I just don't understand it. Did you tell her your feelings for her?"

"Of course I did. I even asked her to marry me."

His mother's eyes rounded and he thought she might be beginning to understand that Sophia had left him and he was doing his best to get over it…and failing.

"You asked her?"

"I just said so."

"With a ring?"

"What?"

"Did you have a ring? Did you get down on one knee like your father and beg her to marry you?"

Jack scowled. "No, of course not."

His mother was now staring at the ceiling as if counting to ten. When her eyes met his, her brows were up and her chin down again.

"What did you say, exactly?"

Now he was looking away. "I don't remember."

She placed a hand on his folded arms. "Jack?"

"I said that if she married me, she'd gain tribal protection against federal prosecution. That I could marry her and the tribe would keep her safe."

"How romantic."

"I was offering to be her husband."

His mother shook her head in a way that signified either disappointment or that he'd blown it somehow. He thought the latter but wasn't quite sure. He shifted from side to side and her hand squeezed his arm, bringing him back to stillness.

"You offered," his mother said. "You didn't ask."

"Mom, she said she didn't need a husband. She needed her job back."

"You made her feel like an obligation. Do you love her?"

"Of course."

"Start with that."

"That's stupid," he said.

"Why? Because you will have to wear that heart of yours on your sleeve instead of keeping it trapped in that big barrel of a chest? That's the point, Jack. You have to take a risk to show her that you can't live without her. You have to say the words and hope she doesn't turn you down. You offered a plea bargain, not a proposal."

Had he? He swiped a hand over his mouth.

"Try again, Jack, and bring the biggest diamond ring you can afford."

SOPHIA HEADED FOR the break room to freshen up her coffee. She had been riding a desk for two weeks. She didn't like it, watching the other agents in her office come and go as she remained behind with the paperwork. Her captain did a much better job at keeping her informed. The official line was that her little round of private explosives were counterterror measures taken by the Turquoise Canyon tribe in conjunction with federal authorities. That sounded so much better than rogue agent. She was under the impression that they'd keep her awhile and fire her when the media coverage petered out. Her union rep and their attorney suggested she get a deal in writing and get out while the getting was good. But where and to what? She thought of Turquoise Canyon and grimaced. The canyon was much wider now and the US Army Corps of Engineers was working up there.

She wanted to call Jack and see how he was doing. Busy, of course. She wondered about Federal Agent Cassidy Cosen. She knew the Anglo had married tribal councilman Clyne Cosen, but what did she do, commute from way up there on Black Mountain all the way down to Phoenix every day?

Logistics. That was not what was keeping her from Jack. It was stubbornness and fear. Stubbornness that he wanted to protect her instead of love her all her life. And fear that if she took him up on the offer to protect her, she'd lose the control she'd gained over her life.

"That's why they call it falling," she muttered.

Like a trust fall, you had to take a risk.

"Knock, knock." She knew the voice without looking up. It was one of the agents in the office, Patrick Gaffney.

She plastered a smile on her face and turned toward Patrick. Why was he verbally knock-knocking on the open break-room door?

"You busy?" he asked.

She shook her head.

"I brought you a visitor." His expression was entirely too manic for the generally taciturn agent.

"Yeah?"

Normally, they went out to meet visitors and did not bring them back to the break room. She had a sudden terror that it was her mother. Sophia set down her mug on the table.

Patrick stepped aside and Jack Bear Den filled the doorway. Patrick poked his head up from behind Jack's shoulder like a prairie dog emerging from his burrow.

"I'll leave you to it," said Patrick and he disappeared.

Jack stood with his hat in his hand. Sophia sucked in a breath as her heart began a jolting beat that made her eardrums pound. It was hard not to rush forward and leap into his arms. How she wanted to do just that. Instead she casually reached for a chair back for support, fumbling her grip. She got a tight hold on the second try and she allowed her gaze to sweep over him, searching for changes.

His attire was more formal than usual.

He wore lean jeans. Beneath the cuff poked large, elaborately tooled boots she had never seen. The leather was obviously gator and some of the stitching and accent pieces were turquoise in color. His belt she recalled, staring for a moment at the familiar enameled buckle— the medicine wheel to help him find which way to go.

Had it led him here?

There was a visitor's pass stuck to the lapel of his gray sports coat. Around his neck hung a necklace of disc-shaped turquoise beads holding a medallion featuring a large piece of turquoise framed by two bear claws set in silver. The ornament was bright against his white cotton shirt. Jack had dressed in his best.

She lifted her gaze to his familiar face. He was clean shaven and his chin dipped as he peered at her from beneath a hooded brow.

"Sophia," he said. "I've missed you."

Her heart continued its silly pounding. She licked

her lower lip and saw his gaze drop to her mouth. Now the pounding moved south and her grip on the chair back tightened.

"This is a surprise," she said.

"A happy one, I hope." He cleared the doorway and she saw he carried a bouquet of red roses mingled with baby's breath. The paper-cone wrapping was crushed tight in his fist as he held the flowers upright like an ice-cream cone. "I brought you these."

Red roses. A dozen, at least.

Her gaze flicked to them and back to him as she tried to interpret the gesture. These were not the sort of flowers a man brought a woman in the hospital or to congratulate or to thank. He knew that, right?

"You look well," he said.

She didn't, but the cover-up helped disguise the circles and weight loss, which she blamed on the surgery.

He continued forward, stiffly, as if his boots hurt his feet. His finger slipped under the collar of his buttoned shirt and tugged. There was sweat on his upper lip.

Now, she had seen Jack in situations that should have made him sweat. Under fire in his SUV. Helping her lay det cord on the canyon and flying across the river in a boat to reroute the explosive series. He had not ever looked this nervous.

"What are you doing here, Jack?"

"Came down to ask you a question."

A question or *the* question?

"These are for you." He approached, arm extended as he thrust the flowers at her.

She collected the bouquet and inhaled the floral perfume. "Thank you."

At first she thought he was bowing because his head

inclined. But then she realized he was kneeling. Jack sank to one knee before her and fished in his pocket.

Sophia stopped breathing.

"SOPHIA?" JACK SAID. His mouth was so dry it tasted like sand.

The darn box wouldn't open. He pulled and realized too late that he had it backward, as the tiny hinge came apart and the top section dangled like a bird's broken wing. He scowled at the damaged black velvet. The slot still held the white gold band set with a low-profile solitaire.

He held out the offering.

"Sophia, I'm in love with you. I want you to be my wife."

Her mouth dropped open and her eyes went wide as she looked at the ring and the box with the dangling top.

He rushed on, trying to assure her. He knew her feelings about commitment and relying on a man to provide for her.

"I want a partner, Sophia. I want you as my partner. You might not believe me, but I will always protect you and provide for you. But I don't expect you to give up anything. I want to join your life, not take it over. Will you at least consider me as a husband?"

Her mouth closed and her chin began trembling. He hadn't seen this before. Should he stand up now and gather her in his arms, or just stay here holding out the ring?

Sophia set the roses on the table and reached, placing her hands on his extended one. She was nodding frantically as if she had suddenly lost the ability to speak.

"Is that yes?" he asked.

"Yes," she squeaked.

He blasted forward like a center tackle coming off the line at the snap and pulled Sophia to his chest. She hugged him around the neck, and he inhaled the sweet familiar scent of her.

How he had missed her. Suddenly everything seemed just right. He set her on her feet and pulled the ring from the slot.

She smiled up at him as he held the tiny ring between them. She gazed down at the glittering ornament.

"The guy said he could size it to fit or that you can return this one and pick something you like better."

She wiped the tears from her cheeks and glanced down at the engagement ring. "I couldn't like anything better than this one."

Sophia offered her left hand and he slipped the circlet to her knuckle. She took it from there, sliding the ring down her slim finger and into place. She took a moment to admire the setting, smiling down. Then she lifted her gaze to meet his.

"I never thought I'd want this," she said.

"I always wanted this," he said. "I just never thought I'd find the right woman. But I have found her in you." He took her left hand in his, picturing the wedding vows and knowing they could not come soon enough. "I'm sorry about the first time I asked you. It was stupid. I made it sound like I was doing you a favor because I was afraid of doing this." He lifted her left hand.

"Asking me?"

"You told me flat out that you would never depend on a man."

"I did say that."

"I think it's just smart to be in control of your life, Sophia. I understand that and only want to be with you, always."

"I love you, Jack. You make me want to believe. You're worth the risk."

He dragged her in for another hug and then a kiss and then another. When they finally came up for air, Sophia giggled and cried all at once.

"I want a honeymoon," she said.

"All right. Where to?" he asked.

"Hawaii."

Now Jack's mouth dropped open as his breath caught.

"I want you to find your father's people, Jack. We'll go together. I'll help you."

"'I'll help you,'" he repeated on a whisper. "Those might be words as important as 'I love you.'"

"What about my job?" she asked.

"I'd never ask you to leave your work, Sophia. It's important, what we do. The world needs protectors."

She smiled up at him and in her sparkling eyes he could see a brave woman, a survivor and a life mate who would walk with him on the journey of their lives. Jack had finally found his direction and his true path, here with Sophia.

* * * * *

Can't get enough of
APACHE PROTECTORS: TRIBAL THUNDER?

Check out the earlier books in the series:

TURQUOISE GUARDIAN
EAGLE WARRIOR
FIREWOLF

Available now from Mills & Boon Intrigue!

He stared directly into her eyes, intense and sincere. "I believe you."

She stamped down the hope she felt at his words, tried to be logical. "Why?"

"My gut is telling me you're innocent." His gaze went to the gun and then back to her face. "Relatively innocent."

A smile twitched her lips, and she felt the sudden, ridiculous urge to laugh at the predicament she'd gotten herself into. She'd never so much as gotten a parking ticket her whole life and in one day, she'd stolen a gun off one federal agent and taken another one hostage.

"Just level with me, Juliette," Andre said, his deep brown eyes imploring, almost hypnotizing in their intensity.

A shiver worked its way up her body that had nothing to do with fear. Letting her attraction for this man lull her into trusting him was a bad idea. Whether or not he believed her story, he was still a federal agent.

BODYGUARD WITH A BADGE

BY
ELIZABETH HEITER

MILLS & BOON

First Published in Great Britain 2017
By Mills & Boon, an imprint of HarperCollins*Publishers*
1 London Bridge Street, London, SE1 9GF

© 2017 Elizabeth Heiter

ISBN: 978-0-263-92892-1

46-0617

Our policy is to use papers that are natural, renewable and recyclable products and made from wood grown in sustainable forests. The logging and manufacturing processes conform to the legal environmental regulations of the country of origin.

Printed and bound in Spain
by CPI, Barcelona

Elizabeth Heiter likes her suspense to feature strong heroines, chilling villains, psychological twists and a little romance. Her research has taken her into the minds of serial killers, through murder investigations and onto the FBI Academy's shooting range. Elizabeth graduated from the University of Michigan with a degree in English literature. She's a member of International Thriller Writers and Romance Writers of America. Visit Elizabeth at www.elizabethheiter.com.

For my amazing agent, Kevan Lyon.
Thank you for believing in me.

Acknowledgments

Thank you to Paula Eykelhof, Denise Zaza, Kayla King
and everyone involved in bringing *Bodyguard with a
Badge* to shelves. Thanks to fellow Intrigue authors
Barb Han, Janie Crouch and Tyler Anne Snell for
#AllTheWords. And thanks to my family and friends
for their endless support, with a special thanks to my
usual suspects for their manuscript feedback and
support: Chris Heiter, Robbie Terman, Andrew Gulli,
Kathryn Merhar, Caroline Heiter, Kristen Kobet, Ann
Forsaith, Charles Shipps, Sasha Orr, Nora Smith and
Mark Nalbach.

Chapter One

Andre Diaz lurched upright, disoriented and unable to see through the thick smoke swirling in his bedroom. He sucked in a breath and instantly choked, even as his tired brain attempted to figure out what was happening.

"Andre! Get up!"

His older brother's voice cut through his growing fear and Andre threw off his covers and jumped out of bed, almost tripping.

"We have to move," Cole told him, his ever-calm voice laced with barely contained panic.

Andre stumbled through the dark room, each breath labored. Out in the hallway, light beckoned, but as he joined his brothers in the doorway, he realized it wasn't because someone had flicked a switch.

The house was on fire.

"Hold on to me," Cole insisted. "Marcos, grab Andre. Don't let go. Come on."

Andre clutched his older brother's shirt and he felt his younger brother's hand on his shoulder as the three of them hurried toward the stairwell. They ducked low to avoid the flames that seemed to be leaping all around them.

The walls were on fire. Andre looked up. The ceiling was on fire, too.

Finally, they reached the stairs and Cole picked up the pace. They were both coughing now, so whatever Cole yelled back at him, Andre couldn't understand.

His eyes were watering, too, and he couldn't see anything but flames lunging closer as he stumbled down the stairs, faster and faster, desperate for air. But every breath brought smoke deeper into his lungs.

Then, he could see it. The door was open. He could see outside.

But could he reach it? His lungs hurt, and his body was starting to shut down from lack of air. His eyes felt swollen and useless, and even though Cole was a step ahead of him, he knew it only because he still clutched his brother's shirt. All he could see was that open doorway ahead, the sun beginning to rise on the horizon.

But finally, he was stepping into the fresh air, falling onto the newly cut grass, coughing and coughing, feeling as if he'd never get oxygen into his aching throat.

Through his haze, he heard Cole screaming. Then he saw one word form on his brother's lips: "Marcos!"

Andre looked back and realized Marcos hadn't made it out behind him. The doorway he'd come through was now engulfed, flames reaching for the front porch.

Andre tried to get to his feet so he could race back to the house, but his knees kept buckling. Then Cole's arms were around him, holding him in place, even as Andre yelled for his younger brother. But no one else was coming through that flaming doorway, and suddenly sparks flew from the post on the front porch, and half of the roof collapsed.

Andre jerked awake in his bed, his heart thundering against his ribs. He was drenched in sweat, his breathing erratic, as though he was still inside that burning house.

"You got out," he reminded himself, throwing his covers aside and getting out of bed on unsteady feet. "We all got out."

The fire had happened eighteen years ago, when he'd been just fourteen. The first few years afterward, he'd woken up regularly, panicking until he remembered that his younger brother had escaped another way. He hadn't dreamed about that night in years.

But he knew what had brought it on: the call he'd gotten last night at work. A family trapped inside their house. The father had set it on fire and was holding a gun on his wife and son, determined that they'd all die together. The firefighters couldn't go inside to save them without being shot.

The FBI had gotten the call from the local police, whose only sniper was out of commission. Andre's team had gone in, and he'd been the one to take the shot from the roof of the house across the street, through the second-story bedroom window.

He'd killed a man in front of his family, but it meant the firefighters had been able to enter the house. They'd gotten the wife and son out, alive and amazingly unharmed. Except for the nightmares they'd both surely have for years, too.

Beside his bed, a persistent buzzing caught his attention and he realized he'd been receiving texts. He swiped a hand over his forehead and grabbed the work cell phone he always kept close.

It was a triple-eight call from his boss at the FBI's elite Hostage Rescue Team, where he'd worked for the past four years as a sniper. Triple eight meant an emergency.

Of course, at HRT, they were already part of what the

FBI called their Critical Incident Response Group. So no call was low priority. But triple eight was as high as it got.

It meant no time for even a two-minute shower, so he tossed aside the boxers he'd been wearing and traded them for cargos and a T-shirt, yanking up his flight suit over it. His FBI-issued rifle and the rest of the gear he carried on a mission were in a lockbox in the trunk of his sedan.

Andre double-timed it down the stairs of his little house and hopped in his car, still trying to shake off his dream, and hoping it wasn't an omen for what was to come today.

The information in the text was minimal, but it was enough to get his adrenaline going for a different reason. They were going to a hostage call at an office building not far from where he worked at Quantico. Multiple gunmen, multiple hostages.

At 7:00 a.m., the sun was just beginning to rise, and it instantly took him back to the dream he'd just left, those moments outside the house, frantic to get to Marcos. He slapped his siren on the roof, punched down on the gas and wove around a long line of cars. "Mind on the mission," he told himself.

He dialed his partner, Scott Delacorte, and soon Scott's gruff voice filled his car. "We don't know much. The gunmen are in a marketing company office up on the third floor. Employees there start early and leave early, to avoid some of the rush-hour traffic. So we could have a lot of hostages, but we're hoping none of the other companies in that building have started the day yet. Police are holding the scene."

"Any news on what the gunmen are after? Any communications? Do we know if they've fired shots?" Was this a hostage-taking situation or an active shooter?

"The call came in to 911 ten minutes ago from a secretary who managed to hide in the storage room. She told the operator there were multiple armed men—at least three—and at the time of the call, they hadn't started shooting. She thought they were searching for someone."

That might be good or bad. Good if the person they were after hadn't arrived yet; maybe the gunmen would leave, and HRT could nab them on the way out. Bad if the gunmen had a specific target they wanted to take out. Once they did, they might eliminate anyone else in their way.

Still, the setup was strange. A single gunman searching for a particular victim—maybe a spouse or stalking target—wasn't that unusual. But multiple gunmen, after one target? That was overkill. What single target at a small, independently owned marketing company would warrant that kind of firepower? It didn't quite fit.

"That's odd," was all Andre said aloud.

"Agreed. But the secretary's in the storage room. Who knows how well she's pegged the situation?" The screaming siren from Scott's end stopped. "I'm here. Gonna set up and get on the scope. Northwest corner, we've got woods, a nice trail that actually leads right out the back door of the office building and up a little hill. The whole thing is pretty hidden. I'm looking through my binoculars right now and I see a good sniper perch about a quarter mile up. How far out are you?"

"One minute."

"Make it faster," Scott said and cut the connection.

Andre pushed the gas pedal down to the floor, blaring his horn over the siren and whipping around the few drivers obnoxious enough not to get out of his way. Thirty seconds later, he was at the office complex.

He flashed his badge to the police officers stationed at the entrance to the complex, which was nestled in the woods. Thankfully it was off the beaten track enough that they shouldn't have to worry about the potential collateral of the pedestrians and gawkers they'd get if they were closer to the city.

The cops let him pass, and he flew into the parking lot, screeching to a stop next to his boss's big green SUV. He yanked his gear out of the trunk as his boss gave him the rundown.

"We don't know much more than what Scott already gave you," Froggy told him. The guy had been a navy SEAL before joining the FBI, and the nickname was a humorous nod to his past. "Go join Scott and get me some more intel."

"You got it." Andre slung his rifle over his back, slipped his gear bag over his shoulder and slid his Glock pistol out of the holster he'd put on while he drove. He popped his earbud in, and turned on the bone mic at his neck. It nestled against his voice box, so all he'd need to do was speak and his whole team could hear him. Then, he was on the move.

He ran around the corner of the office building, Glock ready in case one of the gunmen decided to try to rabbit out the back. Then he spotted the half-hidden trail Scott had mentioned and jogged onto it, increasing his pace even as the incline up the hill got more and more steep. Every minute counted for the hostages inside.

"I cleared you a spot," Scott said, not taking his eyes off the scope as Andre settled into the patch of dirt his partner indicated.

Andre dropped his gear beside him and set up his rifle, dialing in the specifics for wind and altitude that Scott read off to him. And then he was peering through his own rifle scope, into the third floor of the office building.

He scanned from left to right across the whole floor, taking in the situation. A gunman stood in the front room, a Bluetooth receiver in his ear and tattoos climbing out the top of his shirt. He clutched a semiautomatic pistol with both hands, but he kept checking the paper he held crumpled against the stock of his gun. On the floor around him were eight men and women in business clothes. Some held on to one another, two were in tears, and they were all avoiding the gunman's gaze as though he'd already warned them not to look at him. But no one appeared to be injured. Not yet.

Andre pulled back up to the gunman, dialing in a little closer, trying to see what was on the paper that was so interesting. He was speaking angrily, but Andre didn't think he was talking to the hostages.

"Phone's on," Scott said, seeming to read Andre's mind.

They'd been partners for two years now, and Scott had become practically a third brother to Andre. Half the time on missions, they didn't need words at all. "We know who he's talking to?"

"I think it's the second gunman."

Andre swung farther right and found the other guy. He, too, had a cell phone, clipped to his waist, with an earphone in one ear. He held a semiautomatic, and he kept glaring down at a piece of paper as he wrenched open one door after the next, clearly searching for someone.

He pulled open another door and aimed his weapon at the woman cowering inside on the floor, surrounded by stacks of paper and printer cartridges. She yanked her hands up over her head, a phone dropping to the floor.

"Shit," Scott said as the gunman's grip shifted and Andre was able to zoom in closer and get a glimpse of what was on the paper he held.

"It's not her he's looking for," Andre said, keying his mic so the rest of the team could hear. "This guy's carrying a picture of a woman. Mid- to late-twenties, blond-ish-brown hair." A beautiful woman, with a sad smile. Not an easy face to miss. "She's not one of the hostages in the front room."

Andre widened his view again as the gunman waved the woman in the storage closet toward the other hostages. She scurried out of the room, then dropped down next to her coworkers, as the second guy continued to open doors, looking angrier and more frustrated with every empty room.

"I thought the secretary told us there were at least three shooters," Andre said, continuing his search.

"She did, but I've only seen two. We've got operators in place right outside the front door. They're ready to storm the building if these guys start shooting, but ideally we identify the location of all the shooters first. If this goes bad, I've got the one with the hostages, okay? You take the other guy."

"Got it," Andre affirmed. But only Froggy could give the word to take any shots. If that happened, he'd have to shoot through the window and time it when the second gunman was in his line of sight, which could get dicey. The guy was heading into the back of the office now, where Andre didn't have an angle on him.

Scott swore and Andre asked what was wrong at the same time as Froggy.

"I found the last gunman."

"Where is he?" Andre asked, continuing his methodical search.

"He slipped out the back door. He's heading up the trail right now, straight for us. And the woman they were hunting for? She's with him, and he's got a gun pointed at her head."

Chapter Two

He'd found her. After all this time, she'd finally started to feel safe again, as if she didn't have to constantly look over her shoulder. But somehow, he'd found her and sent his goons after her.

These stupefied thoughts ran through Juliette Lawson's mind as she put one foot in front of the other. Her body had gone numb, but she could still feel the exact spot where the cold metal of a gun barrel pressed against her head.

The thug walking behind her had grabbed her just when she'd thought she was going to escape. She'd been in the bathroom when she'd heard screaming that morning. She'd peeked out in time to see three men enter, holding pictures of her. She'd never seen any of them before, but she knew why they'd come.

Initially, she'd darted back into the bathroom, hoping to hide, praying they wouldn't find her, that they'd just leave. But it soon became clear hiding wouldn't work, so she'd tried to slip down the back stairs. Just as she'd been reaching for the door to the exit, this one had come up behind her and put a gun to her head. He'd led her out the back door, out of sight of the police officers gathered in the distance and farther away from help.

She'd considered screaming, but fear had trapped it in her throat and then she'd realized if she did yell for help, he'd probably shoot.

Now, the gunman jabbed her with his weapon every few steps, pressuring her to move faster up the little dirt trail through the woods. But they were moving uphill at a steep angle, and she was wearing heels. If she picked up her pace any more, she was going to stumble. And the faster she walked, the less chance she had of figuring out a way to escape before he reached the next step of his plan.

Juliette knew the next step of his plan was to do one of two things: either get her somewhere secluded and kill her, or take her back to Dylan. It was like comparing a death sentence to life behind bars. She wasn't sure which was worse.

But she did know that if Dylan had hired him, this guy had training. Even if by some miracle, she managed to wrestle the gun away from him, he'd be able to take her down. If she ran, he'd probably shoot. And he wouldn't miss.

She tried to push aside all the regrets she felt, to focus on survival, but one regret kept surfacing. If only she'd never met Dylan Keane. Then maybe she'd still be back in Pennsylvania, still trying to sell the paintings she loved in galleries, instead of trying to be invisible as a graphic designer and spending her days buried in a cubicle.

Now there was a very good chance she wouldn't even be buried in a shallow grave. There was a good chance she was about to bleed out in the woods, and those cops who'd surrounded the office would eventually find her body. She prayed she'd be the only casualty, and the other gunmen wouldn't hurt her colleagues.

They had no idea who she really was, no idea what danger they were in just being near her. She'd never thought she'd been putting them in harm's way, because she'd never expected Dylan would send goons to her work. She'd always figured that if he tracked her down, he'd simply grab her out of her apartment one day and drag her back. Force her to live in that house again, like a prisoner. Or just kill her right there and leave her dead in her apartment until one of her neighbors noticed the smell.

Stop it, Juliette told herself. Morose thoughts weren't going to get her out of this. She needed a plan. And even though running was pointless, it was probably her best chance.

Up ahead, the trail curved. That was the spot. She'd pretend to stumble, ditch the heels. She'd be able to run faster barefoot.

Her heart started pounding so hard she could hear the blood pumping in her ears. It seemed to block out the other noises off in the distance—the birds chirping, the FBI agent in the parking lot yelling over a loud-speaker at the gunmen, even the big, furious guy behind her insisting she pick up her pace.

The curve got closer and closer, until she knew it was time. Her heart felt out of control as she let out a squeak and pretended to trip on a protruding branch, going down on her knees and sliding out of her heels as though they'd come off in the fall. The guy's hand closed around her arm, but the gun came down. It was no longer pointed at her head.

This was her chance.

She readied herself to shove upward, to knock him down and run as fast as she could, zigging and zagging the way Dylan had taught her, back before he realized he might not want her to escape a bullet. But she never had the chance to try.

A figure flew out of a tree, crashing past her and onto her attacker in a tangled blur of arms and legs and guns.

Juliette yelped and scurried free. The new man was armed too, a Glock strapped to his hip, and a whole slew of other equipment attached to his body that suggested he was in the military. He was all motion, just smooth brown skin and bulging muscles and full of confidence as he drew back a fist and sent it crashing into the gunman's jaw.

The gunman took the hit with a growl and tried to flip the new guy, but Juliette didn't wait around to see who'd come out on top or how long the fight would last. She caught a glimpse of intense, dark brown eyes on her rescuer and decided he was some kind of Special Operations soldier. She had no idea what he was doing in the woods, but she said a silent *thank you* and stumbled to her feet, darting off the trail.

She was pretty sure the soldier was going to prevail in the fight happening behind her, but even if he wasn't with the law enforcement surrounding the office complex, he'd surely turn her over to them.

And then there was no question what would happen next: she'd be headed straight back to Dylan, straight back to the life she thought she'd finally escaped.

"WHAT DO YOU think you're doing?"

A strong hand closed around her arm, bringing Juliette to a stop. Her bare feet almost slid out from underneath her on the trail, which was slippery from the leaves that had begun falling off the trees a week ago. Before she could go down, her rescuer dropped his hand from her arm to her waist, catching her.

"It's over," he said, his voice reassuring. His fingers pressed into the top of her hip, keeping her from making another run for it, away from everyone. "The guy's in handcuffs. You're safe."

Juliette stared up at him. He probably had four inches on her height of five foot six, just enough so she had to tip her head back to look him in the eyes. They were deep brown, almost hypnotizing the way they were locked onto hers as though he didn't see anything else in the world right now.

She knew it was only because he was trying to convince her everything was going to be okay, but that didn't stop a shiver of awareness from working its way up from her toes.

Thank goodness he misunderstood the reason. He told her, "I'm Andre Diaz, with the FBI. I promise you, you're safe with me, okay? And we're going to get your colleagues out of there. But right now, I need you to come with me."

Instead of letting go of her waist, he led her back down the trail toward the parking lot, guiding her like she was in shock. Which maybe she was, because she couldn't believe any of this was happening.

She'd been on the run for three years. She'd managed to hide, to somehow stay one step ahead of Dylan all that time. And now it was over.

Those first few months, heck, that entire first year, she'd jumped at every noise and slept with the lights on most nights. But lately, she'd found herself relaxing.

She couldn't remember the last time she'd looked over her shoulder or run to her car clutching her mace in one hand, certain one of Dylan's lackeys was on her trail.

She'd let her guard down, created a new life for herself. It hadn't been a full life, but it had been *hers*. And now it was over.

Glancing at Andre as he helped her down the trail, carefully avoiding any sharp sticks or rocks on the trail because of her bare feet, tears blurred her vision. Not out of fear, but because someone cared enough to bother helping her. She blinked them away.

Now wasn't the time to get emotional because some guy was doing his job, because apparently some members of law enforcement really were on the side of the victims. And now *really* wasn't the time to fixate on the feel of his strong hand grasping the top of her hip as he led her to all those blinking red and blue lights in front of her office building. But she couldn't help but be hyperaware of the pure masculine scent of him beside her, the ridiculously hard bicep pressing into her back.

She dragged her feet as they hit the concrete, glancing up at the third floor where all her colleagues were, terrified because of her. And she realized Andre had carefully led her to a vehicle on a path that kept her completely out of view of the windows up on the third floor.

"Hop in here," he told her, holding open the back of an SUV with tinted windows. When she hesitated, he added, "It's my boss's vehicle. You'll be okay. It's surrounded by my team, and there's no way anyone's getting past them. When this is over, we'll get you home safely."

She hesitated once more, because she could never go home again. Not to any of the places she'd ever called home over the years.

Then, the *tat, tat, tat* of a semiautomatic boomed, followed by two more shots in quick succession, and someone let out a piercing scream.

Juliette spun toward the sound, dreading what she was going to see—who had gotten hurt because of her. But she never found out, because Andre shoved her into the SUV and dove on top of her.

The weight of him flattened all the air from her lungs, and the awareness she'd felt earlier when he'd simply had his hand on her waist multiplied, making her skin seem to buzz wherever it touched his. Even though he was simply protecting her, she was suddenly keenly aware of how long it had been since someone had held her.

She tried not to squirm and prayed she wasn't flushed deep red as he spoke into some kind of communications device she realized went from his ear to a microphone at his neck. Then just as quickly, he was helping her up.

She felt dazed, still trying to catch her breath as he told her, "It's over. All of your colleagues are okay."

"What?" The word came out breathy and filled with disbelief. How could it possibly be over that fast? And how could everyone be unharmed?

He gave her a grin that made a dimple pop on one side and said, "We're good at what we do."

She stared back at him, taking in all the details she hadn't noticed before: his cleanly shaved head, the cleft in his chin, the complete focus in his eyes. Beneath that, genuine warmth, as if he really cared what happened to her and it wasn't just his job to keep her safe for the next few minutes.

Don't fall for him, she chanted in her head. She'd just met him. She knew nothing about him, other than that he was willing to put his life on the line for others.

She'd fallen for Dylan that way: instantly. A sudden, ridiculous attraction that she'd mistakenly thought was love. She'd fallen for all the things she thought she'd seen in him that had turned out not to be true. And she was seeing all those qualities in Andre's eyes right now: the goodness, the honesty, the protectiveness. Except she suspected with Andre, they were actually real.

His gaze seemed to bore into her and then she saw something else: a reciprocal glint of attraction. It made her want to lean closer and tell him the truth about what had happened today. To go through the process she knew they'd want: hours of questioning at some police station or maybe an FBI office, to learn why hired gunmen were after her. To trust that maybe this time someone would believe her story. That maybe this time things could really change. But she couldn't take the chance.

He smiled at her and gave her a hand out of the vehicle.

One of the other agents, dressed as if he was going to war, slapped him on the back and said, "Why don't you give her a ride back to Quantico? The locals are asking us to take the lead, since these gunmen might be professionals. We're going to need a debrief."

She could tell from Andre's dimpled smile that when the questioning was over, he was going to ask her out. In another life, she would have said *yes*.

Too bad she'd never see him again after today.

"AREN'T YOU GOING to stick around and see if you can drive this woman home?" Scott teased, just as Andre thought he'd made a clean getaway.

Andre spun around in the Quantico parking lot, where they'd driven after the situation was contained. The gunman who'd fired in that office had been shot by one of HRT's operators, but the other two had been brought in wearing handcuffs. They had both gone silent as soon as they were arrested, demanding lawyers, but the FBI had been able to ID them quickly anyway, because they had criminal records. Strangely, the woman Scott was talking about had gone just as silent as the gunmen. She claimed she didn't know why they were after her, when clearly she did.

"Which woman?" Andre parried, even though he knew Scott wasn't about to let him off the hook that easily.

"Juliette. Or was it Mya?"

That was the other problem. The woman he'd rescued on that hill had identified herself as Juliette Lawson. So had her colleagues. But the name scrawled next to her picture that the gunmen had all been carrying was *Mya*.

When they'd mentioned it to Juliette, she'd gone pale and made a beeline for the women's bathroom, where she'd been for the past hour, either sick or just hiding out.

The fact was, Andre *had* planned to ask her out. From the second their eyes had met inside his boss's SUV, he'd known he was in trouble. Sure, she was gorgeous, with those wide hazel eyes framed with insanely dark lashes, and all that long, golden-tinted brown hair that had come loose from her messy bun when he'd tackled her. The soft, womanly curves that had cushioned his fall were pretty tempting, too. But what had really done him in was the way she'd stared back at him, the look in her eyes equal parts vulnerable and strong.

He'd driven her back to Quantico, making small talk on the ride, trying to get to know her a little better. She'd seemed shy, shell-shocked, but definitely interested. He'd intended to wait around until the regular agents had finished questioning her, then ask if he could make a detour to dinner on the way back to her car. But that was when he'd thought she was a simple victim.

He should have known from the beginning there was more to it, because the crime itself was so strange. Why send three heavily armed men after one small woman in a third-floor office building?

In fact, why do it in such a high-profile way at all? Why not have one man grab her on the way to her car before she made it into the office?

She was involved in something. The fact was, she was probably guilty of something. And while a woman with a little mystery had always been a draw for him, a woman who would break the law he worked to uphold was of no interest.

Andre shrugged at his partner, who'd been his friend too long not to see exactly what Andre wasn't saying. "I'm not sure I need that kind of drama."

"There's always Nadia," Scott said.

Nadia Petrova was a fellow agent, who worked as a weapons training specialist at the FBI Academy, which was located at Quantico with HRT. She'd made no secret of her interest in Andre, and it was getting more and more difficult to sidestep her hints without hurting her feelings.

"I think I want to be the one in the relationship with the bigger guns," Andre joked. The truth was, Nadia was nice enough, but there just wasn't any spark.

Scott snorted and slapped him on the arm. "All right. Well, after these last couple of calls back-to-back, I'm heading home. Froggy says you can do the same if you want. The other team is up now."

The HRT teams swapped off, so one was always on call if any emergencies came in from across the country while the other teams trained. After the week they'd had, with seemingly one crisis after the next, Andre was ready for some low-key exercises. Like rappelling out of helicopters and practicing with his MP5 for mock hostage situations inside one of the old 747-airplane hulls they kept on hand.

"See you tomorrow," Andre said, digging around in his duffel for wherever he'd stuck his keys as Scott hopped in his SUV and sped away, leaving Andre alone in a lot full of cars but empty of people.

When he'd pulled into the lot a few hours ago, there had been nowhere left to park except at the very back, so he meandered that way now, still digging for his keys. It wasn't until he was a few feet away from his sedan that his agent instincts went on high alert, warning him someone was close. Too close.

He lifted his hands into a defensive position even as his brain reminded him he was in a heavily guarded Marine base and FBI training area. Then he let out a breath and dropped his hands to his sides as he spotted Juliette—or Mya—coming around from the front of his car.

"What are you doing here?" Had she been waiting for him, crouched between the grill of his car and the big tree he'd parked underneath for a little shade? He frowned. Had she been hiding?

"Get in the car," she said, her voice wobbly.

A smile threatened. "That's what I was planning," he said, starting to rethink his plan to ask her out to dinner. Except... "Shouldn't you still be inside, talking to the case agents?"

The hand that had been wedged between her side and

his car came out, pointing a Glock pistol at him. "Get in." This time, her tone was apologetic.

He stared, dumbfounded. "Where'd you get that?" She certainly hadn't come into Quantico with a weapon. Had she taken it off someone inside? If so, that meant she was a much bigger threat than she seemed.

"I'm sorry," she said, and she actually looked it, with her big, teary eyes and her full, trembling lips. "But we need to go. I have to get out of here, which means you're going to drive me off the base."

He leaned against his car, eyeing the distance between them, gauging whether he could disarm her without the gun going off. "Why don't you tell me what this is about? Let me help you." He kept his voice calm. It was the same tone he'd used last night with the traumatized kid who'd come out of that fire clutching his mother, after watching a bullet come through the window and take out his father.

"No. Please." Desperation entered her tone as she shifted her awkward, double-handed hold on the gun. "Just get in, okay, and I promise I'll let you go as soon as you drop me off where I tell you."

She wasn't used to holding a weapon, Andre could tell. "You're going to have a hard time firing that gun with the safety on."

When she glanced down, he took one slow step forward, almost close enough to disarm her without a chance of her taking a shot. Just one more step and he could do it.

But then her eyes locked on his as she leveled the weapon at his center mass, something hard and determined in her gaze. "There's no external safety on a Glock," she replied, all the nerves gone from her voice. "Now get in. We're going for a ride."

Chapter Three

She'd just taken a federal agent hostage.

And not just any federal agent. No, she'd picked some kind of super-agent, a man who could take down an armed criminal with his bare hands. When he'd flattened her against the floor of his boss's SUV a few hours ago, she'd discovered he probably had a negative percentage of body fat. He was all hard, solid muscle.

She should be afraid of what he could do with that muscle, especially after her actions tonight, but for some reason, he made her feel safe.

Andre's hands were tense on the wheel as he drove silently away from Quantico. He hadn't said a word since they'd gotten in the car and driven past the guard and out of the gated complex. But she knew that wouldn't last much longer.

What she didn't know was what she was going to say to him.

It didn't matter that she'd emptied the gun of its bullets back in the FBI office after she'd slipped it out of an agent's holster. There was still no excuse for what she'd just done. Not even if it might well save her life.

The armed standoff at her office building had surely made the news by now. Dylan would know his goons had failed. What's more, he'd know where to find her himself. Heck, if he wanted to, he could probably get into Quantico and drive her away without anyone making a word of protest. Why would they question a fellow law enforcement officer?

"You planning to tell me what this is all about?"

Andre's question was quiet, almost a whisper, but it still made Juliette jump in her seat as his voice brought her out of her reverie.

"And would you mind aiming that gun somewhere else? I'd prefer it if you didn't shoot me accidentally."

"I'm not going to shoot you at all," Juliette blurted, then silently cursed herself.

But her words didn't seem to surprise him. He just repeated his request, and she set the gun on her lap, close enough that she could grab it, but not pointed at him anymore.

"Where are we going?" he asked when she didn't say any more.

She'd directed him to drive out of Quantico but hadn't given him a location beyond that. The truth was, she had no idea where she was going. Back to her office—where her car was—was a bad idea, because police were surely still there. And by now, Dylan would have both her work and home address.

Her apartment was off limits. All the things she'd worked hard to build for herself here, she'd have to leave behind. But that was a small price to pay for her life.

She'd planned to have Andre drop her off somewhere she could hitchhike out of town. But the exact logistics of getting out of town before the FBI found and arrested her? She hadn't quite figured those out.

He must have sensed her hesitation, because he suggested, "How about I drive you to my place?"

"What?" She gaped at him. Was this some kind of trick?

"You obviously have nowhere to go," Andre said, his voice tired. "And I think you need help. Let *me* help you."

"I just repaid you for saving my life by taking you hostage!" Juliette flushed as she said it, both at the absurdity of what she'd done and at how ridiculous she was to argue with him if he was really willing to hear her out.

"You also told me you weren't going to shoot me," Andre replied, still sounding calm and in control, even though she was the one holding the gun.

A gun that as far as he knew was loaded with bullets. And one she'd proven she knew how to use when she'd told him the Glock didn't have an external safety.

This had to be a trick. But what choice did she really have? She was tired of running. She wanted her life back. She wanted a *real* life back. Maybe if she let herself trust him, just for now, Andre could help her get that.

"Okay," Juliette agreed, amazed the words were coming out of her mouth even as she said them. "Let's go to your place."

THIS WAS A *bad idea.*

The words echoing in Andre's head sounded like his older brother, Cole. And even though it was his experience that Cole was almost always right, Andre pushed them aside and held open the door to his house for Juliette.

He watched her glance around the living room curiously, taking in the oversize couch, the comfortable chairs bracketing it, the coffee table stacked with books and coasters. He knew it appeared lived in, the kind of place often overflowing with friends and family. She lingered on the photos lining the table behind his couch—he and his brothers, he and Scott on an overseas mission, his HRT team after a joint training with some navy SEALs. His families.

"You have a nice home," she said softly. "It's cozy."

There was something wistful in her tone, as though she didn't have memories scattered all around her own place. But for some reason, he had a hard time imagining her *not* surrounded by people. Instead of asking about it, he said simply, "Thanks. Make yourself comfortable."

Right now, she seemed as far from comfortable as possible. She'd left her heels somewhere in the woods, so she'd been barefoot ever since, the hem of her slacks collecting dust. She had one hand crammed into the pocket of her cardigan, the outline of the Glock clearly visible. Her hair was a mess, with a few bobby pins valiantly trying to hold up what had started out as a bun, and leaves woven through strands that shimmered under the light. Her pale skin had been flushed from the moment she'd pointed the gun at him.

Maybe if he could get her to relax, he could get a real story out of her. And then he could decide on his next move.

When she just shifted her weight from one foot to the other right inside his door, he closed it behind her and flopped onto his couch across the room, careful not to let the hem of his T-shirt come up. So far, she hadn't thought to ask, and he didn't want to give her reason to suspect he was armed. He might be willing to bring her to his house, but there was no way he was handing over his gun.

He was giving her a lot more benefit of the doubt than

he normally would. Maybe it was the attraction he'd felt for her the second he'd seen her. More likely it was the vulnerability he kept seeing. He was a sucker for a damsel in distress.

The only problem was, there was a good chance Juliette was involved in something she shouldn't be. At the very least, she'd taken a weapon off someone, and he couldn't forget that meant she was more dangerous than she appeared.

Still, he needed her to trust him if they were going to get anywhere. He'd figure out the rest of it from there.

"Have you lived in Virginia very long?" he asked, his tone easy and casual.

She eyed him as though wondering what his angle was, but he just waited patiently, hoping to ease her into conversation.

Finally, she took some hesitant steps forward and settled gingerly on the edge of one of his chairs, far away from him. "A little while."

"I've been here for four years, ever since I got accepted into HRT." When she looked perplexed, he clarified, "The FBI's Hostage Rescue Team. The tryouts were brutal, and when they put me in a sniper role, I had to go through extra training with the marines."

She leaned back into her chair a bit, her expression intrigued, so he kept going.

"The guy you met today, the one who came down that trail we were on? That was my partner, Scott. We've worked together for two years. He's practically my third brother now." He paused, hoping she'd engage, that he could connect with her and get a real story about what had happened today.

"You have two brothers?" Her gaze went back to the

photos, probably searching for someone with any kind of genetic similarity.

"You'll never pick them out," he said with a smile. "They're my foster brothers. We look nothing alike. But we're closer than blood." Even after the fire that had destroyed their house, that had very nearly taken Marcos's life, and had split them apart into separate foster homes, they'd managed to remain family.

"That's nice," she replied, and there it was again, that wistful tone.

"You're not close to your family?"

"No. I grew up in boarding schools." She said it without anger, just a hint of sadness.

Andre cringed. He only had a vague memory of his biological family, before they'd died in a boating accident when he was five. But that vague memory was tied up in his mother's arms, holding him close; in his father's voice, reading him stories. And he had five years of a true, brotherly bond with Cole and Marcos in his second foster home. But before and after that? He knew what it was like to feel all alone, to do his best to go unnoticed because that was the safest way.

He silently cursed. He was already sucked into those wide hazel eyes. He didn't need any more reasons to feel tied to her, to protect her at all costs, even if she really belonged in jail. His gaze shifted to the bulge in her sweater where she'd stuffed the gun.

"Do you want to tell me what really happened today, Juliette? Who were those men after you?"

"I don't know."

He must have looked skeptical, because she immediately insisted, "I don't know them. But I know who hired them. They had criminal records, right? Probably in Pennsylvania?"

He leaned forward. "How did you know that?"

Her face pinched. "Because my ex-husband hired them to kidnap me."

"Your ex-husband?" Andre tried to keep the surprise off his face. He didn't know why he'd expected her never to have been married. It shouldn't matter one way or another, but he found himself disappointed. "Why would he want to kidnap you?"

She gave him a sad smile. "Let's just say that the divorce wasn't amicable. Hell, I don't even know if it's official. I filed, and then I ran. But in order for it to be approved, he has to agree to no-fault. I didn't want to go through a court date, so I didn't dare file a fault complaint."

She fidgeted on the chair, avoiding his gaze, and he knew there was more to the story. Probably a lot more.

Anger heated him, and memories flashed through his mind, images he didn't want to dwell on, from his first foster home. "Did he hurt you?"

"No." She shook her head, but still didn't meet his eyes. "But I saw something I shouldn't have seen, and he knew it. I tried to tell him I'd keep his secret, just to get him to let me go, but he wanted me close. So when I finally accepted that I was in danger, that I had to go, I just filed and ran."

"Why were you in danger?" Andre forced himself not to lean forward, not to show the aggression he was feeling toward her ex. "Why didn't you just go to the police for help? Get a restraining order against him?"

She let out a heavy breath. "I couldn't do that. He was…"

"He was what?" Andre pressed when she went silent for too long. Then his phone rang, and he saw her tense even before he checked the readout. Scott was calling.

He considered letting it go to voice mail, but if someone had spotted Juliette holding a gun on him, he didn't want his teammates swarming his house in a misguided rescue attempt. "I need to answer this," he told her. "But you're safe here, okay?"

He didn't let her argue, just picked up his cell. "Scott. What's going on?"

"You didn't see that woman—Juliette or Mya or whatever her name is—sneak out, did you?"

"Why?" Andre asked, instead of answering, because he hated lying to family.

"She left before they could question her," Scott said. "You're not going to believe this, but she actually managed to get a weapon off of Nadia in the restroom."

"Is Nadia hurt?" If Juliette had disarmed a weapons training agent who could bring fellow agents to tears using her chokehold techniques on the training mats, then Juliette was much more dangerous than he'd suspected.

"Nah, Nadia's fine. Mostly embarrassed. Apparently this woman has sticky fingers."

So, Juliette was a pickpocket. Somehow, that didn't fit. But then nothing about Juliette had fit so far. Still, taking a wallet from an unsuspecting mark on the street was a lot different from getting an agent's weapon out of its holster.

"Anyway, there's a lot more to this story," Scott continued. "And the FBI thinks the woman's in danger."

Andre's gaze sought Juliette's. She stared back at him, her eyes wide.

"What did they get from the gunmen? Are they talking yet?"

"Yeah. I spoke to Froggy. Turns out they took an initial payment for grabbing this woman, and they were expecting more when the job was finished."

"Who paid them?" Was Juliette right? Was it her ex?

"These idiots are claiming they don't know. Which is either true, or they'd worked out their stories together beforehand. They say they were approached anonymously, that it was supposed to be easy money. Grab her, do the job, then get the other half of the money when the deal was complete."

"And they didn't think it was some kind of setup? Or just take the first payment and run?"

Scott sighed. "They both seem to think a cop hired them."

"A cop?" Andre scoffed. "They think a cop hired a pack of ex-cons to kidnap a marketing employee at gunpoint out of her workplace?" He watched Juliette go pale and frowned. "That makes no sense at all. What kind of cop would send these guys in on such a flawed plan?"

"Well, it wasn't the original plan," Scott said. "Right now, because the third guy fired in that office building on FBI agents and they're all going to face some serious sentences, the two we've got in custody are tripping over each other trying to make deals. The case agents have them separated, but they're getting the same story."

"What are they saying?"

"The hostage grab out of the office building was the *criminals'* plan. They wanted it to hit the news, so their anonymous employer would see it. They were planning to grab her and demand a higher payout for her delivery."

"Okay," Andre said slowly. "That does make more

sense. So, the original plan was to grab her more quietly, then make the trade in some deserted location? Juliette for the money?"

"I wish that was the case," Scott answered. "But the plan wasn't to grab her at all. And apparently the second guy—the one you tackled on the path—was trying to double-cross the other two and get all the money for himself, so there's no love lost there."

"So what *was* the plan?" Andre demanded, a bad feeling settling in his stomach as Juliette's words came back to him, her fear of taking her ex-husband to court. And suddenly he knew. Her ex-husband was a cop. Her ex-husband was *the* cop, the one who'd hired three dangerous ex-cons to grab Juliette.

He watched her hands clutch the arms of his chair until her knuckles were bone white. And he could tell she knew the answer to his question without even hearing Scott's reply.

"They were supposed to kill her, Andre. They were told to snatch her quietly, drive her somewhere secluded, kill her and bury the body."

"This was never supposed to go public," Andre said, not taking his eyes off of Juliette.

"No. This woman was supposed to just disappear forever."

Chapter Four

"I need the truth."

Juliette bristled. "I'm not lying to you."

"How'd you learn to snatch a weapon off a law enforcement official?" Andre demanded, resting his forearms on his thighs, making all the muscles in his arms tense and reminding her that he wasn't just strong.

He was also fast.

Juliette scooted to the edge of the chair, in case she needed to make a quick getaway. What had she been thinking, coming here? She glanced at the doorway, gauging the distance.

"Too far," Andre said.

"What?" Panic hitched her voice.

"You're thinking of making a run for it. I'm telling you that you won't make it."

She put her hand on the gun in her pocket, her heart thudding frantically. What if Andre had given his partner some kind of code word in their conversation? Something to let him know to send the cavalry? If they believed Dylan instead of her...

"I'm trying to help you here," Andre said, his soft voice laced with frustration. "We just determined these thugs were supposed to kill you."

She cringed, even though it wasn't news at all. She'd known the second she'd spotted them holding her picture that Dylan had decided to kill her. That it didn't matter those years they'd spent dating, falling in love. That it didn't matter they'd pledged their lives to each other.

"Do you really think it's your best move to run, alone?" Andre interrupted her angry thoughts. "We can protect you."

"Against someone else in law enforcement?" Juliette snapped. "I've tried before. Who is anyone going to believe, me or another cop?"

He stared directly into her eyes, intense and sincere. "*I* believe you."

She stamped down the hope she felt at his words and tried to be logical. "Why?"

"You work in this job long enough and you learn. All the training, all the practice, can only take you so far. At a certain point, you just have to go with your gut. And my gut is telling me you're innocent." His gaze went to the gun and then back to her face. "Relatively innocent."

A smile twitched her lips with a sudden, ridiculous urge to laugh at the predicament she'd gotten herself into. She'd never so much as gotten a parking ticket her whole life, and in one day she'd stolen a gun off one federal agent and taken another one hostage. The truth was, they had more on her than anyone had ever gotten on her ex-husband. The smile faded.

"Just level with me, Juliette," Andre said, his deep brown eyes imploring, almost hypnotizing in their intensity.

A shiver worked its way up her body that had nothing to do with fear and she suppressed it. Letting her attraction for this man lull her into trusting him was a bad idea. No matter whether or not he believed her story, he was still a federal agent. It was still his job to make sure she answered questions about what had happened today, and after her actions over the past hour, the FBI would probably expect her to do it in handcuffs.

Besides, she'd done the whole falling hard for a man with a badge thing before, and it hadn't worked out too well for her then. She doubted things would go better a second time.

"I told you the truth. Okay, so I said he wanted to kidnap me, and I guess that was wishful thinking. I suppose I knew it. Dylan wants me dead. I've been running for years, and now he's found me. And you can believe if he—or one of his hired goons—catches up to me again, he won't make the same mistake."

"You saw something you shouldn't have seen," he repeated her words from earlier. "What was it?"

Juliette heaved out a sigh. "Not enough."

"What does that mean?"

She'd come this far. The man had brought her to his house. He was the first person in years she'd dared to tell even this much. Might as well go for broke.

"My ex was a cop—*is* a cop. I actually met him when he pulled me over for a broken taillight. He let me go with a warning, but when I ran into him a few weeks later at a club, he asked me out."

At the time, she'd thought it was some kind of fate, telling her to give Dylan a chance. Later, she'd learned that he'd run her plates, gotten her name and pulled her up on social media. Someone had tagged her at that club, and he'd gone there, specifically intending to bump into her. When he'd finally told her the truth on their honeymoon, she'd been flattered. Now she wondered if it had been a warning sign she'd been too infatuated to see.

"What's his name?" Andre asked tightly.

"Dylan. Dylan Keane."

"From Pennsylvania?"

"That's right. But if you're planning to dig up his file, don't bother. He's got a perfect record at the department. He actually got a commendation from the mayor right after we were married. No one will ever believe he's dirty."

"That's what this is about?" Andre pressed. "That's what you saw? Something to do with his work?"

"Yeah. Have you ever heard of Kent Manning?"

Andre's eyes narrowed and his head tilted back, as though he was trying to remember where he'd heard the name.

"The businessman who was killed," she prompted.

"That's right. He was a multimillionaire, if I'm remembering correctly. They found him tossed in the lake in some small town in…"

She could tell the instant he realized. "Right. A small town in Pennsylvania. *My* small town in Pennsylvania."

"But they caught the guy who killed him. He's serving a life sentence, isn't he?"

"He is. Chester Loews was Manning's direct competitor. With Manning out of the picture, Loews's company was poised to become the biggest logging supplier in the state."

"All right. That's a logical motive for murder. What does all of this have to do with your husband?"

"*Ex*-husband."

"Sorry." Andre gave her a half smile that made a dimple pop in his left cheek. "Believe me, I didn't forget that part."

Juliette swallowed, her mouth dry, and wondered what the heck that meant. Was it because he was interested in her?

Get it together, she reminded herself. "Anyway," she continued, hoping she wasn't flushed beet red, "what I overheard was my husband meeting with Boyd Harkin. He was Manning's second-in-command, and when Manning was murdered, Harkin took over the company. He was originally a suspect, too, but the evidence against Loews was so overwhelming, it was a slam dunk. Case closed."

"But you think Harkin actually killed Manning?" Andre guessed. "You think Loews was framed?"

"I think they were working together and only Loews got caught."

Andre frowned. "If that's the case, then why wouldn't Loews turn on Harkin? Share the prison sentence?"

"I don't know."

"Okay." He was clearly trying hard to be patient. "Why do you think they were working together?"

"My ex-husband and his partner were working the Manning murder case, and I saw Harkin hand my ex-husband a bag." She'd come home early, unexpected, from her studio because she'd been sick. Harkin had been standing in her kitchen, a big hulk of a man who looked unnatural in a business suit. He'd handed over a brown paper bag, as though he was playing a part in a movie. "Dylan told Harkin he'd keep him out of it, but there was nothing he could do for Loews now."

"Those were his exact words?" Andre asked.

"Yeah. I thought Dylan was getting the bag to make

sure any evidence against Harkin found during the murder investigation would disappear."

From the way Andre was nodding, he agreed. "And you think that bag contained a payoff?"

"I know it did. I found it later, stashed up in our closet. Dylan thought I didn't know he hid things there, but I'd seen him do it before."

"You'd seen him take money before?"

"No." She gave a sad smile, because not all of her memories of Dylan were bad. She'd loved him once, enough to marry him. "Presents he'd bought me."

Andre nodded, understanding on his face. "So, what made you run? Did Dylan know you'd spotted him and Harkin?"

"No. They were so busy talking, they never heard me come in."

"Did he notice the money was moved? What?"

"No. Worse."

"You confronted him."

It wasn't a question, but Juliette answered anyway. "Yes. At first I was sure Dylan would turn him in, but every few days I'd check, and the money was still there. So finally I asked him. I thought for sure he'd tell me there was an undercover operation happening, that they were going to arrest Harkin any day now."

The memory burst forward in her mind, the moment she'd replayed so many times in the past three years. At first, she'd wished she could take it back, that she'd never seen Dylan accept the money, that she could just stay ignorant. Then, she'd wished to take back different moments, like the instant she'd said *yes* to his marriage proposal, practically before he could get the question out. Even the more hesitant *yes* when he'd first asked her out.

"He came home late because he'd been working a big case, but all excited about some cabin one of his buddies was going to lend him for the weekend. He wanted us to go away, just the two of us. Then I told him what I'd seen, and I knew the second I did it that our marriage was over."

Sadness and pity and some other emotion she couldn't quite pinpoint flashed across Andre's face, and she got back to what mattered now. "He told me I needed to forget I'd ever heard that conversation."

A tremor went through her, recalling the fury in Dylan's voice, the hard glint she'd never seen before in his eyes. "He said if I ever told anyone, I was signing my own death warrant."

ANDRE FOUGHT HARD to keep his expression neutral, not to let Juliette see how badly he wanted to smash her ex's face in with his fist right now. He was pretty sure he was failing miserably.

She gave him a shaky smile. "This is why I was trying to run. I can't have my name connected to any kind of investigation or he'll find me."

"You do know there's not some kind of law enforcement bulletin that goes out with everyone's active cases, right?" Andre joked.

"Yeah, well, when the hostage situation hits the news—if it hasn't already—he'll know I'm here. The first thing he'll do is contact the FBI."

"I doubt it. That'd be pretty suspicious."

She snorted. It should have been ugly, but somehow it was cute. "Trust me, he'll come up with a story everyone will believe. He's done it before."

"What do you mean?" Andre asked, remembering

her comment that she'd tried to get help in the past, and no one had believed her. "You tried to report him, didn't you?"

"Yeah." She sighed and sank back into the chair, her head dropping back and her hands going limp at her sides.

It would be easy to jump up and snatch the gun off her lap now, but he didn't. He just waited for her to start talking.

"Stupidly, I went to my local department, where he worked."

"That's not stupid. It's logical," Andre said, even though she probably should have gone to the FBI.

"Maybe it would have made a difference if I'd done it that night, instead of waiting to see if I'd misunderstood. But by the time I finally got the courage to turn him in, he'd already set the groundwork. They were expecting me. He'd told the chief that I'd..." She flushed, her voice getting quieter as she finished, "That I'd had a miscarriage and was suffering from severe depression."

"Did you?" Andre asked quietly, not even realizing that he'd reached out to take her hand until she lifted her head and looked at it, perplexed.

But she didn't pull hers away. She just shook her head and continued, "No. But he said the doctor had put me on medication and I was having delusions that everyone was out to get me."

"And they bought it?" Andre asked with disbelief. "Even when you told them specifics about the money?"

"I never got that far. I tried to talk about Dylan meeting with Harkin, but they just patted me on my head and sent me home. The chief *literally* patted my head, as if I was a child. And when I got home that night..." She trailed off, as a shiver visibly went through her. "Anyway, that was when I knew I had to run. And I've been running ever since."

"Three years," Andre said, doing the math from the time he remembered seeing Manning's death in the news.

"Yeah. Twice before, he's caught up to me, but I managed to keep running, start over yet again. I thought this time I'd finally gotten away. I should have known better. I'm never going to be free of this."

"Everything is different now," Andre promised her.

"How?"

"This time, you've got help." Andre squeezed her hand. "We're going to nail him to the wall for this."

He could see hope spark in her eyes, but just as quickly, she seemed to push it down. She carefully pulled her hand free and twisted it nervously in her lap. "How? All we have is the word of two criminals who don't even know who hired them. And me. A woman using an assumed name who's probably got a warrant out for her arrest now, too."

Andre's mind warred with what to ask next—how she'd managed to get that gun off Nadia in order to earn that possible warrant or what her real name was. He should ask about the gun, since knowing her ex's name meant he could track hers down. But somehow, the question that came out of his mouth was, "What's your real name? It's Mya, isn't it?"

Her nose crinkled. "Technically, yeah. But Juliette's my middle name. I've gone by Juliette most of my life."

"Kind of a strange choice for a fake name, then," Andre commented.

"Yeah, probably, but I'm sure Dylan expected me to use Mya and a different last name." He must have looked confused, because she added, "He called me Mya. He was the only one who did when we met, and we were only married for a year, but over the time we knew each other, my social circle just kept shrinking, and somehow I ended up in his. So by the end, no one called me Juliette anymore."

"Controlling," Andre muttered.

"It's not what you think. He wasn't cruel or abusive or anything, just…" She seemed to search for the right word, finally settling on *manipulative*.

Andre thought about arguing, because her relationship with her husband sure sounded abusive—maybe not physically but definitely psychologically. But the truth was, no matter the attraction he'd felt from the second he'd met her or how he wanted to help her now, her relationship with her ex wasn't any of his business. So instead he just said, "You wanted to reclaim the name for yourself."

"Exactly. I wasn't Mya Moreau anymore or Mya Keane. I was Juliette Lawson. Lawson was my grandma's maiden name." She fidgeted. "I got some fake documents, just enough to get me by—a driver's license and a social security number. I knew how from hearing Dylan talk about some of his cases. Anyway, my grandma and I were close when I was little, back in England. She was my rock, so that's why I wanted to use her name. It wasn't until after she died that my parents sent me away to boarding school here in the US."

He made a face.

"They weren't bad people. They just didn't know what to do with a kid. The boarding school was them trying to provide for me in the best way they could." She shrugged. "I always suspected it was because of my grandma that they didn't do it sooner. I know I should have picked a totally random name, but I didn't think…" She flushed and trailed off.

Still, he could guess what she was going to say. She didn't think her husband paid enough attention to what she wanted or who she was to know her grandmother's maiden name. But he was a cop; presumably, he knew how to chase a trail.

"None of that matters now," Andre said. "What matters is we figure out how to turn the tables on him." He tried to keep his tone even, but he could hear the aggression in his voice when he said, "It's time for Dylan to be the one jumping at shadows."

She stared back at him, shadows beneath her eyes and a weary slump to her shoulders. "How are we going to do that?"

"It's time to call in reinforcements."

Chapter Five

These were *some* reinforcements.

Juliette actually had to work to keep her jaw from dropping as Andre opened the door and ushered in two men who couldn't look more different than him. He introduced them as his brothers.

"We're not blood related," Cole Walker, Andre's older brother, said.

Clearly, he'd misunderstood her gaping. Thank goodness. She wasn't sure what she'd been expecting, but two men equally as attractive as Andre hadn't been it.

Cole had about two inches on Andre, and with his pale skin, light blue eyes and reddish-blond hair, they were total opposites. Throw in Marcos Costa, the youngest brother, with his jet black hair and piercing bluish hazel eyes, and no one would ever pick any of them as brothers. And yet they acted more like family than anyone who shared blood with her.

And, as she'd learned in the past two minutes, they all worked in law enforcement. Andre, in the FBI; Cole, a police detective just like her ex-husband; and Marcos, a DEA agent.

Women probably saw them together at family outings and wanted to suggest a *Hot Men of Law Enforce-*

ment calendar. Still, as attractive as his brothers were, it was just Andre who made her pulse jump whenever she stared at him.

Which made no sense, because they barely knew each other. Besides, she should have learned her lesson when it came to instant attraction.

"—not quite what we were expecting," Marcos said, humor in his voice, and Juliette realized that not only had she not been paying attention, but he'd been talking to her.

"Uh, sorry," she mumbled.

"Juliette had a long day," Andre said, earning inscrutable glances from his brothers.

Clearly, they both wondered why he was risking his career to help her. But the family loyalty ran deep, and they walked into Andre's living room without a word, plopping onto the chairs on either side of the couch.

"What weren't you expecting?" Juliette asked, trying to catch up.

"You," Marcos responded with a dimpled grin as he flung his arms over the back of the chair and got comfortable.

"Knock it off," Andre said.

Although Juliette wasn't quite sure what he meant, she could tell Marcos was trying not to laugh. Cole was giving him a brotherly warning look, but underneath it, he seemed amused, too.

She had the distinct feeling that she was either the butt of a joke she didn't understand, or Andre's brothers thought something more scandalous was happening between her and Andre than a simple felony. Abducting a federal agent at gunpoint was surely a felony, she thought, then tried not to dwell on it.

Andre sat on the couch, and since it was the only seating left, Juliette joined him there, sticking close to the opposite side. No need to tempt herself even further by getting within touching distance of Andre. But nerves still shot through her at his nearness.

She scooted even closer to the far side, shifting so the armrest would hide her weapon. She'd kept her arm strategically placed over the bulging pocket of her cardigan since Andre's brothers had arrived, but she was pretty sure neither of them had been fooled.

"So, what's the plan?" Cole asked. "Get us up to speed here."

When Andre explained the last few hours—glossing over her armed abduction—Cole seemed considerably less amused.

She fidgeted, not liking the idea of Cole and Marcos thinking poorly of her. Their opinions shouldn't matter, but it was obvious how close they were to Andre, and already *his* opinion of her had become very important.

The three men were silent for a long minute, until Marcos burst out, "What a bastard."

It took her a minute to realize he was talking about her ex-husband. A tentative smile bloomed.

"We start there," Cole said, nodding at Marcos as though he was agreeing with his brother's assessment.

Juliette's shoulders slumped and she hadn't realized until that moment how tense she'd felt through Andre's explanation. Although he'd painted it as though her word was all he needed, she'd had no idea what reaction to expect from Cole and Marcos.

Even her own parents hadn't just blindly believed her when she'd tried to ask them for advice. They'd insisted she must have misunderstood what was happening. Then, they'd gone back to their own lives in England and hadn't bothered to check back in with her. She wondered what they thought now, if they'd heard about her in the news during the three years since she'd disappeared, and tried to push down the guilt.

"Start where exactly?" Juliette asked. "I wish I did, but I don't have any proof of the payoff."

"Well, technically, you do. Your eyewitness testimony," Cole said. "But that's not actually what I meant. I think we should investigate this attempt on your life. These cons took a payment for it, right?"

Andre nodded.

"So, there's a trail. We just need to find it."

"How?" Marcos asked. "We don't exactly have the legal authority to go for a warrant. This isn't our case. But I'm sure the Bureau will be doing that. What about Scott? Can he help?"

"I want to give him plausible deniability here," Andre replied. "He doesn't know Juliette came home with me. Right now, the FBI is searching for her. I don't want him to need to lie for me. Besides, HRT won't be handling the criminal investigation. That'll get handed off to the Washington Field Office."

"So, ask the WFO agents," Marcos suggested. "They'll share, won't they?"

"If they can find the money trail," Cole said. "But if these criminals don't even know who paid them, I'm betting it's pretty hidden. I know someone who can help."

"Shaye?" Marcos guessed, that same smile flickering on the corners of his lips that had been there when he'd spotted her in Andre's entryway.

"Yes, Shaye," Cole replied.

"You sure this isn't an excuse to see her again?" Marcos teased.

"Whether it is or not," Andre jumped in, "Cole is right." He looked at Juliette. "Shaye Mallory is some kind of computer forensics genius who used to work for Cole's department. If anyone can find a trail, it's her. Ask her," he told Cole. "But make sure she's careful. I don't want to spread it around why we're digging."

"Not a problem," he said, sitting a little straighter.

Even Juliette could tell he had a crush on this woman. The only question was why Shaye hadn't jumped at the chance to go out with him. She glanced between the brothers. The same was true of all three of them. What if Andre had a girlfriend? Maybe she'd misread his intent to ask her out when he'd saved her life in the woods this morning.

Wow, had it really been less than twenty-four hours since she'd been on her way to work, thinking everything was going to be normal today? Exhaustion hit so hard she couldn't stop herself from sinking into the cushions.

"I think that's our cue," Cole said.

"You take the big hardship and talk to Shaye," Marcos teased Cole, "and I'll start digging into the Manning murder, see if I can get any traction there."

"And I'll check into Dylan Keane," Andre said, a determined edge to his voice.

It wasn't until Andre stood to walk his brothers to the door that Juliette realized they were leaving because of her. She tried to sit upright again, get focused, but the stress of the day had finally caught up to her, and her body didn't want to obey.

"Thank you," she called after them.

Then Andre was back, scooping her off the couch as if she weighed nothing.

She squeaked—actually squeaked—with surprise and looped her arms around his neck for stability. He smelled vaguely of the woods he'd been running through this morning. On him, the scent of pine managed to be an aphrodisiac. Her voice came out breathy when she asked, "What are you doing?"

"Taking you to bed."

Suddenly, she wasn't tired at all. Her body came alive, sensitive to every inch of his arms looped under her back and knees, the solid warmth of his chest pressed against her side. She looked up to discover his face was much closer than she'd expected. If she just tilted her head back and snuggled closer, she could trace her lips over the adorable cleft in his chin, over the tiny dots of scruff just starting to come in, to his mouth.

Her throat went dry at the thought, and her pulse picked up until surely he could feel it. When his gaze met hers, his pupils instantly dilated.

She stared up at him, anxious for him to dip his head and kiss her but not wanting to break the anticipation. She let her gaze slide down to his lips and then back up to his eyes, so there was no mistaking what she wanted.

Some logical part of her was screaming a warning about the last time she'd taken a chance on a man in law enforcement, but logic was *not* winning against the desire in Andre's eyes. She could feel the pace of his breathing change beneath her, and his fingers curled into her arm and her leg where he held her. His head lowered, infinitesimally slowly.

Just when she was gripping his shirt to pull herself toward him, he straightened and picked up his pace, striding into a room and dropping her on the center of the bed.

Surprise made her laugh, then nerves kicked in. Kissing Andre was one thing, but she wasn't sure she was ready for anything more.

But he was already backing out of the room. "You should get some sleep," he said, then disappeared through the doorway, leaving Juliette alone.

ANDRE SWORE UNDER his breath as he paced back and forth in the kitchen, forcing himself to stay away from the guest bedroom where he'd just deposited Juliette. He didn't know what had happened. Despite his attraction to her, his intent had been innocent when he'd picked her up. She was obviously exhausted. He'd planned to let her get some rest.

Then she'd stared up at him as if she wanted to devour him. The memory of it heated him until he opened his freezer and stood in front of it to cool down.

What was it about this woman?

Yes, she was gorgeous, but he knew plenty of beautiful women. And yes, he had a definite thing for a damsel in distress, but despite the challenges Juliette had obviously faced, she wasn't exactly screaming for someone to save her. The woman had stolen a gun off a federal agent, for crying out loud.

He squinted over at the couch where she'd been sitting and realized he hadn't imagined it. When he'd lifted her, the gun had dropped unnoticed out of her pocket.

Andre slammed the freezer shut, then walked over and picked it up. He went to empty the bullets and realized there were none. A startled laugh burst forth. Juliette had taken him hostage with an unloaded weapon.

He knew it had been loaded when she'd swiped it off Nadia at Quantico, which meant she'd purposely emptied it before holding it on him. He wasn't sure if that made the whole situation better or worse, but he took the gun into his room and locked it up.

Then he sank down on the edge of the bed, hearing Juliette toss and turn on the other side of the wall. He should have been polite and offered her a change of clothes to sleep in, a towel and some toiletries to take a shower. But he'd been too desperate to get out of there before he acted on their mutual attraction.

It was bad enough that he'd let her into his house and promised to help her evade the law. He didn't need to jump into bed with her, too. Because if he did, he'd get way too entangled. And no matter how much he might want to, he was still thinking logically enough to know it was a bad idea.

There wasn't a good ending here. Even if he helped Juliette prove her ex-husband was guilty, there was still the matter of her stealing Nadia's weapon and him hiding her from the FBI. If he got involved with Juliette, there'd be even more hell to pay.

As if on cue, his phone rang and the readout said it was Scott.

Andre didn't have to pick up to know why Scott was calling him back. Somehow, he'd figured out where Juliette had gone.

"I can explain," he answered the phone.

"Well, that's good, because Bobby said he thought he saw you on the freeway with this Juliette woman in your passenger seat."

Bobby was one of their friends on HRT, a monster of

a guy who still managed to beat most of the team running the Yellow Brick Road at Quantico.

"I said that couldn't possibly be true," Scott continued, "because Juliette—or should I call her Mya?—was on the run, and the FBI was searching for her!"

"There's more to the story than you think."

"Well, there better be, because I don't think the FBI is going to appreciate one of their own agents hiding a fugitive."

"She was the victim," Andre reminded him.

"Until she took a weapon off a federal agent," Scott shot back.

Keeping her other illegal action under wraps, Andre said, "She emptied the bullets. You'll probably find them in the parking lot."

"Great. She still stole the gun. What's going on?"

"I'm sorry I didn't tell you when you called before, but she's in trouble, okay?"

"So you gave her a lift off FBI property and hid her when you found out she'd snatched Nadia's weapon?"

"Not exactly. I'm just trying to help her. Her ex-husband is the cop who hired those goons to kill her."

There was a beat of silence, then Scott asked, "Can she prove it?"

"If she could prove it, do you think she'd be running?"

"Touché. Well, don't you think she's better off in FBI custody, where we can keep her safe?"

"I'm keeping her safe."

Scott swore. "This isn't exactly a career-advancing move you're making here."

"Yeah, I know."

"I mean, you could be in serious trouble. If she's in

danger, the FBI will help her, but she can't just take an agent's weapon."

"Yeah, I got it," Andre snapped.

"I'm just trying to help you," Scott said softly. "What do you really know about this woman? Don't mess up your career for her."

Scott's argument was perfectly logical. Andre knew he was right. But still… "I can't walk away from her. She's totally alone, and she's got a cop gunning for her."

Although Andre had never found himself in her particular predicament, he did know exactly what it was like to be all alone in the world, and to feel as if the people who were supposed to help you had turned their backs. He'd gotten lucky, moving into the foster home with Cole and Marcos when he was nine. Before that, after his family had died, was a time he didn't want to think about too much.

The abuse had been sporadic. He'd think everything was fine, and then out of the blue, his foster father would knock him down the stairs. He'd tried to get help, but the person he'd told hadn't believed him, and he'd been too young to realize he should try again. Instead, he'd learned to be invisible.

Four years after he'd been put in that house, social services had gotten suspicious. They'd taken all the kids away, and Andre had been moved somewhere else. He'd expected the same thing, but instead, that very first day, Cole had somehow known what he'd been through. He'd told Andre that things would be different now, because he had a big brother to watch out for him.

The memories faded as Andre realized Scott had been saying something. "Sorry. What?"

There was an audible sigh on the other end of the line. "What can I do?"

"I was trying to keep you out of it. I don't want to mess you up here."

"Yeah, well, I should have realized earlier you avoided my question about whether you'd seen Juliette leave Quantico. I'm in it now. We're partners. I've got your back."

Andre smiled, knowing how lucky he'd been to have had Scott assigned as his partner. He'd gotten a whole new brother that day. "Thanks, man."

"Just try not to get us both kicked off the team for this, okay?"

Scott's tone was light, but Andre knew it was no joke. "We need to find the proof to connect her ex to the attempt on her life. And tomorrow, when I come in, I'll bring Nadia's weapon. I'll say I found it in the parking lot. It will be kind of true."

"You're coming in tomorrow?" Scott asked. "What about Juliette?" He paused. "Or do I call her Mya?"

"Juliette." Andre frowned. "Good point. I shouldn't leave her by herself. I doubt Keane could track her to my place, but I don't want to take any chances."

"Keane? That's his name?"

"Yeah. Dylan Keane. He's a cop out of Pennsylvania. She saw him take a payoff connected to the murder of Kent Manning."

Scott swore. "Okay, tomorrow I'll go see my fiancée and my sister at WFO, then use it as an excuse to drop in on the case agents, try to whisper that name in their ears and see what pops."

"I'm going to see what I can find from here."

"Good luck. And, Andre?"

"Yeah?"

"Try not to fall for this woman."

Too late. Instead of blurting his instant reaction, Andre replied, "I'll do my best. Thanks for the help."

Then he opened up his laptop. "All right, Dylan Keane. Time to dig up your skeletons."

Chapter Six

A soft *thud* woke Juliette from a deep sleep. She blinked, her heart racing, as she tried to get her bearings. She was lying under a soft blue coverlet in an unfamiliar room. For a minute, she panicked, until sleep cleared and she remembered. She was at Andre's house.

Everything was fine, she reminded herself. She tried to calm her pulse, which was still erratic, as if it knew something her brain didn't. Then she heard it again: another noise, this time a *thump.* Like someone was in the house. Someone besides Andre, whom she'd heard go into the bedroom, away from the noise, hours ago.

Judging by the darkness of the room, even with the shades partially open, it was the middle of the night. The sort of time someone would try to break in if they wanted to snatch her away while a federal agent slept in the next room.

"You're being paranoid," Juliette whispered to herself, but she slipped carefully out of bed, stepping quietly toward the chair in the corner, where she'd left her cardigan.

She swore under her breath. When she'd taken it off, she'd realized the gun was no longer in her pocket.

Even if there were no bullets, it might have been a way

to hold someone off, unless that someone happened to know she didn't like guns. She understood them, knew how to fire one, because Dylan had taught her. But they still made her nervous, and Dylan knew it. If her life depended on it, she wasn't actually sure she'd be able to fire at another person, even if she did have bullets.

Should she scream, try to wake Andre or his neighbors? If it *was* Dylan, what would he do? If he'd really sent hit men to kill her, would he be willing to take out anyone else who'd dare to help her? A shiver raced up her arms.

Dylan had caught up to her before, more than once. The first time, a month after she'd run, he'd come close. Way too close. He'd broken into her apartment in Cleveland in the middle of the night. Similar sounds had woken her up.

Her breath stalled in her throat at the memory. She'd barely slept in those first months, and every sound used to wake her. Which had turned out to be a good thing, because she'd slid out of bed and peeked around the corner, seeing him as he finally got the latch on her window open and began climbing into the apartment.

She'd run the other way, out the front door, leaving everything behind except her car keys as she leaped over multiple stairs at a time, trying to outrun him. He'd caught up to her on the second-floor landing. She rubbed her arm now, remembering the bruises he'd left behind.

Another *thump* and Juliette ripped herself out of her stupor. Two heavy bookends bracketed a handful of books on the dresser and she grabbed one of them, wielding it like a club in her shaking fist as she pressed up against the doorway, peering around the edge.

Her eyes adjusted slowly to the darkness as she slid

down the hallway, pressed against the wall. Directly ahead, ominous shapes in the living room came into focus: the couch, the chairs, the table with all of Andre's pictures. Her attention was drawn to the window. Closed. No telltale fluttering of the curtains.

A faint creak drew her attention to the room beyond the living area. She hadn't been in there, but she knew it was the kitchen, because that's where Andre had gone when he offered to make everyone coffee yesterday. His brothers had both looked at her and frantically shaken their heads, and Andre had grumbled about his coffee being just fine.

Another creak, followed by something sliding across the floor. Someone was definitely in there, and now footsteps were moving toward her. Slowly, as though the person was trying to be stealthy. She never would have heard it if she hadn't been so close, listening so carefully.

Juliette pressed herself against the wall and lifted the bookend over her head, praying it wasn't Andre she was about to bash with the heavy marble piece. But then, why would Andre be sneaking around in the dark in his own house in the middle of the night?

She held her breath as the footsteps moved a little closer. Then, a figure darted through the doorway and had her pinned to the wall before she could swing the bookend. Her panicked breath caught in her throat and her pulse skyrocketed.

She squirmed, shoving herself forward, frantic to escape and torn between screaming for Andre and keeping him out of danger.

"Juliette. Juliette, it's me."

She looked up, into Andre's deep brown eyes, filled

with concern and understanding, and embarrassment heated her. Along with intense awareness.

He was pressed against her, barely any space between them from head to bare feet. His hands held her wrists against the wall behind her. He'd changed from the cargos and T-shirt he'd been wearing earlier into a pair of pajama pants and nothing else.

Every breath she took put even less space between them, and she was overly aware of how thin her camisole was, and grateful she hadn't slipped out of her bra before climbing back into bed. His bare skin brushed her arms, surprisingly soft over the steel of his muscles.

"Juliette," Andre said again, but this time his voice was almost a growl, and she watched the worry in his eyes turn into something more carnal.

"I thought you were an intruder," Juliette said. Her own voice sounded way too high and breathy.

"I know." A smile lifted his lips, then slowly faded. His grip on her wrists loosened, and he took the bookend from her, dropping it on the carpet with a heavy *thud*.

"I was working in the kitchen." His gaze slid slowly over her face, almost a caress. "I hit the lights, planning on a quick power nap, but I guess I really fell asleep. I knocked over a couple of things, and it woke me up. Then, I heard you and——"

"And you decided to sneak up on me?" She tried to put some indignation into her voice, because he'd scared her, but it was hard to focus on being annoyed when she was working so hard not to loop her free arm around his neck and press her lips to his.

"Honestly, for a minute there, I wasn't sure it was you, the way you were obviously trying not to be heard. I wasn't sure until I came around the corner."

"And then you thought you'd tackle me anyway." Juliette cursed inwardly at the way the words came out, more flirtatious than accusatory.

He smiled again, moving in closer until his breath whispered across her lips, making her shiver. One hand was still locked around her wrist, but he moved it up, threading his fingers through hers over her head. The other hand slipped around her waist, moving slowly, as though he was giving her every chance to tell him to stop.

Instead, she closed her eyes and met him halfway. Desire made her body tingle at the first touch of his lips. He brushed them over hers, again and again and again, until she was glad she was sandwiched between him and the wall because she wasn't sure she could hold herself up. She was letting him set the pace—it was what she was used to—but she couldn't take it anymore, all those slow kisses teasing her senses.

So, she pulled her hands free and ran them up his bare arms, gaining courage at the way goose bumps pebbled his skin under her touch. When she reached his neck, instead of throwing her arms around him, she kept going, bracketing his face with her hands, and ran her tongue over the seam of his mouth.

That was all the encouragement he needed, because suddenly his tongue was dancing with hers, and excitement skipped along her nerve endings. The hand that had been tangled with hers slid into her hair, stroking through it, then down over her neck and shoulder before heading back up. She thought they were as close as they could get with clothes on, but he moved in closer still, until she could feel every inch of him, could tell how much he wanted her, too.

She tensed as doubt set in. She'd never been with anyone besides her husband. And look how that had turned out.

Andre must have felt her panic, because he backed up. Not far, but enough to put air between them. He lifted his mouth from hers and stared down at her, as though he was waiting for something.

"I—I'm sorry," she stuttered. "I don't know—"

"It's okay." He took a step back and she almost fell forward at the sudden lack of contact.

"I'm just— This is…"

"You don't need to explain," Andre said, still breathing as hard as she was. "I get it."

Somehow, she doubted that, but she kept silent. Once upon a time, she'd been sure of herself. Sure of who she was, of what she wanted out of life. She'd worked hard at those boarding schools she'd hated, earned herself a scholarship to a school with a great art program because her parents refused to pay for anything but their alma mater. She'd chased her dreams of making a name for herself as a painter single-mindedly until Dylan had swept into her life.

Then, somehow, she'd slowly lost sight of who she was, who she wanted to be, alongside Dylan. And these past few years running had still been all about him. She hadn't really thought about it—she'd been so focused on building a life as someone new—until this moment. Now it was as if she was waking up from a nightmare and trying to find her footing again.

When she didn't speak, just stood staring at him, her mind on how she'd let her life get so out of control, Andre finally said, "Maybe we should go back to bed."

His words made her want to throw caution aside and follow him to *his* bed, but instead she simply nodded.

She started to move toward the hallway again when she remembered. He said he'd fallen asleep in the kitchen, working. "What were you working on?"

"Your ex-husband."

"What?"

"I was digging into his records to see if I could connect him to Manning or the attempt on you."

Hopeful, she asked, "Did you?"

Andre shook his head. "I'm sorry. On paper, your ex seems clean. As in, perfectly, spotlessly, ridiculously clean."

Disappointment made her shoulders slump. It might not have been Dylan sneaking through Andre's house, but he was here nonetheless, still controlling her life. One bad mistake from which she couldn't ever seem to break free.

"You're not going to be able to hide forever."

The words coming through Andre's phone instantly flashed him back to the dream he'd had two nights ago, right before he'd been called in to the hostage situation. Memories rose up, images he hadn't focused on in years, of him kneeling in the grass, held back by Cole as he screamed for Marcos. Those terrifying moments when the roof had caved in, then Marcos diving through a window and Cole flattening him to the ground, putting out the flames on his pajamas. The rest of them—his foster parents and the other foster kids in the house—all standing outside in disbelief, watching their home disappear in the fire and smoke.

Something was wrong with that memory. He tried to recall more details from that night eighteen years ago, a time he'd tried hard to forget. But something about it was bothering him, and for some reason, Scott talking about hiding had made him think of the fire. He frowned, bringing the memories into clearer focus, but Scott's insistent voice pulled him back to the present.

"Froggy isn't buying that you're sick."

"Why not?" Andre asked, insulted even though he should have felt guilty since it was a lie. He'd called off work today in order to stick close to Juliette, but Scott was right. There was only so long he could do that before he'd have to return to work, so they needed to move fast on her ex.

"Uh, how about the time you showed up swearing you could still rappel out of a helicopter with a 101-degree fever? You were practically delirious, but you were sure you'd be fine sliding out of a helicopter fifty feet in the air."

"It wasn't that bad," Andre mumbled.

"Or when you told Froggy you could go right back to work after busting up your ankle?"

"Hmmm."

"Yeah. You should have been a little less eager then, because he doesn't believe simple food poisoning would keep you away from work."

"He's not going to call me, is he?" Andre had no desire to lie to his boss twice—the first time, over an answering machine, had made him feel bad enough. Besides, Froggy was a human lie detector. If they actually spoke, he'd know for sure.

"No. I told him I'd convinced you not to come in for once, that the guys didn't want to be puked on. But I don't think he really bought it. And how long can food poisoning last anyway?"

"We're off for the weekend," Andre reminded him, "and I've got some vacation days coming."

"Just deal with this mess and get back here. This woman isn't worth losing your job over." Before Andre could reply, Scott said, "Froggy's headed my way now, so I've gotta go. I'll let you know what I hear from WFO."

"Thanks," Andre said and Scott hung up.

Andre was slower to set down his cell, his mind going back to that dream as he absently sipped the coffee he'd poured himself a few minutes ago. It was just after 8:00 a.m., but he'd been up for an hour and a half already and since it had been four before he'd gone to his room last night, he was feeling the lack of sleep today.

Juliette hadn't emerged from his guest room yet, but he'd heard her tossing and turning most of the night, so he wasn't expecting to see her for a while yet. By the time she woke, he wanted to have better news than he'd had last night. Her ex may have known how to stay below the radar, but if he was crooked enough to take a payoff for murder, it was doubtful that was his first step over the line.

If he had really hired three ex-cons to kidnap and murder his ex-wife, there was a trail. And by now, he knew he'd failed and would either be heading to Virginia to try to remedy the situation himself or he'd be frantically trying to bury that trail as deep as he could. So, Andre needed to find it while it was still hot.

"Morning."

Andre looked up at the soft, sleepy voice and found Juliette standing beside him, still wearing the dirt-covered slacks and camisole. Her hair hung in waves down her back, making him want to bury his hands in it, and her eyes were a little unfocused, the way they'd been last night after he'd kissed her.

Realizing he was staring, Andre jumped to his feet and grabbed a cup. "You want some coffee?"

"Uh, sure. Black is good. Thanks."

He poured her a big cup and handed it over, watching as she took a dainty sip and then cringed.

"Sorry. I make it a little strong."

"Yeah, like motor oil," she joked, but she took another drink, this one bigger, and joined him across the kitchen table.

The moment felt strangely domestic and intimate, as if they sat across the breakfast table together every morning. Stranger still, that idea felt somehow right.

He tried not to panic and pushed the thought aside. He couldn't fall for this woman. As soon as they figured out how to pin the attempt on her life to her ex, she'd be answering to the FBI herself. Granted, given the circumstances—if they could prove it—he was sure he could convince them to let her theft of Nadia's weapon slide. But then she'd be free. And somehow, he doubted she'd be returning to the life she'd built here—the little cubicle in the marketing company and the apartment where she'd planned to leave everything and run. She'd be gone, probably back to Pennsylvania, back to the life she'd left behind before she'd married Keane.

And he'd never see her again.

"What's the plan for today?"

Her words made him shake off his morose thoughts and focus on the immediate problem.

She seemed wary, as if she wasn't sure they could really stop her ex, and he didn't blame her, after being on the run for three years. But there was hope in her eyes, too, and the weight of her expectations hit him.

The responsibility to victims was something he was used to, usually in an immediate life-or-death situation, but this was a different kind of pressure. The pressure to help her, not to let her down. Even if it meant that as soon as he succeeded, she'd disappear from his life as fast as she'd entered it.

"You hire three ex-cons for a hit, and it doesn't matter how hard you try to bury it, there's still a trail. We're going to find it."

He could see her forcing herself to look optimistic, but her voice betrayed her. "He's a cop. He's handled too many investigations to screw up. He's not going to make a mistake."

"There's no such thing as the perfect crime, Juliette. I've handled a lot of investigations, too, and I promise you this: I'm going to bring him down."

Chapter Seven

Two hours later, after Juliette showered and tossed her clothes in his washing machine, Andre sat across from her, trying to focus. But with her so close—in a borrowed T-shirt and boxers, with damp tendrils of hair falling out of the knot on top of her head—all he could think about was leaning across the table and picking up where they'd left off last night.

"What?" Juliette asked, fidgeting and making him realize he was staring.

"Sorry. You're cute in my clothes." She smelled good, too. She'd used his soap. Although he didn't think it had any scent on him, on her it was sexy.

She blushed, and he couldn't help it. He had to tease her a little more. "So I have to know. How *did* you get the gun off Nadia? I mean, she's the agent they use at the Academy when they want to scare the NATs."

Juliette's forehead creased. "Gnats?"

"NATs. New Agents in Training. Nadia can get someone in a chokehold in less than thirty seconds." She was fast, and even though she had the sort of muscles that warned you not to mess around, most agents figured they were just as well trained and could hold their own. "I know, because it's happened to me."

Juliette leaned forward, propping her chin in her hands, and grinned at him. "Really? Now, that, I would have enjoyed seeing."

"Maybe I need tips from you." He leaned forward, too, until there wasn't much space between them and the amusement on her face turned into awareness. "How'd you do it?"

She shrugged, looking a little embarrassed. "It's not really that impressive. I don't think Nadia knew I was even there when she came in. She was changing in the stall, and the holster fell close to the edge of the doorway. I just slid the gun out and left the room before she realized it was gone. I'm not even sure why I took it, except I was feeling desperate to get out of there before Dylan showed up and told the FBI some story to take me with him. You know I never would have—"

"Fired on me with no bullets?"

She leaned back, and he wished he'd kissed her while they'd been inches apart. "You knew?"

"Not until you left the gun on the couch and I checked it. But I appreciate the fact that you weren't holding a loaded gun on me."

"And yet, you took me back to your house before you realized. Why?"

He shrugged. "I could see you needed help." He could tell she was going to press for more, so he added, "Besides, in HRT, we're trained to take down people holding weapons. I didn't view you as a particularly big threat."

Her lips pursed, as if she was trying to decide whether or not to be insulted, and then she sighed. "I guess you had the right instinct. I don't like guns."

"And yet you seem to know a lot about them."

"Dylan taught me. The first time he took me to the

range, I think he just wanted to show off and impress me. Then he realized how much I hated shooting and he kept making me go back, said I needed to learn to be comfortable around them. He probably regrets that now."

Andre kept his opinion of her ex to himself. "Let's make him regret ever underestimating you." The words came out with a lot more vehemence than he'd intended.

She fidgeted again, as though she wasn't sure how to handle having someone on her side, and when she spoke again, she changed the subject. "I've been thinking about something you said earlier, and it's been bothering me."

"Okay. Lay it on me."

"You asked me why Loews would take the fall for both him *and* Harkin over Manning's death. Why wouldn't Loews turn in Harkin if they were both guilty? And I don't know."

"Well, if you're right and they *were* in on it together, my guess is Harkin had something on Loews to keep him quiet."

"Something worse than a murder charge?"

"I meant, he was holding something over the guy. Probably a threat to his family."

Juliette asked slowly, "Do you think Harkin could have done the same thing to Dylan?" She fiddled with the edge of his T-shirt, not quite meeting his eyes. "You think Harkin told Dylan to either take the money and keep quiet or he'd hurt Dylan's family?"

When Andre didn't immediately answer, she looked up at him and then shook her head. "You think I'm naive, don't you? I mean, he tried to kill me."

"You married him. Whatever your feelings are now," Andre said carefully, "you loved him once. I get that."

And he did understand it. He didn't have to like it—

especially any residual feelings she might have for the man she'd married—but he definitely got it.

She frowned. "This isn't me trying to make excuses for him. I don't want that life back. I just...I guess I'm trying to sort out in my head if he was ever the person I thought he was, or if I misjudged him from the very beginning."

"I'm sure—" Andre started, but she cut him off.

"This isn't really so much about him as it is about me." She pushed back the chair and stood, pacing in her bare feet across his kitchen. "We were only married for a year. And we didn't date that long, either. I met him about a year out of school. I've been running from him now for longer than I knew him. But the thing that bothers me most about it isn't so much that my ex-husband wants me dead."

She let out a humorless laugh. "Well, maybe it is. But how do I know if I can trust my own judgment about anything anymore? It feels as if it's not only him chasing me, but my own bad choices."

Andre slowly got to his feet, walking over to where she'd stopped and slumped against the wall. "You can't think that way. This isn't your fault."

She threw up her hands. "Maybe it is. I married the guy."

"That doesn't make you responsible for his bad decisions. Some people are really good at fooling others." He threaded his hand through hers, in part because he wanted to comfort her and in part because he'd liked the way her hand had felt in his the other night. "You're not to blame because he's manipulative. Trust me on this."

She stared down at their linked hands. "How?" she

asked quietly. "How do I know I'm not going to let the same thing happen all over again?"

"I don't know," he said softly, because how could anyone guarantee they'd never trust the wrong person? "But you can't let one bad experience stop you from living your life. It's not fair that you've been running from your life because of him. We're going to get it back for you."

JULIETTE LOOKED UP into Andre's eyes, so full of conviction, and she couldn't help herself. She stood on her tiptoes and pressed her lips to his. He tasted like the horrible coffee he'd made that morning, mixed with something sweet and addictive she was already coming to associate as being uniquely *Andre*.

For a minute, he was still, not kissing her back. But then she moved in closer and he growled in the back of his throat and settled his hands on her hips, pulling her flush against him. The sudden full-body contact reminded her that she wasn't wearing anything underneath his boxers and shirt, and from the way he slanted his head and kissed her even more deeply, he'd felt it, too.

She locked her arms around his neck, trying to lift herself up even higher to eliminate the four-inch height difference between them. Then, the hands on her hips shifted lower and in one smooth motion, he lifted her, and her legs seemed to wrap around his waist without conscious thought.

The friction of his cargo pants against her bare thighs, along with his hands stroking over her hips, sliding under the edges of her shorts, made her whimper with a need she hadn't felt in a long time. His mouth migrated from hers to the side of her neck, nipping his way down to her collarbone until her head fell back. Then, his lips were back on hers and he was carrying her down the hall.

Instead of dropping her on the bed the way he'd done the other night, he laid her down slowly, settling on top of her and kissing her leisurely, as if they had all the time in the world. As if this were something real, instead of them being thrown together temporarily. In a flash of insight, she realized this *could* have been something real, if she'd met Andre under different circumstances. If she'd never made the mistake of marrying Dylan, never made such a mess of her life. Of course, then she never would have met Andre at all.

Andre lifted his head. "Where'd you go just now?"

"Sorry." She tried to tug him back down, but he stayed where he was, watching her. She stroked her fingers over the smoothness of his scalp, down over the bunching muscles in his back, and twined her legs with his. "I was just wishing we'd met under different circumstances."

"Me, too." He propped himself up on his elbows and gave her the half grin he used whenever he was about to tease her. "So, if we'd met differently, how do you think it would have happened?" He tipped his head to the side, as though he was thinking hard. "I bet you would have hit on me at the grocery store."

She let out a surprised laugh. "No way. You would have hit on *me*. And I doubt it would have been at the grocery store."

"Why's that?"

"Do you cook the same way you make coffee?"

"Hey!" He tickled her, and trapped underneath him, she squealed. "That'll teach you to make fun of my culinary skills."

"Oh, yeah?" She stroked her foot up and down his leg,

and skimmed her hands up underneath his shirt, until the smile dropped away and his gaze turned hungry. "You make terrible coffee," she whispered, stretching up to drop kisses on his chin and mouth. "Really bad."

"Okay. You can be in charge of making the coffee."

"That's not—"

He didn't let her finish, just molded his lips to hers, until all thoughts of teasing him disappeared. She shoved her hands up higher, tugging his shirt with it, until he helped her toss it aside. Then she was tracing her fingers over the muscles on his chest and abs, and hooking her legs up higher, around his hips.

Andre traced a line of kisses from her lips up to her ear, then whispered, "I must have had a great pickup line, wherever I was."

Juliette laughed, a lightness in her that she hadn't felt in years. "I guess so," she said, then fused her lips back to his.

A sudden vibrating on his leg startled her and he reached down and pulled out a phone, sighing and rolling off of her when he saw the readout. "Give me just a minute," he told her, then put on his serious voice and answered, "Scott. What's up? Tell me Froggy isn't on his way to my house right now."

"Froggy?" she mouthed, but he just grinned at her. His look turned pensive as he listened to whatever Scott was telling him.

"And they don't know who it was?" A pause. "Did they run the number?" Another pause. "Huh. Okay, keep me updated if you hear more. Thanks, man."

Juliette sat up, tucking her knees to her chest and wrapping her hands around them as a bad feeling settled in her gut. She waited until Andre hung up, then asked, "What happened?"

"Scott had his fiancée talk to the case agents investigating the hit on you."

Juliette shivered at the terminology he used, so nonchalantly calling it a *hit*, and reminding her of what he did every day. The lust that had been warming her faded, leaving her cold. "What did they say?"

Andre slid next to her, leaning against the headboard, and tucked her under his arm. "A case with this kind of media attention, and the FBI always gets phone calls from citizens claiming to have information. We have to sort through it all, but most of the time it's nothing. But the agents got a call this morning from someone who was more interested in you than the hostage situation."

She wanted to ask if the agents had given out information about her, but they didn't know where she was, couldn't suspect she'd be here, so instead she asked, "They think it was Dylan?"

"They don't know anything about Dylan, remember? We're trying to drop the name with them, but we need to do it in a way that doesn't send them right to my door."

"Okay, so what are they doing about it?"

"There's not a lot they can do. The number went to a burner phone, so they don't know who made the call, other than it was a man and he asked about you specifically. He called you Mya."

Dread replaced the happiness she'd been feeling only a few minutes ago. "It's got to be Dylan."

"Probably. As far as we can tell, the media didn't get a hold of the name the cons had with your picture, and all your coworkers still know you as Juliette. None of them were told about it either."

"Do the agents know *anything* from this call?"

"Just that it came from Pennsylvania." He shifted to look at her. "I understand your reservations about trusting law enforcement, and believe me, I want to help you. But we're hindering our own investigation here. The best way to prove this was Dylan is to use all the FBI's resources. Which means turning yourself in."

Chapter Eight

"No way!" Juliette lurched off the bed and away from Andre.

He got up more slowly. His hands were out, as though he was trying to seem nonthreatening, but without his shirt, he looked like too many kinds of threats. "I know—"

"If you don't want to help me, fine. But I'm *not* turning myself in."

Andre sighed. "Juliette, the FBI won't let anything happen to you."

"Right." She turned and strode down the hall, into the small laundry room off his kitchen. She pulled her clothes out of his dryer, happy to discover they were mostly dry. "They'll say, 'no, of course it's not a big deal that you stole one agent's weapon and took another one hostage. Of course we're not going to arrest you for that. Of course we won't hand you over to someone else in law enforcement, who's got a spotless record!'"

She took a deep breath, knowing she sounded hysterical, and hugged her clothes to her chest. She wasn't about to strip naked and change in front of him. Funny how only a few minutes ago, she'd been desperate to get both of their clothes off. "If I go to the FBI, he'll find me."

"Not if you tell them what you saw," Andre replied,

standing in the doorway with his arms crossed over his chest, effectively blocking her exit.

"Andre, I appreciate that you believe me, but you said it yourself. On paper, my ex appears perfect. And I... *don't.* I can't take the chance, okay? If you need me to go, then I will, but I can't turn myself in."

Memories flooded, of the humiliation she'd felt the day she'd gone into Dylan's station while he was out on a call. The looks the other officers had given her when she'd come out of the chief's office, half pitying, half disgusted. The way the chief had called out to have one of them "make sure she got home okay," as though she was incapable of driving herself. And then the way Dylan had glared at her when he'd come home that night. The fury on his face had been unlike anything she'd ever seen, telling her she had to get out before he killed her.

"Okay," Andre said softly.

She nodded, staring at the ground and trying not to tear up. She'd been alone a long time. She'd only known Andre for a little over twenty-four hours. He'd made her feel safe, as though she had someone she could rely on, someone she could trust, way too quickly. But she could do this on her own again. She'd run. She'd just have to keep moving this time, not stay in one place so long. "If you need to tell them I was here, please just give me a head start."

His arms went around her before she'd even realized he'd moved closer. "We'll do it ourselves. It'll be harder this way, but you've got a lot of people on your side. We'll figure it out."

"What?" She stared up at him in disbelief.

"You really think I'd let you go it alone?"

Her eyes stung, this time from tears of relief, but she blinked them back. Just because Andre was on her side didn't mean it was over. Dylan knew she was in Virginia now. Since the FBI hadn't given him any information, he'd start searching himself. And although she'd seen Andre in action and knew he was good at his job, Dylan hadn't gotten to be the city's top detective by accident.

Andre hugged her closer. "But just for the record, the Bureau is a good place, and we've got solid investigators. They wouldn't turn you over to a cop that you claim tried to have you killed just because he wears the badge."

She nodded against his bare chest, not bothering to argue. She knew he believed what he was saying, but he didn't know how persuasive Dylan could be. Or how persistent.

It had been three years. Three years where she'd tried to stay under the radar, where she'd kept silent. But that hadn't been enough for him. He couldn't just let her go, trust that she was scared enough she'd never turn him in—though it was doubtful anyone would have believed her anyway. Instead, he'd kept coming after her, no matter how hard she attempted to disappear.

Her jaw tensed as she thought about all the towns she'd tried to start over in, all the towns she'd had to leave—some in the middle of the night, leaving everything behind again. Maybe Andre was right about one thing. It was time to stop running. It was time to make a stand.

She pulled back from Andre's embrace just far enough to look up at him again. "I know you think we're at a disadvantage without the FBI's resources. But you have something better than that. You have me. And I know Dylan. So tell me what you need to know, and let's get started. Let's end this."

"I'VE GOT BAD NEWS." Cole stood in the doorway, holding a box of pizza and a case of beer, looking apologetic.

Andre tried not to let the words discourage him any more than he already was. He and Juliette had spent the day tracking Dylan's activities, digging up anything they could find.

Andre's thinking had been that since Shaye was searching for the money trail to the convicts, his time was best spent hunting down some other way to get Dylan behind bars. It didn't matter to him how, just so long as the guy was locked up. Once they took care of that, they could focus on nailing him for everything else.

But all their searching had come to absolutely nothing. Either the guy was way too good at hiding his transgressions or he really hadn't stepped over the line, except with the Manning murder case.

"What is it?" Andre asked, stepping aside so Cole could join him, Juliette and Marcos in the living room.

"I don't think Keane is behind this."

"What?" Juliette leaped from her seat. "Of course he is! Who else would send a bunch of criminals to kill me? You think I make a habit of pissing off dirty cops?"

Andre shot her a glance, and she visibly took a breath. "Sorry," she told Cole, running a hand through her hair and pulling part of it out of the complicated knot she'd put it in earlier. "It's been a long couple of days."

In his typical way, Cole shrugged it off. "No worries. Here." He tossed her a bag.

She opened it. "Where did you get these?"

"Shaye said you'd need something to wear if you'd been in the same clothes since the shooting. I have no idea about sizes, so she just gave me stuff with drawstrings. You'll probably need to roll the sleeves though—

she's pretty tall. And she sent sandals. She said you could adjust them."

Juliette looked so pleased that Andre mentally slapped himself for not thinking of it. They'd been cloistered in his house for two days, so he hadn't thought much of her going barefoot or wearing his T-shirts. In fact, he liked her best barefoot and in his T-shirts.

"What are you grinning about?" Marcos asked, but the way he was glancing from Andre to Juliette suggested that he already suspected the answer.

"Nothing." Andre got back to business. "What do you mean, you don't think Keane is behind this?"

"You know how good Shaye is, right?" Cole prompted as he set the pizza and beer on the coffee table and Marcos helped himself to a slice.

"Yeah, I remember." Last year, Cole had been involved in a dangerous investigation of a gang with a reputation of gunning for anyone who tried to take them down. Shaye had used her computer forensics skills to dig up a money trail no one else had been able to find, landing the leaders in jail. But not before they'd done a drive-by at the police station, killing several officers and driving Shaye out of police work.

"How'd you get her to help with this anyway?" Andre asked. He knew Cole had tried to get her to return to the department before with no luck.

"It took a lot of begging. But I think it's good for her. She loves the work. It's being at the station that's the problem. PTSD from the shooting. Anyway, she's still searching, but she's already tracked most of Keane's assets. He's definitely living above his means, but there's no trail of money going out. Not the kind of money you'd need to hire three ex-cons for a hit."

"So what does that mean?" Juliette asked. "You think maybe it was some different sort of trade? Maybe he wouldn't arrest them for something if they did this for him?"

Andre shook his head. "No. Both the perps in custody specifically talked about a payment. They got half beforehand and were expecting the rest after the job was finished. There's got to be a trail."

Cole shrugged. "Well, there's not. At least not going from Keane. Not even to some third-party account that these guys could draw from. She's still digging, but she says if she hasn't found it at this point, he'd have to be really skilled at hiding money. If she doesn't get any hits soon, she's going to try it the other way, from the criminals out, but it's going to take longer."

"Why?" Juliette asked.

"Because there are three of them, and she's doing it off-book," Marcos answered, without pausing as he devoured his slice of pizza. "She's got to cover her tracks. It's not as if she has a warrant for this. Not only is she not assigned the case, but she's a private citizen now."

"Oh." Juliette frowned and Andre could tell exactly what she was thinking.

"She won't get caught," Andre promised.

"But if she finds something, we'll have to find a way to give the trail to the case agents, so they can pull the information legally," Cole added. "We have to leave her name out of it. Right now, we're doing it to verify we're after the right guy and to know where to send them. But this won't put him away, because we don't have any jurisdiction here."

"And you guys are okay with this?" Juliette looked from one to the next. "Doing this outside the law?"

"Not really," Cole said, flopping onto one of the empty chairs. "But this isn't a regular thing. Andre wouldn't ask if there was another option."

Juliette fidgeted and then sat forward. "I don't want—"

"Besides," Cole spoke over her, using his big brother protective voice, "if someone in law enforcement had put a hit out on *my* girlfriend, I'd be doing the same thing."

He didn't seem to notice Juliette turning red, but Marcos was clearly trying not to smile at her reaction. Andre just hid his surprise that Cole thought Juliette was better off hiding in his house than under FBI protection. And that Cole had equated her to his girlfriend and already liked Juliette enough to get protective of her.

"I mean, I trust the FBI, and I'm sure they'd put you in a safe house, but they're still going to have to give a fellow law enforcement officer the benefit of the doubt, especially if there's no evidence to support your claim. If the guy knows he's under investigation, he's got the skillset to hide the evidence. And at some point, if they can't pull up any proof?" Cole shook his head.

"I'll be back in danger," Juliette said softly, as if she'd known that all along.

"That's not going to happen," Marcos spoke up before Andre could say the same thing.

"You don't even know me," Juliette said, looking genuinely perplexed. "Why are you doing all of this?"

"You matter to Andre," Marcos said simply, "so you matter to us."

"Thank you," she said softly, and his brothers must have been able to see as well as he could that she was overwhelmed, so both of them shrugged as though it wasn't a big deal and grabbed pizza.

But it was a big deal. And he knew it as well as Juliette. There weren't many people he'd ask his brothers to put themselves on the line for, and he'd known Juliette less than forty-eight hours. He wasn't sure how she'd become so important to him in such a short time, but he knew it was more than just a simple need to protect her.

He felt connected to her, on a level he didn't totally understand. But one thing he did know: he couldn't let anything happen to her.

Deciding to worry about what his feelings meant later, Andre took the remaining chair and popped open a beer. "Scott says the WFO agents got a call from someone digging for information about Juliette. We assume it was Keane, since it was a burner phone."

"Well, he could make the drive in an evening and be back before morning, but he'd have to know exactly where she was first," Marcos said.

"It'd be a stretch," Cole put in. "As a cop, he'd probably take back routes to avoid traffic cameras as much as possible, and that would add a lot of time to the trip. But you're right. He's not going to come out here without already knowing exactly where she was."

What neither of them was saying—and Andre wasn't about to either—was that if Dylan made that trip, it would be to kill Juliette and then drive back before anyone knew he'd left the state.

"The news was reporting our team was at the hostage situation, but he'd have a hard time getting names, even if he knew someone in the Bureau. And then he'd have to narrow it down to me and suspect I was harboring her," Andre said. "That's not going to happen."

"So, what's next?" Cole asked. "Marcos, did you find anything?"

Marcos shook his head and set down his third slice

of pizza. "I wish I had more to report, but everything in the Manning investigation seems above board. Loews had motive, means and opportunity, and they found his prints at the scene. If Harkin was there with him, I can't find any sign of it."

"Maybe they both plotted it, but Loews was the actual killer," Cole suggested.

Juliette shrugged. "I don't know. What I heard was my husband—my ex—telling Harkin he'd keep his name out of it, but he couldn't do anything for Loews. About a week later, they arrested Loews, so I assume they already had evidence against him."

"What about Harkin? He was a suspect before that?" Cole asked.

"Oh, yeah," Juliette answered. "With Manning dead, Harkin took control of the company. It's worth millions of dollars. First, they ruled out Manning's wife—I'm told that's common practice with homicide. After that, Harkin and Loews were the next obvious suspects—his business partner and his biggest competitor."

"And Dylan Keane was the lead detective on the case," Marcos contributed. "He already had a great track record at the station, but this was his biggest case. Still, I'm not seeing any signs of impropriety. From what I can tell, Harkin *did* get investigated and cleared. So, either Keane made evidence against him disappear or…"

"Or what?" Juliette prompted.

"Or there wasn't any to begin with."

"Then why give Dylan a payoff?"

"Harkin wouldn't be privy to what evidence the police had. It's possible Keane took a gamble, told Harkin he could put him away and offered an alternative."

"But if Harkin was innocent, that's a big gamble."

"Not really," Marcos said. "Dirty or not, Keane was a good investigator. Even if he couldn't prove it, he probably knew Harkin was involved."

"Well, if there wasn't any evidence, then he's only guilty of taking a payoff." Juliette sounded dismayed. "Proving that isn't going to put him away forever."

"No, but proving he tried to have you killed will," Andre said.

Juliette nodded, and he could tell she was trying to look optimistic, but didn't feel it. He couldn't blame her. So far, their digging into Keane hadn't yielded anything. But years of working as a regular special agent before he'd transferred to HRT had taught him this kind of investigation rarely happened quickly. It took time. At least with Keane in Pennsylvania on the job, he wasn't here hunting Juliette.

Cole cursing brought Andre's attention back to his older brother. He was staring at his phone and then he shook his head, and he didn't have to say a word for Andre to know he had more bad news.

"Shaye just texted me. Don't ask me how she knows this, but Keane just put in for a week's vacation. Starting tomorrow."

They were all silent a moment, then Juliette spoke the obvious. "He's coming here. He's coming for me."

Chapter Nine

"Who do we know in Leming?" Cole asked.

"Leming, Pennsylvania?" Marcos replied.

"Yeah. Supposedly that's where Keane was going for his vacation, to a friend's cabin out there. I recognize that town. Why?"

"Kendry patrols near there," Marcos reminded him. He told Juliette, "A guy I worked a joint task force with about six months ago. He's a small-town cop, but he's got one of the best eyes for trouble I've ever seen. We tried to recruit him, but he preferred small-town living."

Juliette tried to focus. "Recruit him?" she echoed, her mind still reeling with the news that Dylan was on his way here. She knew he'd come eventually, of course, which was why she'd been trying to run in the first place. But being in Andre's house had begun to lull her into a sense of security.

"To the DEA." When she didn't respond, Marcos added with a lopsided grin, "That's where I work."

"Oh. Right." She sounded as dazed as she felt, and as Andre's brother got on a call with Kendry, all the decisions she'd made in her life that had driven her to this point flashed through her mind.

This was the first time in three years that she'd told

anyone the truth about who she was and why she was running. This was the first time she hadn't felt totally alone. The truth was, she felt safer than she had in a long time, because she knew without needing to ask that any one of them would put himself in front of a bullet for her.

That thought filled her with a terror greater than her fear of Dylan. She looked at Marcos, talking animatedly on the phone while Cole huddled close to listen, his expression serious and intense. Then over at Andre, leaning forward, his elbows resting on his knees, a determined energy radiating from him.

When she'd held a gun on Andre and demanded he drive her out of Quantico, she'd never expected this. She hadn't thought it through, how it might impact him and his family. She'd just been fixated on her own next moment, living to see another day.

It was how she'd approached her life for the past three years. Those years were just a blur of new cities, new states, new names. She'd made what could loosely be called "friends," but she'd never let herself get close enough to anyone that her past might come up. Never close enough to have to explain where she'd come from or how she'd gotten there. The whole time, she'd been going through the motions, never planning for a future she wasn't sure she'd have.

Now, suddenly, she wanted one. Desperately.

She mentally traced Andre's features: the strong profile, the furrow he got between his eyebrows when he was deep in thought, the little dimple when he gave her one of his sly grins.

As though he could sense her staring, Andre turned toward her, that furrow appearing. She ducked her head. She didn't want him to read her too closely now, because he'd see things she wasn't ready to admit yet, not even to herself.

She couldn't let anything happen to him because of her. That thought blared in her mind as if it was coming through a bullhorn.

"He's there."

She looked over at Marcos. "What?"

"Kendry didn't even have to check," Marcos said, sounding surprised. "He said Keane arrived in Leming an hour ago and actually stopped by the station, letting them know, one officer to another, that he was around."

Cole frowned. "That's a little unusual. You think he's trying to set up an alibi?"

"Maybe. But why there?" Andre asked. "It's not any closer to Quantico, and he's less likely to have people who can account for all his time. As alibis go, he'd be better off staying home and sneaking out and back during the night."

"True, but in Leming, he's got a potential alibi *without* so many eyes on his activities. Maybe that's the point," Cole suggested.

"The timing is too suspicious to be coincidental," Marcos agreed. "But at least we have a contact there. Kendry's going to try to keep track of him, let us know if he spots him leaving."

"So, what's next?" Cole asked, eyeing Juliette as though he suspected what she was beginning to realize. "Keane—legitimately or not—seems innocent, and Manning's murder investigation appears above board." He looked at Andre. "You didn't find anything else in Keane's record, right?"

"Nope." The single word was bursting with frustration.

"Any chance he spotted our tracks?" Marcos asked. "It might explain why he took off."

Cole slowly shook his head. "I doubt it. But it's possible. Which means maybe we need to consider a completely new alternative."

"What?" Juliette asked, not following.

Andre took one of her hands in his, either oblivious or uncaring of the look his brothers shared when he did it. "What if someone else put the hit on you?"

"No—" Juliette started, but Andre cut her off.

"Just consider it. You said Keane has been chasing you for years, but has he tried to kill you before? Or was he trying to drag you back home?"

Juliette remembered that moment in Cleveland when he'd caught up to her on the stairwell. Her panic as she ran out of her apartment in her bare feet and pajamas, so fast she'd almost fallen down the stairs. The sound of his boots pounding on the steps behind her. The feel of his hand as he'd gripped her arm so hard she'd worried he'd pulled it out of the socket. The bruises that hadn't gone away for a month.

This time, she focused in on that single moment when they'd stood in the stairwell together. She'd whipped around to face him, terrified. She'd expected to see a weapon in his hand or the same fury that had been on his face when he'd threatened to kill her if she ever told. But instead, there'd been desperation.

She hadn't waited to see what he'd wanted. She'd just screamed as loud as she could and been so grateful when two neighbors peered into the stairway almost immediately. He'd let go of her arm, and she hadn't looked back. She'd just run.

She'd kept what she thought of as her "escape bag"

in her car, with a change of clothes, some money and forged documents for a quick getaway. She'd peeled out of town and driven for days, sleeping only occasionally on the side of the road, before driving again. She'd traveled through multiple states before she'd stopped that first time.

"I don't know," she admitted now. He'd caught up to her again, more than once, but she'd spotted him and run before he could get close. "But he threatened to kill me before I left if I ever spilled his secret."

Andre leaned closer. "But did you ever hear him say he'd planted evidence? Anything other than he'd keep Harkin's name out of it, but he couldn't help Loews?"

Juliette shook her head, wondering what he was getting at.

"What if we're going about this wrong?" Andre asked. "What if Keane wasn't the only one involved?"

"What do you mean?" Juliette asked, her mind spinning from the possibility that she might have been wrong about Dylan's plan in Cleveland. She'd never before questioned that he'd been trying to kill her. But what if he'd actually intended to grab her and drag her back home?

The longer they'd been married, the more possessive he'd become. Maybe he really didn't want her dead—just wanted her somewhere close so he could keep controlling her, make sure she wasn't a threat.

What difference did it make? Death or prison?

"It's a real possibility," Cole said, as if he could read Andre's mind. "Keane must have had a partner on the force, right?"

She nodded. "Yeah, of course. They'd been friends since childhood. They joined up together, were on patrol together, then got their detective shields together.

Jim Valance. They were like brothers." She paled, as realization hit. "You think they were in on the cover-up together? That Dylan was trying to bring me home to protect me in his own stupid way, and that it's *Jim* who's trying to kill me?"

JULIETTE FELT AS though she had whiplash. Dylan was trying to kill her. Dylan *wasn't* trying to kill her. Dylan was guilty. Dylan was innocent—or at least, not *as* guilty. Jim was guilty.

Jim Valance. The first time Juliette had met him had been the day Dylan had pulled her over. Jim had been in the car with him. Then, later, when Dylan showed up at the club, Jim was there, too, playing wingman. A year later, he'd been Dylan's best man at their small wedding ceremony.

Why hadn't she ever considered that Jim might be involved? Juliette mentally kicked herself. It would certainly explain why Jim had been so furious when she'd come into the station to turn in her husband, his silent fuming when he drove her home. She'd assumed it was simple loyalty. She'd never thought she was putting Jim's career in jeopardy, too.

"Dylan used to talk to me about his cases sometimes," Juliette said, as three pairs of eyes, so different physically but so similar in intensity, focused on her. For the first time in years, she thought back to that first year with Dylan and remembered more than just the bad. "I remember when he got the Manning murder case. He was so excited because it was the most high-profile case the department had gotten in years, and his chief had made him lead."

"How did Valance feel about that?" Andre asked when she paused.

"I don't know. I saw Jim all the time, but there was always a little…I don't know, jealousy maybe?…between us. I think he felt as though I sort of took Dylan away from him. I figured he was happy for Dylan about the assignment. I mean, they were partners, so that effectively made Jim one of the leads, too."

"But he wasn't the head detective," Cole said. "That might have been a sore spot."

"Maybe. But he never acted upset about it that I saw. But what I do remember, from early on in that case, is Dylan complaining about Jim. When they started the investigation, Dylan suspected Harkin."

"He talked to you about his cases a lot?" Andre asked.

"Sometimes." It was more like he talked *at* her about his cases. He hadn't really wanted her opinion about them. He'd just needed someone to listen silently while he worked things out aloud. She hadn't really minded back then, but in retrospect, it had been representative of a lot of things in their marriage. He'd wanted to be in control, to have her around when he needed her.

Back then, she'd thought that was love. Her parents hadn't hidden the fact that they hadn't planned to have her and didn't know what to do with her once they did. She'd avoided a lot of entanglements in boarding school. Then, Dylan had showed up and focused all of his attention on her.

It had never really occurred to her to wonder if he'd liked her for who she was or because he could mold her into what he wanted her to be. And it had probably been so much easier for him to do it since she'd had virtually no support system. He'd chipped away at the rest, little by little, so slowly she hadn't realized it was happening, until all her friends were acquaintances.

Still, he wasn't all bad. She'd loved him once, and although she had memories of feeling lonely in their relationship, she also had memories of them laughing together when things were good and leaning on each other when times got hard.

"Juliette," Andre said softly, bringing her back on track, "when did Dylan stop saying he suspected Harkin? Was it after he took the money?"

"He stopped talking to me about the case at all around then. But before that, he complained about Jim. I'd forgotten all about it, because of everything that happened afterward, but initially, Dylan was mad because Jim kept insisting Harkin was innocent." She frowned. "Actually, I think it was Jim who first suggested Loews was a better bet than Harkin as the killer."

"What if *Jim Valance* tampered with evidence rather than Keane?" Cole suggested. "Harkin could have approached Valance first, offered him money to lead the investigation away from him and toward Loews. But Valance couldn't convince Keane that his theory on Loews was right, so Harkin decided to pay Keane off, too."

"It would explain why you just heard your ex talking about keeping Harkin out of the investigation and not about making any evidence disappear," Marcos agreed. "Maybe Valance already told Harkin that he could only do so much—it might have been easier to hide the evidence that Harkin was there than it would have been for both of them."

"Did Valance know you'd overheard your ex and Harkin talking?" Andre asked.

"I don't think so. I don't think he realized I knew

Dylan had taken money until I showed up at the station to report Dylan."

Andre stroked the hand he'd been holding since they'd first started this discussion. "Those times you spotted Keane tracking you when you were running from him— did you ever see anyone else? Did you ever see Valance?"

Juliette frowned, focusing on those days in Cleveland before Dylan had showed up in the middle of the night. She thought of the day she'd spotted him talking to someone in the tiny town she'd moved to in Arkansas, and the time she'd seen him coming out of the post office in the spot she'd picked in Maine. She thought hard, trying to remember if she'd ever noticed anyone else, but finally she had to shake her head. "If Jim was with Dylan, I never saw him."

"If we're right about this," Marcos said, "he wouldn't have been with Keane at all. He would have been either ahead of him or behind him, trying to track you down first."

"What about the ex-cons who showed up at your job?" Cole asked. "Did you recognize any of them?"

She shook her head. "I figure Dylan arrested them at some point or another. They had arrest records from our town."

"And if Valance was his partner…"

"Then Valance was in on those arrests, too." She dropped her head to her hands, feeling Andre's strong fingers beneath her cheek, too. "I can't believe I just assumed it was Dylan all this time, when it was actually Jim."

"It's just a theory," Cole reminded her, but she could hear in his voice that he thought they were on the right track.

She lifted her head and looked from one brother to the next, stopping on Andre. "So, if Jim sent those hit men after me, and Dylan is hiding out in Leming right now, does that mean Jim is gunning for both of us?"

"I don't know," Andre replied. "It's possible. Announcing to the locals that he's there could be Keane's way of giving himself protection. He goes out of town and gets killed and his partner is also away, the partner's an obvious suspect. But the two of them on a job together, day after day? It would be too easy for Valance to set up an ambush."

Juliette shivered, and she knew Andre saw it. She didn't want to go back to Dylan, but she didn't want him dead, either. "So, what do we do now?"

Andre and his brothers started talking strategy, but Juliette didn't hear any of it. Because she suddenly knew the answer.

It didn't matter who was after her. What mattered was that these men had vowed to protect her. They'd put their careers on the line to help her, and she didn't doubt they'd do the same with their lives. And she couldn't let them make that sacrifice.

It was time for her to go.

ANDRE OPENED HIS eyes slowly. The sun was already streaming through the slats in his blinds as fragments of his dream came back to him. He'd been dreaming about the fire again, and it had woken him repeatedly during the night, then he'd fallen back into fitful bits of sleep. Every time he'd woken, he'd thought about getting up and walking into the room next door, where Juliette slept. But he'd resisted.

She'd handled the news that maybe her ex-husband

hadn't been out to kill her for the past three years surprisingly well. But he'd also seen the regret on her face that she'd misjudged him. Maybe even wistfulness for what they'd once shared.

The idea that she might still love her ex-husband made his chest hurt. But he had no claim on her. He'd only known her a few days. It wasn't enough time to form a genuine bond with someone. Or at least that's what he'd told himself every time he'd woken up last night. But the truth was, he felt more connected to her than he'd ever felt to another woman, logical or not.

He identified with how alone she'd found herself, because he'd been there. And he admired how she'd forged forward on her own, using her wits and intelligence to not only survive but to build a new life for herself in each new town. She was a fighter, just like him. And this was a battle he was going to make sure she won.

He noticed the silence in his house and looked over at his alarm clock. He'd slept later than usual. When he sat up, more pieces of his dream returned, and he swore. The thing that had been nagging him about his memories of the fire had surfaced in his dreams.

The sun had been coming up that morning, too, but instead of 9:00 a.m., it had been sunrise. Well before anyone in that house woke up. Everyone should have been coming from upstairs that morning, fleeing through the front door or the side. And yet, his foster father and one of the other foster kids had come around from the back of the house. Why?

The house had burned down that day. The foster family had been totally split up, and he'd never seen those parents or the kids, other than Marcos and Cole, ever again. But years later, he'd seen the report about the fire.

It had been deemed an accident and he'd never questioned that before, because supposedly the firefighters had found candles left burning. Andre had assumed his foster father had forgotten to put them out before going to bed. But the fire had started near the back of the house.

For the first time, he suspected someone had started that fire on purpose.

The idea sent fury and sadness and a hint of fear running through him. Who? And why?

He threw his covers off and stood and it struck him again how silent the house seemed. Was Juliette still asleep?

A new dread crept up on him and he strode into the next room in nothing but his boxers, flinging open the door. But the room was empty, the bed neatly made. And he knew it even before he walked through the rest of the house.

Juliette was gone.

Chapter Ten

"You need to get down here *now*," Scott told him when Andre fumbled to pick up his cell phone as he was climbing into his car.

The car that thankfully Juliette hadn't taken with her. Which meant she'd either walked wherever she was going or gotten a cab.

He didn't like the idea of either one. What was she thinking, sneaking out on her own when someone was searching for her, trying to kill her? Regardless of whether it was her ex-husband or his partner, someone still wanted her dead. And she was giving them a much easier target.

No one would know to search for her from his house, Andre told himself as he belatedly answered Scott. "Get where now? Where are you?"

"At Quantico."

"You are? Why?" They had the weekend off.

"I came in to pick up some gear I left. And you're lucky I did, because guess who's at the entrance gate right now, turning herself in?"

Andre swore. "When did she get there?" And what the heck had she been thinking?

"Just now. I was on my way out when I saw the cab

pull up and she climbed out. Either she admitted to taking the gun off of Nadia or they suspect she's involved
in something herself, because they've got her in cuffs
right now."

"She's not armed," Andre said, starting his car and
racing out of his drive. "I have Nadia's gun, minus the
bullets."

"Yeah, *I* know that," Scott said, "but you really want
me explaining to the guard at the gate that you've had
possession of an agent's stolen weapon for two days? If
Juliette was going to turn herself in—which I think is a
good idea, incidentally—this isn't exactly the best way to
do it. You need to be careful how you play this, or you're
going to be facing an OPR investigation."

That was probably going to happen no matter what.
But he'd known it from the moment he'd agreed to help
Juliette. The FBI's Office of Professional Responsibility
was going to want to review his actions. If he was lucky,
it would be a mark in his permanent file. He didn't want
to think about what would happen if he was unlucky.

"Just get over to the gate," Andre said. "Tell them to
wait for me before they talk to her. I'm coming in now."

"Yeah, well, step on it," Scott replied. "I'm—"

Whatever he was going to say next was cut off by the
sound of a *bang, bang, bang* Andre would recognize
anywhere. Shots fired.

"Scott? What's happening?" Andre asked frantically,
but the call disconnected.

Andre stepped on the gas.

SOMEONE WAS SHOOTING at her. And they were doing it at
an FBI facility!

Juliette pushed aside her disbelief and dropped to the

ground, trying to absorb the weight with her hips and shoulders since her arms were cuffed behind her back. Pain ricocheted through her body, but adrenaline pushed her on. Awkwardly, she scooted toward the guard post, but her too-small sandals snagged the hem of the too-long pants Shaye had lent her, slowing her down. All around her, more weapons went off—she assumed agents firing back.

She had no idea who they were shooting at, because she couldn't see anyone. But she recognized the sound of a rifle, which meant the shooter probably had high ground.

How could Jim have possibly tracked her here? It didn't make any sense, unless he'd been watching Quantico, waiting for her to show up because the news had reported that HRT agents had responded to the hostage situation. But that seemed far-fetched. Maybe the shooting was random, not aimed at her.

Another rifle shot fired amidst the pistols. Pain exploded in her leg and she screamed, any doubt gone. This was about her.

She tried to wriggle into the guard post, out of the line of fire, but before she could go anywhere, a figure leaped into her line of sight, yanking her off the ground and practically tossing her behind the booth. Then she was squashed against it, her wrists burning from the handcuffs and her lungs compressed by a man's back against her.

For a minute, new panic made her desperate to move. Was she exposed here, standing up? Was he? But he seemed to know what he was doing, and as he turned his head and scanned the tree line to the left just as another rifle shot fired, she realized who he was. Andre's partner from the day they'd met.

"Muzzle flash, my seven o'clock," he yelled, and then a new barrage of shooting began. "Whoever is outside the shooting zone, flank him!"

"We've got agents heading there now," the guard in the gatehouse yelled back. "More on their way."

She'd done this, Juliette thought, praying no one had been hit. Besides her, she realized, remembering the flash of intense pain in her leg. She couldn't feel it now—her adrenaline was pumping so hard—but she could stand, so she figured it couldn't be too bad.

"He's after me," Juliette told the agent protecting her. Scott, she remembered. His name was Scott.

"It's his unlucky day, then," Scott replied, his tone hard and too calm. "Because now we're after him."

She prayed he was right, that they'd catch him, and no one would be hurt because of her. She'd come here today because she couldn't bear the thought of Andre or his brothers getting hurt—physically or facing professional consequences—because of her. If her actions caused someone else to be shot, she didn't think she'd ever forgive herself.

Tears pricked her eyes. No matter what she did—run or hide or take a stand—it never seemed to end. He was still after her. Whether *he* was Dylan or Jim, or both of them—she didn't know.

Her eyes dried, and anger hit. She hadn't done anything wrong—at least not until her misguided attempts to get away from Quantico. Someone else had set all of this in motion, chasing after her when she would have kept her silence and stayed hidden. Maybe it was time to really stand up and fight. To finally end this.

If only she knew how.

"Andre's almost here," Scott said and Juliette realized she had no idea how much time had passed.

It felt as if it had only been a few minutes since the shooting started, but if Andre was close, that wasn't possible. How long had they been standing here, pressed against the guard booth, avoiding bullets?

The shooting had stopped, she realized. The air around them was quiet, too still after all the gunshots. "What happened? Did anyone get hit?"

"Everyone is okay. Unfortunately, though, the shooter got away," Scott said. "But he made himself a hide up there. He's been there before, so there's a trail. Plus, we've got his casings. We'll get prints. And then there's nowhere this guy will be able to hide. He shot at federal agents, which tends to piss us off. He's going down."

She tried to move, to squirm out from behind Scott and look at her leg, but he pushed her back.

"You're not going anywhere until I have the hundred -percent all clear. Sorry."

"I'm sorry," she whispered back, but she didn't think he'd heard her, because by then he was talking into a phone and then he was finally letting her move.

But as soon as he stepped away, she almost fell. She steadied herself, hoping he hadn't noticed, but then he was saying into the phone, "By the guard booth. Get over here. I think she was hit."

Juliette looked down, almost in a daze as she watched Scott take out a tactical knife and slice open the side of her pant leg, which was ripped and blood splatdered. He poked at her leg, making her jerk away.

"False alarm," he said, standing again and addressing her while talking into the phone. "A bullet must have hit close to you. It kicked up concrete. It's not going to be fun to have the pieces pulled out of your skin, but there's no bullet wound. You're okay. Turn around," he added, and when she didn't immediately move, he turned her and then she felt the handcuffs click open.

She rubbed her raw wrists and nodded her thanks.

"Got it," Scott said into the phone. Then he held out the phone to her. "Andre wants to talk to you." His tone practically sing-songed, *you're in trouble*.

She made a face at him and he laughed. How he could laugh after what they'd just been through, she didn't know. But maybe that's how he—and Andre—handled this kind of situation. She'd been married to a cop, knew the dangers that even a routine traffic stop could carry. And Andre was in an even more dangerous position, one that sent him into the line of fire when other law enforcement wasn't enough. How was she going to deal with that?

The thought made her freeze. When had she started thinking of Andre as someone she had a future with? She'd known him forty-eight hours, and part of that time she'd spent under fire or holding him hostage. Even if they knew each other well enough for her thoughts not to be flat-out ridiculous, it could never work.

Not unless she finally got free of Dylan and her past, a voice in her head whispered. The sudden, fierce hope she felt, the wish for a real future instead of what she'd been doing for the past three years, surprised her with its intensity.

"Andre?" she spoke into the phone, and her voice came out small and scared.

"It's okay," he told her. "I'm here. I'm coming."

She coughed, tried to sound strong, because she wasn't

scared due to what had just happened with the shooter—
or at least, that's not what was scaring her right now. It
was the realization of how strong her feelings were for
this man. But she couldn't exactly tell him that, not now.
Not until she was no longer on the run.

Instead she cleared her throat again and said, "I'm
fine. I'm sorry I ran out on you."

Scott was staring, listening to every word, so she
turned her back on him for the illusion of privacy and
continued, "I was trying to keep you out of trouble. You
and your brothers. I didn't realize… I didn't want to—"

Suddenly, strong hands landed on her shoulders and
spun her around and then Andre was there in front of
her, and she was crushed in his arms. Over her head,
she heard him say something to Scott, but his hold on
her was so tight, her ears pressed against him, so she
couldn't make it out.

Then he held her at arm's length, studying her intently,
clearly searching for injuries. She started to tell him she
was fine, but he'd already dropped to his knees and was
checking her leg for himself.

"Scott's right. It's not serious. But we'll need to get
you patched up."

Something else Scott had said came back to her, and
she looked at him. "You said the shooter had been up
there awhile?"

"Yeah, well, he set up a hide. The agents said it appears to be well used. He's been waiting for you."

Juliette returned her attention to Andre. "Dylan has
been in Pennsylvania. So this definitely wasn't him. What
about Jim? Has he been off work? Do you think he's been
here since those men came into my office?" She couldn't
bring herself to say *since the attempted hit on me.*

"I don't know, but we're going to find out."

He held up his hands as a pair of agents came running their way. "She's with me. I need to take her to the hospital, and then we'll go to the WFO. We've got information on the hostage situation from earlier this week."

The agents nodded, and although they didn't look happy, no one tried to slap handcuffs on her again.

Andre took her hand. "Let's go."

"Are you sure? Should I stay—"

"We're getting you stitched up and then it's time to lay everything out in the open for the case agents. It's time to end this."

"A COP FRIEND just paid Keane a visit in Leming," Andre announced three hours later. He was sitting at a conference table at the Washington Field Office with Juliette and a pair of agents. The agents seemed less than impressed by their sudden involvement, not to mention their story about why they hadn't come forward earlier.

If OPR didn't already have his name on a short list, Andre was sure these agents were going to insist it was added. He'd never met either of them, but they were both veteran agents who'd been wearing frowns since he and Juliette had arrived.

"So, Keane is still in Pennsylvania?" asked the older agent, a man with a thick head of entirely gray hair and a roadmap of lines on his face. He'd introduced himself as Special Agent Porter and apparently expected even Andre to address him by his title.

"He's still there."

"Well, cross him off the list, then," the other agent said. Special Agent Franks was about five years younger than his partner and only slightly more likeable, with intense green eyes that held a little bit of sympathy mixed in with the annoyance.

"For the Quantico shooting anyway," Andre agreed. "Not necessarily for the hit."

"Don't you think it was the same person?" Porter argued.

"Yeah, probably," Andre said, "but not definite." He angled a glance at Juliette, who'd stayed mostly silent after she'd told them her story, putting a lot of emphasis on how Andre wasn't to blame for her actions. Neither of them had mentioned his brothers. Andre wanted to keep them out of it.

"What about Jim?" Juliette spoke up. "Do we know if he's still working? That should be easy to check, right?" She looked at him rather than the agents on the case.

"We're checking that now," Porter answered her. "And while you two were getting coffee, I put in a call to the profiler we had review the hostage situation. She's on her way now."

"I think her theory was right," Franks said, which just made Porter frown more.

"What was her theory?" Andre asked.

"You can ask her yourself," Porter said, staring at a text on his phone. "She's here. Be right back." He stood and left the conference room.

"Don't worry about him," Franks said when he was gone. "He's always in a bad mood."

Andre tried not to let his amusement show; Franks wasn't exactly a ball of fun himself. But any humor quickly faded as he thought about his own future with the Bureau. He knew he was going to be in trouble— the question was how much. He just hoped he hadn't destroyed his career.

But even if he could, he wasn't sure he'd go back and do anything differently, except perhaps not let Juliette out of his sight. He would have preferred they'd gone in together instead of her showing up at Quantico and ending up back under fire.

The door opened again, ending Andre's musing as Porter led in a woman wearing a well-tailored pantsuit. Her hair was up in a tight bun, her pretty features muted by her serious expression. When Andre stood, he towered over her, even though he was only five-ten.

"I'm Evelyn Baine," she introduced herself, shaking his hand and then Juliette's. "I provided a profile on the hostage case yesterday, but the new details Agent Porter just shared give me a lot more insight." She smiled, and he could see she loved her job. "This will help."

"So, what was in your profile?" Andre asked, curious about what Porter had meant earlier.

She propped her hands on her hips, not bothering to sit as Porter settled back into his own seat. "Well, the fact that someone hired ex-cons for the job, and that the *intent* was for them to grab her…" She paused, looking at Juliette apologetically. "Grab you…and kill you without anyone knowing why you'd disappeared suggests a professional, not a personal grudge."

Beside him, Juliette sat a little straighter. "I'd been thinking it was my ex-husband, and I guess we've just determined he wasn't involved in the shooting at Quantico, but we weren't sure about what happened at my office. So, they were both probably planned by Dylan's partner."

Evelyn's lips twisted. "How well did you know his partner?"

Juliette shrugged. "Pretty well. He was Dylan's best man at our wedding. He was over for dinner all the time."

"Tell me about your relationship."

"It was okay, I guess." She glanced at Andre and Evelyn's keen gaze followed, as though she could read their entire history together in that one look. "I was telling Andre that I think Jim was sort of jealous of the time I took from him. Before Dylan and I married, he and Jim did everything together."

Evelyn nodded, and it was clearly what she'd been expecting. "It could have been the partner who did this. We definitely can't rule him out. He's a cop, and so he knows the more distance he has from a murder the less likely he is to be tied to it forensically. But everything about this attempt screams that there was no personal connection."

"Murder is pretty personal," Porter argued.

"Yeah, but if you've secretly—or not so secretly— envied someone for years, where's the payoff? Juliette ran three years ago. She was no longer competition for Dylan's attention. And with a grudge big enough to kill over, most people want to do it personally. But time and distance will dull that kind of grudge."

"Our theory is that Dylan Keane and Jim Valance were helping cover up who really killed Kurt Manning," Andre said. "Juliette overheard Keane take a payoff. We think the hit was an attempt to silence Juliette."

"I agree," Evelyn said. "But I don't think it's either of them who put out the hit. I think you're searching for a third player."

Chapter Eleven

"Well, Jim Valance is missing," Franks announced, taking his attention off the tablet he'd been typing away on for the past ten minutes.

"What do you mean, missing?" Juliette asked, noticing that neither Andre nor the profiler seemed surprised.

She studied Evelyn, taking in her unusual mix of features—the sea green eyes and light brown skin—and the woman's small stature. It was interesting how someone so tiny compared to the three men in the room could project all that confidence. Especially after essentially being told that the theory she'd just announced could be wrong.

"It's got to be Valance we're after, not some mystery third participant," Porter said.

Franks shot him a look that Juliette couldn't quite interpret, then he said, "Valance's chief says he took a day off earlier this week, and he hasn't returned. He was supposed to be in yesterday, but he wasn't. They've checked his house, and there's no sign of him. No sign of a struggle either, and his car is gone."

"So there's a good chance he's nearby," Porter concluded. "Do you know if he's skilled with a rifle?"

"The shooting at Quantico wasn't skilled," Andre said, and Juliette gaped.

"No one was shot," Andre said quietly. "Given the distance and the angles, if he knew what he was doing, he should have been able to hit you."

"He got close," Porter said, eyeing her leg, which was wrapped after she'd gotten the bits of concrete removed.

"Yeah, but if he already put a hit on her, why shoot to scare?" Franks agreed. He asked Juliette, "Is Jim Valance a good shot with a rifle?"

Juliette shrugged. "He's a cop, so I assume so." Dylan had been good with one, which was why she'd recognized the sound. Early in their relationship, when he'd take her shooting, he'd usually let her use a pistol only, but he'd shoot a variety of weapons, and she'd learned to distinguish the sounds.

"That doesn't really mean anything."

When Porter didn't elaborate, Andre explained, "A police officer would be issued a pistol and probably a shotgun as a backup weapon. But most of them don't shoot rifles on the job, not unless they're in a specialty unit. Being proficient with a pistol doesn't necessarily mean you'd be good with a rifle. The distance is totally different, and he'd have to know how to use a scope properly."

That was what Andre did, Juliette knew. Scott had told her he was one of HRT's best snipers.

"Just because Valance isn't at work doesn't mean he's here," Evelyn spoke up. "Keane left work, too, and he's at a cabin in Pennsylvania. Almost as if he's hiding out."

"Right." Andre spoke up. "We thought he might be hiding from Valance, making it harder for his partner to stage an 'accident' on the job."

"Or someone is after both of them," Evelyn suggested. "What about the person you already suspect has gotten away with murder?"

"Harkin." Andre nodded slowly. "I hadn't considered him."

"Why would he be trying to kill me now?" Juliette asked. "It's been three years. And it's Dylan who's been chasing me all over the country all that time."

"He kept finding you, right?" Evelyn asked.

"Yeah." Juliette bit her lip, considering how long she'd been here feeling safe. Had that just been an illusion from the beginning? "But except for that one time, I always spotted him and ran before he caught up to me. I didn't see him here."

"But maybe he'd found your location and was biding his time. Or he'd narrowed it down to this area but didn't know exactly where. It's possible someone was tracking Keane while he tracked you," Evelyn said.

"Yeah, we thought maybe Jim was," Juliette replied.

"But why *now*?" Evelyn asked.

"Well, that's what I was wondering about Harkin. As far as I'm aware, he never even knew I'd overheard him and Dylan talking. And if he did know all along, why wait three years?"

"That's the key," Evelyn told them, wearing an expression Juliette figured she saved for doing big reveals when she gave profiles. "Determine what the trigger was recently and that will tell you who."

Porter was animated for the first time since Juliette had met him. "You're right. The one thing we know for sure is that Dylan Keane wasn't involved in today's shooting. So, either he's been searching for you all this time and someone else has been helping him, or someone's been following him. And the other person had something happen recently that means you have to go."

"Like what?" Juliette asked, perplexed. She understood Dylan's persistence chasing her until he caught up to her. But why, after all this time, would someone else come after her?

"Someone is threatening to tell," Andre said, and all the other agents in the room nodded. The energy in the room seemed to go up with the feeling that they were onto something. "And one of them decided he needed to eliminate all the loose ends."

SHE WAS A loose end.

Juliette didn't say the words out loud, but it was almost as if Andre heard her, because he took her hand under the conference center table and squeezed.

"Jim was always a big spender," she realized. "Your br—uh, you said Dylan was living above his means recently. Jim *always* did. Or at least it seemed that way. He always had the newest electronics, and he was constantly taking these women he met at the clubs to expensive dinners. Maybe the money ran out."

"Maybe he demanded more from Harkin to keep his mouth shut," Evelyn agreed, not commenting on Juliette's slipup, although Juliette was pretty sure she'd noticed.

"That's risky," Franks said. "If he was the one who altered evidence, he was in pretty deep himself."

"Yeah, but he was investigating the case. He could always say he pulled the file for some reason, noticed something new. I doubt he'd actually do it, given his involvement, but to a murderer who'd gotten away with it, that could be a convincing threat," Andre agreed with Evelyn.

"Can you get Valance's financials?" Evelyn asked the case agents. "That could be the stressor that set off this attempted hit."

"Probably not with what we've got now," Porter said. "But if Valance is having real financial problems, we might see evidence of that even without a warrant. But honestly, the prints on the shell casings at Quantico will probably tell us more."

"What about the convicts we arrested?" Andre spoke up. "They both thought a cop paid them off."

There was silence in the room for a minute, then Juliette said tentatively, "Maybe Harkin was trying to cover his tracks? He's pretty intelligent. He and Manning started that company together. Manning was in charge, but a lot of people in our town seemed to think Harkin was really the brains of it."

Andre nodded. "It's a definite possibility."

"We'll investigate his whereabouts, too," Porter promised, then stood. "Unless there's more you can give us, we need to get back to work."

"Are you going to bring Dylan Keane in?" Andre asked.

"Not yet," Porter said. "Right now, he needs to feel as if no one is onto him. The police department in Leming is keeping eyes on him so he doesn't take off. If we bring him in for questioning now, we're just announcing what we suspect. And we won't be able to hold him, which means he could run. We need something concrete first, then we'll grab him."

Juliette got to her feet slowly, wondering what this meant for her. When she'd shown up at Quantico and tried to explain what had happened, they'd patted her down for weapons and slapped handcuffs on her. It had been humiliating, but she understood it.

"The FBI can offer you a safe house," Franks said.

Juliette looked at Andre, not sure what to do. That might be the most logical thing, but would it mean she'd be trapped in some out-of-the-way house, not involved at all in bringing down whoever had tried to kill her? Even though she wasn't in law enforcement and she knew she couldn't officially investigate, she didn't want to sit on the sidelines. She'd been doing that with her whole life for too long. She wanted to help stop this.

Besides, if she went to a safe house now, would she see Andre again?

"She can stay with me," Andre said, not seeming to care about the smirks from Porter and Franks at his words. "I'll keep her safe."

"WHAT HAVE YOU GOT?" Andre asked, opening the door wide for his brothers and Scott that afternoon. It was beginning to feel like a regular occurrence, all of them gathering to work on Juliette's situation. Although Andre wasn't happy about the circumstances, it was fun to work with his brothers this way. Since all of them worked for different law enforcement agencies, he'd never done that before.

"I've got more pizza," Marcos said.

"I've got beer," Scott contributed.

"And I've got news," Cole finished.

Andre shut the door behind them. "You win," he told Cole. "Let's hear it."

"I've got a little bit of news, too," Marcos said. "I just thought you'd appreciate the food."

"Me, too," Scott said. "But my news isn't case related. Not exactly."

"All right, let's hear all of it," Andre said, ushering them into the living room, where Juliette was waiting, wearing another pair of Shaye's too-long pants and slightly too-tight T-shirts.

When they'd returned from the WFO earlier, she'd changed out of the clothes she'd worn to Quantico, which had been torn and filthy. Then she'd put her hands on her hips and informed him that she might not have investigative experience, but she knew the players best and she could help. He'd already known he was falling hard for her before that, but watching her stand there so determined had pushed him over the edge.

He stared at her now, looking eager to hear the news his brothers and his partner had brought. She was a natural part of the group, and she seemed at home in his living room. They needed to wrap up this case, because once he could be sure she was out of danger, he was going to ask her to stay in Virginia, to give the two of them a chance at a relationship.

The idea unnerved him, in part because he had no idea if she still considered Pennsylvania home or if she'd want to stay in a place that had just been another city in a long line of hiding places. Not to mention she'd spent most of her time since college either dating, being married to, or running from Dylan Keane. Once she was free of him, would she even want a relationship? Or would she want a chance to be totally independent, completely free of any man?

Pushing the worry aside, Andre sat beside Juliette on the couch as Marcos opened up the pizza on his coffee table.

"Well, since I won," Cole said with a grin as he settled in one of the cushy chairs, "I talked to a detective from Juliette's old town, one cop to another. The case agents had already called a few times today, so they'd gotten the lowdown. Apparently, when Juliette disappeared three years ago, it made the department nervous, since it happened right after they'd ignored her claims." He looked at Juliette. "Keane told them you'd moved back to England to live with your parents."

She sighed. "And they believed that? I didn't spend much time with anyone from the department other than Jim, but I saw them sometimes. *Someone* there should have known I had barely spoken to my parents in years."

"I think they did," Cole replied. "But Keane must have doctored photos, because he produced some of you and your parents, so they bought it. He'd told them you couldn't get over, um, your miscarriage."

"He made that up," Juliette cut in, and Cole seemed relieved.

"Anyway, he said you had to get away for a while and I think they bought it, but a few of them thought the whole thing was odd."

Juliette leaned forward on the couch. "Did anyone check into it?"

"No."

Juliette sat back. She didn't seem surprised that no one had bothered to see if she'd really left of her own accord or if something had happened to her.

"What kind of slipshod department is this?" Andre demanded.

"Keane was one of their top detectives," Cole reminded him. "And Juliette had never made any complaints before. By the time she did, he'd laid the groundwork for them to dismiss it. I agree that they should have checked it out, but it's not really surprising they didn't. You always want to give your colleague— especially one who's probably saved your life a time or two—the benefit of the doubt."

Andre nodded grudgingly. HRT was a brotherhood,

which was something he loved about it. A good police department would be the same way. If one of his HRT buddies had been accused of something like this, he probably wouldn't have believed it either. Everyone had blind spots.

The thought took him back to his dream from that morning. "Hey, this is unrelated, but later we need to talk." He looked at Cole, sitting on his big chair, and Marcos, perched on the armrest. "It's about the fire." He didn't need to explain which one.

They both seemed quizzical, but nodded.

"So, anyway," Cole continued, "since the FBI has been asking for information, one of the officers pulled the Manning case and went over it again, and I asked him if I could review the forensic evidence."

"And?"

"And Loews's fingerprint was found at the scene. It was on a pen that was under the body. The theory at the time was that either any prints were wiped down and this one got missed because of its location, or more likely that Loews actually had the pen on him and didn't realize he'd dropped it."

"So, basically, it would be easy for someone else to drop," Marcos said.

"Yeah, but not one of the detectives. The responding officer found the pen. It was fingerprinted at the scene. So, if it was left behind, then the killer did it."

"Well, actually that makes sense," Andre said. "If we're going with the theory that Loews and Harkin were working together and Harkin paid off the detectives. Juliette heard Harkin tell her ex that he'd keep him out of it but couldn't help Loews. That's probably why. Loews dropped the pen at the scene and didn't realize it and it was too late for the detectives to make that evidence go away."

"The detective I spoke to *did* say that he remembered Keane being gung ho on Harkin being the killer, *not* Loews, until one day he jumped in with his partner saying it was Loews. They were surprised, because he'd been insisting so loudly for so long, but they figured the evidence didn't bear it out."

"Any word on Jim Valance's whereabouts?" Andre asked.

"Nope. They're searching for him, but haven't found anything. They've had a bulletin out on his license plate since he didn't show up for work, because they were worried something bad could have happened to him, but there have been no hits on it yet."

Andre looked up at his younger brother, who was already on his third slice of pizza. "What did you dig up?"

"I talked to Kendry again ten minutes before I got here. He checked earlier today and Keane was still at the cabin. But given everything that's happening, I suspect Keane's department is going to call him home soon. And Kendry promises to check again in the morning."

"Scott?" Andre asked.

"Well, not to add any more pressure to this situation, but I need Nadia's weapon. I promised her I'd bring it back to Quantico tomorrow."

Juliette flushed. "Will you tell her I'm sorry? I left the bullets in the trash can outside the bathroom."

"Yeah, we found those," Scott said. "And I will. But you should probably tell her yourself when this is all over, because otherwise, the next time she sees you, she might use her persuasive techniques to get a personal

apology. And by persuasive techniques, I mean her no-
torious chokehold."

He said it as though it was a given Juliette would be
sticking around, and Andre wanted his partner to be
right, but from the surprise on Juliette's face, he wasn't
sure.

"I also talked to someone at OPR," Scott continued.
"Unofficially. He can't promise me anything, and he only
talked to me at all because my sister saved his life a few
years ago." Scott turned to Juliette and explained, "My
sister is a SWAT agent." He returned his attention to
Andre. "Anyway, he says if the investigation shows a
reasonable belief on Juliette's part that she couldn't trust
law enforcement to help her and *if* you weren't unreasonably hindering an investigation, it'll just be a mark in
your file. He says you might get off with a verbal warning, but he doubts it."

"Who decides this?" Juliette asked, nerves clear in
her voice. "What can I do to prove to them that this is
my fault and not Andre's?"

"Don't worry," Andre told her, relieved that the agent
didn't think he would be suspended—or worse. He was
surprised, because part of him was expecting it.

"Well, I am wor—" she started, but the ringing of
Andre's and Cole's phones at the same time cut her off.

"That's weird," Andre said as they both answered,
and then he looked over at Cole, wondering if his brother
was getting the same news he was right now. From the
expression on Cole's face, he was.

"What is it?" Marcos asked as they both hung up.

"They just found Jim Valance. He's dead."

Chapter Twelve

"What?" Juliette gaped at him. "Jim is dead? How?"

"A homeless man stumbled across his body in an old warehouse. The place was condemned, so no one was supposed to be in there," Cole said.

Juliette nodded. She knew exactly which warehouse he was talking about. Everyone in town knew it. The warehouse had been condemned for as long as she could remember, but somehow it never got bulldozed, and every few years, police had to rouse squatters from it. "It's a good place to hide a body. Usually, no one goes in there until it *really* starts getting cold outside, generally December."

"Well, estimated time of death is yesterday afternoon," Andre contributed, his expression hard to read.

"Right before Dylan left town," Juliette said. It made sense, in a way. If Jim was trying to go after Harkin for more money, he was probably putting pressure on Dylan to help, too. She should have realized earlier that Dylan wouldn't have been in this alone—he and Jim always worked as a team. If Jim pushed hard enough and Dylan wanted to put it all behind him, maybe he'd snapped.

But somehow, even though the idea of Dylan trying

to kill her didn't seem far-fetched, she couldn't imagine him turning on Jim.

She shook her head. "You talked about the law enforcement brotherhood? Dylan and Jim were like brothers." It was a connection that had always seemed to go deeper than his loyalty to her. The loyalty she knew she'd completely broken when she'd confronted him.

"He chased you pretty determinedly," Andre said.

"Yeah, but you've been putting doubt in my mind that his intent was to kill me. Either way," she rushed on when Andre seemed ready to keep arguing, "he knew Jim a lot longer than me. They weren't just partners. They grew up together."

"Getting back to Valance," Scott said quickly, not giving Andre time to respond, "What happened to him?"

"He was shot in the head with a small-caliber weapon. They should know more in a day or two, after the autopsy. The locals are handling the scene, and so far if they have anything useful forensically, they're not sharing. They do know the gun was unregistered."

She wondered if that was supposed to mean something to her. Of course a cop would know not to use his own weapon, but she assumed most people wouldn't do that if the murder was premeditated.

"Was he moved, or did someone lure him to that warehouse?" Marcos asked.

"He was killed there," Andre said. "So either it was a meeting place no one would see or someone took Valance there under duress and then killed him."

"Doesn't that mean it was probably Harkin?" Juliette asked. "There's no reason for Jim and Dylan not to be seen together. They're partners."

"Well, I was digging up information on Harkin while

you were in the shower earlier today," Andre began. Somehow, the words sounded intimate, as though they really shared a home instead of this temporary situation. "And he filed a flight plan for his private plane to fly down to an island off the coast of Florida this week. Supposedly, he left at the beginning of the week, which would give him an alibi."

"Supposedly?" Juliette asked.

"It's his own plane," Cole jumped in. "Right now, all we know is that he filed a flight plan. There's a chance he could have filed the plan and not actually taken the flight. Or the flight might have happened with someone else on it."

"Whether or not the flight took off should be easy to confirm, but it'll take a little longer, because we're dealing with private airstrips. As for him sending someone in his place?" Andre shrugged. "Unlikely but definitely possible. We'll have to dig a little deeper on that."

Could Dylan really have killed Jim? Juliette wasn't sure why that was so hard for her to imagine, after the horrible things she'd thought Dylan was willing to do to her. But it didn't feel right. Dylan and Jim's friendship not only went way back, but it was also a bond she couldn't imagine him betraying—maybe because unlike her relationship with Dylan, Jim's had been on equal footing, a brotherhood. "I don't think Dylan did this," she insisted, noticing Andre's frown deepen.

There was an awkward silence for a minute, then Marcos broke it. "Well, with a cop dead and his police force investigating, plus the WFO agents on your case, plus all of us, we'll find answers soon." He gave her a wide grin and added, "You've got a heck of a team on your side."

Juliette managed to smile, because it was true. She

did have a heck of a team. But then her gaze was drawn back to Andre, who was sitting close enough to touch on the couch beside her. All she'd have to do was stretch out her hand a tiny bit and take his. But somehow, he felt far away right now.

Once they had their answers, what would it mean for her and Andre?

THREE HOURS LATER, Andre faced his brothers, who both wore expectant, slightly nervous expressions. Scott had headed home to his fiancée half an hour ago, and Juliette had gone to bed a few minutes ago. She'd claimed she was exhausted from the day, which was probably true, but he suspected her real reason for leaving the room was to give him time alone with Cole and Marcos.

"She's totally crazy about you," Marcos said now, obviously noticing where his attention had strayed.

"Don't mess this up," Cole added, in what Andre and Marcos jokingly called his "big brother" voice.

"This whole thing with her ex…" Andre shook his head.

"One way or another, he's going to end up behind bars. If he's *not* the one who killed Valance and hired the convicts to go after Juliette, there's still the matter of taking a payoff from a murderer." Marcos leaned back in his chair, as though that was all there was to it.

"You're worried she's still hung up on him?" Cole asked. "Because I don't think so."

"Not exactly." Although he had, just a little, when she'd insisted Keane was innocent in his partner's murder. "I guess I'm worried that once this is all over, she won't really even know what she wants."

Marcos made a face at him. "She's a grown-up."

"Yeah, but she spent her life being sent off to boarding schools by parents who had no interest, then she married this guy, who was obviously a real winner, and then she's spent all these years running from him. I don't want to take advantage of the fact that I might be the first guy who's treated her decently."

Both his brothers were silent, then Marcos said, "She seems pretty self-reliant. She managed to stay ahead of this guy for three years, right?" When Andre nodded, he continued, "She didn't lean on anyone during all of that time. That takes a lot of willpower. Besides, she was willing to turn herself in for you. That's pretty huge."

Andre hadn't really thought about that. He'd spent so much of his energy today worrying about her when he'd woken to find her gone, and then dealing with the aftermath. They hadn't really had a chance to talk about why she'd gone to the FBI herself. But suddenly her words during their phone call at the scene of the shooting came back to him.

I was trying to keep you out of trouble. You and your brothers.

"This might not be what you want to hear," Cole said, "but if this ends, and she's finally free, logic says she won't stay in one of the places she was hiding. Especially not with the way she talked about her job the other day. As if it was a placeholder for what she really wanted to do, but she knew the job she wanted would make it too easy for her ex to track her. If she does stay, then I think you'll have your answer."

Andre nodded. His brothers made sense, but there was still a voice in the back of his head warning him that relationships forged in these kinds of circumstances didn't last. Not that they even had a relationship. He wasn't sure exactly *what* they had, but hour by hour, it *felt* more like a relationship, at least on his end.

And Marcos was right about one thing: the fact that she'd been willing to put herself in danger to keep him and his brothers out of trouble? All of a sudden, he wanted to send his brothers home and kiss her for that. Preferably for a very long time.

"So, what was this about the fire?" Marcos asked when Andre went silent.

He shook himself out of thoughts about Juliette, on the other side of the wall, probably tucked into bed in the nightgown Shaye had lent her. "Did either of you ever read the report on it?"

They both sat a little straighter and nodded, and Andre knew his surprise showed. None of them had ever talked about it. But then again, they were similar in so many ways. Probably the same thing that had driven them all into law enforcement had driven them to need answers.

"It was an accident," Cole said. "The fire started at the back of the house. Someone left some candles lit after going to bed. They were close to papers on the desk, and it spread fast from there."

"Stupid," Marcos hissed, and the frustration in his voice took Andre back to those terrifying moments watching Cole tamp out the fire on his younger brother, of the hours at the hospital while their burns were treated.

Cole's had been superficial, mostly to his hands. Over the years, the scars had faded until they were no longer visible at all. Marcos would carry a reminder of the fire on his back for the rest of his life.

"I don't think it was an accident," Andre told them.

Cole leaned forward. "Why?"

"Everyone was supposed to be upstairs, asleep, at the time of the fire, right?"

His brothers nodded.

"But I don't think everyone was. I've been dreaming about that night ever since that call I got a few days ago."

"To the scene where the father set the house on fire with his wife and kid inside," Marcos said.

Surprise made Andre sit back, and Cole added, "Scott told us about it. He thought it might bring back memories."

"You didn't say anything."

"Yeah, well, you got pretty busy right afterward," Cole said, tipping his head in the direction Juliette had disappeared.

"Who wasn't sleeping at the time of the fire?" Marcos asked, bringing them back on topic.

"Our foster father," Andre said. "And one of the other kids." He racked his mind for the name of the girl who'd joined them in the house a few months before the fire started. "Brenna."

"No way," Marcos said instantly, reminding Andre that Brenna had only been a year younger than Marcos then—putting her around eleven—and that Marcos had developed his first crush the day she arrived.

"What makes you think they weren't sleeping when the fire started?" Cole asked, lines furrowing his forehead.

"They were coming from around the back of the house. Everyone else was in the front or coming out the side door, logical if they'd come from upstairs."

"Maybe they came out the front, then went around to the back to see if there was another way to get the rest of us out," Marcos suggested.

"Maybe," Andre agreed. "I guess that could make sense if it was just him. But why would he take Brenna with him?"

"She followed him?" Cole suggested.

"I don't know." Andre shook his head. "The dreams I've been having have been bothering me, as though I was forgetting something important. And then when I remembered where they'd been, it all clicked into place."

Being with Juliette had helped it click, Andre realized now. As they'd worked to unravel who was coming after her, they'd put doubts in her mind about her past—both that it was Keane after her, and that what she'd overheard really meant what she thought it did.

His own past was suddenly the same way—a nebulous thing, instead of set in stone the way he'd always accepted.

"Why would either of them set fire to the house?" Cole asked, always the reasonable one, bringing Andre's mind back to the conversation. "Our foster dad lost his house that day. It wasn't salvageable at all. And Brenna had only been there a few months. What reason would she have to set a fire?"

"Do you think someone was hurting her, and we didn't know it?" Marcos asked.

They all knew it could happen. All three of them had been in multiple foster homes over the years, and all of them had seen both good and bad. And they'd lost track of Brenna after that day, so whatever secrets she had, she'd taken with her.

"She never said anything," Cole said slowly. "And if she set the fire, he didn't turn her in. Which suggests either that she wasn't to blame or that he had something bigger to cover up."

When Marcos's face darkened, Andre said, "There were a lot of kids through that house. It wasn't exactly full of love and sunshine, but I never saw or heard anything terrible or suspicious."

"I didn't either," Cole agreed.

"So then why?" Marcos asked.

"There could be a perfectly logical explanation," Cole stressed, but as Andre knew they were all thinking the same thing.

The fire that day had split them apart, sent each of them off into new foster homes on their own, with no one to have their backs. It had been a defining moment in all of their lives. Having brothers ripped from them after they'd finally found a new family had impacted each of them hugely. If someone had caused it, no matter the reason, Andre wanted to know why.

Once they helped Juliette get out of danger, it was time to dig into their past.

DREAD ABOUT WHAT he might find in his past and worry about what his future could hold consumed Andre as he stood in the doorway to the guest room. But as Juliette stirred under the covers, opening her eyes and staring back at him, the present seemed very clear.

She blinked a few times and sat up. The covers fell to her waist and he noticed she was wearing his FBI shirt instead of the nightgown Shaye had sent.

A wave of possessiveness swept through him.

"What's wrong?" she asked, her voice heavy with sleep.

"Nothing." He didn't move, just stayed rooted in the doorway, watching her and wondering if he should have waited until morning for this.

She held out her hand. "Did you talk to your brothers about the fire?"

It was all the encouragement he needed. Pushing away from the door frame, he went and sat on the edge of the bed, taking the hand she offered in both of his. "Yeah, I did. We're going to worry about it later."

"You want to tell me about it?"

He shrugged. It wasn't why he'd come into her room, but he found he *did* want to talk to her about it. "The house that Cole, Marcos and I lived in burned down when I was fourteen. We always thought it was an accident, but now I'm not so sure."

She swore softly and he had to laugh, because with everything that had happened over the past few days, it was the first time he'd heard her swear.

"That day was really scary," he said, stroking the soft skin on her hand. "But the real tragedy for us was that it split us up. The foster parents we lived with then lost their house and so all the kids went different places. When I moved into that house, it felt like home for the first time since my parents died. Not really because of the foster parents, but Cole. He treated me as if I was his real brother, from day one. And then Marcos came into the house, and it was the same thing. It was this instant connection, as though we shared a blood bond."

Juliette smiled and in the darkness, her eyes had a stormy quality, because he couldn't see the flecks of blue amidst the hazel. "I can see it. The three of you even look alike."

He must have seemed skeptical, because she laughed and added, "Not physically. But there's something about the expressions you make, this intense thing all three of you get. When it happens at the same time, it's obvious you're brothers."

No one had ever told him that before, and the idea made him smile. "Did you know that when Cole got out of foster care, he took on multiple jobs so he could get a place and take me and Marcos in when we hit eighteen?"

"Wow," she said softly. "That's a pretty amazing family you have."

It was, and it made him think of how she'd grown up—with blood relatives who'd left her to tackle life on her own. He twined their hands together more tightly. "What about you? Any family you're close to?"

She shrugged. "My grandma and I were really close when I was young, before she died. It's why I picked her last name to use here, because she showed me what family was supposed to be. But otherwise? Not really. I had some cousins in England I got along with well, but my parents sent me to the US when I hit middle school, so I only saw them once every few years after that."

"You didn't go home for holidays?"

"Not usually."

The sadness he was feeling for her must have shown, because she said, "It was hard at first, but I made friends. In college, too. Honestly, part of my loneliness was my own fault. I've never been good at letting people get too close. I always worry they'll disappear." She flushed, as though the admission embarrassed her.

"I'm not going to disappear." The words came out of his mouth before he'd really thought them through, but they must have been the right ones, because she leaned forward and kissed him.

Unlike the kisses they'd shared before, this one was tender and brief, like a couple who'd known each other a long time. It was less about desire and more about comfort and connection, but as he slid his hand through the silky strands of her hair that fell forward when she kissed him, he wanted more.

She must have felt the same thing, because she slid out from underneath the covers and scooted closer, not breaking contact. Then her arms were around his neck and she was stroking his tongue with hers as his hands found the bare softness of her legs.

"Mmm," she mumbled softly, sliding even closer to him and making his T-shirt ride up her thighs.

She kept kissing him—slow, deep kisses that were making him crazy as he avoided her bandage and skimmed his hands up and down her legs. "This isn't why I came in here," he said semicoherently.

Pulling back slightly, Juliette gave him a seductive smile. "Really? Why'd you come in here?"

"I wanted to talk about the future." He was jumping the gun and he knew it. But despite the fact that he could spend hours on a rifle scope totally still and silent, when it came to his personal life, he wasn't good at waiting. When he wanted something, he dove in headfirst.

She looked wary as she asked, "What about it?"

"When this is all over, and we've got your ex and whoever else is involved behind bars, I'm hoping you'll stay in Virginia."

Surprise flitted across her face, and he wondered if this was a mistake, if he should have just kept pursuing her until she gave him a real chance, rather than giving her time to think too much about it. But since it was already out there, he kept pushing. "I want us to get to know each other under more normal circumstances. I want to take you out on real dates, kiss you good-night on your porch."

She hesitated, and he knew that whatever feelings she had for him, on some level she wasn't ready for another serious relationship.

"It's okay," he said before she could shoot him down. "You don't have to answer right now. Just think about it."

"Right now, I need to—" Juliette started, but whatever she was going to say was cut off by the ringing of his phone.

He scowled at it, not just because of the bad timing, but also because it was late. The readout said Cole.

Cursing, he picked up. "What's happening?"

"Uh, did I wake you?" Cole asked. "I thought you'd still be up, since we didn't leave all that long ago."

"No, I'm up," Andre said, staring at Juliette, who was tugging the shirt back down her legs.

"Shaye's been up late, reviewing the forensic details from the Manning murder."

"What does she think?"

"Well, you're not going to like this, but she thinks this is more than just a couple of cops helping one murderer stay out of jail. She thinks Loews was framed. Shaye thinks he's actually innocent."

Chapter Thirteen

What was wrong with her?

Juliette mentally cursed herself for her idiocy. Andre had offered her a chance at exactly what she'd wanted—him—and she'd frozen. Worse, she knew she was right not to make any promises now.

Even if they brought down her ex, even if she was safe for the first time in years, was she really ready to be in a relationship again? The idea of being with Andre was exciting, but it was also terrifying.

When she'd married Dylan, she'd thought that was it. She'd found her forever. She hadn't had any doubts when she'd said yes to his proposal, hadn't suspected they'd be anything but happy together. The end had come out of nowhere, even if in retrospect she could see that the relationship hadn't been right.

Andre was a good guy—she didn't doubt that. But the fear she'd shared with him earlier hadn't gone away: How did she know she could trust her own judgment about what was right for her? About *who* was right for her? And was she even in the kind of place where she should be in a relationship at all?

Yet, the thought of throwing away a chance to be with Andre made her feel physically ill.

"How is that possible?" Andre was asking into the phone, bringing her attention back to the present.

Finally, he hung up the phone with his brother so she could ask, "What did he say?"

"What were *you* going to say?" Andre asked, setting his phone on the bed and taking her hand again. There was nervousness in the depths of his gaze, and he always seemed so sure of himself that the expression didn't seem right on him.

Her breath came faster. Could she tell him she was scared? That even though she had feelings for him, she wasn't sure she was ready to act on them? It wouldn't be fair to ask him to wait around until she was ready, but maybe they could put this on hold, just for now.

"Can we wait to talk about you and me until after this is over? I need to be able to put this all behind me before I can think about moving forward." It felt like a cop-out, but it was the truth, too. Maybe once Dylan was really, truly out of her life, she'd feel more confident about any decisions she made.

Disappointment flashed across his face, but then he hid it and pressed a quick kiss to her lips. "I get it." He didn't give her a chance to elaborate, and his tone shifted into what she'd come to recognize as his serious work voice. "Cole just heard from Shaye. She studied the forensic details from the case file, and she thinks Loews is innocent."

"What?" Juliette gaped at him. "But the pen was found *under* the body. It had his prints. You think Harkin framed him," she realized. "But what about what I heard Dylan saying to Harkin, about not being able to keep Loews out of it?"

"Are you sure that's exactly what you heard him say? Is there any chance you misunderstood?"

She thought back to that moment three years ago that had changed her life. She'd walked into the house from the side door, and she hadn't taken her car that day, so Dylan hadn't heard her. She hadn't realized he was there, either, because both of them had planned to be out all day. But when she'd walked toward the stairs, she'd heard voices from the kitchen. She'd stopped as soon as she'd heard the unfamiliar voice with Dylan.

She remembered the exact instant she'd recognized it from news footage as Harkin's voice. She remembered her disbelief, then the anger, then the panic.

Could she really be one hundred percent positive of Dylan's exact words from that day? Some parts of it seemed stamped in her memory, but other parts felt hazy, as if they were a dream. Still… "I think so. If it wasn't exact, it was close."

"So, Keane told Harkin, 'I'll keep you out of it, but there's nothing I can do for Loews now'?"

"Yeah."

"Hmm."

"Why does Shaye think the pen was planted?"

"She says that Loews's print was the only one on the pen."

"So?"

"So, it was a perfect print, easy to pull, and yet there was nothing else. No smudges, nothing."

"That sounds a little odd," Juliette agreed. "But maybe the fact that Manning landed on the pen smudged off the other prints? Besides, shouldn't the original forensics expert have noticed that if it were a problem? Or Loews's experts at the trial?"

"Probably," Andre said. "But either it didn't come up, or it didn't sway anyone. But I find it strange. It's not weird to find no useable prints or to find partials from multiple people or just smudges, but to get one print that's exactly what you need and nothing else should have made someone's alarms go off. It sounds way too convenient to me. If I'd been the investigator, I'd have been suspicious."

"So, this is about more than putting away a murderer," Juliette summed up, feeling herself go pale. "If Shaye is right, then by running when I did, I basically helped Dylan put an innocent man in jail."

"WE'RE NOT GOING to know for sure if Loews is innocent until we find Harkin. We need to figure out if he's really in Florida," Andre said, but he could tell by Juliette's stricken expression that she was only half listening.

"It sounded as if Loews and Harkin were in it together, that they were both guilty," she said, her voice baffled and horrified.

"They might have been," Andre said, trying to focus on their conversation instead of their proximity on the bed. "Right now, this is just Shaye's theory."

She gave a smile that didn't reach her eyes. "Cole said Shaye was the best."

"She's pretty good, but my brother has had a crush on Shaye for a couple of years now, so he's easily swayed by her opinion."

"Or part of *why* he's into her is because she's so good at what she does," Juliette said, and Andre knew it was true.

"Let's just try not to get ahead of ourselves here." He knew exactly what she was doing right now, blaming herself for one more thing that wasn't her fault. "You can't make yourself feel responsible for other people's bad deeds."

"If I'd known—if I'd even *suspected*—I never would have—"

"You tried to turn in your husband, and the police ignored you," Andre reminded her. "That took guts."

"Yeah, but I would have kept trying if I'd thought an innocent man was paying for Harkin's crime." Her forehead furrowed, as though she was trying to figure out how she would have done that and stayed ahead of a husband who'd threatened to kill her if she told.

"But you didn't know," Andre said. "So all we can do now is figure out the truth and make sure whoever should pay goes to jail."

A tremor ran through her, so subtle he wouldn't have noticed it if he hadn't taken her hand earlier. Was it the thought of her husband—a cop—landing in jail? They had protocols for that, separation plans, because cops didn't tend to fare well in prison.

He remembered what she'd asked earlier—she'd wondered if Keane might have taken the payoff because Harkin had threatened Juliette. Although he didn't feel any sympathy for the man who'd violated his professional duty and taken money to let a murderer go free, Andre's animosity lessened just a little at the idea that Keane might have been at all motivated by the desire to keep Juliette safe.

"Once we find out the extent of Keane's involvement, if we can get him to cooperate in bringing down Harkin, I'll try to do what I can for him," Andre said. He didn't add that the promise would be void if it turned out Keane *had* been the one trying to kill Juliette. If that were the case, Andre was going to be sure he spent the rest of his miserable life behind bars.

Surprise flashed across Juliette's face, and then she shifted on the bed to face him. "It probably seems—" she frowned, clearly searching for the right words, then continued "—strange that I would care at all what happens to Dylan."

"Not at—"

She cut him off. "I don't love him anymore."

The words gave him hope, strong enough he actually felt it in his chest. If she really meant that, if she'd truly put her feelings for her ex behind her, then they did have a chance. And although he had real concerns about her being in a place where she knew what she wanted for herself, he wasn't afraid to wait. Staring at her now, sitting so close to him in his guest bed, her hair slightly wild from either sleep or his hands a few minutes earlier, he knew that when this was over, he was going to fight for her.

"But once, I loved him enough to promise my life to him," Juliette continued, not seeming to realize he'd made a big decision. "Even after all the things he's done—or might have done—there's still a part of me that feels bound by that promise. Not to share my life with him," she amended quickly enough that Andre wondered what expression he'd made. "But if he *wasn't* actually trying to kill me—if it's been Jim or Harkin all this time—then I feel as though I at least owe him something. Maybe just some measure of forgiveness," she finished softly.

He smiled at her, because that was probably more than he'd be willing to offer someone who'd threatened to kill him, regardless of whether the person ever tried to carry out the threat. The thought reminded him of his suspicions about the fire, and he wondered what the goal was if it had been arson. Had the fire just gotten out of control, or had someone wanted to kill one of the people in the house?

His foster father had held a blue-collar job, his foster mother had worked part-time out of the house, and they'd used the money from having foster kids to bridge the gap. He'd never seen either of them do anything that would put them in danger. And everyone else in the house had been kids. Cole had been the oldest, but he was only fifteen at the time.

It didn't make sense. Could he be wrong?

As soon as he thought it, he dismissed the idea. Whether or not the fire had been intentional, he was pretty sure that his foster dad and Brenna had been in the back of the house where the fire started. And that meant there was a story no one knew. When Juliette was safe, he was determined to figure out what it was, and he knew Cole and Marcos felt the same way.

"You think that's silly?" Juliette asked, and Andre realized he'd gone silent for too long.

"No. I think it takes a special kind of strength to give that kind of forgiveness."

She smiled up at him, her expression soft and almost shy, and he got to his feet before he did something she'd already said she wasn't ready for, like pull her to him and do his best to never let go.

"In the morning, we'll figure out a plan of action to finish this."

Juliette leaned back against the headboard, her mouth forming a silent *O*. He could tell she was surprised he wasn't staying.

Then she sat forward again, and he knew he needed

to get out of there before he broke his promise to give her time to figure out what she wanted. "Good night," he said, then practically ran from the room.

"WE DON'T REALLY know anything until we find Harkin," Andre said softly into his cell phone early the next morning as he nursed a cup of coffee at his kitchen table, alone.

Juliette was still asleep, and although she'd only been in his house a few days, he already missed their easy companionship in the morning, the way her sleepy eyes instantly widened with just one sip of his coffee. If he needed an excuse to keep making it strong, that was it.

"Well, I spoke to the case agents and they're still trying to find him. They're in touch with officials on the island off the coast of Florida where he supposedly flew early this week, but so far, there's no sign of him," Scott said. "They've got a local agent heading over to talk to airline officials at the private airport where his plane landed. They'll try to get a confirmation one way or another."

"If he didn't take that flight, he probably drove here. Did they ever locate Valance's car?"

"I don't think so, but if Harkin has gotten away with killing Loews and a cop, I doubt he'd be dumb enough to take that cop's vehicle."

"True. Do we know what Harkin drives?" Andre asked.

Scott snorted. "A lot. The guy apparently collects cars, both high-end and classic. With Juliette's statement, the case agents got a little leeway in pulling information on Harkin, but that's a lot of cars to try to track down. So far, there's no sign of any of them, but that doesn't mean much. For all we know, he had his secretary rent him a car before he took Harkin's flight to Florida."

"All right. What have you heard about the shell casings used at Quantico?" Andre tried to hide his frustration, but he was sure Scott could hear it. He'd been on HRT for years, so it had been a while since he'd worked a case, but doing it this way—outside the loop—was frustrating. Although HRT required him to sit with his eye pressed to a rifle scope for hours, sometimes days, on end, he'd gotten used to that sort of "hurry up and wait" scenario. This kind of waiting, with the ability to take the next steps with Juliette hanging in the balance, had him on edge.

"Yeah, you're not going to like this. The guy wore gloves to load them. We've got nothing."

"And the hide?"

"It's odd. I went up there myself," Scott said, and Andre was glad, because no one knew hides the way snipers did, because they made hides all the time.

"How so?"

"Well, remember how I said the shooting was obviously someone without a lot of experience on a rifle? The same is true of the hide. It was functional, in a way. He was definitely *trying* to create something to blend into his surroundings, but it was amateurish. I think he got training somewhere, but not professionally."

"You think he took some kind of shoddy civilian training?"

"That would be my guess. It's as though he knew the theory, but not quite how to put it into practice."

"Juliette said Keane knew how to shoot a rifle, and now that we know Valance was dead when the attack at Quantico happened…"

"Harkin is our best suspect," Scott finished. "Yeah, that makes sense. He's got the money to take that kind of training for kicks, and it fits with what I've been seeing in my research. This guy did a lot of weekend training programs—race car driving, skiing, even wine making—but didn't stick with anything. I'll see if I can find anything about firearms training."

"I think our best bet is to locate him now."

"Locate who now?" Juliette asked, yawning as she walked into the kitchen in his T-shirt and not much else.

He loved that look on her. The thought danced around in his mind, filling him with mild panic. Despite how little time he'd known her, his feelings were too strong, too protective, too intense to be simple attraction. He had no idea when it had begun—probably the moment she'd walked through his door—but he was falling in love with her. Fast.

And she didn't know what she wanted when this was all over. He wasn't even sure she'd committed to staying in Virginia.

"What's the matter?" Juliette asked.

"Nothing. Just getting info from Scott," Andre replied, glad to hear his voice at least sounded normal.

She looked suspicious, but didn't press it as she helped herself to a cup of coffee, topping it off with a generous dose of cream.

"Wimp," he mouthed at her.

Scott continued, "Yeah, the case agents are working on locating Harkin now. But one more thing I *can* tell you about him? The guy owned a lot of guns. And I mean, a *lot*. As though he was a collector. So, whether or not it was him who shot at Quantico yesterday—and I'm thinking it was—he owned more than one rifle."

"Well, that's good. So, even if we don't have prints, we'll probably be able to match the casings to a rifle when we arrest him," Andre said.

"Yeah. Now we just need to find him."

Chapter Fourteen

"We found him."

"What?" Andre stood in the doorway of his house, staring at Franks and Porter, who'd shown up unannounced, wearing rumpled suits and excited expressions.

Juliette walked up behind him, thankfully having changed out of his T-shirt and into another set of Shaye's borrowed clothes. "You found Harkin?"

The two agents shared a look, and even though they'd known Andre was keeping an eye on Juliette, he could see exactly what they were thinking. He would have been annoyed, except they were right. There was nothing professional about the way he felt about her.

"Where is he?" Not giving them time to answer, Andre said, "If you're planning an arrest, I want in on it." The guy had shot at Juliette. Andre wanted to be there. Ideally, he'd be the one to slap on the handcuffs and let Harkin know he'd be facing a lifetime in prison by the time they were finished with him.

"That's why we're here," Franks said and Andre knew his surprise showed; he'd expected to need to fight to be included.

Andre held open the door. "Come on in."

Franks seemed amused that they'd only been invited

in after agreeing to let him help, but Porter's usual serious expression didn't change as Andre led them to his living room. They sat on the two chairs, leaving him and Juliette the couch.

Juliette settled in next to him, at the kind of distance they'd expect if she was a simple witness. Andre longed to take her hand in his and squeeze, but he resisted and stared at the case agents instead, waiting for more details.

"Harkin may have killed Valance, who was a veteran police officer. Whatever the circumstances, we're considering Harkin a high threat. Normally, we'd bring in our SWAT team, but given your involvement—" Porter's gaze went to Juliette again as he finished "—we thought you'd be interested in kicking down the door for us."

"Absolutely," Andre said. Normally, as a sniper, he had high ground, meaning it was his responsibility to survey the situation below and to keep his team members safe. But he'd trained as a regular operator too, in all kinds of dangerous setups. Kicking down a door to get to one armed multimillionaire should be simple.

"Good," Franks said. "It's a little atypical and we had to get special permission, but you've assisted the investigation and you have insight into the players that could be useful." Unsaid but hanging in the air was that he'd helped only after he'd hindered it by hiding Juliette.

"What about Dylan?" Juliette asked. "Are you going to bring him in now, too? We know he left town after his partner's murder. Even if he didn't kill Jim, he's still involved in this whole thing somehow."

"No," Porter said.

Franks explained, "Valance's murder is technically a local investigation. We're coordinating with them because of a possible connection, but right now, there's no evidence Keane killed him. We're after Harkin for the Quantico shooting—that's *our* jurisdiction."

"We can bring Keane in, lean on him and try to get him to break," Porter told Juliette. "But your ex is a cop. Not only will he have a union rep and a lawyer, he knows the drill. He'll figure out pretty quickly we don't have anything and then he'll know we're onto him."

"We're hoping Harkin will give us the leverage we need to hold Keane," Franks added. "Because we *do* have more on Harkin. It's not a slam dunk by any means."

"I used up a favor with a judge for this one," Porter grumbled.

Franks rolled his eyes. "But we found a record of a special firearms training course he took last year. I showed his instructor the hide outside of Quantico and she swears that's his work. It won't hold for long, but it'll get us an arrest and a chance to test fire Harkin's rifle. Hopefully our labs can connect the rifle to the shooting and then if he's smart, he'll be begging to help us."

Porter leaned forward, looking antsy. "Let's get moving. Diaz, call your partner and see if he wants in. Then we'll handle the paperwork and get moving. We got a hit on one of Harkin's cars early this morning and an unmarked police car followed it to a residential location. The police are keeping a discreet eye on it, making sure we know if he moves, but this is a good spot to take him down. It's out of the way, so there won't be any collateral nearby."

"It turns out to be the home of one of Harkin's employees, a woman he apparently sees socially on and off. Anyway, she's in Europe, finishing a deal for him, so he knew she wouldn't be there. We talked to her today and confirmed that Harkin has the code to the house. She had no idea he was there."

"You made sure she knew she'd be in legal trouble if she gave him the heads up, right?" Andre asked.

"We did, but that won't be a problem." Porter laughed and it sounded strangely forced coming from him. "She was pissed."

"She was digging for information on why we were asking about him," Franks added. "And she happened to mention that he's always been a hard-ass to work for, but over the past few years, ever since he took over the company, his corporate tactics have gotten a lot more brutal."

"Did she suspect he had anything to do with Manning's murder?" Juliette spoke up.

"Nah, I don't think so," Porter answered. "But she didn't sound surprised that the FBI was investigating him about something. She probably figures it has to do with his unethical business practices. She was going on and on about not having any choice but to do what he told her to do when it came to deals."

"Our white-collar squad might be investigating that business once we wrap this up," Franks said.

Andre tried not to jump to his feet. He was far less interested in what happened with the company once they grabbed Harkin. His goal was making sure Keane paid for his part in the whole thing, once they eliminated Harkin as a threat. "You have details on the house for the takedown?"

Porter stood and Franks followed suit. "We have it at the office. Call your partner. We'll get all the paperwork in order. Join us there in an hour and we'll lay out the plan. This guy goes down today."

"Why is this taking so long?" Juliette paced back and forth in Andre's living room. She knew she should sit down and try to make small talk with his brothers, whom Andre had called to stay with her while he went after Harkin. But every time she tried to relax, she got so jittery she had to move.

She remembered this feeling somewhat from her days being married to Dylan, but it had been different. She'd known his job as a cop was dangerous, but he'd always brushed her off when she wanted details. It might have made her worry less, but it left her feeling disconnected, too. Not Andre. When she asked him something, he told her the truth, even if it wasn't what she wanted to hear.

"It's only been fifteen minutes since he left," Marcos said, amusement in his voice. "He probably hasn't even reached the WFO yet."

"Just relax," Cole said, in his ever-calm voice. "My brother has a ton of training. He's good at what he does. He's going to be fine."

Logically, she knew that. Andre had told her about his training, which was so intense that it was actually a regular part of his job duties. The guy had even trained with most of the military's Special Operations teams. He was more than qualified to take down Harkin.

Emotionally, though, she couldn't stop dwelling on all the little things that could go wrong. In a job as dangerous as his, there were so many variables.

She vaguely heard Marcos ask Cole, "Distraction?"

Cole responded, "Distraction." Then, they were guiding her over to the couch and putting a photo book in her hands.

"What's this?"

"Open it," Marcos said. "I guarantee you it will keep you occupied for a little while."

Curious, she flipped open the cover and then she felt a smile stretch her lips. On the first page were two pictures. She recognized the subjects in the first one immediately: it was a shot of Andre, Cole and Marcos as young boys. They were almost scrawny and wore mudsplattered clothes as if they'd been playing sports right before the shot had been taken. The three stood in a row, their arms looped over one another's shoulders.

"What's this one?" She tapped the other picture on the page.

"That's Andre as a baby," Cole said.

She studied the two people holding him and realized she should have known it instantly. Although the image was yellowed with age and wrinkled, as though it had been carried around in a pocket for years, Andre had his mother's eyes and his father's dimple.

She stared at it for a while, then flipped to the next page, finding more images of him with Cole and Marcos, a little bit older. "You sure Andre won't mind me looking through this?"

Cole gave her a smile she couldn't quite interpret, other than she knew it had something to do with patience. "Of course not."

"You do know my brother is cr—" Marcos cut off midway as Cole elbowed him.

Juliette lifted her gaze from the photo album. "He's what?"

Marcos was obviously trying hard not to roll his eyes at Cole. "Nothing. Hey, Andre said that graphic design wasn't really your first job choice, but you picked it because you were qualified and it wouldn't be a way for your ex to track you."

"Smart," Cole said. "Old habits and unusual activities are one of the ways people who are hiding get tracked down. Well, that and money and hits on your social security number."

"So, what did you do before you moved here?" Marcos asked.

"I was an artist back in Pennsylvania. Oil paintings mostly. I did a bit of everything, but my favorite was portraits," Juliette said, and it felt like a lifetime ago that she'd held a paintbrush in her hands and stood in front of a canvas. She missed the slightly toxic smell of the paints, the calluses on her fingers from holding a brush for so many hours, the pride of finally getting a painting right after working on it for days or weeks.

"You loved it," Marcos said. "I can tell. So, when this is all over, will you go back to painting? We have a lot of good galleries in DC."

Cole tried to elbow him again, but Marcos dodged the hit.

"Uh, I don't know." If things didn't work out between her and Andre, could she bear to stay here? Virginia had never really felt like home, but all of a sudden, she didn't want to leave.

She'd spent most of her time here afraid to do things. Although she'd stopped constantly looking over her shoulder, she hadn't dared to even take a community art class, because she'd been too afraid Dylan would find some way to track her if she did. It might have seemed paranoid, and maybe it was, but he'd found her too many times before when she was sure she'd buried all her tracks.

She'd avoided getting too close to anyone, so they wouldn't probe into her past. She hated lying to people. And without a lot of friends, she hadn't done much socially. So, Virginia had just been the place she lived—and in the back of her mind, she'd always expected it to be one more spot on her list, another place she'd have to leave when Dylan inevitably tracked her down again.

The idea that her need to run might really, truly come to an end felt suddenly overwhelming. No matter what she did, she'd need to start over. It was just a question of how much of a fresh start she wanted.

Would it be enough to simply find a new place to live around here, a new job? Or did she need to go somewhere truly new, a place untainted by Dylan and her own fear?

She thought back to the moment it all started, when she'd been in that club in Pennsylvania, just a year out of school and out celebrating her first painting in a show. Dylan had shown up and asked her out and she'd hesitated, her internal warning system blaring that something wasn't quite right. But she'd shrugged it off and agreed to that first date, and a year later, they were married.

She wondered now if subconsciously she'd known it was too coincidental that he'd been there that night, right after pulling her over, when she'd never seen him before that day. Maybe some part of her had realized he'd tracked her down, had known she should be wary.

Now, her internal warning system was going again, but with Andre, it was totally different. She'd never felt scared or uncertain about him. She'd only been concerned about herself.

She'd thought that, because of her choice with Dylan before, she couldn't trust her own judgment. But maybe the real problem was that she was afraid of herself: of her own shortcomings, of taking a big chance on another relationship and having it end. Of what that might say about *her.*

The realization didn't make her any less certain about what she was supposed to do when it came to Andre or her future, but it did make her wish she hadn't asked him to wait last night. Because today, he was off on a mission for her, and no matter what his brothers said about his skills, no matter what she'd seen firsthand, it was still dangerous.

What if he didn't make it back today and the last thing she'd told him about their future was that she didn't know how she felt? Because the truth was hitting her hard now. As much as it scared her, she knew exactly how she felt: somehow, she'd managed to fall in love with him. Now, she just had to figure out what to do about it.

"A NIGHTTIME ENTRY would have been the better option for this," Scott whispered to Andre as the sedan they were riding in pulled onto the long road leading up to the house where Harkin was hiding.

Andre shrugged. He agreed—since Harkin was a murder suspect, and one they knew to be armed, breaching the house silently while they expected him to be asleep would have been the most logical approach. And despite his desire to take Harkin down as swiftly as possible, he'd backed his partner up when Scott had pressed that point back at the WFO office.

But Franks and Porter wanted to go in now. They'd argued that with a failed attempt on Quantico behind him, they couldn't be sure how long Harkin would stay. They worried if he ran, it could lead to an arrest in an area with more civilians present. At least here, they knew he was contained and almost certainly alone, with no risk of anyone getting in the crossfire if Harkin decided to go out shooting.

But every one of them wanted to bring him in alive. They needed Harkin if they wanted answers. And Andre desperately wanted answers, for Juliette.

"It's one guy," Porter snapped, obviously having the hearing of a bat. "You two should be jumping up and down that we invited you along."

"Oh, we are," Scott said, in such an even tone that Andre could tell Porter wasn't sure if he was being mocked or not.

They'd also considered a ruse approach—having an agent knock on the door dressed as a utility worker— but rejected it as too risky with a suspect who'd killed a law enforcement officer. Instead, they were going with a dynamic entry. It was HRT's specialty: speed, surprise and violence of action.

But today, as Franks pulled the sedan to a stop far enough from the house that Harkin wouldn't see them coming, a bad feeling came over Andre. He had no idea why, since he'd done this kind of entry plenty of times, both in practice and for real. He could practically run it blindfolded.

Franks and Porter pulled on the rest of their gear, and Andre stepped out with Scott to do the same. "Be careful," he told them all and although Scott and Franks nodded back at him, Porter rolled his eyes.

"Let's do this," Porter said.

They ran crouched low just behind the tree line until they were close to the front door. Then they paused only a moment until each man nodded he was ready to go. With a quick hand signal, Andre led them to the front door, racing forward as fast as he could with the battering ram.

With one hard slam, the door split from its hinges and fell into the house. Then, Andre was racing in after it, praying the sudden premonition he'd gotten that something was going to go very wrong wouldn't come true.

Chapter Fifteen

"Move, move, move!" Andre yelled, clearing the doorway fast. It was the most dangerous place in a breach, because until you were through it, you had nowhere to move and you were in a clear line of sight if the suspect expected you.

Then he was moving to the right and Scott cleared behind him, breaking left. A few seconds later, Porter was at his back, Franks lined up behind Scott and the four of them hurried forward. Every second that they didn't contain Harkin was another second for him to grab a weapon and start shooting.

But as soon as he was standing in the massive living room just inside the front door, Andre knew his premonition had been right. The living room was open, with funky modern furniture that left nowhere to hide, and it was clear. But the floor plans for the house they'd pored over before breaching, back at the WFO, were wrong. The owner must have made massive changes since then, and when they'd spoken to her, she hadn't mentioned it. So, the FBI didn't have the new design.

"New plan," Scott said, eyeing the split-level staircase directly beyond the living room. It had been located at the back of the house in the plans they'd seen.

"You take downstairs," Andre said. "Porter and I will keep moving forward through the first floor. Advise us when you're on your way back up." It was the only way to continue the breach without giving Harkin an opportunity to sneak up on them.

Scott nodded, barely looking fazed as he led Franks slowly down the stairway ahead of them. But he and Scott had thousands of hours of training in this kind of search. A regular special agent would get plenty of training at the Academy, but whether they did any afterward depended on where they ended up. Porter's expression was hard, his hands too tight on the grip of his pistol, as Andre glanced back at him, nodding toward the hallway.

"We move fast," Andre reminded him, taking the lead. He had to trust that Porter was behind him, against the opposite wall of the hallway, and ready for the takedown, however it happened.

It felt like minutes, but Andre knew only seconds passed as they rushed down the hallway, fast enough to keep the element of surprise but slow enough to watch for threats. Beyond the short hallway was a kitchen, and if more changes hadn't been made, then there should be a family room to the right of it.

The turn out of the hallway was another dangerous point, a spot where they had no visual. So Andre pulled out a small mirror and held it just past the edge of the hallway, and his pulse instantly picked up. "Family room, behind a chair. He's armed," Andre whispered, both to Porter coming up beside him and over the mic so Scott and Franks could hear.

"Downstairs is clear," Scott replied. "We're coming back up."

Andre kept the mirror steady, happy Harkin hadn't

spotted it. But he'd heard them break down the door, and he was definitely on edge, crouched behind the cover of a big recliner, a gun peeking out, held in shaky hands.

"There's a mudroom behind the family room," Andre said. "Another entrance." He wasn't sure why Harkin hadn't tried to escape that way, but maybe he'd correctly assumed they'd catch up to him before he got far, since his vehicle was parked out front and behind the house was a stretch of open land. It was why they hadn't bothered stationing anyone at the back or blocking the exit before going in.

"Heading toward you now," Scott said.

"Great. I want you to join Porter. I'm going to go around to the mudroom. When I say go, draw his attention. I'll rush him."

"I can go that way," Scott replied.

Although Andre knew it made more sense, he wanted to do this. He needed to be the one to take Harkin down—and to be sure they brought the guy in alive—for Juliette. "I got it."

"Affirmative," Scott replied, and then Andre nodded at him as they traded places. Porter followed him back the way they'd come and around the side of the house.

"I want you out here, guarding the rear exit," Andre told him.

Porter opened his mouth, but then snapped it shut and gave a quick nod.

It was better for one person to make a clandestine entrance than two. Andre slid his pistol into the holster strapped to his thigh and tested the handle on the door to the mudroom. It was locked, so he pulled out his kit and quickly opened it, then slid into the house.

"In five," he whispered to Scott over his mic, then

stepped forward, placing his feet slowly so there'd be no unexpected creaks. He slid to the edge of the mudroom and waited, not daring to even peer around the edge.

He knew where Harkin was. It was up to Scott to keep his attention focused the other way.

He counted down the remaining seconds in his head, then the instant he heard a loud *thump* from the front of the house—as though Scott had slammed his fist into the wall—Andre darted around the corner.

A gun went off, close enough to make his ears hurt, and he landed on Harkin, slamming him into the ground and wrapping both of his hands around Harkin's gun hand. The force of the hit briefly knocked the air from his lungs as Harkin bucked wildly, trying to break free.

Andre smashed Harkin's hand down until his grip broke, and the gun slipped away from him. Andre swept his hand out, shoving it farther out of Harkin's reach, then got his feet back underneath him and yanked Harkin's hands behind his back.

Harkin's head snapped back, almost head butting Andre, and made him lose his grip. Faster than he'd expected, Harkin rolled over, then aimed an uppercut at Andre.

Out of his peripheral vision, he saw Scott run into the room and scoop up Harkin's weapon as Andre jumped back, avoiding the hit. Then he rushed back in before Harkin could recover, using the man's own momentum to propel him forward into the wall.

"You're under arrest," Andre barked, snapping handcuffs on him before he could resist again.

"It's over," Franks said, sounding excited. Andre shoved Harkin forward so they could get him in a car and back to the FBI's holding area for questioning.

"Not quite," Scott said.

"We still need to find Keane," Andre added, watching Harkin's expression.

His face spasmed, then he seemed to collect himself as he demanded, "I want my lawyer."

"You're going to need one," Scott said. "Because we're planning to match casings from Quantico to your rifle downstairs."

There was no response, but Andre could see it in the heavy breath Harkin let out. They were going to match.

Scott grabbed a fistful of Harkin's sleeve and passed him over to Franks as Porter finally came in through the mudroom. "Hang on to him." Then, he nodded at Andre. "You need to come downstairs and see something."

Andre gave one backward glance at Harkin, who looked as though he'd swallowed something foul, and then followed Scott down to the lower level.

They passed a large, open area set up with a bar and seating that would have been quick for Scott and Franks to clear, then went into a small office tucked away in the back. Scott gestured at the wall above the desk.

Pinned to the wall were pictures, dozens of them. All of Juliette.

"Why did you have pictures of Mya Moreau?" Porter demanded, slamming his hands on the table in the interview room where Harkin was sitting, his lawyer beside him.

It took a minute for Andre to remember they were talking about Juliette. It was strange to hear anyone use her given name, instead of the name she'd given herself.

He leaned forward, practically pressing his nose against the one-way glass, watching for Harkin's reaction.

They'd been back at the Washington Field Office for two hours, and although Harkin wasn't being very co-operative, they expected that to change very soon. The rifle they'd found upstairs at the house where Harkin had been hiding was expected to be a match to the casings they'd found at the scene.

They had a firearms examiner testing it now: every casing spent from a rifle left unique markings from the barrel, and they'd soon know if this rifle was a match to the casings found outside of Quantico. When that came back positive, which Andre knew it would, Harkin would be itching to make a deal.

And Andre wanted a reason for officers in Leming, Pennsylvania, to knock on the door of the cabin where Keane was holed up and arrest him. He wished he could be there to do it himself, but it would have to be satisfaction enough to have the man behind bars.

"They're not my pictures," Harkin said stubbornly, shaking his head as his lawyer whispered something in his ear.

"So it's just coincidental that she was at Quantico when you tried to shoot the place up? And that she was the intended target of a hit you ordered on a marketing company?" Franks asked.

"And it's coincidental she witnessed you making a payoff to a police officer in return for not bringing you in on a murder charge?" Porter added.

Harkin scowled, but beneath the anger Andre saw the hint of fear in his eyes. He hadn't realized how much the FBI knew.

"This could be a while," Scott said from where he was stretched out on a chair across the room, snacking on a handful of chocolate candy.

"Yeah, I know. You don't have to wait around," Andre said.

"It's okay. Chelsie's out with my sister tonight anyway."

Andre glanced back at his partner, who'd changed in the time since he'd met his fiancée, Chelsie. There was a new sense of calm happiness about him that Andre envied—and he knew that same kind of peace was within his reach. He just needed to see this case wrapped up and then find a way to convince Juliette that they were better off together than apart.

In the adjoining room, Porter's voice carried loudly as he added, almost conversationally, "You know, when we're finished examining the rifle, we're going to check out that pistol you fired today at FBI agents. I'm betting that comes back as matching the bullet that killed a police officer in Pennsylvania."

Harkin's lawyer leaned forward once more, whispering in his ear, and Harkin jerked away, then stared down at the table for a long moment. Finally, he gave his lawyer a defeated nod.

The lawyer leaned forward. "We want to make a deal."

THE INSTANT THE door opened and Andre stepped inside, Juliette could tell something was wrong.

She jumped up from the couch, setting aside his photo book, and ran over to him, inspecting him from head to toe until she could be certain he wasn't injured. Once she confirmed he seemed fine physically, some of the worry eased. "What happened?"

"We got him. Harkin confessed in exchange for a deal.

Assuming his story checks out and his testimony helps, he'll get some concessions on his sentence—where he serves it and for how long, maybe more."

"That's good news, right?" Marcos asked as he and Cole joined them in the entryway.

Andre took her hand, holding on to it like she was going to need support. "Let's sit down."

Uneasy, Juliette let him lead her back to the couch. She watched him take in the discarded photo album without comment. Once they were all seated again, everyone watched Andre expectantly.

"The takedown went okay?" Cole asked, wearing an expression Juliette could only describe as big brotherly.

She had a sudden wish for family in her life who would stand by her the way Andre's brothers stood by him. Her gaze swiveled from Cole to Marcos and then back to Andre. They'd been there for her, just because Andre had asked. If she and Andre worked out, she'd be gaining a real family. If they didn't, she'd be losing more than just a relationship—and hurting more than one person.

Pushing that worry aside for later, she added, "No one was injured, right?"

"Nah, everyone is fine," Andre replied.

Her heart rate should have gone back to normal, but she could tell bad news was still coming.

"The takedown went mostly as planned. A few snafus but nothing huge. We got Harkin back to the field office and matched the casings from the rifle used at Quantico to the one found in the house."

"So, it *was* him at Quantico." It had seemed to be the only option, with Dylan in Pennsylvania and Jim dead before the incident happened, but it was good to have it confirmed. And if he'd admitted to firing at federal agents—whether or not they had been his actual target—Juliette knew jail time was in his future.

"Yeah. And he fired when we were inside the house." Juliette must have looked a little panicked, because Andre added quickly, "A rogue shot. Didn't hit anyone. Anyway, that pistol is being checked now. We were pretty confident we were going to match it to the bullet used to kill Valance, so the agents brought it up and Harkin's only option was to get ahead of what he could."

"Okay," Juliette said, trying not to fidget as Andre shifted to face her, gripping her hand just a little tighter.

"He admitted to killing Jim Valance and to the shooting at Quantico."

In the chairs across from them, Andre's brothers were silent and Juliette said what they had to all be thinking. "But not to hiring the convicts to kill me? He's saying that was Dylan, isn't he?" That had to be why Andre looked so worried about her.

The idea hurt, especially after starting to have doubts over the past few days that Dylan had ever really tried to kill her, but the truth was that she'd spent three years thinking it, so it wasn't exactly a new concept. Besides, whether or not he'd tried to have her killed, there was no doubt that he'd terrorized her over the years. And if she really wanted to put her past behind her, she needed to find a way to accept that Dylan's mistakes were his own. Even if a tiny piece of her still felt responsible for marrying him in the first place.

"That's not all," Andre said. "What he's claiming is that his murder of Jim Valance was self-defense, and that the shooting in Quantico was during a time when he was temporarily insane."

Cole snorted. "That's pretty convenient. He's not even going to wait until trial to bring up temporary insanity, huh? Just get it on the table now."

"Why would anyone believe that?" Juliette asked, her nervousness increasing with every minute. She wasn't sure where this was going, but she knew it wasn't good. Not for Dylan and probably not for her, either.

"Harkin's story is that during the investigation into Manning's murder, Valance and Keane questioned him repeatedly, getting more aggressive each time. He says that eventually, they coerced him into a payoff, saying otherwise they'd plant evidence for a murder he didn't commit."

"No way!" Juliette interrupted. "I heard him at my house. He didn't sound coerced at all. And Jim wasn't even there."

"Well, according to him, that payoff came *after* they'd made the demand and he'd agreed. He said they were just reiterating what had already been agreed. He says he has no idea if Loews is actually guilty, and he doesn't know why Keane told him there was nothing he could do for Loews."

"That makes no sense," Juliette argued, but as she looked from Andre to his brothers and back, she could tell Harkin's story had planted doubt about the way they'd assumed everything had gone down.

Andre's fingers stroked her palm. "We're still trying to verify all of this, but Harkin's claim does have some internal logic. I think he's lying about some of it, but honestly, the most believable lies tend to be mixed with the truth, and I think at least some of what he's saying is true."

She started to argue, but he continued, "Harkin says

that Keane and Valance continued to harass him after Loews went to jail, demanding more money every few months or they'd 'find' new evidence and try to re-open the case, then name him as a coconspirator. Harkin claims that recently Valance demanded a meeting in a deserted warehouse. Harkin was afraid Valance was going to kill him because he'd been asking for more money and Harkin had refused to make the most recent payoff. He says they argued and that he'd only brought the gun for self-protection, but Valance tried to take it, and it went off by accident."

"Wasn't he shot in the head?" Cole interjected.

"Yeah, so that story is probably twisted to his benefit," Andre said, then turned to Juliette again. "He also says Keane told him you'd overheard him making a payoff and that you needed to disappear for good."

Juliette felt herself jerk at the news, a whole new level of betrayal rushing through her, which was ridiculous. If Dylan had tried to kill her, if he'd sent *hit men* to try to kill her, what did it matter if he'd also sent a murderer like Harkin after her? But somehow, she felt blindsided.

"He had pictures of you at the house he was staying in here. A lot of them."

Juliette felt her hand tighten around Andre's until she knew she was gripping way too hard, but he didn't seem bothered. "What kind of pictures?"

"Shots from a lot of different states over the years. The writing on the back labeling the places doesn't match Harkin's. We suspect it's Keane's, since you already confirmed you'd seen him following you."

She nodded, feeling as though she was in a daze. "Dylan gave them to Harkin to help him find me?"

"We're not sure. That's what Harkin is saying, but it's

also possible he stole them. He says he didn't know where you were until he saw news of the hostage situation online and recognized your picture. Then, he claims he panicked, sure that since Keane's hit men had failed, Keane would take it out on him. He says that drove him temporarily crazy, and he came here. He saw that agents from Quantico had been at the scene, so he waited at Quantico, hoping to see you. That's when he took the shots."

"And you're buying all of this?" Juliette asked, not sure what to think of Harkin's story.

"Some of it," Andre replied.

"From what Andre said, the things Harkin admitted to are basically what he knew the FBI could connect him to forensically," Marcos said.

"Exactly," Andre agreed. "He's trying to put the best spin he can on what he knows we're going to be able to prove, and put the rest on Keane. But that doesn't necessarily mean he's lying. There's consistency to the story, and it didn't sound rehearsed."

"So, what's next? How do we figure out if his story is true?" Juliette asked.

"Officers in Leming are bringing Keane in as we speak," Andre said. "We should have his side of the story anytime now."

As if on cue, Andre's phone rang and his eyebrows lifted. "It's the case agents. I'm hoping they're going to bring Keane here for questioning, but if not, I requested to fly down with them to Pennsylvania to be involved in it." He picked up the phone. "Diaz."

Juliette loosened her hold on his hand just a little as he spoke. The pieces of Harkin's story swirled in her mind, and even though she knew some of it had to be simply about saving himself, parts of it *did* sound like the truth.

After all the years of being sure Dylan was out to get her, and then the few days of uncertain hope that maybe her instincts about her ex-husband hadn't been entirely disastrous, disappointment crashed in on her.

Then Andre hung up the phone, his grim expression filling her with dread. "Keane is gone."

Chapter Sixteen

It had been twenty-four hours and there was still no sign of Keane.

"How did this happen?" Andre tried to keep the frustration out of his voice, but it rang through clearly.

Marcos shook his head, angrier than Andre had seen him in a long time. "I don't know. Kendry was watching him. Keane must have known it. Honestly, he was probably counting on it, so everyone was distracted, thinking they knew where he was. It gave him a head start." His gaze jumped to Juliette. "I'm sorry. I honestly thought we had him pretty contained."

"So did his department," Andre said, not wanting Marcos to feel responsible. "Everyone was confident about that."

"It's not your fault," Juliette said. "But how did he get out? Do they know how long he's been gone? They were checking often, right? So they must have a window when his car disappeared."

"Well, that's just it. He fooled them all. He set automatic timers in the house so the lights went on and off at expected times. And his car is still there, right out in front of the cabin. They don't know how he slipped past them, but the cabin is in the woods, so he could have gone on foot. We have no idea how long he's been gone. The last time Kendry saw him personally was when he checked in at the station a few days ago. The cop who checked on him after the Quantico shooting just checked the outside, didn't actually speak to Keane."

"He couldn't have gone far on foot. If he stole a vehicle, that should have popped up by now," Cole said, his shoulders slumped as he downed his third coffee in as many hours.

Since Andre had made the coffee, he knew Cole had to be wiped out to be drinking so much without a word of complaint. All of them were exhausted. His brothers had been at his house practically nonstop between working, and the strain was starting to show. But he knew they wouldn't have it any other way: the three of them always stuck together.

"Yeah," Andre agreed, downing the rest of his own coffee even though it had long ago gone cold. "I bet he had a vehicle waiting nearby. He had this well planned."

"But what's his next goal?" Marcos asked, and everyone turned to Juliette.

She shook her head, obviously bewildered. "It makes the most sense that he's going to just try to disappear, right? Try to outrun the investigation?"

Her voice held a mix of hope and doubt, and Andre knew why. Keane had spent so many years tracking her; would he give up now?

"The most logical answer is that he's had this planned for years," Cole said. "He set up a failsafe, a way out if the situation with Harkin ever became public. Obviously he knew it was possible, between Valance demanding more money from Harkin and you out there somewhere, knowing the truth. As a cop, you get caught doing *half* the things we suspect Keane of, and you're in serious trouble. No cop wants to end up behind bars, with the people they put away."

Juliette looked a little nauseous and Andre wasn't sure if it was the idea of some criminal coming after her ex-husband in jail or simply the idea that Keane was still out there somewhere, unaccounted for.

The way he always did when she seemed worried, he slid his hand across the small space separating them on the couch and wove his fingers through hers. He wasn't sure when the action had become so natural, almost instinctual, but it must have been for her, too, because her hand curled into his before she glanced at their connected hands. She smiled up at him, seeming almost surprised.

"Shaye never found the trail of money to pay those cons," Marcos interjected. "Wherever that money came from could be his backup funds if he had to run."

"The FBI didn't find it either," Cole said, "but Shaye's still searching."

"Isn't that going to be a dead end?" Juliette asked. "I'm sure he was smart enough to use cash."

"Sure," Cole agreed, "but that much cash? Even if he didn't take it all out at once, we should see something that lines up. Anyway, Shaye's stopped hunting it from Keane's end and now she's trying to go from the criminals, tracking their payment backward. That might work better if Keane used a fake name to set up the account, which he probably did."

"The case agents are still hunting for that trail, too," Andre said. "They're also arranging interviews with just about everyone in Keane's life, from his family to his co-workers, trying to find places he could consider safe or contacts who might help him." He'd gotten off the phone with them a few minutes ago, and they'd both sounded discouraged, their resources spread too thin.

A police detective who'd spent a decade on the force would know all the tricks. He'd know how to avoid detection. And it sounded as though he already had a fake identity set up, that he'd been planning this all along.

"Chances are, his goal is to get out of the country," Cole said. "His best bet is to go somewhere without extradition."

"If he makes it, we might never know," Juliette said. Andre could tell what she was thinking: her days of hiding might never end.

"He's not going to make it," Andre vowed.

Keane had managed to stay one step ahead of them so far, but now the FBI's attention wasn't split among Valance and Harkin and Keane. Now, the focus was solely on Keane. And Andre wasn't giving up until he was behind bars and Juliette was free from this nightmare.

"WELL, I'VE GOT good news and bad news," Cole announced. He emerged from Andre's kitchen after taking a call from Shaye.

Juliette felt like she'd been on a roller coaster the past few days. Everything seemed to be two steps forward and one step back, except when it came to Dylan. Then, it was the opposite.

Cole and Marcos had slept on Andre's pullout couch last night, sticking close in case something broke and they were needed. Ever since they'd learned Dylan had gone missing yesterday, everyone seemed to be on high alert.

Juliette had no idea if Andre's brothers were off work anyway or if they'd taken days off for this. She hardly knew what day it was anymore. Everything had become a blur of investigations, and her past and her future tangled together as though they were never going to break apart.

"What is it?" Andre asked. In the past day, his constantly optimistic attitude had started to slip a little, and even he was starting to show the strain of trying to battle her demons for her.

He hadn't asked for this. She'd waited for him at Quantico that day because he'd been nice to her. Not even so much because he'd been the one to save her life when the gunman had led her out of her office, but because she'd instinctively known he wouldn't hurt her. Even if she held a gun on him and demanded he help her escape.

She wanted to put this behind her, and not just so she could move on with her life, although that was a big part of it. But she wanted the dynamic of their relationship to change, too. She wanted to be here with Andre because they both wanted it, and not because he was still trying to protect her. It was time for her to be his equal, and not a pawn in her ex-husband's schemes.

"Are you okay?" Andre asked, and she realized they'd all been staring at her.

She blinked, trying to clear whatever expression had been on her face, and nodded as she waited to hear what her ex had done now.

"Shaye tracked the money."

"That's great news," Juliette said, surprised. "That means, what? She figured out what name he used? Can't we try to track him with that?" She glanced from Andre to Marcos, thinking it was a good lead and wondering what she was missing. But they were just staring expectantly at Cole and she remembered she hadn't heard the bad news yet.

"Looks like Keane didn't use cash. He sent wire transfers and Shaye tracked it back from the criminals' accounts. Keane set up an account with a fake name and paid the cons out of it for the hit."

"Is she sure it was Dylan?" Juliette asked softly.

"Yeah," Cole said. "I'm sorry. Shaye hacked the bank's security. We've got a picture of him that lines up exactly with when the wire transfer was sent. She confirmed it all. We can't use it in court, but it's him."

So there was no question. Juliette expected to feel surprise, or even sadness, at the final confirmation that her husband had been the one to put out the hit on her, but somehow, all she felt was numb. The weight on the couch shifted as Andre scooted closer and slid his arm around her shoulders and she leaned into him, waiting for the rest of it.

"Apparently, this account was only set up a few months ago. The money that went into it was probably the payoffs from Harkin. Shaye's guess is that he kept it as cash until recently. Not smart to hoard that much cash, but—"

"He had a good hiding spot," Juliette said. "He always said he trusted a hidey hole more than a bank."

"With someone like Shaye on your trail, that's probably a good instinct," Cole said.

"That woman is a genius if she's on your side and a serious threat if she's not," Marcos said. "Especially if she's working outside the law."

"Yeah," Cole agreed, but he seemed guilt-stricken about asking her to go outside the law. "Anyway, that would line up with what Harkin was saying about Valance demanding more money lately. We've confirmed that Valance was having money troubles because of a gambling problem. So, Keane might have realized the whole thing was going to go south on him and it was time to take action."

"So, we still don't know if he was chasing after me for three years to kill me or drag me back," Juliette said, although she wondered if it really mattered now.

"No. What we do know is that Keane paid the three cons out of this account and he had plenty left to start over. Before Shaye could tag the account, he transferred the rest of the money. She knows it went overseas, but she can't find it."

"It sure sounds as though he's trying to run," Marcos said.

"No." Cole's expression was troubled as he looked at Juliette. "Right before he transferred the rest of the money, Keane withdrew a bunch of cash. He did it in Maryland, just outside Washington, DC, earlier today."

Andre's hold on her tightened.

"He's in Maryland?" she repeated.

"He was three hours ago," Cole replied.

"He's close," Marcos said unnecessarily.

"Yeah, but why is it taking him so long?" Andre wondered. "He slipped away from Leming more than twenty-four hours ago. He could have been staking out her apartment by now."

"He's coming in slowly, maybe going through DC instead of passing it by because it's an unexpected route," Cole said. He nodded as if that's the way he'd do it if he were on the run. "He's being careful."

"Then, he's not leaving the country," Andre said. "At least not without making a stop first. Because we're on pretty high alert for him in Virginia and DC. He has to know that he'd be better off making a run for it by heading the other way."

"He's got everything ready to run, but he's going to come here and eliminate me first." Juliette said the words everyone else was dancing around.

"He'll be caught before he makes it anywhere near you," Cole said. "Every officer and agent within a hundred miles is watching for him. It's harder than you think to slip through that kind of net."

"He got this close," Juliette said. "You said he's right outside of DC already." Really, what Cole had said was that Dylan had been outside of DC three hours ago. For all they knew, he was here now, waiting for her to go home.

"Even if he could get close," Marcos contributed, "he's not going to be able to track you to Andre's house. And just in case, by some crazy fluke he manages to get Andre's name, we can move you somewhere with no connection to my brother. We'll stay away from FBI resources totally and use a DEA safe house. We can move you within the hour."

"Even if he found us," Andre said, gripping each of her arms and staring intently at her, projecting total confidence, "he'd never get past me."

A smile trembled on her lips, but she couldn't hold it. "I've put you in danger long enough."

"*You* haven't put me in danger at all," Andre said, so quickly she knew he actually believed it.

"I don't want you to have to stand in front of me. Any of you." She'd come to know all of them pretty well over the past few days. Any one of them would put his life on the line for her, and if any of them were hurt protecting her, it would be far worse than Dylan catching up to her, whatever his intentions.

"It won't come to that," Andre said, but something in

his voice told her he almost wanted to face Dylan one on one.

"I'll take the FBI up on the safe house they offered me. I want to be far away from you if he does manage to evade everyone."

Andre pulled her close, hugging her against him so tightly it was almost hard to breathe. "That'll never work. I'll just volunteer to be on your protection detail."

"I just think it's safer for everyone—"

"It's not going to happen," Andre cut her off.

"Okay," Juliette said as a whole new plan flashed through her mind, a plan she knew would end this, one way or another. And it was long past time to take her life back. "Then I know a way we can draw Dylan out and finish this."

She leaned back, pulling out of Andre's embrace so he could see her eyes, see that she wasn't going to back down about this. "We use me as bait."

Chapter Seventeen

"That is never going to happen." Andre put his hands on his hips, using the glare he usually saved for uncooperative suspects.

It should have made Juliette back down, but instead her lips trembled as if he'd said something funny.

"I'm not kidding," he snapped, keeping his voice near a whisper even though he knew it made him seem less intimidating. His brothers were sleeping in the next room, and he didn't want to wake them.

Ever since Juliette had announced her dangerous plan earlier that evening, she'd been stuck on it, ticking off all the reasons it was their best chance for bringing Keane down and sounding way too logical. He, on the other hand, had come off as too emotionally invested. But bless his brothers, they'd taken his side.

Still, Juliette hadn't given up, and after his brothers had finally announced they needed to call it a night, she'd dragged him into the guest room to keep pushing her case.

"Everyone is out there searching for him. You flaunting yourself as bait isn't going to change the end result. We'll catch him, and we'll do it without putting you in unnecessary danger."

"Andre," Juliette said softly, still so calm it was starting to piss him off. "What happens if he gets here and he can't find me? What happens if he gives up and he uses whatever fake name he's cooked up and goes overseas, somewhere you can't bring him back? I want this to be over. I want him to pay for the things he's done."

"So do I," Andre said. "But not if it means exposing you to danger."

"I'll be fine," she insisted. "I'm not planning to run screaming down the streets until he finds me alone. We'll set it up so the FBI is watching me. He comes close, and you guys arrest him and bring him in."

"If it's too easy, he'll suspect a setup and disappear," Andre said, trying to sound reasonable. The truth was, if he spotted a setup, he'd probably still come. If Keane was willing to risk all the heat in Virginia to get back at his ex-wife, he'd willingly walk into a setup, too, as long as he thought he could outwit them. And with someone confident enough to think he'd get away with all the things he'd done already, Andre had no doubt Keane believed he could.

The problem was, even if they had all the advantages, there was one scenario that no law enforcement agent wanted to face, because it was a no-win. It didn't matter how much protection they put around Juliette if Keane was willing to trade his own life to take her out. And if things seemed dire enough, he might hit that point. Andre wasn't willing to take the risk.

"You know that if we give him a chance to grab me, he'll try," Juliette said and she didn't look scared about what that meant.

"What if we set you up as bait and he just shoots you?" Andre asked harshly. "At this point, he may not care if you see him first. He sent hit men in to take you out, remember?"

She blinked, and he saw a hint of fear behind the determination. "It's a chance I'm willing to take."

"Well, I'm not."

"Andre." She pulled his hand off his hip and held it with both of hers, sparks of determination in her hazel eyes. "This is my life. I need to be able to live it again, without this shadow hanging over everything I ever do. If it means I have to put myself in danger, I'm okay with that. I need to be free of this, and I need to help bring him down."

Andre tried to interrupt, but she kept going. "After everything he did, to so many people, I need to finally take a stand. I can't keep hiding and hope someone else takes care of this problem for me. Can't you understand that?"

Fear clenched his chest, because he *could* understand it. The fact was, it was exactly what he'd be doing if he were in her position.

"I don't like it," he muttered and cursed himself silently, because it sounded as if he was giving in.

"I know," she said, stepping closer and keeping hold of his hand. "But I trust you to keep me safe. I'm ready to be free from this fear." She gazed up at him, only inches away now. "So that we can move forward."

He didn't know if it was a promise for what the future held for the two of them or not. Instead of asking, he tugged her closer still, pulling her flush against him. He didn't give her a chance to explain, just slipped his arms around her and lowered his mouth to hers.

She rose up on her tiptoes, looping her arms around his neck. She kissed him back, picking up the pace instantly.

He slowed them down, keeping his arms tight around her when she would have pulled his shirt off, pressing his lips along the column of her throat until she whimpered. He stayed there for a long time, until she was squirming in his arms, before he finally brought his lips back to hers.

Her hands slid up underneath his T-shirt. Her nails dug into his back as he stroked her tongue with his, trying to tell her without words what she meant to him. He forced himself to keep the pace slow, but she moved as though she was trying to get even closer to him. His hands seemed to act without permission, sliding down over the curve of her butt.

She arched up even higher on her tiptoes, her whole body rubbing against him, until she had to know exactly what she was doing to him. "Andre," she breathed into his mouth.

It was easy to scoot his hands down farther, and he gripped her thighs and lifted her so she could loop her legs around his waist. Then he turned and walked the short distance to the bed, his mind and body battling.

He'd promised her that he'd wait until she had closure on her past before they moved forward. And he knew exactly what she was doing right now, from the frantic, almost desperate taste of her kisses. She was trying to create a memory, in case they didn't have a future. In case her plan failed and her ex-husband killed her.

Determination made him hold her tighter. No matter what it took, he was going to keep her safe. And he was going to prove to her that he deserved her.

He lowered her slowly onto the bed, easing himself on top of her and trapping her wrists up over her head. He slipped free of her too-tantalizing mouth and settled his tongue on her earlobe, trying to gain control as she arched beneath him.

She twisted her head, capturing his mouth again and biting on his bottom lip, making it throb. His eyes closed as she pulled her hands free, yanking his shirt up as high as she could. She dropped her hands back down and slid them under the waistband of his pants.

He rolled over, taking her with him, and laughed at her when she tried unsuccessfully to tug her arms free from underneath him.

"Hey!"

"Let's slow down," he panted. "We have plenty of time."

"Well, I was hoping for a couple of times before your brothers woke up," she said, her cheeks going pink and weakening his resolve.

He groaned and closed his eyes, then opened them again before she could distract him with her mouth. "I meant, we have our whole future ahead of us."

She jerked back slightly, but with her hands underneath him, she couldn't go far.

"I know you said you wanted to wait until this was behind you, and you don't have to make me any promises right now. But I'm going to make you one: when this is over and you're safe—because you will be safe—I'm still going to be here. I know the people in your life have let you down, and I understand why you're nervous and even why you might not want to jump into a relationship, but I'm willing to wait. I want to be with you, so I'll do whatever you need so we can really give this a shot."

It was more than he'd intended to say. She was staring at him, her mouth moving as if she was about to respond, but she didn't know how.

So, he beat her to it, rolling to his side so she could slip her hands free, then tucking her in close to him. "You don't need to say anything. I just wanted you to know."

He reached over and flipped off the light on the side table, then wrapped his arm back around her. "Tomorrow, if the FBI doesn't have Keane in custody, we'll figure out a plan. Tonight, I just want to lie close to you."

"ARE YOU SURE you want to do this?" Agent Franks asked her.

It was midday and they'd put this off long enough already, hoping someone would catch Dylan before he slipped out of the country. Andre's jaw was tight, his mouth in a hard line. Juliette knew he wanted her to call it off and either trust the FBI to catch Dylan or accept it if he managed to get away from them again.

But she also knew that if the roles were reversed and this were him, he'd be doing exactly the same thing. "I'm sure."

If it was possible, the dark expression on Andre's face got even more stern, but she also saw pride in his eyes.

There had been a possible sighting of Dylan earlier today, along a back road coming into the county where she lived, and she'd had a brief burst of hope that he'd be caught and she would get a reprieve. But he'd managed to lose the officer tracking him before backup could arrive.

They couldn't find him. But they knew he was close. It was time to do this. Time to end Dylan's hold on her for good, one way or another.

She gazed at Andre, remembering the feel of his arms around her as she'd drifted in and out of sleep last night. When she'd shared a bed with Dylan, she'd always slept on her own side. But with Andre, it felt right to spend the entire night snuggled up against his warmth and his strength. As if she belonged there.

Whatever doubts she'd been having fled. If she couldn't face her past and forge her own future, then she didn't deserve a man like Andre.

She let her gaze sweep the conference room. The case agents, Franks and Porter, were there. They'd been brought in by Andre, since this was their investigation. Andre's brothers were in the room, too, and Juliette knew some kind of special deal had been made to allow their involvement since neither was FBI and neither had jurisdiction. She'd heard the words "task force" and "paperwork" and a lot of grumbling from Porter, but Andre had insisted. Andre's partner, Scott, was supposed to be here, too, but he'd been called in for HRT at the last minute when one of the other team's snipers had fallen ill.

"Let's go over this one more time," Porter said now, bringing her attention back to him.

He'd settled himself at the front of the room, and although technically he was in charge, Andre had devised most of the plan for today. It gave her confidence that Dylan would bite.

The idea of facing her ex again made fear slide through her, but she tried to force it down and focus. This was it. Today was the last day she'd ever run from Dylan.

"We've evacuated your apartment building and replaced a few of the tenants with agents so it doesn't appear too empty," Porter said. "The news report about spotting Keane driving into Maryland and asking citizens to be on the lookout for him is going to air in half an hour. We're hoping that will give him confidence we're going in the wrong direction, get his guard down a little. Then we'll send you home. We're going to have a marked police car out front, because we don't want him thinking it's too easy."

"Meanwhile," Franks took over, "Agent Porter and I will be in the apartments on either side of you. Officer Walker—" he gestured to Cole "—and Agent Costa—" he looked at Marcos "—will be hiding in the apartment with you."

"And I'll be across the street, on the rifle," Andre finished.

She knew he wanted to be in the room with her, and she'd seen the struggle in his eyes as he'd laid out the plan, putting himself farthest away. But she also knew his skills as a sniper. If Dylan got too close and they had to take him out instead of making an arrest, Andre wouldn't miss.

Besides, she knew there was no one he trusted more to watch over her than Cole and Marcos. The three of them had conferred in the living room this morning while she'd been getting dressed and snippets of their conversation had drifted back to her. She'd heard Cole and Marcos assuring Andre she was going to be just fine and she didn't think she'd ever heard Andre sound so nervous as when he'd told them, "Don't let anything happen to her. If you have even a second's doubt it's going to go bad, just be sure you stay out of my line of fire and I'll take him down."

The idea of the man she might want to spend the rest of her life with shooting the man she'd once pledged that same thing to made bile rise up in her throat. She prayed it wouldn't come to that, but she knew Andre would never shoot unless it was a last resort, maybe especially because it was her ex-husband. He'd never want to hurt her.

The thought bounced around in her head and she

locked gazes with him, giving him a shaky smile. She knew it was true. No matter what their future held, it was going to be totally different from her life with Dylan. Her ex had always thought of his own needs first and hers had been a distant second. But with Andre, even in the short time she'd known him, she came first.

She wished she'd spoken out loud the words that had been rattling in her brain as she kissed him last night. *I love you.* She stared at him, wishing he could read her mind, wishing she'd told him. Just in case.

Don't think that way, she scolded herself. But as Porter gave the go-ahead and they left the office for the cars that would take them to her apartment, dread settled in her chest and refused to budge.

Dylan had been so determined to kill her that he'd chased her for three long years. He'd hired hit men to take her out. Even with law enforcement all over the country searching for him and a certain life sentence waiting for him, he was coming after her again. With someone that single-minded, would they be able to stop him?

Andre pressed a kiss to her lips in front of everyone and then she climbed into the car with Agent Porter. He'd be posing as a neighbor dropping her off. Juliette closed her eyes and said a quick prayer. They were about to find out.

Chapter Eighteen

It had only been an hour since Juliette had been back in her apartment, but she'd been antsy since the second she'd walked through the door. Cole and Marcos had arrived ahead of her and were out of sight, in the other room. She was supposed to move around as if she was returning home after a while away, and she wasn't to talk to them just in case Dylan managed to get eyes on her.

Chances were extremely slim that Dylan could see her, because Andre had made agents sweep any building with a view to her apartment. It was probably overkill, but he'd remembered her talking about Dylan being skilled with a rifle and insisted. The building across the street was already empty—they'd confirmed it earlier, but now it was closed off with only Andre inside.

She resisted the urge to peer out her living room window and across the street to the brand-new apartment complex being built. Even knowing where Andre was, she'd never spot him. And that was the point.

Before they'd returned to her apartment, Andre had made her practice what to do if Dylan managed to get inside with a weapon. It was Juliette's job to move him in front of the window and stay out of the line of fire without being obvious. She'd practiced over and over at Andre's house until it felt almost natural.

But Andre had insisted it was a last resort, that it wasn't going to come to that. Chances were almost zero that Dylan would make it past the agents watching throughout the apartment building and get up to her place on the third floor. And if he did, he'd still have to contend with Marcos and Cole, both of whom had arrived looking ready for battle.

She longed to have her phone ring, to have agents tell her it was over, that they'd caught him. With every minute that went by without word, she got more nervous that Dylan would see through their plan and just run. Because if they didn't catch him today, she'd always wonder when he might reappear. How could she pursue a future with Andre if one day Dylan might show up again and take out his wrath on both of them? On their kids?

She froze, the thought taking her by surprise. But for the first time in a long time, she was anticipating a future, and she could actually envision kids with Andre. A little girl with her eyes and Andre's dimple. A little boy with her smile and Andre's cute little nose. Happiness mingled with panic. It was all too much, too fast, as though after putting her life on hold for so long, she was suddenly heading into warp speed.

She settled stiffly on the couch in her living room, trying to act normal. But she couldn't help glancing around the room. It had only been a few days since she'd left this place, thinking she'd return at the end of the day, but it felt like much, much longer.

The room was a boring beige color, from the walls to the carpeting to the counters in the attached kitchen. Her furniture was functional, and there was just one painting hanging on her wall. It was a bright, cheery watercolor she'd picked up at a fair this summer, her first foray back into normalcy. She'd felt so daring when she'd hung it, as though she was making a statement: *this time, maybe I won't have to run.*

Back in Pennsylvania, her walls had been overrun with paintings. When she'd married Dylan and moved into his house, he'd thought it was too much, so she'd only hung half of what she'd owned. But she missed the splashes of color, the quirky oil paintings, some of which were her own.

She clenched her fists. Dylan had taken that from her: not just her ability to feel safe, but her ability to feel like *her.* Even though she was terrified to confront him again, she desperately wanted him to walk through that door, wanted the chance to tell him that he'd underestimated her.

But where was he? She looked at her watch, wondering if they'd given him enough time. Had he seen the news reports? They'd been broadcasted widely. Maybe he'd seen through the trap.

Her gaze drifted from the window, with the shades pulled wide, to the door, locked and bolted just in case. What were they going to do if he didn't show up today? How long would they keep this ruse up, waiting for him?

She didn't know why, but she'd imagined it all happening fast. She'd been so sure that as soon as she returned to her apartment, he'd be there, furious and anxious to eliminate her for good. But she should have known better. Dylan may have been dangerous and too caught up in his own vendettas to take his best course of action and run, but he was still a cop. An ex-cop now, she amended. And he was still smart.

He might want her dead badly enough to return here, but he'd still conduct surveillance on the apartment building first, make a plan for the best way to get to her.

Would he spot the agents? When she'd walked through the building, she'd seen someone doing laundry downstairs and another supposedly getting mail and both appeared to be regular tenants. But she knew the truth. Would he realize it? Did he have some kind of law enforcement radar, since he'd lived that life for so long?

She wondered for the first time what had turned him. She'd initially thought that Harkin had bribed him, maybe even threatened her, and that had been the start of it. But what if Harkin had been telling the truth? What if Dylan had set it up from the beginning?

If he'd taken money before that day, she'd never seen it. Never suspected anything. They hadn't been hard up for money, but they hadn't been flush with it either. If he'd been hiding it away all along, what had he planned to do with it?

It didn't matter now, she told herself, peering through the doorway into her equally bland bedroom, where Marcos and Cole were waiting out of sight. What was she going to do if he didn't show at all? Would she go through her normal routine, go to sleep and get up and…what? She hadn't returned to work after the shooting at her office and she doubted they'd want her back.

Once this was over, she would really be starting fresh. Again. It felt scary, the way it had every time Dylan had caught up to her in yet another town and she'd had to run again. But this time, it felt exciting, too. She'd never had anything to anticipate before, and now there was a lot.

She would go back to painting. She'd been socking away her savings, so she might even wait before going back to work, see if she was still good enough to sell her art. She'd go out with Andre on real dates. She couldn't help the goofy smile she felt on her face as she remembered his words about kissing her goodnight on her porch. She was going to have to find a new place, one with a porch.

But before any of that could happen, she needed Dylan to show. She leaped to her feet, anxious again. Where was he?

JULIETTE LOOKED JUMPY.

Andre studied her through the scope on his rifle, watching as she hopped off the couch in her living room, then paced and sat back down. She'd been that way for the past twenty minutes, as if she was desperately trying to stay still but couldn't take it.

He was feeling antsy himself.

Everything about this setup was right. The layers of protection around Juliette were solid but invisible. He shifted his rifle from left to right, watching the exterior of the building before moving back up to the apartment again.

By all appearances, the apartment building had a normal level of activity, and they'd gotten lucky with the agents Franks and Porter had recruited, because none of them *looked* like agents. The cops in a marked car out front, taking turns reading a paper and watching the front entrance, finished the ruse. It should have led Keane around the back, into Andre's line of sight, where he could warn the agents on the bottom level to go out and arrest him before he even made it inside.

But so far, there had been no sign of him. And as Andre checked in for what felt like the thousandth time, but was actually only every thirty minutes, the other teams confirmed it. Either Keane wasn't here yet, he wasn't taking the bait or he was waiting.

But waiting for what? With every minute he stuck around, the greater the chances were he'd get caught. As someone with a decade in law enforcement, Keane had to know that. If he wanted to come for Juliette—and Andre was sure he did—he had to come soon.

Right now, Andre was wishing for Scott on the scope beside him. With two of them, one could be constantly scanning while the other stayed focused on one spot. With Juliette already so well protected, it wasn't really necessary, but maybe that was why his neck was tingling. He felt as though he was missing something. He never ran missions without his partner.

Andre shifted, settling into his position more fully. He was prone on the ground, his elbows up underneath him to give him a little height. The rifle was lined up at the bottom of the big open space that would become a window, resting just above the sill. It gave him a perfect vantage point, while allowing him the most invisibility. Someone would need to be above him to spot him, and Andre had been watching the roofline of Juliette's building, too, just in case Keane was a daredevil or getting creative.

"We've got a possible," a member of Porter's team came on the radio.

Andre's pulse kicked up slightly. It would have skyrocketed if he wasn't well trained. To take an accurate shot on the rifle, everything needed to be calm and steady: pulse, breathing, hands. "Where?"

"Coming around from the west side of the building now. He should be in your line of sight soon. A male approximately Keane's height and weight. He's wearing a ball cap pulled low and a bulky coat. It's hard to see his face."

"Got him," Andre said, dialing in closer on the scope. It might be hard for the ground agents to get a match, but Andre could get close enough to see the guy's nose hairs if he wanted. Just as soon as the man tilted his head up.

He was walking briskly, heading for the back door of Juliette's apartment building, both hands in his pockets.

"Watch the hands," Andre warned. "He might have a weapon."

The man kept walking, closer and closer to the door of the building until Andre knew he was going to have to tell agents inside to grab him soon. But he didn't want to do it if it wasn't Keane, because that could scare him off.

"Come on, look up," Andre muttered, dialing in even closer. But all he could see was the guy's jaw. It wasn't enough. He took a step even closer to the door and Andre got ready to key his mic when a creak behind him made goose bumps instantly rise on his arms.

He started to spin around, but he wasn't fast enough to stop the butt of a gun from slamming down on his head. Pain exploded and then he crashed onto his rifle.

A man swam in front of Andre's wavering vision and an angry voice snarled, "You shouldn't go after someone else's wife."

Then the stock of the gun crashed down once more and everything went black.

Chapter Nineteen

"Something's wrong." Juliette wasn't sure how she knew it, but a feeling of dread hit her and wouldn't let go.

"You're okay," Marcos said in a stage whisper, breaking the plan not to speak, probably because of the terror in her voice. "They stopped the man just inside the apartment building. It wasn't Keane. He seemed a little more nervous about the whole thing than he should have, so agents are questioning him just in case."

"You think Dylan would have sent someone else after me, instead of coming himself?"

"No," Cole said calmly. "But maybe this guy was a distraction. The agents are on alert." Then his voice got quieter and she knew he was on the radio when he said, "What's Andre's status?"

Juliette strained to hear the answer, finally leaving the couch and standing in the door to her bedroom as the reply came back: "He went offline. We think his radio died. But he's only been off for a minute. I'm sure he'll come back. I've had this happen before with the radios."

"Someone should check on him," Juliette said.

"If he doesn't come back in a few minutes, we will," Cole replied. "He's right. If the radio went off, it should come back. Or Andre will call."

"Let's just call him." She knew it was ridiculous, but something about this felt wrong.

"He's okay," Marcos spoke up. "I just got a text from him. He says his radio died on him, the guy downstairs isn't Dylan, and he'll call if he spots anything."

Juliette let out a heavy breath. "Sorry."

"It's okay," Cole said. "This is stressful. Just try to act normal, okay? There's a pretty small chance he can see you, but we don't want it to be obvious you're talking to anyone. Especially if this guy we just stopped was a decoy."

She must have looked perplexed, because Cole explained, "A distraction. Or a test, to see if the place was being watched. Agents grabbed him inside, so hopefully if Keane is watching outside, everything will seem fine to him. But it could mean he's here." He tapped the radio again. "Let us know when you have word on the man you're questioning."

Twenty-five minutes later, the radio went on and Juliette stood, walking into her bedroom so she could hear the news.

"Someone gave the guy we stopped a hundred bucks to put on a ball cap and keep it low, his head down and hands in pockets, and walk to the back of the apartment building at exactly the time he did. The description of the person who paid him matches Keane. He's nearby."

She was already jumpy, but her nerves increased so much her hands started to shake. She shoved them into the pockets of her borrowed pants and tried to appear unaffected.

"It's going to be fine," Cole promised. "We won't let him get anywhere near you."

So much for nonchalant. She nodded her thanks as Marcos said, "I'm going to text Andre, let him know."

A minute later, Marcos muttered, "This makes no sense."

"I don't know what that is," Cole said. "An autocorrect error?"

Juliette got off the couch and went into the bedroom. "What's happening? Did Andre spot him?"

"I think he's too focused on the scope. His message makes no sense, maybe something weird with autocorrect. Hang on."

"What does it say?"

Marcos jumped to his feet and let out a string of curses, then yanked up his radio and barked, "Someone get to the building across the street, now! Trace my brother's phone. Hurry! Keane has him."

"What?" Juliette grabbed the door frame as her whole world seemed to tilt.

Vaguely, she felt Cole grab her shoulders, as if he was afraid she was going to fall, and then lead her to sit on the bed. She blinked a few times, bringing everything back into focus even as her heart thumped a terrified beat. "How is that possible? Dylan can't have Andre."

"I got a picture from my brother's phone," Marcos said. "Someone else sent it."

Cole was already back on the radio and peering out the window across the street. "Hurry!"

"We should join them," Marcos said, heading for the door.

Cole grabbed him. "We stay here. What if Keane hired someone to help him? He could be trying to draw away Juliette's protection to get her while everyone is distracted."

Juliette jumped to her feet. "Who cares? Go find

Andre! Let Dylan come for me. Just make sure Andre is okay!"

Marcos's jaw bunched, but he nodded at Cole. The brothers seemed to come to a silent agreement. Marcos drew his weapon, his expression more fierce than she was used to with his easygoing, teasing grins. "Let's get her out of here."

"No," Cole argued. "We wait for the agents to check on Andre, then move with security around us." He studied Marcos's phone. "That picture was taken in the back of a car. Our best bet is to trace Andre's phone."

"What picture?" Juliette demanded, yanking the phone out of Marcos's hand, even as he tried to pull it back.

She gasped as she got a glimpse of it. The image showed Andre, his eyes closed and his head bent at an awkward angle, bound on what had to be the bench seat in a vehicle. There was blood on his scalp from a nasty gash.

Tears gathered in her eyes until she could barely see the picture. "Is he dead?"

She wasn't even sure the words had passed her lips until Cole said, "No. He's tied up, Juliette. He's just unconscious."

As the phone beeped once more, Marcos swore. "Well, he's not coming here. Keane wants to make a trade."

Juliette blinked the tears back, swiping a hand across her cheeks in case any had gotten free. "Me for Andre," she realized.

"Don't worry—" Cole started.

"Do it," she insisted. "Make the trade."

HIS HEAD WAS killing him. It throbbed with every beat of his heart, and nausea rolled in his stomach, until he knew it was a real possibility he was going to throw up. Except that there was a gag over his mouth and if he threw up, he might choke to death.

Andre focused on breathing in and out through his nose, slowly, until the nausea lessened. He cracked open his eyes, and flashes of light danced in front of him. Beyond that, he could see…something.

He squeezed his eyes shut again and tried to move his hand up to his head, but that just sent pain through his wrists. His hands were trussed behind his back, locked at the wrist by what had to be a zip tie. Slowly, what had happened came back to him: the sudden realization someone was behind him in the empty building. Turning around, but not fast enough. The blow to the head. The furious voice of a man who'd come unhinged. Keane.

Andre opened his eyes again, forcing them not to close against the painful light, until the world around him started to come into focus. He was in a dingy hotel room, lying on his side on disgusting carpeting. A radiator rattled noisily in the corner and a bed was in sight. Off in the distance, he saw a door, presumably to a bathroom.

It was the kind of place you paid for by the hour. Only people who were desperate or wanting to pay in cash and stay out of sight would visit. Since Keane was a cop, Andre doubted there was anyone within screaming distance. Or if there was, they wouldn't care.

The bathroom door opened and then a pair of work boots strode toward him and stopped. Andre looked up.

Dylan Keane was stocky and muscular, with dark blond hair and eyes the color of an angry storm. He was obviously strong, if he'd carried Andre down three flights of stairs and then into this place. Or—from the achiness all over Andre's back and legs—he'd been dragged part of the way. Dylan might have been attractive at one time, but the stress of having everyone learn his true character was written all over his face.

The other thing written plainly on his face was fury. And it was directed right at Andre.

He sensed the kick coming before Keane drew back his foot and slammed it into his ribs, but with nowhere to go, bracing didn't help much. Andre's head throbbed even more, and the nausea returned, but he tried not to let Keane see how badly it hurt.

From the smirk on Keane's face, he wasn't successful. "You make it a habit of chasing after other men's wives?"

Andre wanted to tell him the fact that Juliette had run from him for three years should tell him something, but he could barely even move his mouth with the rag shoved in it.

"Don't worry," Keane said. "You won't have to wait long to see her. I've told her how to find me. We'll see her soon. And then it's bye-bye, Mr. FBI."

JULIETTE REMEMBERED SITTING at a diner with Dylan maybe six months into their marriage. She'd been going on and on about an exhibit she'd seen at the art museum, talking about all the different artists. She recalled the flush of excitement from knowing the gallery next to the museum was going to take one of her paintings. She thought Dylan had been excited for her.

Then, all of a sudden, he'd exclaimed, "Renoir! That's it."

"What?" she'd asked.

"That will be our code word for danger."

She'd stared back at him, uncomprehending and frustrated, and then he'd explained, "If there's ever any kind of danger and I need you to get up and get out, no questions asked, I'll say that. Renoir. No one would use it in regular conversation, so it will be perfect."

"*I* was just using it in regular conversation," she'd reminded him. "I was telling you—"

"Just remember the code, Juliette," he'd cut her off. "If I ever say Renoir, you get up and go. No explanation, nothing. Just do it."

"Juliette," Cole said now, and from his tone she knew he'd been saying her name repeatedly.

She snapped herself out of the memory and focused on his face. "What?"

"What does this mean to you?" He held Marcos's phone up again, this time scrolled back to the text that Marcos had said didn't make any sense:

Renoir. 3A. At the Grind.

He wasn't showing her the last message that had come in after the picture of Andre, but she'd seen it earlier:

Send Juliette alone or Andre is dead.

"Uh, I don't know," she said, but from the expression on his face, Cole was suspicious.

The fact was, she didn't know. Not for sure. But she suspected. *Renoir* meant get out, get away from the agents. *3A* had to mean 3:00 a.m. Dylan had often only used the first letter when jotting down times for things. *The Grind* was what he'd always called his job, and it was the only part she wasn't sure about.

His work was back in Pennsylvania. She doubted he was sending her to a police station nearby. He must mean her work, she realized. The marketing company would be empty at 3:00 a.m.

Her life for Andre's. It was a trade she was willing to make.

"Renoir was his code for danger," she told them, because she knew they wouldn't believe that she didn't understand any of it. "But I don't know about the rest of it."

"Is there a location called The Grind?" Marcos asked. "Maybe a coffee shop?"

"We can look it up," Cole said, still staring at her questioningly.

She tried to keep her expression confused and upset, which wasn't too difficult, and eventually he must have bought it, because he got to his feet and spoke into the radio, telling everyone they were changing locations.

They took her to Shaye's house to hide, because she was far enough outside the loop they didn't think anyone could track her there. While Shaye tried to distract her, Cole and Marcos huddled in the kitchen on a multi-hour call with the case agents. They had tracked Andre's phone only to find it discarded on the side of the road.

Juliette heard them realize that *3A* was probably 3:00 a.m., but they were having no luck with *The Grind.* Apparently, there were at least three locations within a thirty-mile radius with those words in the title.

"He's going to be okay," Shaye reassured her now, and Juliette resisted glancing at her watch, knowing it was just after one.

The past few hours had been a jumble of fear and second-guessing herself, but she knew she couldn't risk deviating from what Dylan wanted. Not with Andre's life on the line.

Juliette refocused, staring at the woman across from her who'd opened her home and shared her clothes. Shaye Mallory was tall and thin, which Juliette could have guessed from the fit of her clothes. She had long, curly red hair that didn't seem to want to stay in a clip, and deep brown eyes filled with compassion.

When they'd arrived, Shaye had looked at Cole with barely concealed adoration and embarrassment. There was a story with those two, and Juliette prayed one day, not long from now, they'd have Andre back and she'd get to hear it.

Juliette gave her a shaky smile. "I hope so."

"Maybe you should try to get some sleep," Shaye suggested.

Juliette tried not to look too happy. She'd been hoping for the last twenty minutes that Shaye would suggest that. "I probably should. Wake me if anything happens, okay?"

"Of course." On the way out of the room, Shaye flipped off the overhead light, just leaving on the lamp.

Juliette waited a few minutes after she'd gone before she stuffed pillows under the covers. She changed into something from Shaye's closet, tossing the clothes she'd been wearing over the end of the bed. She hoped if anyone came in to check on her that it would be enough to fool them. She turned off the lamp, plunging the room into darkness.

Her heart racing, she carefully slid the window open, inch by inch, praying it wouldn't squeak. She had no idea how long it would take her to get to work on foot, or if she'd be able to hitchhike once she got far enough out from Shaye's house. All she knew was that she couldn't let anyone catch her.

Cole and Marcos were well trained, but so was her ex-husband. And he meant what he said. If she didn't come alone, she had no doubt he'd kill Andre.

She knew she was doing the right thing as she climbed

out the window, closing it again behind her. Then she started to run.

Dylan had kidnapped Andre almost six hours ago. What had Dylan done to him in that time?

That worry propelled her on foot until she was panting and a cramp shot through her side. The calf that had been pelted with bits of concrete a few days ago ached. But none of it mattered, because a truck was coming. She jumped out in front of it, waving her arms.

The vehicle slammed to a stop and the man in the driver's seat rolled down his window. "Are you crazy, lady?"

"I need a ride," she gasped. "Please. It's an emergency."

He stared at her a minute longer, probably trying to decide if she really was crazy, then reached over and opened the passenger door. "Get in."

Ten minutes later, after she'd directed him to her old office, he stopped outside the front door, clearly skeptical. "It's closed. Are you sure this is where you need to be?"

"Yes. Thank you for the ride." She jumped out of the truck, glancing around, searching for any sign of Dylan. But everything was dark and empty, almost spooky.

"You want me to wait in case you need a ride back?" the man persisted.

"No," she snapped. She needed him to leave, so Dylan didn't think she'd brought backup. Why hadn't she asked him to drop her down the street? "Sorry. I'm fine. Please go."

He shook his head, muttering something under his breath, but he drove off, leaving her all alone.

And she sure felt alone. She crossed her arms over her chest, cold as she looked around, from the dark building and empty parking lot to the woods out behind the office where a hit man had dragged her, intending to keep her as leverage before putting a bullet in her head.

A car raced around the corner, then slammed to a stop in front of her so fast it made her jump backward.

A tinted window rolled down on the passenger's side and Dylan glared back at her from his place behind the wheel. His furious expression was ten times worse than when he'd scared her enough to send her running for her life three years ago.

She resisted the urge to take another step backward.

"Get in."

"Let Andre go and then I will," she replied. Her voice only shook a little bit.

"You get in the car in the next five seconds or I shoot Andre in the head," Dylan barked.

Juliette got in the car, and it shot backward out of the parking lot so fast she slammed into the dashboard. Grabbing it for support, she looked in the backseat. It was empty.

The car did a three-point turn fast enough to make her head spin, then raced away from her office.

Chapter Twenty

"Guess who I found," Keane announced.

Andre stopped his useless attempts to free his hands and looked up just in time to see Keane shove Juliette toward him, hard enough that she hit the bed and bounced off the edge, then landed on the ground beside him.

In his mind, he screamed her name, but he still couldn't make a sound with the gag in his mouth. Keane had insisted he was going for a drive and that he'd be back with Juliette, but Andre hadn't believed it. How had she gotten away from his brothers? No way would they have let her go alone.

For a second, he hoped they were somewhere behind her, but the sorrowful expression on Juliette's face told him she'd come by herself.

He said a silent prayer that his brothers were tracking her. Wherever Keane had met up with her, it couldn't have been far, because he hadn't been gone more than ten minutes.

Juliette scooted toward him, reaching her hand out to his face, but Keane grabbed her arm and yanked her to her feet, roughly enough that it had to hurt.

Andre tried to yell, but the gag swallowed it. As hard as he'd worked on his binds while Keane was gone, he hadn't been able to get free. He'd managed to push himself against the bed and he'd been sawing the zip tie on the metal frame. But although he was making a small pile of plastic shavings under the bed, it wasn't going fast enough. Not even close.

He'd tried pushing himself to his feet only to discover his ankles were tied together, too, and there was a loop going from his ankles to his wrists. Essentially, he wasn't going anywhere.

How had he let this happen? How had he not considered that Keane would make a grab for him instead of Juliette? Now she was going to pay for caring about him. And how much she cared was written all over her face. His breath caught at the love he saw there, and he willed her to hide it before Keane saw, too.

"You promised you'd let him go," Juliette said, yanking her arm free of her ex's grasp. "I'm here. You have what you want."

Keane smiled at her, and it was so cocky and full of gloating that Andre wished he could knock it off the man's face with a swift punch. But he couldn't stand, and if he tried to swing a punch, there was a good chance he'd throw up.

"Well, originally, I thought I might," Keane said, and his voice was so full of hate that Andre could hardly believe he'd once been married to her.

He also understood in that instant every hesitation Juliette had ever had about diving into a new relationship.

"But I see how you care about him, and I think I'll hold on to him a little longer."

Juliette instantly blanked her face, but Keane just laughed, then leaned close so they were nose to nose and whispered, "I know you too well."

For a second, she seemed to be considering fighting him and then Keane pulled a gun from his waistband and shook it at her. He took a step back and sank into a chair. "Go ahead. Take a seat. Let's chat."

Juliette seemed wary as she glanced from him to Keane, but then she sat gingerly on the edge of the bed. "What is there to talk about? You came to kill me? Fine. Do it. But leave Andre out of it."

At her words, Andre redoubled his efforts to break free of the zip ties, but all he succeeded in doing was bloodying his wrists worse than he already had. He'd never felt so helpless in his life.

Juliette sank to her knees next to him. Her eyes were broadcasting all the things she was trying to keep off her face as she untied the gag from around his mouth.

For a second, he thought Keane was going to argue, but he let her do it, then gestured with the gun for her to stand back up.

Free of the gag, Andre's throat felt like he'd gargled sand and his mouth felt like someone had shoved cotton in it, but he managed to rasp, "You think she cares about me? You're wrong. She turned me down because of you. If you hadn't blown it by threatening to kill her, she'd still be with you."

Juliette looked shocked, blinking at him as though she wasn't sure if he actually believed his words or it was some kind of ploy. Keane looked suspicious, then a little hopeful.

Andre prayed it would work. He knew his only chance was that the FBI would track them down in time, and he didn't think it was probable. But Juliette had a shot, because underneath all of Keane's anger and hate was something else. He still loved her, in his own sick, twisted way.

And if they could convince Keane she loved him too, he might let her live.

JULIETTE BIT BACK her instant response to Andre's ridiculous comment. For a second, it had stunned her silent, because she'd thought he really believed it, that he didn't know she loved *him*. But that moment of surprise saved her, because she recognized what he was doing. He was trying to get Keane to keep her alive, no matter what happened to him.

And she realized he was right. Dylan's biggest flaw had always been his own ego. If she could convince him she still loved him, maybe she could find a way to talk him into leaving with her—and keeping Andre alive.

The thought of going anywhere with Dylan gave her chills, but she fought them and did her best to appear embarrassed, as if Andre was right. She wasn't sure Dylan was buying it, but as long as he was talking, he wasn't shooting, so she put as much indignation as she could into her voice as she asked, "Did you send those men after me? Did you really try to kill me? Because I kept your secret all these years."

He frowned at her, glanced down to Andre and then back up, as if he didn't know what game they were playing. He settled the gun on his lap and shrugged. "Sorry, babe. Harkin was freaking out at the idea of you still being out there somewhere, knowing the truth."

"And so you decided you'd kill me instead of dealing with him? He's the murderer!"

"Yeah, well, he was a problem I was planning to take care of, too. I would have, if the FBI hadn't rushed into that house when they did. I'd been in Virginia for days by then, tracking him. It was crappy timing for me when the FBI found him."

His words felt like a sucker punch even though she'd known it had to be him. Still, some part of her had foolishly hoped it was Harkin. And yet... She squinted at Dylan, trying to figure out what about his blasé tone felt wrong to her.

He scowled at Andre. "That really screwed me up. Before you did that, I thought I could go back to work. But I assume he's told all, probably skewing the story to make himself look good, right?"

"He said you harassed him for a payoff on a murder he didn't commit, otherwise you were going to frame him."

Dylan snorted. "Oh, he did it. When Jim told Harkin I'd figured out he was the one who framed Loews, he offered to let me in on what he was giving Jim. And yeah, after that, he was fair game. I gave the guy a free pass on murder, so he owed me. But I never threatened to frame him for something he didn't do. That guy was guilty."

His scowl deepened. "And I can't believe you fell for that trick in Leming. I've been here for days. I followed Harkin to Quantico, the idiot. I would have taken care of him then, but I realized what he was doing and I wanted to find Juliette, too." His gaze shifted back up to her. "I saw you with this *Fed*. You sure seemed cozy."

Juliette recalled that moment when Andre had run up to her at the entrance to Quantico and swept her into his arms, and she'd felt safe again. The fact that Dylan had seen it all made the moment feel slightly tainted.

Andre had taken her to the field office from Quantico, Juliette realized. Dylan must have lost her there and gone back to Harkin's house, then seen the police car nearby and held off on killing Harkin yet again.

"When did you turn into…this?" Juliette asked softly. She knew it blew Andre's plan, but she couldn't keep it up. Dylan was never going to buy that she still loved him unconditionally. Not only had he just admitted he'd tried to have her killed, but as much as she knew his flaws, he knew hers, too. He might have always put her feelings second when they were together, but she hadn't sat silently in the background. She'd spoken her opinion.

Dylan leaned toward her, his hands gripping the edges of the chair as though he'd forgotten the gun was in his lap. "You know how awful it is, being a patrol cop? Even a detective? Dealing day in and day out with these civilians who call you names, who you have to worry will pull a gun on you because you want to give them a speeding ticket? Being a detective was worse, like wading into the scum of the earth. Jerks like Harkin were out there getting rich, and I was barely paying the mortgage risking my life for them. I deserved some of that."

How had she not seen this? She stared at him now, barely recognizing the man she'd fallen in love with so many years ago.

He scoffed at her, leaning back in his seat. "You still love me, huh? If you want to play that card, you might want to wipe the look of disgust off your face, babe."

"Don't call me that," she snapped, standing up and striding toward him.

He lifted the gun, pointing it at her. "Uh-uh. Don't get a backbone now."

"What are we doing here, Dylan? What's the point of this?" She could practically hear Andre behind her, telling her not to antagonize him, but she couldn't stop.

All those times Dylan had caught up to her over the years came back to her in flashes of memories. He probably could have killed her any of those times. But he hadn't. Instead, he'd sent hit men after her, and staring into his eyes now, she knew why.

He could take a bribe from a murderer, he could even pay off criminals to kill his ex-wife, but he couldn't do it himself. She might have been playing a ruse, but he was, too. On some level, *he* still loved *her*.

She stood right in front of him, making sure her body blocked Andre from the gun, the way he'd taught her to stand in the apartment. Only this time it was backward, not giving Dylan an angle.

He got slowly to his feet, and for a terrifying instant, she thought she'd misjudged him. But then he set the gun beside him on the arm of the chair and reached up, gripping her upper arms hard enough to bruise. "I haven't really decided yet. I guess it's up to you whether I take you with me or kill you here." His voice turned careless. "Your boyfriend, though? He's dead either way."

He dropped her arms and lifted his eyebrows, as if he was waiting for an answer.

She moved fast, grabbing the gun off the chair, and jerked herself backward. She practically fell onto the bed as she dove out of range before she turned it around and got her finger under the trigger guard.

Dylan gave her a smirk as he pulled a switchblade from his pocket and flipped it open. "That wasn't a good idea." He took a step toward her.

"Don't move," she barked, her voice almost as shaky as her hands. She hated guns. She'd always hated even holding them, but Dylan had taught her to shoot. He knew she could hit a target, but he also knew a target was all she'd ever been willing to hit, no matter how many what-if scenarios he'd thrown at her. She'd told him she didn't think she'd be able to shoot another person if her life depended on it.

He took a step toward her.

Out of the corner of her eye, she saw Andre jerking around on the ground, trying to gain purchase to rush him.

"I know you, Juliette. You can't shoot me."

"You don't know me anymore," she swore, but her hands were still shaking, and she knew he was right. She couldn't shoot him. Not even to save her own life.

Dylan's smile grew and then his attention shifted to Andre on the ground. And in that instant, she saw his intent: after he disarmed her, he *would* kill Andre.

Juliette pulled the trigger.

Dylan fell backward but didn't hit the ground. It was as though he was on drugs. He roared when the bullet hit, then rushed toward her, his arm dripping blood.

She fumbled to fire again, but he was almost on her, the knife outstretched, and she panicked, twisting to get away.

Then, suddenly, Dylan went down, toppling to the ground, away from her.

For a second, Juliette didn't know what had happened. Then she realized that Andre had somehow managed to get up on his knees and tackle Dylan. The two of them were on the ground, locked together so Juliette knew she couldn't shoot.

Dylan's hands were on Andre's throat and his hands and feet were still tied behind him.

The knife had fallen somewhere, but Juliette didn't waste time trying to find it. Instead, she dropped the gun and leaped on top of her ex-husband, wrenching his hands away from Andre's neck, tears in her eyes as she heard Andre gasping for breath.

Then Dylan flipped her over, climbing on top of her, the fury on his face more horrifying than when he'd threatened to kill her, and she wished her hands hadn't shaken at the exact wrong time, sending that bullet wide.

His hands went for her throat and she grabbed his wrists, trying to hold him off, but he was stronger and slowly he pushed back, even with his injured arm. Her arms started to tremble with the effort and then he got them over her head, pinning both of her hands with one of his.

She kneed him in the groin with all her strength and he fell forward with a yelp. She didn't waste time, shooting her hand out and hitting as hard as she could right on his injury. He fell backward, but before she could move, he was coming for her again.

Then, all of a sudden, he flew off her and Andre was there, blood dripping down both of his hands, the zip tie gone. His feet were still bound, though, and Dylan was coming back.

Andre turned, lifting his arms in a boxer's pose, but she could tell he was unsteady on his feet, and Dylan was enraged, racing back for more.

Juliette tried to push to her feet and then she saw it: Dylan's gun, on the ground beside her. She grabbed it, gripping it with hands that barely shook now. "Don't move or I swear this time I'll aim for your heart."

Dylan froze and she could see him trying to figure out if she'd really shot to wound last time or if she was bluffing. Before he could decide, Andre's fist darted out, landing solidly in the center of Dylan's face. He fell to the ground, out cold.

For a minute, Juliette watched him, sure he'd get back up. Then she looked at Andre, swaying on his feet but still willing to stand in front of her, and she set the gun on the bed and took a step forward. She wanted to stand beside him now.

"It's over," he told her.

"I love you," she replied, then kissed him.

Epilogue

Three weeks later, Juliette stood on the front porch of
her brand-new house. It was a rental, but it was a step toward permanency. She'd decorated inside with so many
pieces of artwork that Andre called it her own private
gallery. He joked that she should sell tickets for a tour
of her house.

He'd let her put up paintings in his house, too, which
was good, because as much as she liked her new house—
and her new job at a gallery in DC that Shaye had helped
her find—she spent more time at Andre's house. She
loved the artwork, loved the sense of having something
that was hers, but her favorite thing about Andre's home
were his photos. She'd been working on adding more
personal photos to her place, too.

"What are you thinking about?" Andre asked, coming
up behind her and wrapping his arms around her waist.

She leaned against him, her head fitting perfectly underneath his chin. "The future."

She'd finally put the past behind her. It would always
be a part of her, but her life was no longer in a holding
pattern.

The Manning case had been officially reopened and
Loews had been released from jail after Harkin had fi-

nally confirmed that Loews was innocent. Both Dylan and Harkin were in prison awaiting trial, and the FBI had assured her neither one would ever be getting out. Not long ago, that would have caused her some heartache, knowing the man she'd once pledged her love to was enduring a life in prison. Now, she'd learned to accept that Dylan had made his own choices and she was free to make hers.

She still had moments of panic about being in a new relationship, about trusting someone enough to let him into her heart. But Andre had managed to sneak in there despite her best defenses, and she was glad.

"What about the future?" Andre asked.

She spun in his embrace, looping her arms around his neck as she stared up at him. "I'm glad it's going to be with you."

He smiled down at her, and she could barely see the stitches on his head anymore. "Me, too. Have I told you lately that I love you?"

She pretended to consider it. "Not for the last hour or so, at least."

"I better remedy that," he whispered, then pulled her even closer and pressed his lips to hers.

She went up on her tiptoes to kiss him more deeply, loving the feel of his heart thumping wildly against her.

After a minute, he pulled back to whisper, "I did promise to kiss you good-night on your front porch someday."

She grinned. It was a promise he'd been keeping every day since she moved in. "Good night?"

He smiled back and then she squealed as he scooped her into his arms. "Well, time for bed, anyway."

The dimple that popped on his left cheek made her

skin tingle. But staring up into his eyes, full of all the things she'd seen on that first day he'd swept into her life—the goodness, the honesty, the protectiveness—she got serious. Palming his cheek, she told him, "I love you. I want you to kiss me on this porch every night for the rest of our lives."

His smile turned soft and tender. "That promise will be easy to keep."

"I'm ready for a new life, Andre. And I want it to be with you."

Andre pushed the door open with his shoulder. "Then, let's start right now," he said, striding inside. Toward their future. Together.

* * * * *

Don't miss the next book in
THE LAWMEN: BULLETS AND BRAWN,
POLICE PROTECTOR

And check out previous titles in
THE LAWMEN *series:*

DISARMING DETECTIVE
SEDUCED BY THE SNIPER
SWAT SECRET ADMIRER

Available now from Mills & Boon Intrigue!

Join Britain's BIGGEST Romance Book Club

50% OFF your first parcel

- **EXCLUSIVE offers every month**
- **FREE delivery direct to your door**
- **NEVER MISS a title**
- **EARN Bonus Book points**

Call Customer Services
0844 844 1358∗

or visit
illsandboon.co.uk/subscriptions

∗ This call will cost you 7 pence per minute plus your phone company's price per minute access charge.